The Arcane Arcade

By

Leonard Streitfeld
&
Jay Dubya

Published by
Jay Dubya
4754_9

ISBN 978-1-63498-899-5

In Memory of Dr. Leonard Streitfeld, (1922-2019)
and
Dr. Stephen Streitfeld (1951-2020)

Contents

Introduction

The Arcane Arcade is a collection of sixteen short fiction stories. The general theme of the book is paranormal experience, and the tales are presented as short stories, novellas and novelettes. The stories have been rewritten and edited many times until they have evolved into their finished form.

The characters and events depicted in *The Arcane Arcade* are strictly the products of the authors' imaginations. Any resemblance to any real person or persons is absolutely coincidental, and it is the hope of the authors that readers will appreciate the pure fantasy identities, personalities and plots in the sixteen fictional works.

"The Chess Set"

Betty Wilson was busy packing for a European trip that she and Harry had been planning for several years. The wife was nervously waiting for her spouse's return home from his downtown Market Street office. She didn't want to be late for their evening flight from *Philadelphia International Airport* to Bucharest, Rumania.

Harry Wilson was a very successful businessman, and he and Betty lived on the Mainline, a wealthy residential suburban district just west of Philadelphia. Their fabulous mansion was situated on a sprawling two-thousand-acre estate. Wilson had made his immense fortune in plastics, and the CEO's principal hobbies were playing chess and enjoying horseback riding.

Harry had built a six-stall stable adjacent to his luxurious Tudor mansion that housed several prized thoroughbreds, which were exclusively used for fox hunting on the enormous grounds. The large estate was the perfect setting for the fall foxhunts that the mogul would conduct for his rich and pompous Mainline friends.

After a "chase," the old cronies would return to the luxurious mansion and then enter the expansive den, which featured a splendid stone floor-to-ceiling fireplace. A handsome-looking mahogany bar complemented the room's beautiful wooden tables and soft black leather chairs. There, Harry Wilson and his snobbish acquaintances would play chess for hours and reminisce about the day's rather out-of-the-ordinary activities. The men were all expert chess players, but Wilson's skill was vastly superior to that of his peers.

During *World War II,* Harry had served as a pilot on a *B-24*. The daring aviator had participated in one of the famous raids on the Rumanian Ploesti Oil Fields. The former captain had often thought about *that* dangerous attack, since Harry's plane had barely made it back to its base in England. Wilson had a yearning to journey back to Rumania, to tour around the rugged countryside and to again visit legendary Ploesti. The multimillionaire dreamed of again seeing the extensive oil fields that his bomb squadron had virtually obliterated in August 1943. Many other *B-24* fliers that had participated in the raid shared a similar passion.

The plastics guru finally arrived home from his downtown Philadelphia office. Then, Wilson and Betty continued packing for their "great Rumanian escape." His wife asked Harry what had kept him so late. "Betty, I drove over to the Malvern Chess Club from the office. A serious game-in-progress caused me to lose track of time," the husband apologetically explained.

"I don't know what you love more, your chess matches or your devoted wife!" Betty facetiously joked. "I hope it's the latter!"

"You have me *'checkmated'!*" replied the jovial millionaire. "In fact, Betty you' always have me' checkmated!"

Harry was an avid collector of chess sets, having many fine boards and chess pieces on display in four separate rooms of his colossal mansion, and the valuable sets came from various sectors of the globe. His most cherished board figures were made of very ornate ivory, all sculpted in caricatures. Wilson hoped to supplement his treasured collection on his much-anticipated European excursion.

And after consuming a few light snacks, the husband and wife were finally ready to depart for their weeklong vacation. The Wilsons' owned two limousines, one white and the other black. Charles, the couple's faithful butler, carefully carried their luggage to the white limousine. Gregory, the estate's chauffeur, then drove the anxious pair to *Route I-95*. The Mainline aristocrats soon arrived at *Philadelphia International* with little time to spare. After passing through tight airport security and clearing customs, the two eager vacationers anxiously boarded the *747* and prepared for their long flight to Bucharest.

"I've been looking forward to this trip ever since *World War II*," admitted the former pilot turned industrial tycoon.

"Whatever you want, Dear, I also want!" agreed the supportive wife. "It's like you now wish to relive your earlier life!"

Harry was accustomed to long flights from his military pilot days. As a habit he always brought along a pocket computer chess set. Wilson and Betty got comfortable in their first-class seats, and soon the jumbo jet was airborne, heading east over New Jersey and then the vast *Atlantic*. Refreshments were quickly served, and next, a wonderful in-flight dinner that included Burgundy wine followed. The Wilsons remarked how courteous and pleasant the stewardesses and male flight attendants were.

"This is like being on our second honeymoon," Betty observed and stated. "I trust that Rumania will be fascinating; just as you've always described it."

"I blame myself for not returning to Rumania twenty years sooner," answered the regretful chess authority. "Betty, it's like I had left a part of my soul in Europe, if you know what I mean."

Harry was becoming mellow after a second glass of Burgundy and presently was in the mood for a game of chess. He removed his handheld computer from his sport jacket, and several minutes later the addicted fellow was in the middle of a serious man-versus-machine competition. As Wilson incessantly played, his eyes became heavy, and after three consecutive chess victories, the Mainline champion gradually dozed-off to sleep. Betty thought that rest and relaxation were the best prescriptions that any doctor could order for both Harry and her, and soon the spouse also closed her tired eyes.

The *747* arrived at *Bucharest Airport* precisely on schedule. After being processed through customs, the Wilsons retrieved their luggage from the airport terminal's second carousel, and soon the pair found van transportation to their hotel. The driver was a strange, sinister-looking man with thick, bushy, black hair, and he also possessed a dense black mustache curled-up at both ends. A short coarse beard highlighted the driver's piercing, distinctive, dark brown face. The strange-looking guide spoke broken English with a very heavy local accent.

While en-route to the hotel, the man behind the wheel conversed with Harry and Betty about their intended itinerary. Wilson told the driver of the crucial bombing raid over Ploesti in 1943 and of his desire to revisit the historic site. "My wife and I plan to tour the countryside and visit some of the so-called mysterious places in the Transylvanian Alps," indicated the determined plastics mogul.

"My husband is also looking for a special Rumanian chess set to add to his marvelous collection," Betty quite plainly added. "He's a very enthusiastic collector."

The van driver suggested a "mountain Gypsy" with whom he was familiar. The man then gave the Wilsons exact directions to an isolated Gypsy mountain camp. The couple's van soon arrived at the designated hotel, and after registering at the main desk, the fatigued American tourists were promptly conducted to their room. In the meantime, the suspicious-looking van driver made a quick telephone call from a lobby pay phone and told his listener that a vacationing visitor from the United States was in quest of an unusual chess set. He then added in a low whisper, "This is our chance to get rid of *it* once and for all."

The next day, the Wilsons visited the historic Ploesti oil fields, and then explored several museums where the Pennsylvania tourists studied many photographs of the significant 1943 famous air raid. Harry snapped plenty of pictures to document memories and familiar scenery on film. But now, the multimillionaire and his devoted wife were ready for their trip to the *Alps*. On their second day in Rumania, the pair rented a compact car and their goal was to locate the remote Gypsy camp recommended by the mustached van driver.

The country roads required major maintenance, but the mountain scenery was magnificent and the views more than compensated for the rough ride. The Wilsons traveled a full day, and by late afternoon the elderly visitors were becoming weary. Few towns and villages were situated in the high mountains, so the two itinerant Americans were hoping to find suitable lodging in their new environment. Soon, they came upon what appeared to be a quaint old Alpine inn.

The travelers stepped inside the small establishment and conversed with the proprietor, who commanded just enough basic English to understand that they were seeking lodging for the night. The owner introduced himself to the Wilsons as Alexander, who wore a dark red and brown plaid sweater and puffed rather diligently on an ancient-looking pipe. A cloud of smoke billowed around him as the accommodating host invited his guests to come down for dinner in an hour after freshening-up.

Harry and Betty lugged their heavy suitcases upstairs, settled in their room but had little time to relax. The wealthy Americans prepared for dinner, and then wandered downstairs to the modest lobby. Alexander directed the Wilsons to a dining room where a waiter escorted the duo to a table set for two. A fireplace to their left dimly lit the dismal-looking room, and on the wooden table were a candle and a bottle of cheap wine. Soft classical music was filtering-out from several antiquated wall speakers, and the added touch made the perfect atmosphere for a tranquil dinner.

After Harry and Betty had sat-down, Alexander entered the dining room, and the flattering host amiably served his guests a variety of native foods. It wasn't long before the table abounded with delicious ethnic delights common to the region. When the Wilsons were finished their meals, the husband and wife invited "Alex" to join them at their table for an attempt at conversation, since he was the only other person inside the large dark room. The gracious host asked about his visitors' travel destination.

"We intend to go to a remote Gypsy camp," Harry rather frankly stated. "Do you know anything about it?"

Alexander frowned and advised the tourists to be cautious. "The Gypsies have evil powers. Many residents fear their strange magic," the inn owner informed in a low tone of voice, even though no one else except the Wilsons and him were seated in the dining room.

"What about buying exotic items or tokens?" Betty curiously inquired. "My husband and I like shopping for certain souvenirs."

"Be very careful," again warned the proprietor. "Let the buyer beware as they often say. Many Gypsies' gifts are cursed! And believe me, it is more than just idle superstition I'm telling you."

This new-found information was a bit frightening to Betty, but Harry was intrigued with the eccentric apprehensions associated with local mountain folklore.

It was getting late and the American travelers were exhausted from jet lag and also from Alexander's terse anecdotes, so the twosome retired to their room. An early morning departure was scheduled for their Gypsy camp trip. After a wonderful breakfast of eggs and muffins, the Philadelphia pair paid their lodging bill, said "Good-bye" to "Alex", and slowly motored-away from the secluded mountain lodge.

The aggregate-stone roads were steep, and traffic was sparse in both directions. But the scenery was spectacular and quite enjoyable, and it wasn't long before the vacationers noticed a colony of black canvass tents visible in the distance.

"Betty, there's the Gypsy camp up ahead," Harry recognized and pointed. "Gypsies are such fascinating people, living independently outside mainstream civilization. To tell the truth, I'm rather curious about their isolated existence!"

"We ought to do foreign vacations more often," responded the wife. "It certainly has rejuvenated your spirit of adventure."

Harry rotated the steering wheel to the right, and the compact vehicle veered onto another unpaved road. Then, the Wilsons' automobile had to travel almost a mile upon a mixed gravel and sand surface before reaching the foreboding black tents picturesquely nestled near a gorgeous mountainside.

An inhabitant in the Gypsy colony spoke accented English, and the guide led the Wilsons to a camp elder. The dark, wrinkle-skinned, old man greeted them. Soon, Harry told his host of his heart's desire.

"I'm searching for an exquisite chess set to add to my collection," the visitor indicated. "Do you know of any in the area?"

The camp elder slowly led Harry and Betty to a large, faded gray tent. The three entered the canvass enclosure rather deliberately. The interior was dimly lit by candlelight, and rows of tiered votive candles gave-off a scented aroma that smelled much like perfumed incense. A frail Gypsy woman (who also spoke rudimentary English) introduced herself as Katrina, and then the withered old man politely excused himself' and left the eerie premises, returning to perform his various campsite chores.

Throughout the scary, elderly woman's tent were many handmade products. Blankets, painted dishes, jewelry, and other interesting items cluttered the confined and dusty display counters. However, Harry was in quest of just one objective and that was a special chess set to gladly add to his fine collection. Every visible item on display inside the dingy tent seemed to elude his scrutiny.

"Katrina, do you have any chess sets for sale?" the on-a-mission visitor inquired. "That's the only thing I'm interested in buying."

The woman's expression changed from a forced smile to a slight frown as she momentarily hesitated. "I'll show you something very unusual!" the Gypsy lady confidentially revealed in a whisper. The old hag then displayed to Harry and Betty a majestic well-crafted chest made of dark ebony. Katrina carefully opened the lid, and inside the handsome wooden case was the most extraordinary chess set Harry's eyes had ever perceived. The pieces were next very meticulously removed, one at a time, and strategically arranged upon the accompanying chessboard, which had also been placed on the counter. The elaborate figures had been hand-carved from bone, and each marvelous article had very outstanding characteristics.

The four horses to the set immediately captured Harry's attention. The two black knights had rubies for eyes, and the accompanying white knights had emeralds embedded within their eye sockets. The splendid stallions stood on their hind legs, and each knight wielded a gleaming silver sword. The weapons were pointing straight-out as though the armor-clad cavaliers were about to enter battle. Each of the four knights looked menacing and when viewed together, exuded a macabre quality that sent a sudden chill down Harry's spine.

"Are there any other sets like this?" asked the inquisitive, on-a-mission American visitor. "I've never seen any chess set quite as wonderful as this one."

"No, Sir. I assure you; there is no other set like this one on this entire Earth," the toothless saleswoman emphasized. "It is one of a kind and it could be yours."

The old Gypsy next told the husband and wife that the set had never before been shown to any other customers. The old shrew did relate that the artisan who had carved the fabulous characters had died in 1943 during *World War II* under mysterious circumstances. The gypsy woman's recollection of the tale gave Betty the creeps, since her husband had bombed the area oil fields in *that* year, but Harry was so entranced with observing the fantastic chess set that he ignored his better judgment and instinctively decided to purchase it.

The acquired merchandise was wrapped in a special cloth and then nestled into the ebony container. The item Wilson had bought was extremely expensive, but Harry was not at all perturbed by the two-thousand-dollar cost. Price was of no object because the exquisite set was sure to make his pompous friends residing back on the Mainline 'green with envy'.

"I'm so glad you've gotten the nice chess set. Must you leave so soon?" asked the withered-faced woman. "Won't you stay for a cup of tea?"

"I'm sorry Katrina but my wife and I have already made supper plans back at our hotel in Bucharest," explained and apologized the chess set collector. "We would've loved to stay and find out more about the history and background of this terrific chess set that I've just bought."

When Harry and Betty carefully exited the tent, the Gypsy woman had an evil smile appear on her wrinkle-skinned countenance. Katrina knew exclusive information about the chess set, and her knowledge was something that she intentionally hadn't revealed to her rich American customers.

"At last, I'm rid of *that* accursed gift!" Katrina declared to her reflected image in a handheld mirror. "May God have mercy on that greedy man!"

The thrilled tourists departed the remote gypsy camp and retreated back down the steep mountain path to their rented car. They motored for seven hours until finally reaching Bucharest; their return route being a two-hundred-kilometer odyssey along dangerous winding mountain roads. The Wilsons wanted to reach the hotel as soon as possible, and much to Harry and Betty's mental relief', the ride back to the capital city was rough but totally uneventful. All the way toward Bucharest, Harry was contemplating and discussing the precious chess set and how his aristocratic friends would admire it.

When the itinerant couple finally arrived at the hotel and promptly took the elevator up to their third-floor room, reservations were confirmed over the phone to take the next scheduled morning flight back to Philadelphia. The following day, a cab conducted the Wilsons to the Bucharest Airport, and in several hours, the elated vacationers were airborne, jetting west back to the *Quaker City*.

* * * * * * * * * * * *

The *747* arrived at the *Philadelphia International Airport* on time, and the black limousine was waiting to transport Harry and Betty to their opulent Mainline mansion. Since Gregory had the day off, Charles had driven to the "International Terminal" to meet the two recent arrivals. After satisfactorily passing through customs, the Wilsons wasted little time having their heavy luggage stacked neatly onto carts. Then, the durable items were transported and deposited into the black limousine's trunk by the substitute chauffeur, taking special care not to damage the elaborate ebony coffer containing the newly obtained "impeccable chess set." Soon, the "glad-to-be-home" twosome was being driven onto congested *Route 30* and heading west toward their Mainline destination.

It had been a rather turbulent and tiring flight, and both Mr. and Mrs. Wilson were physically and emotionally spent from their overall travail. The duo decided that they would unpack their suitcases in the morning, leaving their four luggage pieces on the master bedroom's floor. The inimitable chess set remained in the ebony enclosure overnight, and Harry couldn't wait to closely examine it at dawn.

Before the Wilsons had traveled to Rumania, Harry had purchased an elegant table exhibiting a fancy inlaid chessboard, which was checkered in black and white polished marble. The furniture piece had been specifically procured to accommodate the prospective new chess ensemble that Harry now proudly possessed.

The intricately carved Rumanian chess set had been haunting Harry's mind all night, but finally, the owner managed to fall asleep from sheer tiredness. It was 7:00 a.m. when the Wilsons awoke and in a short while, the two were dressed and having breakfast in the splendid home's spacious custom-designed kitchen. After enjoying his standard bacon, toast and eggs, the husband was determined to open the chess set in the mansion's den, so that the marvelous ebony and bone pieces could be very meticulously arranged upon the new black and white marble-top table.

Harry and Betty gingerly unwrapped each of the pieces, and before long, the entire chess set was in place on the aforementioned black and white checkered tabletop. It was the most magnificent and striking collection either had ever seen, and Harry coveted the inspiration of being the first to play "an initial game" on it with a carefully selected friend.

"Aren't these pawns incomparable, Betty?" the husband proudly boasted. "This most-terrific set certainly made our superb Rumanian vacation worthwhile."

"If the set brings you joy, Harry, I wholeheartedly endorse its existence with my entire soul," Betty poetically affirmed. "Yes, Dear; it certainly is beautiful."

Later that afternoon, Wilson invited his best friend Mort Jeffries to come over to the mansion to aggressively compete in the first game upon the novel chess set. Mort had only been playing chess for one year and was not nearly as accomplished as Harry was. It wasn't long before the competitors began maneuvering their pawns and rooks in intense intellectual combat. Harry played white, and Mort commanded the black figures, which were accurately stationed upon the marble-top table.

As the game progressed, Harry became very aware that Mort was playing with virtual invincibility. The mere novice was confidently making incredible and intrepid moves, especially demonstrating particular calculated charges with his ferocious-looking black knights. All of Mort's dangerous advances were both unbelievable and unpredictable. Soon, Harry realized that he was destined to lose the first match to 'an inexperienced novice'.

The frustrated tycoon wanted to win the initial game so badly and consequently, Harry was extremely disappointed by his very quick and systematic demise, losing decisively to a 'greenhorn student of the game'. Wilson insisted that the two foes play again, and he especially demanded once more to have "white" to even the score. The capitalist mogul was certain that his superior knowledge would handily vanquish Mort, who had in the past only beaten "the master" two games in all of their dozens of previous personal tournaments.

Once more, the avid contestants proceeded with their standard original moves, and soon Harry again found his white pieces being devastated and easily conquered by his 'amateur opponent'. The black knights, in a series of bewildering and brilliant manipulations, had Harry's assorted pieces in such disarray that the game swiftly and abruptly ended. Jeffries had adroitly checkmated his foe's queen with the clever positioning of the more belligerent black knight, which had attacked Harry's vulnerable royalty from various unexpected and imaginative positions.

Harry found it quite disturbing and embarrassing to lose two consecutive games to 'an awkward beginner' like Mort Jeffries. Wilson tried to reason that his mind still had been mentally drained from the long-distance European trip, and that when he would be fully refreshed, "the master" would have no trouble in devastating and humiliating Mort on another occasion. The now-frustrated tycoon diplomatically called it a day, for Wilson remembered that important business had to be decided and enacted at his corporate office the following morning.

"Mort, I must admit that you were a formidable adversary today!" Wilson glibly congratulated his chosen chess opponent. "But I guarantee that next time I'll make you into chopped liver."

"Harry, I could never duplicate that inexplicable performance in a million years," Mort candidly and guiltily answered. "Tonight, I felt invincible! Tonight, I feel that not even Bobbie Fischer in his prime could've beaten me!"

After Mort Jeffries left for home, the chess articles were then correctly organized upon the magnificent table-board and left there until their next scheduled parry. Harry usually orchestrated the practice of carefully arranging the pieces, so that he wouldn't have to waste time resetting the board prior to the upcoming "mental combat challenge".

The remainder of the day, Wilson spent seated behind his desk in his stately walnut-paneled center city office. His bewildered mind assessed over and over again the two games he had lost to a 'rank beginner like Mort'. The wealthy plastics product manufacturer and distributor couldn't wait to resume engagement in intellectual warfare with another targeted foe. When Harry Wilson had finally finished catching-up with his boring work responsibilities, the rattled entrepreneur rushed home to swallow-down dinner and to then invite his loyal colleagues over to officially inspect the new chess set.

Seven of Harry's chess playing partners arrived at 8:00 p.m. to examine and admire the tycoon's most recent acquisition. The affable group proceeded from the library to the den to enviously scrutinize the new "absolutely stunning Rumanian chess set". Harry immediately sensed that something in the room was very different. The sundry pieces were not set-up exactly as Wilson had so fastidiously placed them on the board the night before. Each item appeared to have been slightly moved out of place. 'Perhaps the butler had looked at the chess set and had carelessly tampered with the wonderful pieces?' the confused baron-of-industry imagined.

"This is the most magnificent chess set I've ever seen," remarked a jealous neighbor. "I'll bet it's one of a kind!"

"Wilson, your Epicurean taste is above and beyond criticism," stated another of his garrulous, phony friends. "Congratulations!"

The entire chess set sparkled from light given-off and reflected by the overhead crystal chandelier, and each attending gentleman coveted the notion of playing either the resplendent black or white figures. Harry watched intently as each game progressed. George Harrington, who was playing black, had the superior position and was guaranteed a win over slightly-mortified Mort Jeffries. George was not the most accomplished chess player on the Mainline, but he seemed to demonstrate astounding sagacity and strategy with the utilization of his black knights.

Everyone took turns experiencing the feel of the beautiful set, and as the intense games continued, strangely, black had won over white every single time. Harry Wilson was the only spectator who seemed to have noticed the noteworthy coincidence after four games, but the estate owner did not want to discuss or even divulge his keen observation with his enamored Mainline comrades.

Eventually, Harry got his chance to play a game against George. Wilson deliberately selected white to prove that "black" was simply a 'quirky aberration having a good luck streak.' Wilson felt certain he would emerge victorious since the "master" was by far the most advanced chess authority seated in the room.

The new game started and Harry Wilson quickly realized that no matter how intelligent a move he would make, and no matter how accurate and wily his strategy was, it was never sufficient enough to defeat his rival George Harrington. The more offensive of the two black knights was astoundingly infallible while situated upon the marble-top chess table. The awesome nemesis always compromised Harry's pieces into either elimination or into distressful submission. The game swiftly ended, and Harry's white pieces had dramatically lost to his 'relatively unskilled foe'.

"That's the damnedest thing I've ever witnessed," exclaimed Harry's astonished opponent. "That one black knight was almost supernatural and invincible!" George incredulously exclaimed.

"I'll bet you're still unsettled from your recent European hiatus!" consoled Mort Jeffries to his fully stunned host. "Under normal circumstances, Harry, you easily prevail over any of us rookies ninety-nine times out of hundred."

The extraordinary debacles were starting to erode the haughty entrepreneur's general confidence. The most recent surprise loss had tarnished Harry's highly prestigious reputation as the Mainline's top-notch "chess master", and Wilson was even more perturbed because his closest friends were now collectively ribbing him with an abundance of false praise. The host laughed it off as just a bad game he had played, but deep down within his weak heart, Harry Wilson was both paranoid and livid. 'Perhaps my concentration and quality of play are slipping,' he sadly guessed.

The wealthy socialites decided to call it a night when the late evening news appeared on the game room's enormous ultra-modern TV screen. The spirited guests merrily left the stately mansion, and then addled Harry stubbornly reset the chess pieces upon the black and white marble-top board. Next, the obsessive/compulsive fellow very deliberately stepped upstairs to retire to the massive master bedroom chamber.

Wilson had a restless night, and while he was twisting and turning in his sleep, the defeated chess player discerned a distinct noise coming from outside his bedroom window. The nervous man suspected that the mysterious sound had originated from the horses' stables, located adjacent to the mansion. Wilson rose from bed and shuffled his feet across the room to the window, trying not to disturb Betty's rest. Harry quickly peered-out towards the horses' quarters. It was dark outside, but when the man-of-the-house opened the window, Wilson heard his thoroughbreds loudly neighing and snorting in a frightened manner. The animals were deathly scared, and the chess-master wanted to know why. As the 'light sleeper' continued staring-out into the chilly night air, Harry thought he had seen under the pale moonlight the fleeting shadow of a ghostly figure on horseback whisk-by in the distant meadow.

The troubled observer flicked-on the outside floodlights and soon frantically rushed downstairs and out the back door, dashing to the estate's stables. The horses were extremely unsettled and sweaty from frenetically kicking inside their stalls, but the alarmed property owner could not interpret the true source of their nervousness. Something or someone had created the recent loud disturbance, but the anxious tycoon couldn't precisely determine exactly what.

The curious inspector then trekked outside the equine domicile to survey the immediate vicinity, and the on-the-prowl investigator quickly noticed freshly-made hoof prints in front of the nearby red barn. The imprints then led to the vast open field where he and his 'gainfully unemployed friends' often enjoyed their exciting fox hunting escapades. It all seemed very baffling and quite unusual, and Harry Wilson determined that he would have to perform additional probing into the evening's baffling enigma in the morning.

The remainder of the night, the befuddled mogul was plagued with insomnia. Harry finally did doze-off for a short interval until the clock radio rudely startled his uneasy slumber at six a.m. Wilson soon was fully awake, out of bed and showering.

At the breakfast table, Harry discussed with Betty the unexplained event that had transpired during the chilly night. The stressed-out husband asserted that he would have to delve further into the conundrum to thoroughly satisfy his intense curiosity.

"It was the closest thing to paranormal I've ever experienced," the distraught husband concluded and shared. "I'm at wits end."

"Don't worry, Harry. Your active imagination has gotten the better of you because you're still suffering the after-effects of intercontinental jet lag," reassured his devoted wife.

Before leaving for his downtown Philly' office, the prosperous businessman entered the den to closely study the room's stellar new addition. As Harry Wilson approached the black and white marble- top chess table, his eyes noticed a few blades of grass randomly scattered onto the usually spotless, wood parquet floor. Some traces of dirt were evident and smeared upon the surface of the recently purchased chess table. The multimillionaire surmised that the grass and dirt had been accidentally deposited from the shoes of several of his clumsy drunken companions the night before. Wilson then instructed his butler to clean-up the annoying mess.

"Charles, have you been curiously inspecting my new chess set?" the confused master of the mansion asked.

"No, Sir, Mr. Wilson. I only do what *you* direct me to do and nothing more," the servant respectfully and obediently replied.

At his downtown office, Harry was so busy attacking his accumulated business/work backlog that the perplexed man was not able to sufficiently evaluate anything in the realm of problem solving about the prior night's suspicious horse disturbance. Wilson only hoped that it wouldn't occur again.

That evening, the chess connoisseur again invited his trusty Mainline companions over to engage in cerebral duels performed on the expensive black and white marble-top chessboard. Harry insisted on playing the first match while utilizing the black pieces. His opponent again was George Harrington, who had easily bested Wilson twice in their previous matches. The intense parlor contest soon commenced.

The host instantly became aware that his hands would automatically maneuver the black pieces with uncanny deftness, as if he himself was being manipulated by an evil remote control. Wilson was advantageously making bold forays that were both spectacular and ingenious. The more bellicose of the black knights adequately corralled its white counterpart into complicated, entrapped positions, and then the black cavalier expertly created great havoc among the remaining white pieces.

Harry euphorically won the game handily and felt much better because of the thrill of conquest, which had effectively regenerated his failing self-confidence. But Wilson was a little uneasy because the sagacious moves he had brilliantly demonstrated had been improvised without *his* complete volition or intention. It wasn't until after each machination had transpired that the reputed chess-master realized how good of a strategy maneuver had really been implemented. The mansion owner's recent stellar play had just transcended his notorious highly-skilled chess acumen, and *that* alien notion extremely bothered Harry Wilson's conscience.

Next, the American industrialist and land baron again challenged George Harrington in order to gain full revenge for losing twice the night before. This time Wilson plotted to play "white" to amply demonstrate to his enamored audience his awesome, omnipotent chess superiority.

Soon George was making incredible moves with his indomitable black knights, and his remarkable play exhibited great discipline, daring and military precision. Harrington swiftly and adroitly had Harry's queen cornered into a surrendering position. It was, once again, the more combative black knight that had been responsible for the astonishing total defeat.

No one else in the crowded room wanted to believe what had actually and undeniably transpired. The other talkative, spellbound eyewitnesses only assumed that the more fortunate player had won by a stroke of luck and that Harry had not yet fully recovered from his European vacation and from the mammoth mound of paperwork that occupied his downtown office desk. Everyone eventually got an opportunity to indulge in the strange amusement and on every occasion, the one who had played "black" amazingly won.

The evening ended and the bewildered visitors hastily departed the Mainline mansion in a group quandary, chattering furiously amongst themselves. Harry directed Charles to clean-up the opulent den and to put the new chess equipment back onto the board in perfect alignment as the host then graciously showed his vociferous guests to the foyer door.

"You have a most remarkable chess set there," confessed George. "It's an absolute classic! Perhaps you'll someday sell it to me!"

"Good night!" replied Harry. 'Good riddance!' Wilson thought.

"Please invite us over again," Mort sincerely requested. "I'm sure Harry that your chess prowess will return as soon as you get back to normal from your trip and from your taxing office demands."

The multimillionaire marched up the spiral staircase to bed, kissed his wife "goodnight", and after changing into his warm pajamas, was soon sound asleep. During his slumber, Wilson was again startled by a peculiar noise originating from the adjacent horse stables. The chess expert feverishly rose from his bed, rushed to the window, and then focused his bleary pupils outside. The very apprehensive spectator was certain that he had noticed a foreboding form riding upon a formidable galloping horse, speeding away from the stables, and then promptly moving into the gloomy darkness of the distant meadow.

The stallions in the stables were once more in a state of anxiety, agitated and quite sweaty. Immediate action had to be taken to capture whoever was causing the recurring dilemma. The next night, the still-alarmed chess fanatic planned setting a trap to discover the identity of the culprit trespasser and thus 'putting an end to *his* obnoxious pranks'.

"Harry, are you sure you shouldn't call the police?" asked Betty, who had awoken and had exited the mansion wearing her pink bathrobe and matching slippers. "The police are trained to deal with prowlers and hooligans. This is no time for you to learn how to become a vigilante!"

"No, Betty; I can handle the problem myself!" answered the fiercely independent self-made man. "When I need the police, I'll call them! I'm sure that this is some sort of impractical practical joke being played, perhaps by either Mort or George!"

Harry and Betty reentered the stone Tudor-style mansion, proceeded to climb the spiral steps and soon go back to bed. While Wilson was attempting to doze-off into dreamland, he thought his ears discerned an odd noise coming from the newly named "Chess Room." The resident cautiously descended the spiral staircase and flicked-on the downstairs lights to comprehensively assess the disturbance. 'Maybe it's Charles getting a midnight snack,' the rich fellow hopefully thought.

The "Chess Room" was empty, except for some random grass blades that had been carelessly scattered and strewn upon the floor. 'Could it be my careless drunken friends who had again brought that disgusting debris in on their shoes?' Wilson speculated.

As the befuddled man was about to exit the game-room chamber, Harry took a glance at the very singular chess set. Wilson suspected that his pupils had glimpsed a slight movement, but again, the observer was very tired from excessive sleep deprivation. The mogul theorized that it all simply was his vivid imagination running amok.

The next evening, the now-neurotic chess enthusiast set an imaginative trap for the stealthy horseman encroacher. Just when Harry Wilson would normally step up the stairs to the master bedroom right before midnight, but this time the plotter stealthily ambled out to the stable and saddled-up his prized white horse. The obstinate schemer was going to chase and collar the 'prankster phantom' that had been boldly riding and illegally trespassing across his sacred landscape.

It was a misty and drizzly late autumn evening. The self-appointed commando patiently waited in the stable for 'the foolish intruder' to make his predictable appearance. Wilson was standing there, mentally measuring the uncanny phenomenon of the Rumanian chess set and how he could not win to save his life with 'white'. Then the prospective ambusher was becoming exhausted and drowsy. Harry Wilson inadvertently fell asleep lying upon scattered straw in an empty stall only to suddenly be aroused by the sound of fiercely frantic horses. The alarmed animals were squealing in a frenzy; jumping, panicky, kicking and wildly braying inside their separate stalls.

With exceptional difficulty, the self-appointed estate sheriff mounted his saddled beast. Wilson managed to press a wall button while positioned atop his restless white steed, and soon the stable doors electronically opened. The pursuer sallied-off into the darkness in quest of the anonymous interloper. Peering through the heavy night mist, the intense equestrian could barely perceive an obscure figure impetuously galloping-away upon a speedy black steed. The chase was on.

The multimillionaire was an excellent horseman and thought he had the dexterity and the willpower to overcome the 'bizarre mystery rider'. However, the faster that *his* white stallion accelerated, the faster the black horse and rider pulled ahead. In short time, Harry could not see the intruder's silhouette any more. The shadowy specter had lost Wilson inside the brambles of the labyrinth-trailed woods remotely situated on his immense thousand-acre estate.

The disappointed equestrian gave-up his pursuit and violently tugged the reins of his favorite white stallion to the right, pointing the creature back in the direction of the recently constructed stables.

After the alarmed beasts inside the stable finally calmed-down, Wilson left his cherished steeds, entered his mammoth manor house and then returned upstairs to bed. Harry spent another restless night, not ever completely falling asleep. The greatly unnerved fellow was surprised that his unwary wife had soundly slept right through the entire commotion.

"You had better stay home from work and rest all day today and also tomorrow," Betty wisely suggested at the breakfast table. "You can't accomplish much while being so upset!"

"You're right, Honey. I must be suffering from the business counterpart to combat battle fatigue!" Wilson defensively admitted. "I'll try and heed your caring and wise advice."

After breakfast Harry casually sauntered into the den and was shocked when he perused the downed chess pieces on the normally immaculate black and white marble-top table. All the items had been knocked over except the Black King's armored Black Knight. A further inspection of the room revealed tufts of grass strewn-around as well as thick clumps of mud blemishing certain areas of the imported parquet floor. Whatever was happening (both inside and outside the mansion) was certainly cryptic in nature. Harry was indeed paranoid and terror-stricken. Something rather sinister, surreal and unearthly had been occurring that exceeded the man's comprehension.

* * * * * * * * * * * *

A foxhunt had been scheduled for the first Sunday morning in November. When *that* "special event day" finally arrived, the sky was dreary and a slight drizzle was falling. The hunt had never before been canceled, and Harry Wilson was adamant to his loyal Mainline companions that it was not going to be postponed to a later date. "I refuse to break with tradition," the host obstinately argued. "Tradition rules!"

"Let's call it off, Harry. I have a bad feeling about this ugly weather pattern," Mort Jeffries begged. "I always trust my instincts."

"Don't be silly Mort. Don't let a little dismal low-pressure front put a damper on our fun!" returned the domineering chess fancier. "Where's your sense of adventure? It's too damned easy chasing foxes around these woods under perfect conditions."

Wilson kept his hunting dogs caged in a separate outbuilding, and readily had all his special canines assembled on leashes outside their kennel, all waiting for the slated fox pursuit to commence. The riders soon were all mounted in their saddles, the fox was released from its pen, the horn was blown and the hunt was on. The fleet horses galloped into misty, muddy, rain-soaked fields with barking beagles leading the way. The sleuthhounds soon located the desperate fox's scent and chased the frightened prey into an isolated bracken', with the now-motivated men on horseback following *their* wild initiative. Soon the scared-to-death fox had been successfully surrounded, the animal being trapped inside a hollow log.

The wealthy plastics merchant deliberately lagged behind his 'aristocratic posse'. Being in a good mood, Harry desired giving his friends the first chance at hunting-down the elusive, sly creature. As Wilson nonchalantly rode high in his stirrups, he viewed what appeared to be the same black horse along with its bizarre jockey whizzing along in the distance. Their vague forms were speeding through the thick mist in the opposite direction of the aforementioned hunt, traversing the gigantic field from east to west. Harry stubbornly advanced at full speed toward the nebulous figures, which at that moment appeared as a single apparition about to vanish into the thick morning haze.

It was a wild pursuit and when Wilson succeeded at closing the gap while riding upon his favorite white stallion, the black equine and its hellish rider oddly stopped, and next rapidly turned around. What Harry witnessed soon terrified him right down to his bone marrow. The phantom rider was a pernicious, armored, black knight fiercely wielding a shimmering silver sword. The fearsome crusader shouted a foreign medieval battle cry, and then eagerly charged his intended adversary. Wilson had no chance of protecting himself from the superior evil enemy.

As the black knight's charger sped onward, the recent visitor to Rumania was absolutely petrified. With one swift lunge, the anonymous champion drove his sharp steel sword into Harry shouting "*Checkmate!*" Then, after committing his heinous deed, the diabolical *Lancelot* rode-off into a nearby woods'. Harry fell from his still fleeing horse upon the ground, mortally wounded, and a victim of the supernatural black knight's lethal blade.

The multimillionaire's preoccupied friends were currently unaware of their neighbor's horrible fate. Mort, George and the other hunt participants were still frivolously cornering and tormenting the overwhelmed fox. When the horsemen finally ascertained that Harry was not in their presence, the riders rapidly dispersed into two search parties. The dual groups thoroughly canvassed the various surrounding fields on horseback, and soon one group came upon a body lying prone upon the damp ground.

George summoned the second search party by blowing into his foxhunt horn. Harry's familiar form was miserably lying on the muddy turf, and Wilson was profusely bleeding from a large open chest wound. The corporation chief executive was still alive, barely clinging to life. The victim had just enough strength to whisper to his appalled friends, "It was a knight on a black horse that mortally wounded me. I swear to God it was!" The unfortunate chess martyr then lapsed into deep unconsciousness, and a minute later, ceased breathing.

The host's loyal companions were in a state of total shock. The Mainline neighbors respectfully conveyed their friend's limp body back to the manor house and then notified the police, who immediately converged on the scene with sirens blaring. The detectives questioned everyone about the peculiar sequence of events leading-up to the horrible tragedy. The investigating authorities were told Harry's "irrational last words", and then a detective skeptically jotted them down on his notepad.

The very methodical interrogators found the entire story extremely difficult to believe. The police sleuths closely analyzed the contents of every item in every room of the ornate mansion, and when they entered the den where the chess set had been located, the on-the-scene inspectors became aghast with horror.

The room's parquet floor was covered with weird hoof-prints along with an array of unsightly mud clumps. The hoof-prints were normal-sized at the door entrance but became smaller and smaller as their trail approached the chess pieces situated upon the black and white marble-top table. There, the floor marks diminished into even smaller detail and then reappeared upon the marble-slated black and white checkered chessboard, and the ominous hoof imprints eerily led-up to the specific block reserved for the very antagonistic Black King's more brutal, dominant Black Armored Knight.

The now tiny black-painted swordsman had a silver sword drawn in his right hand, but much to the detectives' consternation, the shiny weapon was completely smeared with recently shed blood. The following week, detailed laboratory tests were performed on the retrieved blood samples that had been obtained from the Black Knight's lethal weapon. The distinct "O Positive blood type" was determined to be the same as Harry's, along with accompanying *DNA* evidence.

* * * * * * * * * * * *

An attentive airline hostess shook Harry Wilson's right shoulder and instructed him to buckle-up his seat belt. The jet airplane was making its final approach to *Philadelphia International Airport.* Betty smiled at her spouse as he escaped the frightening spell of his terrifying *747* airborne night-mare.

The wealthy chess-master's mind and heart were in emotional conflict as the jumbo jet safely descended to the runway. Should Harry Wilson destroy his treasured, newly-purchased chess set upon returning to his comfortable mansion on Philadelphia's exclusive Mainline? Was his disturbing nightmare on the return flight from Rumania a bad dream, or was it an arcane, occult omen being mysteriously generated from the mystical, invisible world?

The supernatural powers that were representative of the dreadful and more hostile Black Knight reigned-over Harry Wilson's fearful consciousness as the enormous *747's* wheels finally touched-down in Philadelphia, the City of Brotherly Love.

"The Cups"

The morning sun rays were streaming through the bedroom window and shining directly into the brown eyes of Albert Martin, who quickly awoke from his light slumber. The aroma of freshly brewed coffee sifted its way into the upstairs bedroom. Dawn was always a pleasant refreshing time for the computer wizard. Albert always looked forward to hustling downstairs and then enjoying that first cup of delicious java with Marian.

Albert and Marian Martin lived in Avalon, a small town on the southern New Jersey coast just above Stone Harbor and Wildwood. Their attractive blue-vinyl-sided, two-story-home commanded a panoramic view of the vast *Atlantic*. Albert and Marian were raised in Cape May, fifteen miles inland from the pounding surf, and they always desired to live near the ocean's charm and fury.

"Breakfast is ready!" the wife yelled upstairs. "Coffee's on!"

"Marian, I'll be in the kitchen before you can walk to the toaster," Albert hollered down to his gorgeous spouse.

Albert Martin was age forty and possessed thick bright reddish hair. The man's seemingly chiseled chin and cheekbones made him quite an attractive specimen to the eyes of the opposite gender. The healthy, former college athlete was also well-built and vigorously exercised at the local fitness club three times a week, if his busy schedule permitted.

A distinctive mole blemished the right side of Albert's forehead, and the noticeable growth was the husband's sole facial flaw. The mark always suggested imperfection to those who would meet the otherwise handsome man for the first time. And the avid surfer preferred wearing casual clothes to formal attire, even on his long-distance business flights. Albert's favorite color was blue, which explains why Martin owned several blue sweaters, which he proudly flaunted on domestic and international excursions.

Marian was a fantastically beautiful woman in her middle thirties. Her wavy blonde tresses draped-down to her shoulders. Lovely blue eyes complemented her fair-skinned appearance. The faithful wife maintained a well-proportioned figure. Men would crane their necks for another glance whenever "the doll" passed by on the downtown Avalon-By-the-Sea sidewalks. In short, Marian and Albert made quite an appealing couple.

The Martins had recently returned from a pleasurable European trip the month before. The couple had spent several adventurous weeks abroad and stayed at two expensive resorts on the dazzling Mediterranean Coast. The enjoyable getaway was highlighted by visits to many exotic tourist meccas situated on the beautiful *French Riviera* and in Monaco.

Smelling the coffee aroma, Albert Martin donned his blue bathrobe and then dashed-down to the recently refurbished kitchen. The instant the man of the house gave his wife an affectionate peck on the cheek, the wall phone rang. Marian immediately knew that a 7 a.m. call meant a distant request seeking Albert's in-demand business expertise.

After swallowing a piece of blueberry muffin and then listening to the 'urgent call' on the answering machine, the husband meandered to the kitchen countertop where the coffee had been perking. Marian already had the outside table set on the screened-in porch with toast and strawberry jam awaiting Albert as he carefully carried the two full coffee cups to his breakfast destination.

"Are you still tired?" the wife asked. "You do look rested!"

"I was a bit until I smelled the fresh coffee," Albert confessed, "but then I saw your face and forgot about the delicious brew."

One hobby that Albert and his wife immensely enjoyed was collecting coffee cups and mugs originating from all over the world. The Canadian oak kitchen hutch displayed many valuable cups and mugs that had been purchased as souvenirs on previous vacations. Albert and Marian had a unique family tradition. The couple would drink from two different cups each morning until they had made a full rotation through their entire collection, and then begin employing the process all over again. This rather eccentric habit was a real joy, since the cups reminded the Martins of many romantic foreign locales.

Several cups in the collection had been purchased on the Martins' most recent journey to the *French Riviera*. The couple hadn't had a chance to closely examine the nostalgic vistas pictured on the Monaco and Cannes cups, since upon returning from Europe, the marital partners had been preoccupied reminiscing about their whirlwind sightseeing activities, and readjusting to their Avalon living environment.

Each of the cups hanging in the kitchen hutch exhibited a notable geographic setting, including the colorful ornate beer steins that Albert had once purchased in Munich during the German city's annual *Octoberfest*. And on *that* morning when the Martins got comfortably seated at their white rattan porch table, the opportunity to examine the *Riviera* cups presented itself. Albert and Marian conversed and carefully studied their new possessions.

"Aren't these fabulous scenes exquisite?" Marian marveled and remarked. "They make me want to return to Cannes!"

"They sure are pretty sentimental," Albert agreed. "I'm glad that we began this nifty collection hobby in Aruba back in '82. Honey," continued Albert with a smile, "come to mention it, we've traveled to almost every exotic vacation paradise on the globe."

"Too bad you aren't back in high school," the wife giddily replied. "You'd be able to get an A in geography instead of the C you had earned!"

Albert was a much-relied-upon consultant for a large Philadelphia-based computer firm. The "guru" was dutifully on call for troubleshooting assignments twenty-four hours a day. Frequently, the specialist had to jet to the West Coast in response to sudden corporate database emergencies, and Martin was his firm's chief problem solver and was paid handsomely for his expert skills.

Marian became accustomed to the hectic lifestyle generated by the proliferating computer/Internet age. The accelerated pressure and pace all went with the territory of being modern-day Americans. The wife's devoted spouse made an excellent living, and Marian was quite ecstatic that she did not have to toil daily in the competitive economic rat race. Mrs. Martin was free as a lark, and the woman loved every minute of her domestic liberty.

In his work responsibilities, the computer glitch and virus diagnostician was generally gone for several days at a time and when those departures happened, the electronic wizard's wife was left alone to pursue her random personal interests. Marian often kept busy reading, and occasionally the wife also had friends visit for impromptu coffee chats. One particular confidanté was Martha Howell, an old Cape May Regional High School friend and regular guest whenever Albert was on one of his lengthy Pacific Coast or Great Lakes special assignments.

"Honey, I have to fly out to L.A. to investigate a major computer virus," Albert regretfully stated. "I'm sorry to report that I won't be home until Wednesday at the earliest."

"Don't those California work stations ever get bacterial infections?" his wife joked, referring to the word "*virus*".

"No, just occasional *terminal* illnesses," her husband cutely jested. "And when you fly over Los Angeles, UCLA!"

"Whatever you do, leave the El Niño Effect on the West Coast," Marian requested, ignoring her husband's ridiculous joke. "Forget the *Pacific*. I love the majestic *Atlantic,* especially when it's warm and tranquil!"

"I'll gladly do that," her husband promised with a grin.

"Al, the *French Riviera* was absolutely heaven on earth," Marian recollected. "We just have to re-visit it!"

"Sugar," the husband cheerfully replied, "if I could, I'd take you back there right now. Notice our conversation has gone from the *Pacific,* to the *Atlantic* and has ended-up at the *Mediterranean.*"

"I hope you can get a seat on the plane at such short notice!" Marian answered, expressing her concern. "Airports today are such a terrible hassle!"

"They know me at the ticket counters and if worse comes to worse, there's always 'Stand-by'," the husband indicated. "I'm used to the constant turmoil."

The considerate spouse then kissed his beautiful soulmate goodbye. Albert loved his wife with all his heart and was never reluctant or afraid to show it.

* * * * * * * * * * * * *

After Albert Warren Martin departed scenic Avalon in his green *Buick Park Avenue* heading for the *Atlantic City Airport,* Marian had a chance to more closely scrutinize the memorable *Riviera* cups that the lovebirds had recently purchased. The delicate, hand-painted porcelain mementos had cost a very expensive twenty-five Euros apiece, and each one exhibited very elaborate and colorful artwork. Then honoring a casual whim, the housewife nonchalantly walked over to the kitchen hutch and surveyed the other splendid cups individually hanging inside.

The multicolored tableaus that decorated the cups were indeed quite intricately designed. Three of the memorable scenes depicted typical street renditions featuring human activity. Pedestrians were walking on sidewalks in St. Thomas, in Tokyo, and in Paris. Two particular cups depicted boats floating on placid lakes in Chicago and in Rome. Another cup displayed a familiar desert scene where a camel caravan was shown in the arid forefront with the *Egyptian Sphinx* and pyramids being in the background. Another elaborately created cup portrayed a remote cave's entrance in the *Carpathian Mountains.* Still another pictured a fabulous tropical sunset, which beautifully illuminated a picturesque Samoan volcano's summit.

Marian returned her attention to examining and admiring the two new *Riviera* cups. The perceptive woman immediately detected something rather unusual and irregular. Every time the perceptive woman glanced-down at the handheld objects, the scenes seemed to undergo subtle changes that ever-so-slightly altered the original settings. 'Perhaps I need my eyes examined by an optometrist,' Marian thought. 'Maybe I'm overly stressed-out from my exhaustive European hiatus.'

Soon, the lady-of-the-house ignored the peculiar distinctions being represented by the Cannes scene, dismissing the manifestations as small visual aberrations that resulted from lack of sleep and from last Saturday's six-hour limo' ride from New York City, where Albert had surprised his wife with a scrumptious Four Seasons dinner, followed by a fabulous *Broadway* musical.

'My mind's playing cruel and wicked tricks on my eyes,' mentally speculated the wife, who was now feeling a degree of heightened anxiety. Marian paused momentarily to gather her thoughts. 'I'm also a bit angry because Al had to leave for Los Angeles so suddenly. I was hoping that we could've driven to Atlantic City where we could've enjoyed strolling the boardwalk and spending some time playing slots at Bally's Casino. But I'll be all right once I make a few mental adjustments.'

Albert would usually phone Marian the morning of his return flight, which (even from the West Coast) was ordinarily the following day, after the computer network's defects had been satisfactorily corrected. A full week had elapsed and still there had been no call from her devoted spouse. Mrs. Martin was now somewhat concerned, since Albert hadn't told her the identity of the California bank or corporation where he had been assigned to perform his high-tech magic. She considered calling the company's main office, but decided that her concern might make her seem (to Albert's bosses) like an alarmist or a worrywart pessimist.

The following afternoon, when Marian was out grocery shopping at a Cape May Courthouse ShopRite, the house landline phone rang. A brief message had been left on the answering machine, but upon returning home, Mrs. Martin couldn't understand the erratic voice, which was garbled in dense static. The male speaker sounded excited, but the severe interference destroyed the quality of the voice transmission. Then, the call abruptly terminated. The high-tech phone tracer did not capture a return number.

Marian immediately dismissed the incident as a rare 'Twentieth Century error in telephone communications.' Still, the anxious wife pondered where the call had originated. The woman was convinced that the speaker had been her ever-faithful mate, but why had Albert's 'reliable cell phone' been unresponsive to her many calls?

"I'm going to definitely switch long distance companies," the housewife promised herself. "This is not at all like Albert to not call home if he's delayed. I'll give it another day and then call his boss in Philly'. Neither my landline nor my cell can make contact!"

Several more frustrating and lonely days elapsed. The wife was now in a state of consternation, wondering exactly what had happened to her normally predictable marital partner. Finally, the suspense was too much for the spouse's delicate psyche to endure.

Marian Martin picked-up the telephone and notified the Avalon Police about Albert being a missing person. The Sergeant on duty initiated an all-points bulletin search, but cooperative attempts on both coasts were to no avail. The *California Highway Patrol* and the *LAPD* proceeded to investigate the matter, but no tangible leads or feedback ever materialized.

The abbreviated garbled-voice phone call that Marian had received amounted to another mysterious dead end. The source had been traced to a pay phone in Chicago, Illinois, which was not the city in California where Albert had gone for his now overly prolonged assignment. Mr. Swanson, Albert's boss in Philadelphia reported that the job in California had been completed in three days, that the repair was done on schedule, and that Albert should have been safely back in placid Avalon, New Jersey.

All Marian could do was to wait and pray for Albert's well-being and return. As the depressed wife held a vigil near the kitchen phone, she took another glimpse at the neatly hung cups suspended inside the solid oak hutch. This time Marian Martin was certain that the scenes had been radically (and not mildly) modified. The boats on the Chicago Lake were not in the same position as before, and the waves in the Bay of Naples now seemed wilder and more intense. Marian then noticed that there were more people strolling upon the sidewalks of Paris, Tokyo, and St. Thomas, and the worried wife observed that there were fewer camels in the Egyptian caravan cup than had been represented before, and that the sky above the Samoan volcano was darker and more ominous than she had formerly remembered it. Also, to her befuddlement, the Carpathian Mountain cave had Transylvanian bats flying out of it that hadn't been evident in previous observations.

"My God! Am I hallucinating or am I going certifiably insane?" speculated the alarmed woman out loud. "This series of events is becoming a wretched, extended living nightmare."

The local police and the California authorities had amassed no clues as to Albert's whereabouts. The Avalon cops indicated to Mrs. Martin that they would stubbornly continue the seemingly futile search. Airline records indicated that a passenger named Albert Martin had flown from the *Atlantic City Airport* on Flight 287, which had landed in Chicago to take on additional passengers. On the return flight Albert had failed to transfer at O'Hare in Chicago to board Flight 132 to Philadelphia.

"Your husband was supposed to take a shuttle from 'Philly to the *Atlantic City Airport*," the Avalon Sergeant explained over the telephone. "He never boarded the plane! His car is still parked at the A.C. Airport."

"Thank you for your time!" Marian sadly said over the telephone. "Please keep me posted if anything further develops!" Click.

Three heart-wrenching weeks had elapsed, and the duration seemed like an eternity to Marian. She had lost weight and her appetite had diminished considerably. And worse yet, the distraught woman was panicking and was now on the verge of having a nervous breakdown. Mrs. Martin had in the meantime developed bad cases of colitis and abdominal discomfort. Her husband's sudden disappearance into obscurity had escalated the Jersey Shore woman's mild apprehension to the height of supreme fear.

The out-of-sorts woman had a Nikon camera and decided to take pictures of each cup scenario in an attempt to give logical proof of her contention that the various scenes were gradually changing. Marian planned to later compare the present photographs with what she believed were the ever-evolving representations displayed upon the actual self-altering cups. She snapped photos' a few days apart, and after a roll of pictures had been taken, the beleaguered woman delivered the disc for development at a local RiteAid pharmacy.

Marian Martin hurried in the direction of home to scrutinize the photographic details but was caught in an unexpected delay. The wife's car had inconveniently stalled at a downtown Stone Harbor traffic light. The flustered lady had to contact a local gas station by cell phone in order to send-out a service truck to jump-start the battery on her brand-new Lexus. 'Now it'll require at least an aggravating two-hour delay before I can analyze the photos' in the sanctuary of my own home,' Marian Martin lamented. 'I need to compare the newly developed snapshots to the present appearances of the extraordinary cups.'

While waiting for the AAA truck to arrive on the scene to recharge the faulty car battery, Marian considered her current dilemma. "If I don't die from a massive heart attack, I'll die from sheer fright!" sobbed the grief-stricken woman as she cupped her hands to her worried face, while sitting and waiting for help behind her car's steering wheel. "This horrible torture is hell on earth!"

After having her vehicle towed, and then enduring the excruciating two-hour gas station wait, the auto's electrical problem had finally been identified and finally corrected. A new battery cable had been installed after the terminals had not responded to being "jumped". It was the end of the workday, so Marian nervously paid the old mechanic on duty and gracefully thanked him for his indispensable services.

An abundance of busy rush hour traffic was clogging the major arteries on the narrow Stone Harbor-Avalon barrier island, which additionally slowed-down Marian's homeward progress. The normal fifteen-minute errand from the pharmacy had proliferated into four hours of intense, stressful aggravation.

The phone was ringing when Mrs. Martin eagerly entered the side-door to her attractive shorefront property. It was loyal Martha Howell compassionately calling. The longtime friend and former high school cheerleader wanted to lift Marian's spirits with a "surprise dinner".

"I'll be right over!" assured the self-invited guest. "You sound like you desperately need a visit from your old Cape May High School cheerleading partner! We can chat about how we executed the difficult pyramid formation!"

There would be no time for Albert's wife to closely study the pictures until later that night. Marian dared not disclose her 'crazy theory' about the changing cup scenes to Martha Howell or else her conscientious friend might spontaneously report her for mandatory psychiatric examination.

The delicious roast beef dinner that Martha Howell had brought over was anything but enjoyable to Marian. Her curious mind was preoccupied and distracted, contemplating the changing cup phenomena, along with the relevant corresponding truths captured in the still photographs. All the while, Martha prattled-on about random, insignificant subjects and awkwardly engaged in sharing general community gossip. But Marian's troubled mind could not be deflected from rehashing the huge enigma of Albert's inexplicable absence. The perplexed woman, who usually savored listening to juicy, local shore gossip, suddenly found her garrulous visitor's trite conversation quite annoying.

"Would you like more roast beef?" asked Martha. "It's absolutely delectable! I got it at the ShopRite over in Somers Point."

"No thanks. I don't wish to sound rude, but I only want to get some much-needed sleep so I can relax and ease my troubled mind," answered the despondent hostess with a degree of false courtesy. "As you know, Martha, Al's been missing for nearly half a month and there's no sign of his whereabouts, anywhere. You don't suppose he's run off with another woman, do you?"

"Al's a handsome guy," Martha sympathetically acknowledged, "but he would never leave you for someone else. I'm sure there's a simple explanation that'll account for his strange absence. Maybe he's secretly in Hong Kong buying you a new diamond ring?"

Martha left at 11:00 p.m., just when it was starting to rain along the Jersey Coast. The late spring storm soon intensified, and severe winds howled and swirled around the many expensive barrier island homes. Thunder, lightning, and waves of torrential rain dominated the formerly serene evening sky while mercilessly drenching and flooding the general landscape.

After undressing and putting on her favorite robe, the unnerved housewife finally opened the plastic bag obtained from the RiteAid pharmacy. Marian Martin readily removed the recently developed pictures, and then the woman hastily arranged them on her bedroom dressing table. The photographs were then carefully organized into the exact sequence in which her dependable *Nikon* had taken them. The twelve transforming cups were next lined-up in front of the corresponding pictures, and the neurotic wife feverishly compared each of the past photos to the present cups.

All the time of Marian's incredulous analysis, the fierce northeaster was wildly raging outside. Cracks of nerve-shattering lightning, blasting the sky like powerful Roman candles, lit-up the entire master bedroom every minute or so. The fierce storm was frightening, and Marian was absolutely terrified by its great intensity. The wife was afraid that she lacked the necessary fortitude to persevere the duration through her very grueling, overwhelming psychological ordeal.

The extremely nervous woman was about to comparatively make definite distinctions between the recently developed photos' and their co-relative cups. Suddenly, the bedroom lights flickered and then went out, and Marian Martin was desperately alone and horribly enveloped in total darkness.

The hysterical wife fumbled her way through the dismal house in quest of a flashlight. After discovering one inside a remote laundry room drawer, Marian endeavored to click it on, but the flashlight failed to illuminate. The batteries had gone dead, just as the battery in her car had done.

Then, Marian had to find an alternate source of light, candles. The unlucky victim of circumstance had discovered only one small votive while searching every probable drawer throughout the entire dark house. Her trembling hand was barely able to light the wick with a shaky match, as intimidating thunder and lightning raged outside, definitely challenging the woman's faltering courage.

The tallow finally gave-off a weak, yellow, shimmering glow, but the shadowy photographs lying upon the bedroom dresser were hardly perceptible in the faint candlelight. Marian closely compared the first picture with the associated facsimile cup. Both renditions featured stationary boats on a lake in Chicago. There was no question about it;

the boats on the cups and the boats shown in the photos were indeed stationed in different positions. The wife then planned to again view the objects in the sanity of daylight. Despite the savage electrical storm, Marian's mind and soul were determined to eventually verify the results of her mortal eyes incredible cup and picture differences.

The out-of-kilter homemaker tried resting on the king-size bed, but the rattled wife awoke an hour later when the thunder and lightning became even more terrifying than before. Mrs. Martin rose from the bed and again approached her dresser where the votive's feeble flame was about to expire. But one thing was for certain. Each of the photographs now clearly showed a distinct differentiation from its actual cup counterpart. Marian held her head and felt faint, confused, and very alone. Her face was ashen, and her mouth suddenly became excessively parched. Thunder and lightning electrified the sky and compounded her enormous bewilderment. In her now-distorted mind, morning seemed light years away.

"This is no optical illusion," the woman whispered and then cried to her faint image reflected in the bedroom's blurry bureau mirror. "I can't stand any more of this unbearable torture! I need to be committed to a state hospital for psychiatric evaluation!"

Albert's wife had enjoyed little additional slumber that night. She cringed with fright when the bedroom table-phone abruptly rang. 'How could there be phone service if all of the power lines are out?' she wondered. Marian swiftly lunged for the receiver, but no voice was on the line. Five seconds of heavy static was followed by a series of clicks. Then only a dial tone emanated from the inoperable device. Could it have been Albert? Perhaps it was Martha? Was it a crank call? Maybe it had been a wrong number, and the caller had been too embarrassed to identify himself' or herself during the culmination of such a brutal coastal storm.

It was still a hostile downpour, raining heavily at 4:00 a.m., and the well-built shore house's dim hall lights were incessantly blinking on and off. Marian's bedroom seemed to reflect a very dreary Gothic-like atmosphere with the petrified woman now being too afraid to even move one iota in her bed. The defeated wife could only sob and whimper, waiting and hoping for the apathetic storm to subside, and for the blessed sun to rise.

The pictures and the cups were still situated upon the bureau. With her' mind being in a frenzy Marian felt compelled to get out of bed and again compare the rowed items. The small candle still emitted a minor degree of light as the wife rose from her mattress. An eerie draft circulating throughout the room made the tiny candle flicker and glimmer, and at that dark moment, the votive was Marian's only visual link to interpreting the real, physical world. She awkwardly bent-down at the bureau and closely stared at the dim cups and pictures lying before her eyes.

The cups' presentations were definitely dissimilar from those of the pictures. The once-familiar settings and objects appearing in the cup photographs were obviously smaller in comparison to the same scenes and objects depicted in the actual cups, and Marian ascertained that she would need the aid of a magnifying glass to confirm her nebulous discernment. In the dark, the wife rummaged through dressers and drawers and eventually found a magnifier, after desperately searching and fumbling for fifteen frantic minutes under extreme duress.

"I've never been so scared in my entire life," she cried out loud. "I'd rather die than see this haunting insanity continue. I'll die of fright before I'm ever institutionalized!"

Mrs. Martin was rapidly becoming more and more hysterical and delirious. She nervously removed the magnifier stashed amidst assorted clutter in her husband's unkempt dresser. She held the tool up to the first cup, which showed a street scene with pedestrians strolling on the Parisian sidewalk. With a shaky right hand, the woman then meticulously examined each person duplicated in the cup painting. Suddenly, Marian let out a piercing scream and then fainted upon the bedroom's Oriental rug. Sweat beads slowly formed on the unconscious woman's forehead. An incoherent Mrs. Martin woke-up ten minutes later, noticing that the magnifier was still being held firmly in her hand. The woman's entire body was presently soaked in a cold sweat.

"My God! Spare me this horrendous torture!" she gasped. "I don't deserve this! I don't deserve this!"

Marian Martin stood-up from her weak knees, stepped to the bureau and again looked at the cup's scene with trembling hands, and was shocked at seeing her husband's singular appearance. Albert was standing on the French sidewalk with his arms in the air, and the husband's frozen image appeared to be beckoning for immediate recognition. Albert Martin was wearing one of his familiar blue sweaters, and the raised mole on his forehead was quite visible under the lens of the powerful magnifying glass.

Mrs. Martin quickly scanned the other cups with the aid of the flickering votive. Amazingly, each one now featured a different representation of Albert. The cup with the camels showed the husband riding one, but now Albert's camel was attached to and being pulled by a dromedary. It was as though Martin was being led somewhere, but to where?

"This is beyond bizarre," Marian whispered and panted in raw astonishment. "This living nightmare is evil at its ugliest moment!"

Another of the snapshots depicted the entrance to the dark Carpathian cave, and in the corresponding cup, Albert's image appeared dressed in Arab garb being surrounded by flying bats. His facial features could still be distinguished, and his forehead mole was quite evident and prominent under the magnifying glass. The cup with the *Thames River* boats clearly presented Martin sitting alone in a small dingy. The wife by then had become completely demoralized. "I feel weak and sick. I'm going mad. I'm deathly frightened and don't know what to do!" the woman screamed as more intense thunder and lightning encompassed the coastal home.

Finally, upon additional scrutiny, the cup with the Samoan volcano presented Albert shown near the crater, standing at the summit. Martin was desperately extending his arms as though he were attempting to signal and attract Marian's attention. Each porcelain cup's illustration was now completely revised from its original design, and each current setting had evolved in content far beyond the previous scene that was still accurately represented in each snapshot. And Albert's physical existence was both present and prevalent in each photo'. His attempts to escape captivity and simultaneously communicate his encumbered difficulty to Marian weirdly haunted each cup's new visual portrayal. A dial tone was then heard emanating from the bedroom phone, which had inadvertently been placed out of its cradle on a nearby bedside table.

Feeling disconsolate, Marian Martin was on the verge of an emotional meltdown. The mentally disheveled victim was now hyperventilating and foaming at the mouth. She frenetically lifted the rejuvenated phone and dialed Martha Howell's number, wanting her closest friend to speed right over and give her emotional support. Albert's wife's nostrils and lungs could not inhale sufficient oxygen throughout her current mental crisis. The affected woman had become totally traumatized.

When Martha finally arrived at the home, the storm had subsided, and so the friend used her house key to gain entrance. She rushed upstairs and quickly discovered that Marian had fainted. The unfortunate woman was lying prone on the floor directly beneath the dressing table where she had been viewing the bland photos' and the incomparable shocking, ever-evolving cup images.

Martha called her fiance, a family physician, to do her a big favor and drive over to 127 Dune Lane. When Dr. Adam Saunders arrived at the plush shore home, the physician determined that his new unconscious patient should be immediately transported to the local hospital to undergo a battery of tests. An ambulance was instantly dispatched to the beachfront residence.

The doctors at *Burdette Tomlin Hospital* kept Marian Martin in the intensive care unit for two whole weeks until the besieged wife finally regained consciousness. Upon her being released, the baffled medical experts still could not explain the exact cause for the woman's confused mental state, and the attending doctors put little credence in her nonsensical cups and photos' testimony.

Mrs. Martin ended-up returning home by ambulance. The former Miss Wildwood's spirit lacked enthusiasm, and her daily actions were performed listlessly. The former beauty queen vainly tried forgetting and discrediting exactly what her still-disoriented mind recollected. Her unique and arcane paranormal experience was truly beyond the dimensions of Einstein's time-space continuum.

"I need stronger medication. Albert's absence has altered my sense of reality," Marian hypothesized and mumbled. "And those evil cups! I must destroy each and every one of them!"

Mrs. Martin finally garnered sufficient courage to bring the cups to a team of renowned scientists. The erudite gurus witnessed the scenic pictures evolve and mutate, just as Marian had dramatically described, but with all of their technical knowledge, the doctors, psychologists and professors could provide no feasible explanation for the unearthly phenomenon. The academic authorities were as much in a quandary about the uncanny transformations as Marian Martin was. The metamorphic cups undoubtedly defied the normal boundaries of commonplace laboratory investigation.

Mrs. Marian Martin continued to live in the expensive Avalon oceanfront house at 127 Dune Lane for several years, but she experienced terrible recurring hallucinations that severely affected her overall mental health. The dispirited wife obsessively dreamed about her missing husband in California, about the haunting photos,' and about the scene-changing "mystical cups". The disturbing nightmares resurfaced and were painfully endured almost every night. In both fantasy and reality, Albert was never found, and his inexplicable disappearance still remained a bizarre mystery.

"Please, Dear God, let me be with Albert again. If my husband is dead, please allow me to rejoin his presence. I can't live without him!" the aggrieved woman nightly prayed.

One cold February night, Marian went to sleep and she again dreamed of Albert. The fantasy was so intense that the woman felt as though she was actually in *his* company. The wife imagined that she could feel his hand touching hers.

Every morning, Martha Howell would respectfully phone her grieving friend, but on one particular late February morning, there was no answer. The concerned confidanté had an uneasy suspicion that something was drastically wrong. Marian's habit was that she would always be up and around early in the morning. The alarmed companion rushed to the familiar blue-vinyl-siding house at 127 Dune Lane to verify that everything was in good order.

Martha found Marian lying in bed with her eyes closed. The dear friend had the most peaceful, angelic expression dominating her motionless facial features.

"May you rest in peace," sobbed Martha as she held her dearest friend's cold limp hand. "You were truly my closest kindred spirit!"

The local scientists at *Richard Stockton College* had been assiduously studying the cups daily, but on the day of Marian's unexpected death, as the professors were carefully examining the porcelain objects, the laboratory experts became extremely startled. The laws of science had once again been violated. On the cup that featured the lake scenario, Albert and Marian were standing together locked in an amorous embrace. A caption beneath the scene oddly read, "Lake Michigan, Chicago."

The following week, the *Stockton College* experimenters detected strange developments on each of the other fantastic transformative cups with new images of Albert and Marian being represented. The young couple was again caressing, this time on the Parisian street, and the next day, standing and tightly holding hands in front of the erupting Samoan volcano.

Several weeks passed with no noticeable changes involving Marian and Albert's appearances occurring in each of the cups being scientifically analyzed. From that day on, no further alterations in the cup settings were ever again evident, but indeed, in each portrayal, the couple's warm love had been forever frozen in time.

"A Christmas Doll"

Edward Thomas Brown was swiveling back and forth his new roller chair from computer screen NASDAQ stock indices to a monitor showing the *New York Stock Exchange* ticker tape and general sales volume. Now, all Ed had to do was check-off the list of last-minute mutual fund details, along with certain municipal bonds the stockbroker had to add to an important client's lengthy portfolio, in order to finally end the busy, early winter workday. Then, Brown would be driving his luxury automobile home to his suburban Chicago palace. Tomorrow would be *Christmas Eve,* and Ed was now all set to leave his *Merrill Lynch* office early at 4:30 p.m.

While his mind was mentally reviewing his often-neglected family responsibilities because of his important job commitment, the very busy account executive's conscience was suddenly invaded by a rare surge of guilt. Amidst all of Ed's business duties, the financial advisor had forgotten his promise to buy his young daughter a *Christmas* doll. Jennifer had asked Santa for one in early December at the red and green North Pole setting at a suburban mall, and Ed just remembered that he couldn't disappoint his pride and joy. It was still early enough to purchase the desired item in the expansive toy section of a nearby downtown *Windy City* department store, but Ed had to hurry because nasty weather was on the way. "*Merry Christmas,* Grace," Brown sincerely said as the stocks and bonds guru handed his grateful, very efficient secretary her well-deserved Holiday Bonus Check! "Buy yourself that new laundry room washer and dryer you've been telling me about.""Thank you so much, Ed," Grace Mitchell excitedly replied. "I'll also use some of this cash to cut-down my fat credit card balance. I've maxed-out my *Visa* card on Christmas gifts for my immediate family and also for all my nieces and nephews' presents."

* * * * * * * * * * * * *

The Chicago based *Wall Street* investment manager donned his black leather overcoat and gathered the expensive gifts he had purchased for his wife at a downtown department store the day before. When Ed Brown finally reached his black *Lexus* in the nearby multi-tier Chicago parking garage, the investment consultant carefully arranged the three neatly wrapped gifts inside the trunk, and soon thereafter was driving off the exit ramp and heading north on State Street. It would take Brown about five-minutes to reach the large popular "Miracle Mile" shopping haven, which was scheduled to close its doors in only forty-five minutes.

It was snowing heavily, and the dense city traffic was annoying because of standard center-city gridlock. The aggravating vehicle congestion made the simple errand-at-hand take much longer than Ed had anticipated. The financial wizard feared he wouldn't have adequate time to choose an appropriate doll for Jennifer. The department store (to his recollection) always had an excellent selection, and the well-to-do father felt that it wouldn't take too long to locate a special one that his precious daughter would absolutely love. If Ed hastened, the fatigued driver could swiftly acquire the best doll available.

Brown readily parked his car in a typical downtown tiered garage, paced a block down Michigan Avenue, and quickly entered the revolving doors at the enormous department store's main entrance. The on-a-mission customer remembered that a huge assortment of dolls had been displayed on the third-floor toy section during his last Thanksgiving weekend visit. When the harried customer stepped off the escalator, the occasional patron scanned the designated display, which still contained a good selection from which to choose. Most of the more expensive dolls were positioned on a large table exhibit, but the inventory was in disarray with so many retail customers having handled and mishandled the assorted holiday merchandise. At that moment, Edward Brown's very fastidious selective taste didn't discover anything special that the anxious shopper considered genuinely exquisite or unique.

A cheerful saleslady approached the serious-minded doll department customer, and after the stocks and bonds merchant described his desire, the cooperative employee escorted Ed to a remote cabinet where a finer variety of dolls had been showcased.

"This is the store's *Rolls Royce* department," joked the affable saleswoman. "It's here for our elite clientele that prefer the finest dolls in our inventory. You appear to possess discriminating taste," the saleslady complimented. "This is definitely the area for you!"

"Thank you. These items are much more to my liking," replied the appreciative customer. "It shouldn't take me long to find and buy exactly what I want."

"Do you have any particular preference?" the store employee courteously asked. "I know this section inside and out."

"No. Just as long as it's not a voodoo doll," chuckled the exhausted but highly motivated Big Board stock evaluator. "I don't think that my daughter would like receiving a voodoo doll for *Christmas;* that's all that I would reject!"

The various dolls on display were dressed in the colorful uniforms of different adult occupations. There were male and female representations of police officers, judges, teachers, nurses, doctors, farmers and train engineers.

While studying the wonderful selection, the last-minute shopper noticed a certain doll clad as a white-coated male hospital surgeon. The figure's brightly painted face had a mustache, dark hair, tinted glasses, and featured a weak, wry smile. While examining the novel item more closely, Ed detected a small bloodstain upon the doll's bone-white jacket, so the suggestion of physical pain soon convinced the *Merrill Lynch* account executive to immediately disregard the originally fairly-interesting male physician gift. The prospective buyer could not determine whether the crimson stain had been painted onto the small white coat, or whether the distracting red mark had been caused by a finger cut from another customer, or perhaps from another store employee's hand.

The perceptive *Christmas* shopper continued surveying the extensive toy department collection, and after a short time, his fancy discovered a magnificent doll that Brown was sure his treasured daughter would cherish. The adorable figure was a Russian ballerina, and the business executive immediately had an inclination that Jennifer would positively love it.

The harried impulse-shopper told the very busy on-the-go saleslady that his eight-year-old daughter would be fascinated with the elegant *Bolshoi Ballerina,* and while the cordial woman began gift-wrapping Ed's acquisition, the ecstatic customer again browsed around the doll department. Determined to get home before the snowstorm became worse, Edward Brown returned to the cash register counter and instructed the polite saleswoman that since it was getting late, he would instead have his wife gift-wrap the delicate-looking present at home.

"Are you sure?" the saleslady politely asked. "We specialize in gift wrapping!"

"Yes," Ed diplomatically replied. "My wife by now has closed her floral shop and she's very skilled at gift-wrapping. And I know you're rushed with last minute shoppers like me and have other more urgent things to do."

"Your kindness and consideration are really appreciated," answered the saleslady quite sincerely. "I must admit it's more than a bit busy right now with late holiday shoppers."

The merry father left the mammoth-sized shopping emporium and ventured into what constituted the beginning of an intense Midwest blizzard. The severe, skin-piercing wind gusts had already caused the accumulating snow to form massive drifts next to the Michigan

Avenue storefronts. Ed held his felt hat upon his head as the Wall Street savant trudged the slippery pavement to the high-rise parking garage. Then moments later, Brown eventually exited the elevator at the third-floor to finally reach his luxury vehicle. Next, the relieved man placed the rectangular box containing the charming *Bolshoi Ballerina* doll upon the back seat, and after paying his ten-dollar parking fee at the exit, the driver was soon motoring home.

The dense Chicago traffic was still unbearable, and honking horns abounded. Dusk was rapidly transforming the dull gray winter sky into shadowy evening darkness, and the general gloom along with swirling winds made the early winter snowstorm assume an eerie atmospheric effect.

The automobile congestion moved slowly, and most of the downtown arteries between "the Loop" and Michigan Avenue were bottlenecked as if the city's main thoroughfares were a hundred long-neglected clogged sink pipes.'If this was an *artery* leading to my heart, I would definitely be having a major cardiac arrest,' Ed Brown mused and smiled as the *Lexus* navigator widened his eyes to defensively gaze at his rearview mirror. 'Why do there have to be so many people meandering about in this world?' the driver thought in a mental complaint. 'Oh well, the more people, the more capital there is to invest and profit by!'

While waiting for a signal light to turn green, Ed felt a compulsion to glance once again at the splendid Russian ballerina doll. The curious fellow reached behind his bucket-seat to grasp the box situated in the back, grabbed the unwrapped package, lifted it to the front, and clumsily placing it on the passenger seat next to him. The traffic light finally changed exactly when Brown felt compelled to remove the ballerina out of its cardboard container. Then, Ed reconsidered and rationally decided that he would endeavor admiring the quaint gift while his black luxury automobile would again be stationary at the next bothersome light.

The metropolitan traffic was predictably thinning-out as the driver was exiting downtown Chicago, now heading southwest toward his eighteen-room mansion in suburban Oak Lawn. Up ahead, the next traffic signal was switching to red, and Ed was still curious about inspecting the "magnificent *Bolshoi Princess*".

As soon as the *Lexus* came to a slow halt, Brown anxiously flipped the box lid open and immediately recognized that the pressured saleslady/cashier had erroneously inserted the wrong doll inside. The driver was angry and shocked to see the male surgeon with the bloodstained hospital jacket inside, instead of the totally beautiful Russian ballerina.

Ed Brown's impromptu examination further detected a slight change in the surgeon's facial expression, which now seemed to portray more of a wry semi-smile than the broad grin that had originally appeared upon its weird countenance in the exclusive doll section of the department store. It was now getting close to the reputable department store's holiday closing, but the frustrated driver decided to turn his vehicle around and attempt a calculated chance for a viable doll exchange.

All of the other dolls on display seemed more tolerable to the purchaser's sophisticated taste than the 'grotesque one' presently existing inside the sturdy cardboard box, but the very different-in-appearance 'male surgeon' currently gave the astute buyer the distinct impression of extreme 'hostility and sadism'.

Soon, disgruntled Ed found himself behind the wheel mumbling a litany of mild profanities about how inefficient the garrulous saleslady had been by accidentally inserting the wrong doll into the sturdy box. "Oh well, I should balance my cynicism with authentic Christian spirit. Tis' the season to be jolly," muttered the account executive to his disappointed image being reflected in the otherwise ineffective rear-view mirror. "I hope I have better luck the second time around!"

Brown again glanced at the appalling male surgeon doll situated near the gearshift panel, next to the driver's comfortable bucket seat. Ed was certain that the hideous grimace apparent on the doll's countenance was not the same wry semi-smile that he had noticed when he had first taken a casual inspection. The original wry smile had somehow mysteriously transformed into a sarcastic sneer.

"It must be my wild imagination playing havoc with my vulnerable, overtaxed mind," the doll customer uttered as he negatively shook his head. "I'm so angry that I'm not being at all logical and civil. It was all an innocent error committed by an overworked and underpaid, part-time *Christmas* employee," Ed uttered to himself' as the disappointed man drove the black *Lexus* around the block, turned right, and headed back in the direction of center-city. A pregnant moment of silence prevailed as the irritated *Merrill Lynch* financial adviser again scrutinized with livid eyes the standard downtown Chicago Christmas traffic gridlock.

"If I goofed like *that* lady on *Wall Street* investments, my boss would understandably tar and feather me," Ed Brown lectured to the male doll surgeon possessing the hostile frown, lying horizontally inside the aforementioned open cardboard box. "*Christmas* is supposed to be fun and not a big ugly aggravation like *this* particular one is becoming!"

The *Lexus* owner slowly drove through the intensifying blizzard and finally reached the vicinity of the prominent department store. Ed Brown's reliable highway machine reentered the tiered-garage, and the distressed man once again parked his luxury vehicle, After taking the elevator down to ground level, much to his delight upon stepping onto Michigan Avenue, the shopper recognized that the reputable merchandise palace had not yet locked its doors because of a big volume of last minute *Christmas* season clientélé. Brown rushed his cadence up the crowded escalator to the familiar third-floor toy department and quickly stepped to the notorious high-end doll section.

Luckily for Ed, the beleaguered saleslady that had taken care of him before was still on duty. Brown approached the still-pleasant woman carrying the undistinguished doll box wedged under his right arm. The returning patron proceeded to explain his unfortunate predicament, and after expressing his dissatisfaction, then the stock market expert declared his wish to exchange the male surgeon doll for the magnificent *Russian Bolshoi Ballerina*.

"Oh Sir, I'm so terribly sorry," the flustered saleslady genuinely apologized. "We've been so deluged today, and I must've made the mistake when I rushed your purchase while I was taking care of three customers at the same time! I guess I've just proved the Ben Franklin maxim, 'Haste makes waste'!"

"That's quite all right," Ed amiably replied, admirably concealing his mounting irritation. "Actually, I'm really quite happy that the store's still open for business."

"You don't think I'm incompetent, do you?" the worried attendant sincerely asked. "Please don't report my honest mistake to my ill-tempered manager."

"No. I simply think that you made a rather simple mistake," Ed concluded and stated.

"Well, I want you to know that I once had a bout with amnesia. Maybe it's somehow reoccurring?" the slightly-embarrassed store clerk admitted. "It's a lot of pressure working here on holidays."

Ed accompanied the slender, middle-aged woman to the now-familiar doll cabinet where she immediately reached for the aforementioned elegant ballerina, and then the apologetic sales-woman roughly reinserted the frowning male surgeon into the glass cabinet display enclosure.

The department store employee and her emotionally-soothed customer strolled-back to the toy department's main counter, and the store clerk carefully placed the pretty ballerina into a new box. Brown thanked the accommodating woman for her personal assistance in completing the exchange and then speedily stepped through the doll area toward the store's central escalators.

The satisfied customer turned-around and afforded one last glimpse at the dolls stationed inside the glass cabinet. Ed Brown swore to his conscience that the doctor doll was now really nastily scowling at him, expressing an extremely menacing grimace shown upon its painted face. A chill shot through the customer's already stressed-out heart, and stark fear directly attacked his unprotected soul. Again, the purchaser's rationality conjectured that the peculiar perception could only be his rather weary imagination running amok.

The lateness of day and the advent of night, along with the dangerous howling blizzard, motivated Ed to once again rush out of the prominent department store and gingerly amble through the drifting snow down Michigan Avenue, his careful steps pacing toward his luxury vehicle situated inside the parking garage. The determined trekker quickened his stride through a choir of sidewalk *Christmas* carolers that were braving the snowstorm's violent onslaught, and next the ambler darted past a dedicated *Salvation Army* band collectively gathered around a hanging black pot. And then with his head down and his left-hand holding his felt hat upon his head, the encumbered doll shopper quickly ambled the final hundred-feet toward the multi-tiered parking facility.

An approaching automobile slammed on its brakes and skidded wildly across a thin sheet of ice, hopped the curb, and careened through a snowdrift situated between the snow-laden avenue and the icy sidewalk. The unwary pedestrian suddenly lost his balance and began falling forward onto the pavement. The unfortunate victim was instantly rammed into the air by the out-of-control car's left front fender. The gift box flew-up out of Ed's grip as a result of the impact, and the unfortunate accident victim had been immediately knocked unconscious from the violent collision.

All traffic moving on the busy thoroughfare ceased. A knot of curious onlookers gathered around the helpless shopper lying face down on the snow-covered asphalt. An ambulance was summoned to conduct the severely injured pedestrian to the nearest hospital emergency ward.

At the exact moment the ambulance arrived at the accident scene, the toy department saleslady had been exiting her place of employment. Upon leaving the huge building's revolving door, the woman was immediately attracted to the throng of curious-but-sympathetic accident bystanders. After the saleswoman trekked over to see the object of *their* scrutiny, she shuddered when realizing that the injured man lying upon the snow-covered pavement was the one who had requested the doll exchange just fifteen-minutes earlier. The department store clerk also alertly noticed the wide-open 'ballerina's box' that had been deposited into a snowdrift located beside the frigid Chicago thoroughfare. The formerly flawless and entrancing Russian dancer/doll had fallen out of its enclosure and was now wet, dirty and quite inelegant.

"Oh my God! If only I had not made that terrible mistake. Then, this unlucky man would've never suffered this horrible fate," the saleswoman guiltily sobbed. The saleslady's troubled mind then acknowledged feeling the instant great remorse that had completely saturated her entire conscience.

"I must exchange the dirty ballerina for another before the ambulance arrives," she whispered to no one in particular.

By coincidence the flustered lady had in her possession the last remaining *Bolshoi Ballerina* doll that she planned on giving to *her* niece for *Christmas*. Without anyone observing, the *Good Samaritan* soon replaced the stained ballerina doll with the brand-new impeccable *Bolshoi Princess*. The honest-but-saddened female then orally entrusted the 'new substitute ballet dancer' to the ambulance paramedics and instructed them that it had been the property of the unfortunate man who had been seriously injured in the regrettable automobile-pedestrian incident.

"Don't worry lady, we'll make sure either he or his family gets it!" the ambulance driver promised. "Oftentimes, little things like this mean a lot!"

"Please do so," the guilt-laden woman begged. "I feel like I'm partially to blame for *his* misfortune!"

The ambulance sped-off with sirens wailing, and soon, the emergency vehicle urgently arrived at the nearest hospital's "Operating Suite". Ed Brown was still unconscious but his vital signs remained strong. The very competent team of *O.R.* specialists worked diligently cleaning his multiple body wounds and abrasions. The afflicted man had been badly injured, and surely, extensive surgeries would be required in order to neutralize the new patient's serious internal hemorrhaging.

The top surgeon on duty was instantly summoned, and Ed's wounds were professionally inspected and assessed. There was no time for x-rays, and little time for evaluation. Surgery would have to take place at once, or else, Mr. Brown's death would be imminent.

The *Wall Street* expert's gurney was swiftly wheeled into an operating room, and a team of hospital nurses efficiently prepared Ed Brown's injuries for impending incisions. Just as the chief surgeon approached the recent accident victim, the immobile *Merrill Lynch* executive opened his eyes.

Ed Brown saw something startling that had almost frightened him to death. When the accident sufferer had opened his pupils, he was staring directly at *the surgeon,* who was an actual living replica of the white-coated doll that Ed had just returned to the department store's toy counter. The operating room doctor's dreaded appearance included dark hair, tinted glasses, a thick mustache, a sarcastic sneer, along with the same disturbing blood smear in the precise same spot as that which had stained the frightening doll's white jacket.

The man lying upon the operating room table was now in a state of total shock. Ed Brown's inner spirit was so terrified that it lifted out of his battered body and mystically ascended, rising in an out-of-body experience while arcanely approaching the threshold of the macabre death realm. The ghastly experience of Ed witnessing a human version of the sinister male doctor doll was too great of a jolt for the stock-broker's already weakened heart to endure, and the O.R. patient immediately had gone into cardiac arrest. Sadly, Ed Brown passed away into eternity with a frozen, gruesome expression of utter horror evident upon his formerly handsome face.

Ed's wife had to be notified of her husband's unexpected demise. Roseann Brown rushed in her *SUV* from suburban Oak Lawn to the metropolitan hospital. After the very upset woman arrived with her hysterical daughter, she was informed of the devastating details of her spouse's horrific misfortune.

A compassionate nurse who had witnessed the final minutes of *her* husband's life attempted to console Roseann and Jennifer. As Mrs. Brown was sobbing and slowly regaining her composure, another nurse came to her and presented the department store gift box that had been intended for Jennifer.

The upset child was very reluctant to receive this last token from her deceased father. A very distraught Jennifer Brown carefully and sadly opened the lid and gently removed the contents. Inside was a doll, but the figure was not the beautiful ballerina; instead, the object was the little surgeon doll now wearing a spotless white jacket. The expression on the doll's face was one of sheer contentment, and its appearance reflected a very cordial smile.

Another emergency room nurse came urgently rushing out of the swinging doors and jubilantly shouted, "It's a miracle! Mrs. Brown, it's a wonderful miracle! Your husband has miraculously come back to life and is amazingly breathing again!"

"Reflections"

It was Friday at 5p.m. and another grueling workweek had been completed. Fred Stewart entered some final insurance data into his desktop computer terminal and inhaled a deep breath. Then, the corporate employee instinctively donned his winter overcoat, getting ready to board the next crowded train home. 'TGIF,' the relieved man gladly thought. Fred had endured an especially challenging day and was anxious to escape the drudgery associated with working in the always-pressure-packed New York City corporate headquarters. Surely, the *Madison Avenue* middle-level executive was running late, and Fred didn't want to miss the regular northbound express out of "The Big Apple".

The weather had been miserable that dark and dreary Friday in February. Fred did not relish the prospect of trekking three long city blocks in the rain and slush from his corporation's comfortable skyscraper to the definite city madhouse known as *Grand Central Station*. Stewart knew that he didn't have much time to make his monotonous daily connection that would safely transport the commuter to his familiar suburban Connecticut residence.

While walking to his late afternoon suburban commute, the insurance executive passed an unkempt-looking beggar standing with his back against a brick wall. The deadbeat was holding a cup for contributions and orally soliciting any sort of charity from apathetic, hard-working New York City pedestrians rushing by. The hideous-looking mendicant had a lengthy gray beard, a shabby blue woolen hat, and a dark brown hole-infested leather jacket. Obviously, the dreg and his shoddy apparel both had seen better days. The derelict's hole-laden woolen pants were soaking wet, and the hapless panhandler was aggressively pleading for meager pittances from the cold-hearted rush hour crowd.

The all-too-dependent tramp frequented that particular location, which was situated just before the main entrance to *Grand Central*. Fred Stewart had noticed the vagabond soliciting there many times before, although *he* never bestowed upon the vagrant a penny. Stewart wondered why the 'lowlife freeloader' couldn't obtain a minimum wage job somewhere in the metropolis and abandon the rather dishonorable disgrace associated with 'the despicable art of public begging'.

"Would you be kind enough to show me some Christian Charity?" the grimy fellow asked Fred, shoving the tin cup up to the harried pedestrian's chin.

"I do contribute to charity," Fred very gruffly and indignantly indicated. "It's called the *Fred Stewart Foundation!*"

The repugnant bum gave the cynical passerby a glaring frown when no silver coin was deposited inside his dirty tin cup. The petitioner's eyes followed Fred's brisk locomotion down the puddle-ridden sidewalk of bustling *Park Avenue*. Instinctively, Fred pivoted around and perceived the solicitous codger still sneering at his appearance through the throng of self-preservation commuters, who were actively clogging metropolitan uptown New York City.

"Get a job and get a life, and learn the dignity of working for a living," Fred repeated to himself while alluding to the disgruntled, disgusting moocher. Soon, the insurance expert descended the well-traveled steps to the subterranean platform reserved for boarders of the "Connecticut Northbound Express".

After passing through the all-too-familiar turnstile, Fred Stewart managed to squeeze his anatomy into the packed train, and was fortunate to find the last vacant seat that to his surprise, was actually situated next to a recently cleaned window. The veteran passenger perused an edition of the *New York Times* that he had tucked under his arm and had brought along from the office in case the walker had to protect his head from the relentless rain. 'I should've taken my umbrella to work as Karen had suggested,' Fred thought.

The harrowed and exhausted insurance executive occasionally glanced at the underground lights flashing by his subway train's window and creatively imagined the flickering to be a remarkable shower of shooting stars. It was dark outside, but finally, the Connecticut-bound express ascended to an elevated level as the madhouse rat race known as *Manhattan* had been left behind for another grueling work day. Urban congestion had always distressed Fred Stewart, and the weary passenger was very happy to abandon its demanding tedium.

The express train then descended into another big-city concrete tunnel. Fred ceased reading the metropolitan section of the daily paper when the passenger suddenly felt a trifle uneasy. Glancing out the tinted glass window, the rider imagined he had seen the fleeting reflection of a stationary person. When the man's vision turned his focus of attention across the aisle, Fred's pupils made contact with those of a young brunette woman passively sitting, intermittingly reading a thick romance novel and then nonchalantly glancing around. But the attractive female did not fit the description of the male form that had just mysteriously appeared in the window's reflection. The now-restive Stewart assumed that the visualization was merely a fanciful figment of his stressed mind, the quite weird experience following an incredibly busy day at his company's downtown, skyscraper corporate headquarters.

The remainder of the redundant, monotonous northern excursion was routinely uneventful. Soon, the slightly disturbed commuter had arrived intact to his Fairfield, Connecticut destination. Wife Karen was waiting for Fred in the couple's white *Grand Cherokee Laredo*, and soon the reunited pair was on their way to the well-earned comforts of suburban living.

"You look tired today, Dear," Karen noted. "Thank God it's Friday! Just think. When you retire, every wonderful day will be a fantastic Saturday!"

"It's reached the point where I think I'm starting to hallucinate," commented the frustrated husband. "I think my eyes are playing deceitful tricks on me. I have a theory that dangerous Corporate America can do *that* punishment to a person, you know."

* * * * * * * * * * * *

The following Monday, Karen drove Fred to the familiar Fairfield Train Station, and the breadwinner robotically boarded the morning express back to *Gotham* to register another stressful eight-hour encounter with his sometimes-insubordinate office personnel. This tedious and repetitious round-trip pilgrimage was loyally repeated every weekday, both sunrise and sunset. The twice a day grind would usually require two hours of hectic travel time, which made Fred Stewart feel as if he were an overactive ping-pong ball without a much-needed table net. 'I'm really working a ten-hour day when you factor-in the lousy two hours of commuting,' the middle-management executive mentally assessed. 'And I still have to endure this same stupid commute a dozen more years until I finally reach Social Security.'

Feeling besieged, Fred decided to share his accumulative grief with another southbound passenger. "Twelve more years to *Social Security* if I don't die from urban pressure beforehand," Stewart joked to his fellow grim-faced rider. "I should've listened to my mother's advice and became a successful undertaker back in suburban Philly'."

"I know exactly what you mean," the elderly gentleman piped-up and cheerfully agreed. "Sometimes, I wonder why I was ever born on this extremely harsh planet!"

Another day of distressful, challenging "customer acquisitions" awaited the despondent Connecticut to New York City commuter. That Monday, Stewart agonized redundantly performing his myriad job responsibilities. New customer quotas had to be achieved, and it was great pressure attempting to motivate his staff to accomplish *that* lofty company goal. The repeated ritual was beginning to eclipse Fred Stewart's sense of sanity. The beleaguered man's troubled spirit would occasionally wander adrift from reality, and soon the company administrator would commence engaging in science-fiction daydreaming. When the office supervisor's fertile imagination had deeply drifted into fantasyland that Monday afternoon, Fred recollected the peeved, bearded beggar brandishing the cheap tin cup while impatiently standing and shivering outside *Grand Central Station.*

"I thought New York got rid of the bums when the *Dodgers* moved from Brooklyn to Los Angeles," laughed the agent to his convivial secretary. "Bring back Duke Snider and Jackie Robinson!"

"Why do you say that?" Bonnie Jenkins asked her fatigued boss. "That all happened well over fifty years ago."

"Bonnie, I guess you're right," Fred answered and grinned. "I really should live in the present and shouldn't imagine what was ever wrong or right with the past."

The frantic rush that accompanied late afternoon relief from corporate adminis*trivia* again intensified the standard homeward bound hustle and bustle between *Madison* and *Park Avenue.* As Fred Stewart trudged down the busy avenue to the familiar chaos of *Grand Central Station,* the confounded executive was confronted once again by the annoying, persistent beggar, who now predictably and tenaciously stood before the *Grand Central Concourse.*

Fred tried to avoid eye contact with the repugnant vagrant, but his weak attempt was in vain. A quick glimpse revealed the tramp's glaring facial expression, which immediately sent a morbid chill racing-up the insurance executive's vulnerable spinal column. The rattled commuter again endeavored ignoring his newfound nemesis, and soon Fred's brisk stride conducted him well-past his unpleasant late Monday afternoon 'lowlife encounter'.

Stewart rapidly descended the station steps, and by coincidence, was occupying the exact same seat he had filled the Friday before. Looking for an appropriate diversion, Fred read the stock tables in *The Wall Street Journal* and while alertly studying his high-tech portfolio holdings, the Connecticut-bound passenger had an uncomfortable sensation that someone sinister was stalking him. The neurotic rider's observation of the other passengers detected that everyone else seated was preoccupied reading popular paperbacks, magazines, pamphlets, and tabloid newspapers.

The train departed from the enormous station and moved swiftly down its subterranean tracks. Ten minutes later, the worried commuter's eyes turned towards the side window and caught the fleeting reflection of a strange-looking man. The illusive image had instantaneously vanished before Fred Stewart could ever distinguish any specific defining characteristics. 'I need a vacation bad,' the apprehensive observer nervously concluded. 'Bellevue Hospital seems perfectly okay to me!'

Several moments later, the anxious passenger's head again turned towards the same side window and the appalled viewer witnessed the exact same fleeting reflection as the express train loudly whizzed through the tunnel. The 'haunting illusion' had again evaporated into thin air before the puzzled passenger could discern and interpret any of the phantom apparition's further physical details.

The total experience was both unique and eerie, a definite unwelcome departure from the day's excessive, ongoing boredom. The odd image did not correspond with anyone who had been present (either standing or seated) inside the noisy Northbound Connecticut-bound train. 'What was the source of the uncanny manifestation? Was it an illusion? A mysterious anomaly?' Fred's avid curiosity wondered. 'This is beyond peculiar. It's also way beyond bizarre,' Stewart neurotically concluded.

Once again, the befuddled commuter speculated that his 'superstitious imagination' had been rampantly running amok. For distraction, the perspiring gent tried reading the "Metro News" section of an abandoned *New York Times* in order to forget the recent chilling enigma, but the improvised solution was to no avail. The executive's mind could not think about anything else other than 'the haunting reflection'. Stewart kept meditating about experiencing an 'optical illusion or aberration', and the affected fellow pretended to be reading the wrinkled-up newspaper until the train finally arrived at the sanctuary Fairfield train platform.

Karen was parked near the station steps in the white *Jeep Grand Cherokee Laredo,* and the out-of-kilter insurance office supervisor was soon transported home and having dinner with his faithful spouse. After two hours of mediocre sitcom television viewing, Fred and Karen retired for the evening. While falling asleep, the unsettled corporate traveler's mind was again contemplating the arcane, obscure reflection that Fred Stewart had twice seen from the speeding train's window. Its intrigue still dominated and bothered his now-susceptible psyche.

"Are you sure you don't need a day off?" Karen asked as she noticed her husband's incessant tossing and turning. "I'll call Mr. Williams and tell him you're sick."

"No, Karen. Maybe I'm stubborn, but I refuse to be defeated by a bout of mental exhaustion," Fred replied and insisted. 'I dare not tell

Karen about the reflection, or she might take me to have a thorough psychiatric evaluation,' the husband thought before again attempting to doze-off. Sleep was elusive, but the usually dependable Sandman was still able to pay Fred a belated visit.

The rest of the workweek passed without notable incident. On Friday morning, the Connecticut-to-Manhattan traveler again waged economic combat in the competitive New York business world, and the perplexed insurance hustler was glad that another appreciated *TGIF* had finally arrived. A much-needed weekend off from mind-wracking tedium would be both welcomed and cherished. Friday's workload progressed quickly and after eight wicked and demanding hours, it was eventually time for Fred's routine, all-too-familiar *Grand Central Station* afternoon rendezvous.

Stewart had been boldly approached and solicited every day that week by the confrontational *Grand Central* beggar, neurotically holding the dirty tin cup. That late Friday afternoon Fred decided to utilize another walking route to the congested station in order to deliberately avoid encountering the persistent bum with the grizzly, draping gray beard. The city hiker arrived safely at the customary station without experiencing any difficulty, happy to have successfully evaded the disgusting, emboldened filthy man's daily preamble. Frederick Robert Stewart felt relieved that his amble had not engaged the aggressive, petulant beggar.

Taking a seat on the northbound, the rejuvenated passenger eagerly perused a copy of *Investors' Business Daily*. The completely full train smoothly chugged out of the underground station. After a short while Fred again had the uncomfortable feeling that someone contemptible had been spying on his privacy.

The deeply disturbed rider quickly inspected his immediate environment. Everyone seated was preoccupied with their standard newspapers, magazines, pamphlets, and paperback books. Seeing no suspicious or unsavory characters aboard, the perceptive observer suddenly turned his attentive eyes towards the train's side glass window. This time Fred Stewart got a good look at 'the reflection'.

The strange vision was a mere extended glimpse of three seconds' duration, but there was no doubt about its true recognition. The vague fleeting personage was definitely a replica of the bearded beggar'. A macabre gloom suddenly filled Fred's racing heart. The brief manifestation of the tramp's terrible silhouette had been exceedingly alarming and frightening.

"Oh my God! This can't be! This has to be some sort of paranoid delusion!" the reflection's observer softly panted and whispered as his heavy breath fogged-up the side train window.

In a moment, the very unnatural reflection had mystically disappeared, but the dreaded memory of the manifestation lingered as intense fear inside Fred's very concerned mind. The visual recipient was quite certain of the image's true identity. The baffled passenger decided to transfer to 'a new vacant seat'. Hopefully, 'the hideous mirage' would not encroach into the posterior section of the busy train.

Fred felt beads of perspiration rolling down the sides of his chest and also down his thighs. Luckily, the distraught commuter managed to locate a vacant seat next to a young woman indulgently reading a mystery novel. Fred refused to look out of the side window again, and never even took a forced glance in that direction.

When "The Express" loudly rumbled into Fairfield, Stewart finally got the gumption to reveal to Karen his insidious alarm about "the reflection". His intrigued wife laughed his testimony off, saying that her husband had been working too hard "in the sweat factory". Fred reluctantly agreed with Karen's seemingly objective evaluation. On the way home in the *Grand Cherokee Laredo,* the couple decided that a thrilling weekend "Second Honeymoon" adventure to the scenic and inspiring *Catskill Mountains* was in order. "A pleasurable two-day hiatus is what the doctor ordered," Karen casually evaluated and declared.

* * * * * * * * * * * *

On Saturday morning, the inspired pair alternated driving the white *Grand Cherokee Laredo* to placid, snow-covered Villa Roma near Monticello. The Stewarts mutually agreed that a weekend of rest and relaxation would do wonders for Fred's mental and emotional stability.

The couple did some early spring skiing during the day and some club dancing at the New York State resort's excellent disco in the evening. This welcomed "change of environment away from stress" appeared to be the ideal remedy to alleviate Fred Stewart's apparent mental anguish.

"Karen, this is just what the doctor you had alluded-to would've prescribed," the husband ecstatically commented. "Already, Honey, I now feel like a refurbished new man."

"You're right, Fred. Sipping delicious *Amaretto* by a cozy ski lodge fireplace is better than any pharmacy's finest prescription drug," the supportive wife concurred. "I knew that this *R&R* cure would be just what your mental health needed."

The wonderful, tranquil Catskills' weekend quickly ended, and the Stewarts reluctantly motored back to Connecticut late Sunday night.

After enjoying a decent night's sleep, the conscientious insurance representative awoke and set his mind on being involved in another arduous "Manhattan workweek". Fred punctually arrived at his cluttered desk at precisely 8:30, and like clockwork, picked-up on pursuing his myriad corporate duties right where the workaholic had left off the Friday before. But now, Fred temporarily felt vibrant and energized.

"My batteries have definitely been recharged. I'm ready for anything and everything," Fred bragged to Bonnie Jenkins, his loyal and dedicated secretary. "I actually feel revitalized, renewed," Stewart confidently reported to his surprised assistant.

"You'll need plenty of pep just to make it to Tuesday!" Bonnie sarcastically answered. "I wish I could be so euphoric about anything as you are!"

The day's normal schedule seemed to expire more quickly than usual. Fred purchased a copy of the *New York Times* from a hawking street vendor and paraded his usual route from *Madison Avenue* to *Park Avenue* to *Grand Central Station*. Stewart suddenly recognized the provocative bearded vagrant standing in the same spot, ambitiously soliciting silver coin handouts. The wary pedestrian felt a trifle queasy so the trekker intentionally hastened his cadence. Then, the rapid-stepping ambler felt a surge of panic electrically speeding through his nervous system.

The ominous beggar was staring at Stewart again with a frightful, menacing frown abundantly occupying his hideous countenance. "Hey cheapskate!" the tramp insolently yelled. "Yeah, you! How about donating a damned quarter, you' miserable tightwad!"

The flustered commuter never turned-around to verify the origin of his very obvious disenchantment. Soon, the Fairfield native was again safely aboard the familiar express train and gladly heading back home to Karen and to Connecticut.

"That lousy moocher gives me the absolute creeps," Fred whispered softly to the gloomy darkness outside the moving train's window. "The world would be a much better place without him!"

Shortly thereafter, while reading the *New York Times* bleak front-page headlines, the commuter once more had a subtle awareness that someone was secretly spying on his presence. This time Fred instinctively and quickly craned his neck towards the tinted side window. The horrible reflection of the bothersome bearded mendicant was instantly seen there, again grinning mockingly at the targeted spectator. The sensational reflection persisted for a full ten seconds during the terrifying interaction.

"This train must be a traveling mental hospital!" Fred Stewart gasped. "What has happened to sanity? To my sanity?"

Fred was now totally petrified. He immediately moved to another sector of the noisy train. All that his sensitive ears could discern was the clickety-clack, clickety-clack of the train's metal wheels rubbing against the parallel steel rails. Again, Stewart nervously peered out the window and the occult reflection of the surreptitious bearded derelict once more overwhelmed his sensibilities.

Fred Stewart confided his distress to a stranger who was sitting next to him. The alarmed senior citizen thought it best to sympathetically and intelligently placate his emotionally-disheveled fellow commuter. Each man gazed out the window; the uncanny specter was no longer there.

The recollection of the unearthly apparition started to consume the daily rider's all-too-weakened spirit. The nervous Connecticut-bound passenger felt like vomiting, but the now almost-delirious insurance company office manager breathed deeply to avert the undesirable risk of public embarrassment.

* * * * * * * * * * * *

Fifteen minutes later, Karen was faithfully and habitually waiting at the Fairfield Station platform in the recently-washed white *Jeep Grand Cherokee Laredo*. After a friendly and affectionate greeting, the loyal spouse desperately tried pacifying her unsettled husband's tortured spirit.

"Maybe you need the professional services of a shrink?" Karen Stewart constructively suggested. "Now Fred, there's nothing humiliating about seeking psychiatric help. Many important and prominent people often consult psychiatrists. It's nothing to be ashamed about."

"No, Karen. I think I need an exorcist! And I really mean it!" Fred angrily ranted. "What's been happening to me is without a doubt of evil origin! Did you hear me, Karen? Evil I said!"

The following workday, Frederick R. Stewart obediently reported to office duty against his wife's wishes. That afternoon, Fred was back riding on the crowded Connecticut northbound train, again being grossly apprehensive about the inexplicable recurrence of the totally weird reflection. The restive commuter tried ignoring the side window, but then Stewart's suspicious pupils were drawn to the abominable glass's almost magnetic attraction.

The ghostly reflection of the disdainful bearded vagrant had again horribly reappeared. Fred was beside himself. Was it an accursed phantasm? Was he losing his blessed mind?

"This torture is hell on earth," the distressed man kept repeating, much to the astonishment of a distinguished-looking, well-dressed elderly female commuter, who then very comprehensively and incredulously peered at Stewart while sitting mum next to him.

The express train's itinerary caused it to rumble through a long dark tunnel before loudly ascending to daylight. The overhead lights would habitually go out and then predictably flicker for a few seconds, and now the powerful steel locomotive was swiftly approaching the dark tunnel's entrance.

Total blackness soon enveloped the onrushing 5:30 express, which was hastily pulling its chain of attached coaches. In a matter of seconds, the noisy vehicle had expeditiously exited the dark hollow. But Fred was no longer a disturbed passenger sitting inside the train. The victimized fellow was horrified to find himself standing alone upon an abandoned, out-of-service subterranean train platform, staring directly into the passing tinted windows of the awesome, speeding Connecticut-bound express.

Fred Stewart caught a brief glimpse of a passenger's face racing-by on the northbound express. The repulsive and grotesque-looking bearded derelict was sitting and occupying Fred's former seat. The ever-haunting bum was reading a discarded copy of the 'New York Times Homebound Edition', which had been in Fred's personal possession just moments before.

Fred futilely shouted at the fleeting windows to gain someone's attention. Not one of the tired, self-indulgent passengers ever noticed *his* distressful circumstance. Stewart then heard the haunting echo of the bearded man's ghostly voice asking through the abandoned train platform's overhead loudspeakers, "Now Sir, how do *you* like being on the outside looking in?"

When the *Connecticut Express* finally arrived at the Fairfield Station, Karen Stewart was faithfully waiting for Fred inside the couple's white *Grand Cherokee Laredo*. The anonymous bearded passenger exited the express, casually sauntered-over to a dull green *Volkswagen Beetle,* and unceremoniously slid inside. The repugnant bearded man's devoted wife asked, "How was your week away from home, Sam?"

The loathsome, recently-exchanged vagabond answered, "Fine Lisa. I thought I'd never get back to Fairfield alive!"

For the next several months, Karen Stewart sat daily and impatiently waited behind the wheel of the white *Jeep*. Fred never again set foot onto the Fairfield, Connecticut train platform. Only an occasional, periodic one-second reflection of Frederick Robert Stewart's soul remained to be viewed by the apathetic, commuting, northbound public.

"Spiritual Transfer"

Julius Rubicon ironically was born on March 15, 1962 in a Buffalo, New York hospital. His middle school friends naturally nicknamed Rubicon the rather predictable monicker "Julius Caesar," and one inconsiderate eighth-grade rascal would often satirically state to the likable young fellow, and much to the delight of *their* cafeteria lunchroom colleagues, "Forget the vicious Brutus assassination on the Ides of March! The class is studying *you* in Social Studies, Julius, because we've learned that you have epileptic fits just like Alexander the Great did," the sarcastic adolescent then continued his harangue. "Does your soul really leave your body when *that* wild twitching happens?"

"Yeah, Julius!" a second impish antagonist exclaimed. "When you have those out-of-control epileptic fits, are you Julius Caesar, or are you Julius Seizure!" the smart-aleck punned.

The other male students sitting at the cafeteria table all erupted in a boisterous clamor, obnoxiously pounding their fists upon the structure's top until a teacher on duty approached their misbehavior and threatened to report the obnoxious rascals to the main office for disciplinary purposes, should the raucous misconduct fail to cease and desist.

Eighth-grader Julius Rubicon was able to shrug-off the loud peer hilarity being generated at his name's expense because the youth fully understood that his teenage buddies would only kid him if he had been regarded as their bona-fide chum. Julius's family had moved to Philadelphia during the model student's junior year, and Rubicon attended West Catholic High where the studious scholar again earned high academic honors.

And after graduating magna cum laude from Villanova University four years after his public-school graduation, in 1985, Julius landed a respectable job as a crime-investigative reporter for the very reputable *Philadelphia Inquirer.*

For recreation, the now-muscular specimen often trained in a West Philly' neighborhood gym and soon became quite adept at boxing, judo and karate, where Julius's due diligence had merited the dedicated over-achiever a black belt. The 185-pound athlete took great pride in maintaining himself in excellent physical condition, and although the Wynnewood resident never married, many young women gladly sought his social company.

Keeping his exercise regimen philosophy in constant practice, each night Julius left his well-maintained row-house abode and took walking rambles through the newspaper reporter's relatively safe West Philly' neighborhood. The nightly routine covered a repetitious route where the recently hired writer's agile gait passed a line of lampposts, designed by the city's electric company to be situated at hundred-foot intervals. Since the late evening environment was commonly tranquil and calm, each regular midnight hike was so quiet that Julius was able to hear his own footsteps.

In his daily *Inquirer* work scenario, Julius's responsibility was to report front-page stories about tragic automobile accidents, warehouse conflagrations, and criminal robberies and murders, but without a doubt the frequent thefts and the brutal killings terribly bothered Rubicon's very vulnerable psyche. The reporter's intense loathing of illicit vile acts was often exacerbated because many of the felonious suspects being pursued by the police were never arrested and ultimately never brought to justice.

'Maybe my strict Catholic background makes me resent sinners and crooks,' Julius conjectured while sitting at his newsroom desk. 'I wish that I could more effectively combat the urban crime that threatens the lives of normal, hard-working citizens. Perhaps I should suggest to my over-the-top editor that I wish to be transferred to either the newspaper's Entertainment or its Sports section!'

That midnight, Julius was preoccupied ambling along his familiar neighborhood itinerary when the trekker's perceptive eyes noticed a strange occurrence that Rubicon had never before observed. The first lamppost would always cast its particular shadow as Julius swiftly paced by. And as the health fanatic would step past the bright illumination, his shadow would always become longer.

'What's this?' Julius curiously wondered as the area resident stopped to survey his novel situation. 'My shadow is non-existent! This can't be! What an odd deviation from normal!'

Looking-up at the dark sky, the perplexed observer recognized that there was no full moon reflecting light-beams back toward Earth. 'This is really weird!' the puzzled walker assessed, shaking her head in mild confusion. 'It's a new moon up there! That dark disc simply means that no light rays are being shot-down to good old Wynnewood!'

The other four lampposts lined in straight succession all (according to expectation) cast Julius's shadow when he slowly moved by them, but the first one (not displaying his shadow) still represented a major concern that dominated the objective-oriented fitness buff's mind. After returning home somewhat fatigued at 1 a.m., the newspaper journalist drank a glass of pineapple juice from the refrigerator, checked his landline phone messages, and then carefully climbed into bed. Wondering about the lamppost aberration before closing his eyes,

Julius spent the entire night tossing and turning during what was an extremely restive sleep. Upon awakening on Monday morning, the resident's disarrayed mind gradually became more rationally active.

'I don't have to go into the newsroom until noon,' Julius pondered. 'I'll make a cup of coffee and swallow-down a bowl of *Cheerios,* watch the morning TV weather, and get caught-up with the latest national and international news.'

The opening story delivered by the local Philly' anchor (whose steady eyes remained fixed upon his teleprompter) involved the discovery of a felon's lifeless body found lying in a dark center city alley. "The unfortunate victim, twenty-nine-year-old Thomas Archer, was pronounced dead at Temple University Hospital," the Action News commentator suavely related. "Detectives on the crime scene are baffled as to the motive for the murder, but evidence in the form of blood drops and footprints found next to Archer's body are being meticulously analyzed by police lab' experts. More details about this callous murder will follow on this station's evening newscast at 7."

'Wow!' Julius marveled and realized. 'I had written a background article on Thomas Archer's apprehension last November. The thug had murdered two innocent old women who tried to interfere with *his* audacious small-time robbery of a Chestnut Street convenience store. Archer's demise and subsequent descent into Hell under any and all circumstances is definitely no big loss to humanity! I absolutely despise anyone who intentionally does anything that is unethical, illicit, but especially, immoral!' strict-minded Rubicon evaluated and generalized.

Dressing for his short drive to work on North Broad Street, the newspaper reporter promptly noticed four tiny spots of blood, two on each of the shoes he had worn during his previous vigorous 'midnight constitution'. Thinking little of the minor irregularity, Julius cleaned-off the hardly-visible red stains with a wet paper towel over the kitchen sink. The ultra-moral man's singular thought was totally focused on exactly who had the decency to murder the notorious killer Thomas "Pistol" Archer.

That afternoon, the front-page editor assigned Rubicon to visit the alley where Thomas Archer had been disposed of and to take pictures and then seek-out and interview possible witnesses. Julius's story appeared in the *Inquirer's* Tuesday morning edition, but the article received little public interest and was virtually forgotten by the ravenous TV and press media within a week's time.

Karen Murray, an inquisitive, pretty brunette, and the avid journalist's favorite female companion, enjoyed visiting the writer's

Wynnewood residence to learn about (and discuss-in-depth) potential news stories before they actually became headlines.

"What were Thomas Archer's reasons for murdering the two elderly ladies at the mom-and-pop convenience store?" the St. Joseph University senior asked Julius. "That heinous, detestable criminal act was worthy of receiving the gas chamber!"

"The crook's motive was simple and certainly done in low regard for human life," the knowledgeable boyfriend answered. "The two old women basically got in the way of him robbing the small business's cash register in what proved to be a botched armed holdup. Scumbags like Thomas Archer have no moral compass," Julius opined. "Imbeciles like Archer just react on raw impulse; their brains not weighing the punitive consequences of their actions; their selfish minds never consider the devastating impact that their crimes have on innocent victims, who were simply sharing the killer's same physical environment."

"Confidentially and off the record," Karen desired knowing, "are there any new clues or developments about why Mr. Archer has been permanently erased from civilization?"

"The ongoing investigations at the newspaper and at Police Headquarters still continue. But Karen, besides you and me, no one else wants to even think about Thomas Archer being eliminated. It's as if each and every city murder and heist is ephemeral; a fleeting-but-ugly moment in time to be publicly ignored and soon erased from both print and TV existence."

After Karen left to study for a major upcoming Western Civilization exam, Julius watched television reruns for several hours, exited the house, bought some DVR music discs at a corner retail outlet, and after returning home, Rubicon read two chapters from an Arthur Conan Doyle Sherlock Holmes novel. Feeling a need to experience some invigorating exercise, just before midnight, Julius again participated in his 'nightly constitution' to 'respectfully honor the spirit of Harry S. Truman'.

Everything was copacetic until Reporter Rubicon recognized that his shadow did not appear opposite his form from the first street-light's illumination. 'Here we go again,' the frustrated health fanatic pondered. 'As Hamlet must've stated, 'There' is something rotten in Denmark'! Make *that* famous William Shakespeare quotation into 'There's something rotten in the Wynnewood section of West Philadelphia'! I'll have to pay high attention the next time I venture past this confounded first lamppost. The absence of a shadow during *my* initial time encounter was possibly a fluke, but nevertheless, beyond a shadow of a doubt,' Julius mused in a lame effort to obviously allay his deep worry, 'This second strange streetlight misadventure defies both science and common-sense reality.'

The following morning, the same aberrant sequence of events transpired with Julius surprisingly again discovering fresh blood stains shown upon his black leather shoes. Feeling uneasy, yet greatly suspicious, the nervous fellow grabbed his TV remote control and hastily switched from watching the cable business channel to viewing Philadelphia Action News.

The all-too-familiar male news anchor stated that an on-the-loose Quaker City criminal named John Warren, who also was a fugitive from justice wanted by the FBI, was mysteriously murdered while exiting a popular Market Street movie theater. Warren had been cleverly evading police scrutiny for the past six months, and the treacherous felon had been futilely pursued all over the Delaware Valley by law enforcement dragnets. Aerial surveillance cameras located outside the downtown cinema had captured the sought-after crook being shot, but strangely, there was no filming of either the killer or the murder weapon. Again, the only remnants of the gruesome crime were several drops of blood originating from the victim's chest that had been found on the sidewalk next to John Warren's expired body.

That Wednesday evening, Karen drove her blue Ford Focus to Wynnewood to honor a dinner commitment she and Julius had arranged. The chosen Italian restaurant was only three blocks from Rubicon's row-house, so the duo made the short hike on foot. Karen was still unaware of the odd lamppost shadow phenomenon, but as the couple sauntered past the first light standard, Julius glanced at the pavement, and to his absolute befuddlement, only Karen's shadow was visible to *his* usually keen vision. 'Lucky that my favorite girl didn't notice the inexplicable illusion, but my eyes certainly did!'

On Thursday morning, Julius awoke, and after hopping off his mattress, the first action that the reporter took was to examine his black leather shoes. Six new, wet bloodspots were randomly speckled upon his oxfords in no particular pattern. The disturbed resident next turned on Channel 6 Action News, and the boring teleprompter reader (in his dispassionate monotone voice) bluntly declared that Matthew Harper, a three-time convicted rapist and notorious woman molester, had been brutally stabbed multiple times while checking into a crowded pizza shop located opposite Thomas Jefferson University Hospital.

'Oh my God!' the astounded viewer emotionally contemplated. 'Karen is the only mortal I can trust. I'll definitely have to consult with her tomorrow night about this astonishing series of eerie parallel events between my bloodied shoes and the stranger-than-fiction invisible streetlamp shadows! Perhaps my soulmate can also *shed some light* on this baffling skein of Philly' thugs that are being systematically murdered, and maybe she can help me comprehend evasive details about the illogical lamppost shadow anomaly!'

* * * * * * * * * * * *

"Julius, you said over the cell phone that you had something urgent to tell me?" Karen asked as the college student and her beau sat on the row-house's living room sofa. "What gives?"

"Plain and simple, I want you to spend the night in my house," the boyfriend replied, cutting right to the chase. "This might sound like a science fiction or paranormal TV intro', but I want you to stay up all night and keep an eye on me, and in particular, especially pay attention to my shoes," Julius orally specified. "I can't explain it Karen, but for some obscure reason, blood drops are appearing on my black shoes that I wear to work. I just have to find the solution to this rather intriguing matter, or else I feel like I should be committed to a funny farm for thorough psychiatric observation."

After daybreak, much to Julius's alarm, Karen testified that her boyfriend had a period of almost an hour where his "sleep state" had been borderline comatose, and another hour experiencing wild bed gyrations, and remarkably, eight blood stains somehow appeared on the man's left shoe along with another five on his right.

"But I never awoke and left the room!" the now-baffled reporter gasped. "How did the stains get there? This is a paranormal enigma that neither Dick Tracy nor Sherlock Holmes could ever solve. It's genuine *Twilight Zone* or *Outer Limits* sci-fi stuff, but it's all happening to me!"

"You don't have to be at work until noon. Let's get distracted from your horribly uncanny problem and watch the early morning news," the girlfriend suggested. "Get your fertile mind off of thinking about those nasty, inexplicable bloodstains. Too bad Rod Serling is dead, or else you could give him a call and solicit his educated opinion."

The one-toned, tedious news anchor again appeared upon the living room wall's flat-screen and informed his generally apathetic audience that a wanton arsonist named Peter Swanson had been maliciously murdered outside a Wendy's Restaurant in midtown. "This is another execution-style killing of a dangerous felon," the news messenger somberly indicated. "The police investigators are happy to see another depraved menace to society off the streets, but authorities caution the public not to turn vigilante and take the law into their own hands. We'll have further updates to this irregular development at our noon broadcast."

"Dog bites man, not a story. But Karen, man bites dog, well that's tabloid sensationalism! Arsonists are much more dangerous than pyromaniacs because they desire to start huge fires and not small ones," Julius related to his fascinated listener. "But in all honesty, Doll, I'm worried about the recurrent bloodstains on my shoes that just happen to correspond with four murders that have recently been administered to desperate Philly' fugitives and escaped convicts."

"Look, Julius, I'm convinced that you're entirely innocent about these dregs of American society being eliminated," the sympathetic college sorority girl observed and encouraged. "But I do insist that you notify the local police about this incredible ongoing riddle that's now wickedly haunting your mental stability. Truthfully, it's also making a genuine basket-case out of me, too!"

"You mean you're willing to testify under oath that you were in my home maintaining a vigil while I slept the night when the thug's murder had been committed," the somewhat relieved *Inquirer* employee remarked. "But I washed the blood off the shoes every time, so the cops will think that I'm trying to cover-up important evidence."

"I'll vouch for you," Karen Murray sincerely pledged. "But first, you must alert the investigating detectives about this totally bizarre crime wave and about your parallel arcane bloodstain experiences."

* * * * * * * * * * * *

Karen contacted Police Captain James Flanagan, a burly former patrolman possessing a ruddy complexion and sporting amber-colored plastic lenses worn over his dull brown peepers. Flanagan habitually smoked vintage El Producto cigars and spoke in a raspy, gruff, bass voice.

"Those four punks got what they deserved," Captain Flanagan admitted as the head cop slowly lit and puffed on his huge cigar, deliberately violating precinct regulations. "And your jazzed-up story about the bloodstains is rather sensational, to say the least. But I gotta' tell ya' Miss Murray, the lamppost shadow incidents seem like they belong in the realm of Hollywood studios; that is, in the domain of production companies that release lousy B movies!"

"What do you recommend we do?" Karen asked the skeptical veteran cop. "Is there some sort of legal experiment *you* can conduct to prove my boyfriend's innocence?"

Police Captain James Flanagan recollected a certain case from his yesteryear detective days, and then communicated his seemingly plausible scheme to his two incredulous visitors.

"Julius, I'll contact the big shots over at the *Inquirer* and let them know that you'll be out of commission for a while; that is, you'll be clandestinely working undercover for the police department. As a precaution, we'll temporarily incarcerate you in a city prison and guards will be assigned to monitor your activities 24/7," Captain Flanagan stipulated. "If anyone from the Mafia syndicate, or if any other FBI Post Office poster felon is rubbed-out during your temporary imprisonment, then you'll be officially off the hook and can rest easy about any remote involvement in *this* drastically complicated Philly' murder spree. Any question?"

No high-profile murders of wanted felons had occurred during Julius's two-week prison stint, so Captain Flanagan had the mentally relieved reporter (who had been costumed in zebra stripes) released from custody. That evening, just before midnight, the two lovebirds (accompanied by an assigned policeman) were enjoying a casual stroll in the direction of the all-too-familiar series of the Wynnewood street's lampposts.

"Prison life wasn't too bad after all," Julius softly related to his trusted female companion. "The food was moderately good, and I was kept under guard, living in almost complete isolation. But really Karen, it was like a vacation, or a fourteen-day hiatus of sorts. A color TV had been provided for my viewing pleasure, and I even enjoyed watching afternoon soap operas," the boyfriend humorously admitted. "And in my solitude, I even figured-out why the mediocre shows are called soap operas; the sponsors are mostly detergent companies and soap manufacturers!"

Upon approaching the problematic first lamppost, the *three* walkers all immediately perceived and understood that only two shadows were being projected and displayed upon the side pavement. And upon returning to the reporter's Wynnewood row-house, Julius suddenly felt exhausted, and contrary to his usual energetic self, remarked that he wished to retire to bed.

The policeman and Karen kept a vigilant watch all night, and the cop recorded in his precise notes that the sleeping reporter had been actively disturbed during a portion of his difficult siesta. And at seven o'clock the next morning, the three-bedroom spectators were stunned to comprehend that fresh bloodstains were quite prevalent and boldly visible on both of Rubicon's black dress shoes.

* * * * * * * * * * * *

The following morning, Inspector Flanagan decided that Julius Rubicon should again be put into solitary confinement and be constantly observed by two newly-installed video cameras, each object being equipped with sophisticated night vision capability. Karen was now the official ambassador to the local police precinct, and Miss Murray and Captain Flanagan had gradually become frank acquaintances, getting along royally.

"I've been in touch with my friend Professor Arnold Fitzgerald of the LaSalle University Psychology Department, who incidentally specializes in studying certain convoluted, paranormal out-of-body experiences," Captain Flanagan conveyed to Julius's significant other, while sitting inside his musty, cigar-fume-laden office. "Dr. Fitzgerald is regarded by his peers as being the most eminent national expert in this rising quasi-scientific field that incidentally, has been slowly gaining a reputable academic status. Do you follow my gist, Karen?"

"And what does eminent Dr. Arnold Fitzgerald theorize?" insisted Julius's fond female visitor. "Does he think I'm some sort of psychotic quack, and that Julius is positively stir-crazy? I mean to say to you, Captain Flanagan; this paranormal stuff is not the type of information I study in college!"

"Not at all," calmly responded Flanagan. "I assure you, Miss Murray, the professor's nutty explanation is the only thing I think is *crazy!* The LaSalle guru believes that the first crucial street lamppost is some sort of spiritual signal transmitter; the professor thinks that an arcane, anonymous otherworld instruction-giver has been mystically communicating that your beau is about to leave his body and surreptitiously engage, as a designated, recruited apparition, if I might add, assigned to rub-out malicious, most-wanted criminals. Dr. Fitzgerald speculates *this* rather bizarre hypothesis because the forecasting paranormal authority believes that Julius has been especially selected by mysterious supernatural forces, since your boyfriend positively deplores anything immoral; or should I say, your young Mr. Rubicon totally abhors anything that his religious conscience views as being either sinful or illegal."

"Then, you believe that Julius *is* a murderer whose wandering spirit methodically stalks and kills felons without *his* knowledge or consent!" Karen interrupted, an expression of full-fledged dread now appearing upon her usually smiling face. "You think that my boyfriend is a demented religious fanatic being subconsciously influenced by Satan and his hellish minions? If that's the case, the Devil has stolen my boyfriend's free will?"

"Your words, not mine!" Flanagan coyly countered. "Please don't cry Miss Murray. I'll vouch for Julius in court if I have to do that. I'm on your side of the fence! Please remember that!"

"What's next on the agenda?" Karen inquired in a more rational and less emotional voice. "I'm not used to this level of stress! What must Julius do to keep the two of us out of the nuthouse?"

"Well, Karen, we'll see what happens to your boyfriend the next three nights that he's placed in a cell back at the prison," Captain Flanagan supportively declared. "We'll then be able to gauge, or should I say *fathom* Julius's predicament with a greater degree of accuracy. The results of our complete monitoring will then be forwarded to LaSalle University for further study."

That night, the guinea pig jailbird was handed a Tarzan adventure novel to read in order to occupy his besieged mind during his rather exceptional confinement. Several hours after the jail cell occupant's imagination entered dreamland, the overhead video cameras recorded Julius turbulently tossing and turning upon his hard mattress, and then under extreme duress, the afflicted fellow commenced breathing heavily and very erratically. An hour of subconscious tribulation finally elapsed, and after five subsequent minutes of relatively sedate, rhythmic respiration, the confined subject gradually settled into a more normal sleep pattern.

Despite the fact that Julius Rubicon had discarded his black dress shoes and had been specifically instructed by the precinct brass to wear his favorite white sneakers, the following dawn revealed that no traces of blood had been visible upon his new informal footgear.

* * * * * * * * * * * *

"We have to get the weird street lamppost incidents inserted back into our crime-fighting equation," Captain James Flanagan informed Michael Harris, the very competent North Philadelphia prison warden. "Release Rubicon from your custody right away. Dr. Fitzgerald has advised me to have the tormented subject living back in Wynnewood with the newly installed infra-red lens cameras now active inside his residence. Then, if our longshot theory is correct and we inadvertently hit the jackpot," the Captain sternly stipulated to the doubting Warden, "some valuable paranormal evidence can possibly be professionally filmed and documented."

Julius Rubicon returned home from his boring prison monotony on Monday morning, and feeling extra stamina energizing his unexercised corporal existence, the young reporter took his standard midnight stroll past the notorious lamppost, and predictably, didn't see his shadow. Later on, after enjoying a potato chip snack, Julius watched the late-night cable TV news, and finally, the temporarily laid-off newspaper employee went to sleep.

At 9 a.m. on Tuesday morning, the phone rang in the police precinct's dispatchers' room. A body belonging to Hugh DeVries, a chronic burglar and embezzler with a criminal record forty pages long, had been discovered lying in a horrid pool of crimson outside the Union League Building on South Broad Street. Blood samples were immediately taken, and then soon conveyed in a quick manner over to the city police laboratory for instant test analysis.

Simultaneously, the newly acquired blood traces that had been isolated from Julius's white sneakers were quickly preserved and swiftly transported to the same lab' to enable precise scientific comparisons. At three that afternoon, the landline telephone rang inside the Precinct Captain's infamous smoke-filled office. The rather agitated call recipient nonchalantly picked-up the phone.

"Flanagan here. What did you say? The fresh blood from Rubicon's white sneakers and the blood samples from the knifed body are the same? That's utterly impossible. Let's get real here! There must be some major screw-up somewhere!"

"It escapes plausibility, but it's absolutely true!" a totally fazed Dr. Spencer attested over his secure laboratory phone. "I've never come across anything quite like this in my entire thirty-year career. Captain, I think I'm now ready for insane asylum retirement after partaking in this wholly mystifying episode, or should I say, *this* far-fetched insane sci-fi drama!"

"Look, Spencer, notify everybody in the department that *this* incredible news is to exclusively stay in-house and that the TV stations and the local tabloid papers have to be kept in the dark until further notice!" the Head Precinct Detective demanded with arteries protruding from his throat. "Got the message, Spencer! It's all strictly confidential and highly-classified material that's not available for public consumption! Now run those damned tests again, just to be sure there was no freakin' foul-up!"

Detective Morse, who had been quietly researching and updating recent files inside Flanagan's office when the surprise lab' telephone call had been received, abandoned his ordinary reticence and had a reasonably interesting contribution to make. "Captain, perhaps some wily felon has cleverly developed the wherewithal to game the system," the normally laconic office wonk declared. "Let's try using infra-red lenses in our cameras, and then we could more validly determine what our observations will reveal. If we can't fight fire with fire, we'll fight technology against technology!"

"Brilliant deduction Einstein; you incompetent bungling idiot!" yelled the fully irate Captain. "Now Morse, I want you to know that your ingenious idea has already been implemented and is currently in operation. Get back to performing your own mundane police business, and stop your damned irritating eavesdropping," Flanagan vehemently admonished his non-helpful subordinate. "I don't need your unwarranted and unsolicited advice. Actually, in all honesty Morse, I need you like I need a second appendix!"

"I was only trying to be helpful," Detective Morse humbly apologized. "I should've listened to my mother and became a wimpy Presbyterian minister, or a hated used car salesman!"

"I'm sorry, Tim," Captain Flanagan softly replied, momentarily completely out of character. "I can't hold Mr. Rubicon in custody indefinitely because the troubled guy hasn't been officially charged with murder; obviously, for a lack of hard evidence. We'll be releasing the distraught reporter because we're now set-up to conduct our already established infra-red lenses experiment. Quite frankly Tim, I worry that since the guy's a well-read city reporter," Captain Flanagan elucidated, "the unstable fellow might leak-out confidential information about the dual blood test results oddly being identical. Such a deleterious disclosure would be a terrible and embarrassing disaster for the whole department. That's why we gotta' keep *that* unbelievable blood analysis secret from Rubicon's knowledge as long as this outrageous in-progress investigation continues! I'm tellin' you up-straight Morse," Flanagan loudly vociferated. "If this abominable detective business were a religion, those oddball blood samples appearing on those white sneakers would be considered wonderful miracles!"

"I think I'm now very ready to visit both Fatima and Lourdes!" Detective Timothy Morse humorously summarized. "I believe I need to be permanently cured of my terrible psycho melancholy!"

* * * * * * * * * * * *

The next three nights, Julius Rubicon and Karen Murray again walked past "the occult-but-ordinary-looking first lamppost", and seven hours later, upon waking-up from a restless Friday night's sleep, bloodstains had again magically materialized on Rubicon's white sneakers, which were soon rinsed and cleansed immediately after evidence had been derived by the precinct's arriving murder investigation unit. And remarkably, the same familiar, meticulous process had also been performed the previous two mornings.

"The infra-red cameras detected a ghostly vapor that had mysteriously exited your body and then reentered it an hour later," Karen informed her beau, five-minutes after consulting with Captain

Flanagan over the phone. "Your out-of-body specter has become a stalker-killer!"

"Oh my God!" an exasperated Julius frightfully exclaimed. "I'm an agent of Satan, and I'm involved in committing revenge murders on fugitives, on convicted killers, and on FBI most-wanted villains. Karen, I'm going to burn in Hell for all eternity! I believe I'm nothing more than a robotic demon puppet being used by Lucifer himself! What did I ever do to ever deserve this terribly atrocious curse?"

* * * * * * * * * * * *

"Four days passed and then Karen Murray had some more bad news to convey to her despairing love-mate. "Flanagan told me that three additional criminals named Joe Bowers, Frank Salvo and Stephen Marducci have been killed earlier in the week in separate sections of the city. Julius," the distraught girl sobbed, "I'm really petrified beyond belief about these unaccountable murders and also by your obvious implication in them."

"Did the blood tests match-up?" Julius asked his favorite lady. 'I'm beginning to detest myself. Why the hell was I ever born? I don't want to be Satan's condemned surrogate! It isn't right for an evil supernatural creature to be able to manipulate a mortal human like me. It's like I'm *his* pathetic marionette, obediently enacting his diabolical beck and call! It just isn't right or fair!"

Karen patiently explained that Dr. Fitzgerald had disclosed to Captain Flanagan that Julius's disruptive catatonic states probably initially began as sleepwalking. "Did you sleepwalk as a child?"

"Yes, I did," the boyfriend recalled and replied. "Many times, and once I even tumbled down the stairs at my parents' old house on Frankford Avenue."

"And this is truly amazing Julius. Dr. Fitzgerald believes that the sleepwalking habit eventually evolves into out-of-body experiences in the more serious cases," Karen Murray rhetorically resumed telling her new knowledge. "Yesterday I learned a bit of fascinating history from my phone conversation with the distinguished LaSalle professor. Dr. Fitzgerald stated that during medieval times, a popular notion that had been condemned by the Catholic Church was the odd, bizarre theory described as 'the transmigration of the human soul'. Out-of-body experiences were commonly regarded by the Church as being the practicing of witchcraft, and those people that claimed out-of-body experiences to be reality were horribly persecuted and often cruelly executed by the Inquisition."

"Yes Karen, I know. And Galileo was even brought before the Inquisition because the early astronomer scientifically proved with his telescope that the Earth was not the center of the solar system and that our puny planet revolved around the sun, and not vise-versa. If I correctly recall, his truthful findings were regarded as heresy punishable by death!"

"Let's forget for a moment sleepwalking and out-of-body migration done by you to kill a criminal on the loose. How about Phase 3 of Dr. Fitzgerald's theory when you'll travel as a spirit and dwell inside another person's body?" the now-harried girl desired knowing. "How will you and me be affected then?"

"But I haven't gotten to *that* evil third stage yet!" argued the equally upset astral traveler. "I think my soul can leave my body during deep sleep. I believe that I can then dial my subconscious-consciousness into a beyond human comprehension spiritual instruction bank, which directs me to whom I am to assassinate next. This unworldly instruction bank can somehow obtain the physical murder weapon to be utilized by me during the assigned killing. I then methodically perform the dastardly misdeed and finally, my itinerant spirit concludes my nocturnal exploit, and next I swiftly flit away like an invisible gust of wind to speedily reunite with my sleeping body. And after completing my wicked malice," Julius sadly elaborated, "I adroitly filter back into my sleeping body and leave my bloodied shoes or sneakers lying beside my bed. Is that Hell on Earth or what?"

"You make me quiver with fear!" Karen candidly confessed. "I love you more than words can express, but I don't love what you're doing! It's not done of your own free will! You're being controlled by nefarious, evil forces!"

"Thank God I haven't yet evolved to the point where my soul can inhabit another person's corporal form," Julius apprehensively contemplated and shared. "I believe I might have the propensity to do so, but fortunately for now, I haven't progressed to *that* frightening third stage. Maybe Flanagan can consult the Pope and have me expertly exorcised by a qualified priest!"

* * * * * * * * * * * *

"Julius, the FBI and the Philadelphia Police think that you're pretty damned indispensable. Now Mr. Rubicon, we have a very strategic assignment for you," Captain Flanagan requested and embellished while addressing his Thursday morning office visitor. "And Karen, you can sit down also. Now Julius, all of these dirt-bag thugs and punks that you believe your out-of-body spirit has been rubbing-out, did you ever write about them in the *Inquirer* before your subconscious felt compelled to extinguish each of them from American mainstream society?"

"Yes Captain, as you're keenly aware, I hate anything illegal, unethical and immoral as a result of my most-strict Catholic upbringing. And after I researched each of the mob-related scumbags that my lethal, migrating-spirit has executed, I gotta' admit; I felt especially vindicated without the least trace of guilt surfacing from my subconscious."

"Julius," Flanagan said before deeply clearing his throat, "the FBI and the Precinct want you to write an *Inquirer* expose on the nefarious drug cartel boss El Gordo. The vindictive Mexican mobster has secret hangouts all over the East Coast, one of which we've just located. It's over in Bucks County in nearby Bensalem, and it's situated just north of the Philly' line."

"So, you're asking me to write a scathing column for the paper on this El Gordo personage as a precursor to me murdering the villain after walking past the signal-assignment lamppost at midnight," the first-year rookie reporter grievously summarized and stated. "That's a pretty demanding tall order, Captain!"

Karen Murray felt a dire need to then speak her mind. "Are you going to prosecute Julius for committing all of these horrible murders, even though the victims are contemptible gangsters, hoods and racketeers," the girlfriend courageously challenged. "No matter how reprehensible this El Gordo jerk is, Julius will still be violating the felon's sacred right to live by performing a totally sinful act. And furthermore Captain…,"

"Will El Gordo be alone when my mobile, stalking spirit egregiously executes him?" Julius interrupted his emotionally torqued soulmate. "If so, this job deployment might wind-up being bigger than the Chicago Valentine's Day Massacre!"

"The wealthy, fat lowlife is usually guarded by a dozen or so enormous bodyguards," Flanagan shared before puffing exceedingly on his mammoth El Producto cigar. "Now Julius, here are the pertinent details that the FBI has given us. And quite candidly Mr. Rubicon, I cannot actually guarantee that you won't be prosecuted by the D.A.'s office, but I promise that I'll testify in court on your behalf that you should be placed in the government's Witness Protection Program. I think you've loyally assisted law enforcement on your most interesting and vital past and present missions."

The head Precinct Detective next proceeded to disclose to his two civilian guests that corpulent El Gordo Garcia had hangouts and headquarters in Bensalem, in New Haven, Connecticut, in Atlantic

City and also in Saddle Brook, New Jersey. "The disreputable bully has several other bases of criminal operation that are yet to be specifically identified and surveilled by the FBI."

"So why does my night-stalking spirit have to erase El Gordo Garcia off the face of the Earth?" Julius defensively questioned. "What evil misdeed other than general extortion and drug sales is the notorious creep about to enact?"

"You're much smarter than the average Action News reporter," congratulated Flanagan. "Last week the FBI deftly intercepted and translated certain coded, encrypted messages from the El Gordo syndicate that reveal Garcia and his henchmen's plan to explode a dirty nuclear bomb over, outside or inside Lincoln Bank Stadium during the upcoming Philadelphia Eagles and New York Giants NFL professional football game. The FBI knows that Garcia has recently imported a large cargo shipment into the tiny Hammonton Municipal Airport over in South Jersey," the now-animated Captain divulged. "The usually dependable New Jersey State Police slipped-up and never confiscated the explosive nuclear contraband, which has now been clandestinely transported to a location that only *your* itinerant spirit will be able to find."

Since thousands of Philadelphia sports fans' lives would be placed in imminent jeopardy, Julius Rubicon felt obligated to consent to initiating his next most perilous midnight expedition. The outlaw-hunter's lethal night-prowler ghost would magically receive the hideout location of Garcia's horrendous plot transmitted by the next life supernatural Powers That Be, would arrive upon the demolition scene with an automatic machine gun having a huge cache of rounds in its magazine, and then Julius Rubicon's spirit would systematically mow-down the entire aggregation of worthless knaves and scoundrels.

* * * * * * * * * * * *

True to enacting Captain Flanagan's incisive directions, Julius Rubicon organized and authored a lengthy, scathing front-page article on El Gordo Garcia and his loyal-but-corrupt Mexican confederates. And two days before the highly anticipated Sunday afternoon Eagles/Giants NFL football game, Julius Rubicon and Karen Murray took their routine midnight stroll past the conspicuous Wynnewood street lamppost, and unlike the famous-but-unreliable February 2nd Pennsylvania groundhog, Julius again did not see his shadow shown on the pavement.

The next morning Rubicon awoke with heavy blotches of blood smeared all over his white sneakers, over his light blue shirt, over his tan-colored pants, and over his hands and his face. The following afternoon the stunned and shocked newspaper reporter and his attractive lady friend had a rather meaningful conversation while seated inside the row-house's living room.

"My final roaming-spirit mission has been accomplished," Julius mentioned to his favorite woman. "I hope this is the end of it all. The last several months have been one perpetual nightmare that's been moving in perpetual motion."

"Julius, stay positive! Perhaps Professor Fitzgerald's prescribed plan for your complete spiritual rehabilitation will be successful and that you'll once again be the regular guy that I happen to dearly love. You often claim to be devoutly religious! Show me' more faith in your moral thinking!"

"The outline to all-wise Professor Fitzgerald's scheme seems very comprehensive in both scope and content," Julius credited and readily acknowledged. "And I'm thrilled to know that I've been granted prosecutorial immunity by the Feds for my efficient machine gun disposal of El Gordo and his ruthless mob. Flanagan told me so on the phone earlier this morning."

"But there's a gigantic missing piece to this intricate jigsaw puzzle," Karen wondered and commented. "What was El Gordo's motive in wanting to blow-up Lincoln Bank Field?"

"Flanagan told me that a foreign terrorist network couldn't get their suicide bombers into the U.S. to perform the heinous attack, so the insolent jihadists paid Garcia and company ten million bucks to go do the dirty work for them!" Julius Rubicon explained to his faithful girlfriend. "Let's hope that now I can return to living a nondescript, lackluster-but-happy life right here in West Philadelphia. Honestly, Karen. I'm looking to taking full advantage of that opportunity."

"And where is the nuclear bomb right now?" Karen Murray asked. "Has it been recovered?"

"The stolen dirty bomb had originated in Pakistan, and thanks to me working for the Philly' Police Department, the threat is now safely in the custody of the United States military."

* * * * * * * * * * * *

Renowned professor Dr. Arnold Fitzgerald of LaSalle University had ingeniously organized and implemented a rather extremely interesting rehabilitation program for Wynnewood's all-too-modest unsung hero/reporter. First, a North Philadelphia priest was assigned to perform a thorough exorcism on Julius Rubicon's psyche in order to purge his wandering spirit of harmful demons. Then, a qualified team of crackerjack psychologists and an eminent contingent of esteemed psychiatrists professionally deprogrammed young Rubicon, so that his human needs and basic drives could satisfactorily return to everyday normalcy. And finally, the grateful City of Philadelphia had the first aforementioned Wynnewood street lamppost removed and quickly replaced with a suitable-but-adequate substitute source of nighttime illumination. Thus, the night-stalker trigger-mechanism had been permanently eliminated.

"Photographs"

It was a glorious, crisp autumnal New England morning. Jack and Margie Major were fully awake and eager to escape the confinement of their large, cozy Springfield, Massachusetts home. All of the myriad lawn and garden chores had been completed during the past week, and now it was time for some well-deserved relaxation to be enjoyed in a beautiful natural setting.

The couple had been planning to accompany their fifteen-year-old daughter on a Sunday afternoon photo' outing amidst the majestic grandeur of the Vermont countryside. Lisa Major loved her new *Nikon* and would bring it faithfully on every excursion to the nearby *Green Mountains*, once made famous by Ethan Allen and his "boys" during the colonial *American Revolutionary War*.

The Major family's favorite small village in Vermont always attracted many "Indian Summer tourists" each October. The nature-loving tourists assembled each fall to admire the multi-colored foliage. Over the years, the small New England hamlet had evolved into a popular mecca for camera buffs and fledgling artists.

Jack Major was thirty-nine years old and thrived as a very prominent New England commercial real estate developer. The successful entrepreneur had an effervescent personality that featured a genuine and robust sense of humor. Jack had thick light brown hair, and his well-groomed curly locks strongly contrasted with his dark blue eyes.

Wife Margie was a gorgeous thirty-seven-year-old natural blonde. Mrs. Major had become very prosperous in her own right, being the proprietor of an art gallery conveniently located in the Springfield business district, and the woman was planning to open two novel satellite art centers in Boston and in Providence, Rhode Island. The very independent lady took great pleasure in joining Jack and Lisa on their "weekend communions" with nature. Besides being an avid art merchant, Jack's fully energetic spouse was also an accomplished artist. Margie would paint natural scenes on canvas while the two amateur family photographers practiced their camera craft in the general vicinity. The trio made a close-knit family, and all three participants loved experiencing the splendor of Vermont's pristine outdoors.

Lisa simply adored her father. The blue-eyed, curly blonde-haired girl quite enthusiastically pursued her father's favorite hobby. And Jack Major really relished his weekend photography escapes from the massive pressures associated with effectively functioning in competitive corporate America.

Soon, the family would be motoring north on *Interstate 91* to their special Vermont *Green Mountains* "nature retreat". Jack's specialty was taking still shots of rustic wooded landscapes. Major spent many hours assiduously laboring to skillfully capture unique pictures of trees, meadows, and lakes on film. The dedicated photographer had a terrific knack of recognizing the exact forest settings that would synthesize various elements into excellent award winning "environmental statements".

"Well, Lisa, are you ready for another special rendezvous with Mother Nature?" the motivated father bellowed across the kitchen breakfast table. "I just gotta' commend your overall initiative. Your skill is progressing beautifully with each new session."

"Daddy, I'm anxious to earn my first trophy," Lisa surprisingly intimated. "I want to have an awards room in *my* house when I'm your age, just like you do!"

"I get the *picture*," joshed the ever-jovial real estate developer, whose silly punning propensity was virtually indefatigable.

Jack Major had some exciting news to disclose to his eager, young protegé. The proud father had entered Lisa's name in an important area photography contest. Jack was still the sagacious pedagogue and Lisa his precocious student, but her dexterity with a camera was beginning to rival her dad's reputable ability. The girl had very rapidly mastered all the subtle tricks and finer points of contemporary art form. The teenager's *Nikon* prowess had almost advanced her skill development to professional level status.

"Pretty soon the public won't be able to distinguish between the teacher and the student," laughed Jack before imbibing a mouthful of orange juice. "Then, I'll be able to take lessons from you."

"Dad, any recognition that I'll ever receive, I'll owe to your teaching!" Lisa stated with pure admiration. 'You're the absolute best instructor I could ever want!"

"Your father attributes your ability to you having a *photographic memory*," laughed Mrs. Margie Major from her end of the breakfast table. "But always try to improve your craft, and never take your talent for granted."

Just after the morning meal and its subsequent clean-up had been completed, the trio packed their individual lunches and left their large suburban Springfield home in the Majors' four-wheel drive red *Ford Explorer*. Their chosen destination was a remote wooded area, high-up in a secluded ravine between two gorgeous Vermont mountain peaks. The "retreat" was so isolated that not even the local *Green Mountain* natives were knowledgeable of the stellar site. The trip required about a three-hour drive to reach the isolated "retreat" from the Majors' spacious Massachusetts home, a hundred-and-fifty-miles distance.

The last half-hour of unpaved mountain trails brought the red *Explorer* into a scenic virgin wilderness stretch of land. The view on all sides was positively magnificent. There was an abundance of rolling hills, and the deciduous trees abounded with inspirational shades of red, green, yellow, brown and gold.

The Columbus Day weekend panorama was complemented by the presence of a rambling brook, which coursed a serpentine path through the hilly, lush woodlands. This "special gift of nature" added another terrific dimension to an already ideal mountain setting. The overall spectacle was highlighted by the sound of many birds melodiously chirping sweet serenades, producing a symphony of rhythmic sounds emanating from the multi-hued limbs and branches.

"This is the perfect place to enjoy a picnic and to shoot some phenomenal still pictures," declared the father. "Half of winning a contest is finding the right location and the proper atmosphere."

"I just have a good feeling that I'm going to get my finest picture ever," Lisa boldly predicted. "I think I'm now ready to win my first public award."

"You two are babbling more than that brook over there," humorously added Margie Major. "And you're also doing more chirping than those garrulous birds off in the distance."

The great outdoors inspired Jack Major to be in a very jovial and giddy mood. "Lisa, maybe if you're lucky, you'll accidentally get a close-up of *Big Foot.*"

"Daddy*, Sasquatch* is out in Oregon or roaming around western Canada, not here in New England!" corrected the knowledgeable daughter, whose academic geography awareness was much keener than her weak mastery of algebra.

Jack and Lisa carefully unpacked their cameras, tripods, telephoto lenses and filters. Margie simultaneously removed her paints, brushes and utilitarian easel. After an impromptu early lunch of roast beef sandwiches and apple cider, the family triumvirate separated onto three divergent paths. Each nature lover wanted to discover good vantage points from which to pursue their particular interests. All three clan members respected the others individual privacy, a necessity that is prerequisite to being a serious-minded artist, so that father, mother and daughter could then have proper perspectives of capturing the marvelous mountain vista either on film or on canvas.

"Art expression is not collective group work," Jack had often lectured to Lisa. "It involves an inspired individual interpreting his or her environment in a sincere effort to make a valid statement."

"Lisa, your father is right. *Da Vinci* painted the *Mona Lisa* all by himself without any group work assistance involved," articulated Mrs. Major. "And Vincent van Gogh didn't allow anybody snooping around either when he felt in a creative mood!"

Being a devout contrarian, Lisa Major was enamored with the notion of selecting an opposite-angle forest view other than the one chosen by her father. Then, the girl could feel comfortable snapping-away after doing her standard due diligence. The excited daughter wanted to respond on her own to the same external challenges as those encountered by her award-winning father/teacher.

And each photographer desired to capture on film the fabulous kaleidoscope of stately trees and gradual creeping shadows. Both Lisa and Jack would be maneuvering around hills and dales to obtain as many quality photos' as possible of the ever-wondrous forest's pristine beauty. In the meantime, Margie was applying an array of shapes and colors upon her canvas, which already rested upon the sturdy easel's frame.

During the next several hours, Lisa and her jovial dad had already separated and taken dozens of awe-inspiring "photographic statements", and Mrs. Major had managed to eventually finish her dynamic "still-nature" painting. Growling stomachs dictated that it was now time for a scheduled three-thirty late afternoon food break.

The three picnickers congregated and soon sat on a log situated close to the aesthetic babbling stream. Each person was munching-away on a second round of roast beef sandwiches and drinking cold cans of *Pepsi-Cola*. Margie had brought along some tasty homemade chocolate chip cookies and three orchard fresh apples, which nicely supplemented the delicious afternoon meal.

"It's so peaceful up here in the Vermont hills, far away from the noise, crime and pollution of the city," Margie pleasantly observed and commented. "I feel much safer here than back in 'so-called civilization', if you know what I mean!"

"I've never been as happy as I am right now," Lisa convincingly insisted. "The gorgeous mountains are food for the soul, that's for sure. What's your opinion, Dad?"

"There *is* a pure beauty that exists in nature. Only certain humans bring evil into the world," Jack Major philosophically maintained.

"Then. why are we corrupting nature with *our* presence?" laughed and argued the sometimes-witty wife. "We' aren't exactly dedicated full-time conservationists, now are we?"

After a half-hour of relaxing and pleasant chitchatting, the stimulated trio again retreated to their regular picture taking and oil painting activities. As the late afternoon hours progressed towards dusk, the mountain shadows lengthened, and it was unanimously decided to assemble the array of equipment and begin the three-hour drive back to suburban Springfield. Jack, Margie, and Lisa all felt very content and fulfilled with their individual expeditions into the realm of creativity, and their positive emotions made the long return journey seem like a mere delightful jaunt. Lisa had fallen asleep in the rear of the red sports utility vehicle, but before she could complete her lengthy siesta, Jack was piloting the four-wheel-drive *Ford Explorer* into their tan brick driveway.

"Back to drudgery, mayhem, and civilization," observed and complained the talkative driver. "Oh well, we do live better than Neanderthals once did!"

"I think that primitive *Neanderthal* men appreciated nature more than twentieth-century humans do," quipped the sometimes-cynical wife. "And Cro-Magnons did even more."

An hour later, Margie started preparing supper in the kitchen while Jack and Lisa carefully unpacked the family's gear that had been removed from the red vehicle. Within an hour, the Majors were discussing their fun day of enjoying photography and canvas painting over delectable sirloin steaks and French fries.

The next evening, Jack would cautiously develop the postcard setting forest photographs in his dark room. The Majors had no idea that several pictures that had been captured on Lisa's film would have a very dramatic impact on their very passive and tranquil lives.

* * * * * * * * * * * *

Monday morning, Lisa rose from bed early for a special reason. The neophyte photographer was quite anxious to commence working on her "prize-winning Green Mountain gems", since her school had been closed because of the *Columbus Day* national holiday. Margie was already in the kitchen making breakfast when Jack Major and Lisa made their belated appearances. Pancakes with pure Vermont maple syrup would predictably delight their palates.

"We'll leave the dishes for Mom to wash," suggested the daughter, who was all-too-thrilled to get started developing the rolls of film from the day before. "I'm sure she understands."

"That unsolicited decision ought to really make your mom's day less satisfying," affirmed the real estate entrepreneur. "I don't want to sound too chauvinistic, but dishes and wives often go together!"

"Mother's Day isn't until May!" the teenager quipped. "That's when you and I do all of the household chores!"

"It's about time you two freeloaders became more domesticated," argued Mrs. Major. "Jack, I know you like science fiction. How would you like for a flying saucer to hit you in the head right now, and not the *UFO* kind, either!"

After the father and daughter laughed at Mrs. Major's ridiculous comment, Lisa felt incentivized "to get rolling", and the girl made an anxious beeline to the fully-equipped dark room in order to commence developing her "Vermont Mountain portraits".

Jack ordinarily escorted Lisa into the dark room with him to teach her exactly how the intricate procedures should be performed, but after three years of astute learning, the observant daughter knew every phase of the development process by heart.

On the way to the Dark Room, the daughter recalled that when she was twelve, Lisa had wandered into the "Forbidden Zone" while Jack had been developing "competition pictures" in his pan. The unwary girl had inadvertently flipped on the light switch to inspect her father's activity and had accidentally ruined an entire roll of high-quality photos'. The family now laughs when recalling "the unintentional incident", but at the time of its occurrence, the damage had been a traumatic experience for the budding master photographer. Lisa had never forgotten her father's impetuous temper, exhibited especially when Mr. Major was suddenly disturbed and ever since, the teen has discreetly valued caution over curiosity.

Over two-hundred colorful Vermont forest pictures had been taken by both avid photographers. The father finally arrived at the "Forbidden Zone" and politely knocked on the "laboratory door" to assist his daughter in completing her first-time endeavor. As usual, the many negatives would require much patience to be processed. As one roll of film was finished, another was carefully placed in the dark room's "conversion tank". After three hours of very prudent and diligent labor, Jack determined that the "laboratory proofs" were ready for printing.

The Vermont photographs appeared in 4" X 5" size, and later, the better ones would be enlarged for quality evaluation. Jack and Lisa had *their* individual pictures separated into "designated areas", so that the proper artist would be given credit for *his* or *her* individual achievements. Jack's finest photos were first to be gently exhibited on display racks. Lisa's final endeavors were being printed while her father's "pictorial statements" were still drying.

The two camera buffs first examined the father's initial picture batch, and the evaluators were thrilled to acknowledge that each photo' was rather beautiful, each one seemingly appearing better than its predecessor. The most outstanding representations were then isolated to be enlarged for later inspection.

"Daddy, your pictures are going to be really hard to beat," Lisa admitted. "I still have a long way to go to catch up to you."

"Let's see what you've managed to catch on film," replied the proud tutor. "I think you're catching-up to me pretty fast."

When the daughter's first roll of pictures had been aligned on the table, both she and her father were quite satisfied after viewing the terrific results. The singular representations were every bit as edifying as Jack's, and some of the renditions even appeared to be decidedly better. There was no doubt in Jack's astute mind that one of Lisa's remarkable pictures was destined to win a coveted prize in upcoming contest competition.

"Lisa, I think you've finally arrived as a master photographer. Today, you've ceased being a student and have advanced to the level of mentor," Jack Majors maintained. "Congratulation!"

"Daddy, I want to win the Boston contest so badly and then tell the whole wide world I owe it all to you," the devoted teenager praised. "Thanks to you, my confidence is building every day."

The remaining photo' development of additional Vermont Mountain rolls and their subsequent time-consuming printing ate-up most of that Monday morning. After a brief lunch with Margie, the camera addicts were so enthralled and so engrossed in their great enterprise that they had completely lost track of time. Jack still had stamina to again flick-on the dark room lights.

After another hour of passionate labor, the two looked at the laboratory clock soon alerted "J and L" Enterprises" that an entire afternoon had elapsed, and that supper would be ready. The aroma of freshly baked ham greeted the father and daughter's delayed entrance into the dining room. Margie diplomatically chastised the two new arrivals for having created more domestic work for her to perform after "just cleaning up after breakfast."

"Thanks for leaving me those greasy dishes to wash this morning," admonished Mrs. Major. "You're both so into your addictive picture development that you two obsessed camera buffs are ignoring your basic household chores."

"Honey, we're very sorry," Jack apologized. "But getting to those photos' and getting them printed became quite a noble quest."

"Daddy's right, Mom," Lisa assertively concurred. "I feel like someday I'm going to become just as famous as *Mathew Brady*."

"Well, I have some bad news to report. You two are going to have to clean the dinner dishes. I have to prepare my notes for an upcoming exhibit at *my* Art Gallery," demanded the fiercely independent self-employed woman. "I have other things to think about too, you know."

"Don't worry, Lisa. I promise I'll do the dishes right after supper," Jack informed. "I'll volunteer to be Mr. Mom for the night. You go right ahead and finish-up with your important work in the Dark Room," Jack insisted. "I must admit that now you know exactly what you're doing."

"You two better wash your hands before you have supper," declared Margie Major. "Sometimes it's necessary for me to remind you two hobbyists to get back to basics, including sanitation!"

After the luscious baked ham had been eaten, Mrs. Major brought to the table a homemade pumpkin pie, which was the family's favorite dessert. The previously starved photographers were both very contented with the supplementary highlight of the evening meal. Afterwards, Lisa again eagerly marched down the lengthy hall to the special Dark Room" to further analyze the exquisite forest snapshots that she alone had taken.

'I can't wait to sort-out my best dozen images. I'll select the best rendition to enter into the upcoming competition,' the girl excitedly thought. 'I wonder which one will be my best snapshot?'

While examining the next batch of photos', Lisa suddenly felt an intense chill travel down her spine. The daughter found the image inside the rectangular "4 X 5" spectacle being held in her hands very frightening. So disquieting was her total shock and fear that the girl, feeling quite sick in her stomach, had to immediately vacate the Dark Room at once.

Meanwhile, Jack was busy reading a sports magazine in the den and wasn't aware of Lisa's sudden alarm. The girl would not reveal her suspicion to her over-protective dad because the teen was uncertain whether or not she had seen an actual image, or had incidentally noticed and reacted to some sort of inexplicable photographic aberration. In the morning, "the truth" captured on film would be enlarged, and Lisa would then be better able to ascertain with more clarity the exact nature of 'the ugly human' her eyes had vaguely perceived inside the Dark Room.

The clocks throughout the Majors' home indicated that the evening was gradually advancing to 11 p.m., the time of the late-night TV news. Lisa was very tired from her time-consuming laboratory toil, and very nervous about viewing 'the horribly ugly image' her alert eyes had perceived. But still, the girl feigned normal behavior as she kissed her parents "Good Night", entered her woolen pajamas, and then reluctantly climbed into bed. The recurring recollection of 'the horrible picture' dominated Lisa's fragile psyche, and the jittery girl had trouble falling asleep.

Jack and Margie lingered in front of the TV to watch the remainder of the late-night news. One of the reported highlights was that a prominent Boston political figure's son had mysteriously disappeared. The TV was shut-off shortly afterwards, and then Mr. and Mrs. Major shuffled down the hall to their sleeping quarters, quickly took hot showers, changed into comfortable pajamas, and finally reclined in their very soft bed. Soon, the house was dark, and the family was sound asleep, that is, except for Lisa.

During the night, the fidgety girl could not make a viable connection with evasive *Mr. Sandman*. While lying in bed, Lisa contemplated the alluring Vermont mountain pictures; she gradually mustered-up sufficient courage and decided to secretly revisit the printing room and further examine 'The Horrifying Picture'. Then, the persistent daughter could effectively focus her full analysis on evaluating its initial disturbing content.

The relevant photos had been taken at a different vantage point than those that had been snapped by her father. Lisa had captured her own unique variations evident in the plethora of unique scenery presentations. The comparative foliage shown in Jack's photos had lighter shades than the hues that were captured in Lisa's pictures, and the father's collection was a degree clearer with his color combinations being a trifle more lucid.

While studying her own superb graphics, the anxious teen suddenly experienced an even greater Dark Room chill than the one she had felt before. The second peculiar sensation made her entire body tremble. "Could this be real?" she whispered to herself' in a stunned state of mind. "It can't be true!"

The amateur photographer had been frightened to the point of tears that were quickly accompanied by hysteria. The young searcher was now afraid to move an inch. She stared-down and perceptively examined the obscure manifestation once more. Her reason for apprehension was indeed wholly justified. Lisa shuddered at the prospect of what the tangible illustration before her disbelieving eyes portended for her and her parents.

"I should really show Daddy his horror, but I must be absolutely certain. This must be some simple printing error that I'm seeing," she whispered to herself' after assessing the very frightening photo'.

The huge suburban house was now fully dark, and Lisa's parents were sound-asleep, completely unaware of their child's extreme emotional anguish. The completely awake girl was becoming increasingly upset and scared with each passing second.

Gathering adequate courage, Lisa flicked-off the Dark Room light and then brightened the illumination of the hall by gently twisting the dimmer wall knob to the right. The distressed, mildly sobbing-teenager then softly stepped to her bedroom in an intensely frazzled frame of mind. The scared girl was under the covers immediately, whimpering and alternately weeping. Her disturbed thoughts remained solely concentrated on 'The Grotesque Picture', which still aroused extreme terror within her young heart.

The entire notion of a devious stranger dreadfully stalking her and her parents within the pristine Vermont Mountains was too harrowing for the callow girl to carry in her head. The photograph's harrowing content transcended logic, and it also defied the now-apparent vulnerable innocence of the aforementioned Vermont "retreat" setting. Obviously, the horrid mountain photograph caused great trepidation to reign supreme in Lisa's panic-stricken soul. The girl recalled that inside the dense forest shrub background was the visage of a very suspicious person; an anonymous man's face, stealthily staring and hiding inside the dense foliage and peering directly at the remote lens of the then unaware, very innocent, amateur photographer.

* * * * * * * * * * * *

Tuesday morning Jack Major awoke early. The man had an important appointment to honor with several local commercial building contractors. The very competent real estate developer had left early to his office in order to attend his scheduled agenda of meetings, all the while curiously wondering, 'Who had left the hall dimmer switch on?'

Margie woke Lisa up for school. After the two dressed for their daily weekday rituals, the mother and daughter shared a breakfast and out of habit were slowly shifting-back into their humdrum weekday regimens. A half-hour later, Freshman Lisa was being dropped-off at high school in the wife's dark blue *Infiniti,* and Margie was currently considering how she was going to complete some last-minute responsibilities at her Springfield gallery.

"Is everything all right, dear?" the all-too-perceptive mother asked. "You seem to be a little edgy this morning."

"I'm all right, Mom," Lisa poorly lied. "I just have to take a wicked algebra test this morning, and I feel a little tense about it."

"That's perfectly understandable," the mother compassionately answered. "I despised that all-too-challenging subject too when I was an unsophisticated sophomore. The best part about an algebra test is the after*math,"* the mother awkwardly joked.

84

While nervously seated in her advanced math' class, Lisa thought about 'The Horrendous Picture' and couldn't focus on her algebra test's very difficult quadratic equations. The distracted student was certain she would fail the examination, but academic mathematics was not at that moment paramount in her mind. The monotonous school day went by slowly, including the normally fun-time cafeteria period. Finally, the three o'clock bell sounded at the end of *English,* and boring grammatical tedium would not be resumed until Wednesday. The melancholy pupil quickly exited the two-story edifice to meet her mother, who was waiting patiently in the dark blue *Infiniti* for her daughter's arrival.

"How was the algebra test, dear?" Margie inquired.

"Dreadful," Lisa replied. "I think I flunked it royally."

"You'll probably have to be tutored just like I had to be all throughout high school," the mother sympathetically returned. "Weak math skills must be genetically inherited in our family. I think it involves the scientific side of the brain as opposed to the artistic side! I even had to go to summer school for Trig!"

When Lisa arrived home, the freshman darted to the printing room to attempt disproving her real reason for experiencing academic dismay. The amateur photographer once more studied her inventory of pictures and then comprehensively compared each with photos' that her dad had taken of the almost identical forest environment. Soon, the same spine-chilling, disconcerting anguish entered her heart. An instantaneous numbness totally saturated her entire being. In one of Lisa's photos', a hideous-looking man's scowling face could vividly be discerned, and the 'forest villain' was indeed nastily peering straight at the girl's camera lens.

At that moment, Mrs. Major sternly summoned her daughter to set the dining room table. Lisa tried regaining her diminished composure as the girl promptly exited the film laboratory. The confused junior photographer was momentarily relieved to be able to abandon the terror of the now foreboding Dark Room horror in deference for the security of ordinary family interaction inside the non-threatening dining room.

En route to the regular eating area, Lisa furtively promised her conscience that she would wait for her father to return home and then confide in *his* wisdom about the scope and sequence of her new-found dilemma. Some rational explanation had to reasonably account for the bizarre appearance of the mysterious spy hiding behind the forest bush in the anomalous Vermont *Green Mountain* photograph. At least, that is what Lisa's mind had conjectured.

Jack Major arrived home for dinner right on schedule, and soon the family was seated for supper. The father immediately sensed that something was wrong by deftly studying his daughter's general mannerisms. "You're mighty quiet today, Lisa!"

"I'm sorry, Daddy, but I failed another algebra test!" the girl moaned with real tears forming in her eyes. "I can't seem to understand the fundamentals of that subject!"

"Don't let it get the best of you," replied the supportive father. "Maybe next week you'll see the educational light and the entire discipline will magically come together for you! That's how it was for me with high school Chemistry."

When the family finished eating their pork chops, carrots, and mashed potatoes, and after all three members washed and dried the dishes, Jack and Lisa stepped-down the hall toward the printing room to enlarge the special pictures that the now-accomplished young photographer had selected for entry into the upcoming Boston contest. One by one, the best shots were deftly enhanced, and the larger editions were meticulously hung to dry. This time-consuming Dark Room process would require several hours to finish, so the fervent photography buffs finally terminated their grueling laboratory activities for the night. The newly magnified versions would be thoroughly analyzed in the morning.

Lisa was still hesitant to share her new-found apprehension about 'The Gross Picture', which starkly contained 'the forest prowler's' hostile-looking countenance. Perhaps it was merely a weird optical illusion after all. If it were, it was a very horrifying optical illusion to someone as impressionable as Lisa Major.

The Major family watched TV for the rest of the evening, their viewing culminating with the eleven o'clock news. Lisa pretended to be dejected about failing her advanced mathematics exam while simultaneously camouflaging the true reason for her discontent. Her parents desperately tried alleviating their daughter's disconsolate, upset mood about the non-importance of algebra, mentioning certain failures in the performance of their adult occupations, but the parents' efforts were to no avail.

"Don't worry," encouraged the girl's loyal and concerned father. "We'll return to Vermont before *Thanksgiving*. A little bit of fresh air and a healthy dose of *Mother Nature* will snap you right out of your doldrums, and it'll instantly make you forget all about algebra."

In the middle of the night, Lisa again became extremely restless, and while lying in her bed, the girl had an irresistible urge to revisit the photo' printing lab. The Dark Room seemed to have a magnetic attraction that strongly tugged at Lisa's mounting intrigue. The wide-awake teen was very quiet as she slowly progressed down the home's dark, drafty hallway.

The daughter flicked on the room's lights, and within a minute was intensely gazing at the newly finished enlargements. The nervous teen was desperately searching for any additional observations about the unsightly intruder possessing the gruesome-looking facial features. Every picture the girl had painstakingly taken and developed was intensely scrutinized in full detail. As the young sleuth was mentally synthesizing the elements of 'The Terrible Picture', she again experienced sudden consternation, and then once more felt extreme shock.

"Am I becoming neurotic?" the paranoid investigator whispered to herself as her throat inhaled a deep breath. "This is like a crazy horror movie!"

The flabbergasted photo' examiner reflexively grabbed Jack's powerful magnifying glass, which ordinarily was used to detect outstanding defects in the final prints. The secretive picture inspector started to systematically study every iota vaguely depicted in 'The Horrendous Picture'. Lisa methodically maneuvered the large glass magnifier from leaf to leaf, from limb to limb, from tree to tree, and from bush to bush.

Suddenly, the girl let-out an ear-piercing scream, and her legs buckled as the high school student collapsed to the floor. Lisa Major had seen that same sinister snoop's enlarged ugly face in the second photo'. His menacing glare was still partially hidden inside the maze of autumn leaves, but nevertheless, it was indeed the same repugnant face. The stealthy forest witness had again been staring directly into the *Nikon's* lens. The anonymous subject had brown hair, a mustache, was wearing a weatherworn leather jacket, and the secret subject had a blue-stoned ring shown on his left fourth finger.

After hearing the loud shriek, Jack and Margie came sprinting down the hallway into the now well-lit Dark Room. The parents found their daughter lying prone on the tile floor, and her pallid face exhibited a terrifying grim, macabre expression. The alarmed adults cautiously raised Lisa up and together carried her limp body to the living room sofa. After Mrs. Major applied a cold compress to her daughter's sweat-laden forehead, the emotionally stunned girl eventually snapped-out of her temporary semi-conscious state.

Feeling embarrassed at remembering her screaming incident, the all-too-tormented teenager revealed nothing about the exasperating spectacle she had just noticed. Lisa did not want to frighten her parents over something that might have remotely been 'a printing error'. But what the daughter really feared was her disconcerting premonition that the two disturbing pictures would soon trigger a parade of diabolical nightmares.

* * * * * * * * * * * *

It required several days for Lisa Major and her parents to recover from the nerve-wracking "inexplicable fainting episode". Since the daughter never divulged the nature of her real fear to her loving mentors, Jack and Margie were unaware of Lisa's actual concern, and the parents attributed the extraordinary fainting incident to "an overwhelming phobia about failing algebra".

"Maybe you can talk with your guidance counselor and take a remedial math course until you're ready to confidently tackle polynomials," suggested the all-too-concerned shopping center and mall developer. "That would be a discreet thing to do."

"No, Daddy," Lisa adamantly objected. "I'll manage just fine once I gain a little more skill with equations."

Later that afternoon, Lisa concealed 'The Two Unnerving Pictures' in the back of her personal diary. Only their distant recollection could haunt her normally happy-go-lucky disposition.

Jack Major planned to surprise his beleaguered daughter with a new advanced *Canon* camera, and so the doting father bought her the latest model, which flaunted many marvelous new features. The sophisticated device was an expensive gift, which Lisa had intimated to her mother she would absolutely treasure *after* winning her first important competition. But when it boiled-down to spoiling his beloved daughter, money was no object to generous Jack Majors.

"Oh Daddy, thank you so much!" the appreciative girl screamed, temporarily forgetting about the exceptionally hideous-looking man existing in her two diary photos'. "I promise to do better in algebra."

"Baby, you're a sight to behold, but your new *Canon* camera is a sight to *be held,*" the proud real estate/film developer creatively jested. "I know you'll have good luck with it!"

The important Boston photo' contest was getting closer with each passing day, and Jack Major pasted his precious daughter's Vermont *Green Mountain* pictures into a special album for the event's judges' comprehensive scrutiny. Lisa didn't habitually examine "her contest album" too carefully because the Vermont photos' in the girl's portfolio reminded the prospective entrant of the two terrible renditions that she had secretly hidden inside her personal journal. But Miss Major's anxiety was somewhat mitigated when the aspiring contestant seriously contemplated the upcoming photo' competition in "Bean Town."

Saturday morning arrived, and it was now the big scheduled calendar date. The Majors' motored from Springfield to Boston in their red *Ford Explorer,* their family dialogue being mostly news events as seen on TV. At the gallery, throngs of photo' apprentices had registered for the vital competition, and the waiting-in-line audience soon filled the auditorium to capacity. While handling the mounting tension, Lisa practiced taking some indoor shots with her new *Canon* camera. In truth, the teen wanted to experiment with the item's new features, which included a built-in automatic flash, a telephoto zoom lens, and an advanced self-winding film mechanism. An optional attachment to filter-in the desirable degree of light could be easily added to achieve certain "unique atmosphere effects". Also, the compact unit was lightweight and not at all cumbersome. To relieve stress, Lisa snapped a variety of people attending the show, and the camera aficionado felt more-at-ease while deploying her new-found utilitarian gift.

'Maybe this new camera can capture raw nature instead of imaginary forest molesters on film,' the young photographer mused. 'Maybe my out-of-control imagination is making a small biscuit into a heavy loaf of bread.'

The moment had finally arrived when a panel of veteran judges would assess the competence of the competing photo' virtuosos. Since the contest's reputation was quite prestigious, over one-hundred hopeful candidates were vying for the coveted honor of "Grand Master Photographer", which was generously sponsored by the revered *Boston Photography Exposition.*

As the finalists' albums were being scrutinized, their entries were then displayed upon sturdy easels for public viewing. The fortunate winners were then announced over the stage microphone, and First Prize was unanimously awarded to "Lisa Major". Jack's appealing collection that had been meticulously arranged in *his* Vermont photo' album had merited "Second Runner-up." A large trophy was then presented to the excited Springfield teenager, and the victor was extremely ecstatic with her exemplary accomplishment. Everyone in attendance applauded Lisa's splendid album presentation.

"If this was a horse race, you would've *won* and I would've *showed,*" Jack enthusiastically congratulated his momentarily happy daughter. "Maybe I'll next buy you a racehorse as a reward!"

"This glory I owe all to you, Daddy," said Lisa who then simultaneously hugged her mother and her father. "Thanks to this wonderful prize, I've already forgotten about that stupid trivial algebra test I had flunked."

There was plenty of excitement occurring throughout the noisy, crowded auditorium. Complete strangers approached the stage to congratulate the young winner and to gain a closer glimpse of the award-winning collection. Lisa desired capturing all of the jubilation on film, which naturally would officially document the most renowned success ever achieved in her young life.

The boisterous "congratulations" lasted for a full hour, but then the jostling attendees conducted a peaceful pilgrimage to their cars that were parked inside the building's spacious in-door garage facility. As the family departed the premises, Jack and Margie Major were especially euphoric about their daughter's sublime triumph.

"I'll tell you, Honey, I think that Lisa is a prodigy!" the proud father bragged.

"Maybe this new-found confidence will transfer over to her algebra class," the elated mother speculated and answered.

The next evening, Jack developed the photos of the people whom Lisa had snapped for "scale" and for "room light testing" while participating in the *Boston Photography Exposition*.

"I can't wait to see how my new *Canon's* zoom lens performed," the still-thrilled daughter confessed to her dad. Demonstrating zeal for the task at hand, in the Dark Room Jack and Lisa fastidiously printed and hung the set of new photos' up to dry. A minimum of two hours would elapse until the anticipated results could be fully appreciated. Then, human fingers could gently touch and handle the exhibits, so the two photo' enthusiasts decided to wait until the next day to fully complete their labor of love.

Much to Jack and Lisa's culinary delight, Margie then unexpectedly served the pair tasty apple pie ala mode. The vanilla ice-cream desserts were soon rapidly consumed. Later in the day, lackluster television situation comedies were viewed until the standard eleven o'clock news appeared upon the screen. The local station always seemed to engage in transmitting sensationalism, and Jack often complained that the area network affiliate used "tabloid journalism" to increase ratings and to garner commercial sponsors. The family seemed disgusted with the litany of nondescript fires, robberies, criminal molestations, drug confiscations, homicides and suicides, and Jack, showing his typical cynicism, criticized each and every on-the-scene "redundant" local news report.

"Doesn't anything nice ever happen to anyone anymore?" Margie Major skeptically squawked, endorsing her husband's negative point of view. "The nightly news on all the main channels has become a definite, lackluster turn-off!"

"We live in a sick demented society," concurred the equally pessimistic husband. "The TV news only reflects what kind of messed-up world exists out there."

"Thank goodness for photography and good old *Mother Nature,*" concluded and opined Lisa. "There *are* certain constructive things in life that do bring joy and comfort."

The man-of-the-house was about to shut-off the annoying media apparatus, but Jack hesitated when the glib anchorman announced that a forest hiker had incidentally found a decomposed female body, and that the grisly discovery had been made in the *Green Mountains* of Vermont. This extraordinary coincidence immediately caught the Majors' undivided attention, and the threesome listened intently to the remaining dramatic details.

According to the on-the-scene commentator's report, the local police were stumped and had no viable clues or leads in which to investigate. Jack finally shut the TV off, and after discussing the parallel development of them frequenting the same mountains where the female's body had been discovered, everyone felt uncomfortable and wanted to "call it a night".

At midnight, Lisa was again awake, lying in bed and thinking about the poor victim's corpse being found. The worried girl was wondering if the ominous-looking 'thug' hiding in the forest bushes (who she had inadvertently captured on film) had anything to do with the atrocious Vermont Mountain felony.

Throughout that night, the teen could not achieve a sound sleep. Lisa tossed and turned wildly upon the mattress of her queen-sized bed, her mind besieged with frightening thoughts, all rehashing the memory of the sinister-looking suspect whose scarred face had been isolated in the intriguing forest photos'. Soon, the unpleasant phenomenon evolved into a grotesque repetitious newsreel being repeated over and over again in the girl's neurotic psyche. As the contest winner continued her restless tossing and turning, Lisa's brain kept recalling the formidable facial features of the phantom depicted in the pictures. Only she knew about 'the forest prowler'.

After a second hour of traumatic wiggling and wriggling, the teenager still wasn't able to soundly fall asleep, so Lisa rose from her warm queen-sized bed and silently ambled ever-so-slowly down the dimly lit hall to again revisit the printing room.

After slowly opening the creaky door, the nightwalker then quietly flicked-on the overhead light, closed the portal, and again closely examined the assorted pictures that she had snapped at the *Boston Photography Exposition.* The first four seemed quite ordinary and professionally done, and the observer was somewhat pleased with their overall excellence, recollecting that she had taken and processed a total of thirty-six on three rolls of film.

Suddenly, the recent insomniac experienced another spine-tingling chill which then caused the girl to frantically dart-out of the film laboratory. The petrified daughter was so nervous and so panicky that the pounding of her heart throbbed from deep within her chest, rising all the way up to her aching eardrums. The fearful beholder's sixth sense communicated to her intelligence that something very terrible was about to happen, and the intensity of the girl's absolute terror was all too palpable and surreal for her to endure.

'Maybe the light of dawn will bring some sane relief,' the apprehensive teen desperately hoped as she paced down the hall back to the sanctuary of her bedroom. Five minutes passed, and Lisa lay virtually paralyzed, wholly still upon her bed. Only her relentless low sobbing was discernible to her sensitive, all-too-jittery ears. The traumatized girl felt that she could not bear her horrific secret any longer. The truth needed to be shared with her parents.

* * * * * * * * * * * *

At 4 a.m. Lisa Major awoke from a very incoherent nightmare. The first agenda that dominated her confused mind was the verification of the hellish third observation recently made inside the "print room". The daughter slowly tiptoed down the all-too-familiar hall straight for her father's laboratory. She then very anxiously arranged the new photos from the "Boston Exposition" upon the examination counter.

The pictures were indeed very clear, and the exact amount of desired exposure and detail was quite evident in each one. Lisa had taken random snapshots of almost everyone that had attended the event, but her eyes again assiduously searched for the 'phantom killer' possessing the antagonistic, grotesque face. The girl speculated that his 'mug-shot' was akin to the ones adorning the 'FBI's Most Wanted Men' wall posters in the local post office.

As the freshman high school student viewed the newly developed collection, the teen again felt strange, experiencing the same horrid shiver descending her spine. Lisa continued scrutinizing the new pictures and trembled upon recognizing the faces of many of the Exposition's attendees. One new picture in particular corralled her very vivid observation. An adult male guest had been examining the winning album as though he were studying for a Doctorate in Minutia. His distinct presence had appeared in several of Lisa's other candid shots. In one freeze frame, the subject-in-question had been clearly isolated on film. In her more accurate inspection, Lisa lucidly recognized that same haunting, very cold, conspicuous, eerie stare. The perturbed viewer gasped as her eyes beheld the same sordid individual who had formerly been partially obscured in the previous Vermont Mountain photos'.

The thoroughly distressed amateur photographer rapidly sifted through other pictures to obtain more precise definition of the forest prowler's facial characteristics. One portrayal had captured the stalker's cameo profile while the scar-faced man was leaving the Exposition's exhibit area. Lisa Major was again staggered and overwhelmed upon her further Dark Room analysis when she noticed that the furtive forest scoundrel was wearing a blue-sapphire ring upon his fourth left-ring finger.

"This is not just a sensational coincidence!" Lisa gulped and shuddered in sheer terror. "This is an absolute frightening reality!"

That wild obsession was no figment of her active imagination. Miss Major's Dark Room inspection was indubitable confirmation of the actual existence of a 'wanton murderer'! And then, a very ethereal idea infiltrated the girl's erratic train of thought. Either Lisa had captured on film the purported murderer when the killer had returned to the scene of the female murdered in the forest, or Lisa was the sole owner of a supernatural camera, the existence of which had been described on the *Sci-fi Channel* as somehow being able to freeze and seize 'residue', much the same as photos' of ghosts are believed to be spiritual 'residue' hanging around a scene of violent death. If that were the case, could the nebulous image that Lisa's *Nikon* camera had accidentally captured in the mountain bushes be the murder victim's 'residue' lingering in the forest, and not the 'residue' of the heinous 'killer' taken in real time?

'That creep has to be the killer,' Lisa subjectively reckoned. 'The victim is dead and could not have attended the *Boston Photography Exposition,* but the vicious killer most certainly could have!' she irrationally theorized. 'This is more like a horror movie than a *sci-fi* documentary,' the thoroughly upset girl concluded.

During the next few months, Lisa Major took hundreds of random photographs at many different events, just to get her mind off of 'the on-the-loose murder suspect', and also, off of the problematic algebra failure theme. Her latest efforts involved street scenes depicting pedestrians ambling around, partisan fans cheering at a high school football game, and still other photos' having area skiers zooming-down a steep slalom course. A singular snapshot froze the beauty of a majestic Massachusetts waterfall, and still another portrayed the serenity of a nearby placid lake. Indeed, Lisa Major had amassed a totally beautiful and enviable picture collection. But all along, her principal objective was to forget about the 'residue' of the 'killer' and secondly, to put on the back burner the humiliating shame that was associated with failing Ninth Grade algebra.

One rainy Saturday morning, Lisa was in the mood to again examine 'The Compelling Pictures' compiled in her vast collection. It had taken the ninth grader a whole month to garner the essential courage to resume her personal research into the violent criminal activity that had transpired in the Vermont Mountains.

The high school freshman expeditiously proceeded sorting through her extensive picture inventory, but Lisa's main purpose was now more akin to a detective's pursuit than to a photographer's personal methodology. The selfsame strange alien feeling again swiftly invaded the girl's consciousness. Using her father's trusty magnifying glass, Lisa carefully studied the various candid pictures much closer, industriously searching for additional evidence of 'the repulsive stalking phantom'.

Were the girl's three photos', one of which had luckily caught the 'hideous molester's' attendance at the "Boston Exposition" enough collaborative proof to warrant police notification? Were her two Vermont forest photos' hidden and locked in her personal diary sufficient corroboratory evidence? Should Lisa Major finally show her unaware parents the basis for her very real fear, and should she alleviate her guilt and voluntarily share her outlandish hypothesis?

The young photographer now suffered the mental agony that perpetually suggested to her aggrieved psyche that she was undoubtedly being stalked for the purpose of being murdered. As the days and weeks passed and the prospect of summer school became more real, the freshman was becoming increasingly despondent regarding her regular, formerly satisfying, picture-taking activity. During *that* troubling time frame, Lisa Major was always suspecting that the wretched 'felon' was prowling in her immediate vicinity, and that the aggressive stalker was scheming to cause her evil, physical harm. But why, and what was his selfish motive? There had to be a plausible explanation to validly justify her trepidation.

Whenever Lisa held her new *Canon* camera, the girl would always pivot around quickly as if she was ready to shoot a pistol. Her sixth sense suspected that she had been specifically targeted as the killer's next female victim. Miss Major could only sense his cold, alien surveillance from a distance, with his devious eyes attempting to spy on and relish her every move. And the truth of *his* undeniable existence persisted in the reality of her possessing three very distinct 'indicting photographs'. Or was the daughter's fertile imagination tailoring a wild, bewildering detective-story; a supreme fantasy designed to weirdly validate her intense, accumulated, very real emotional fear?

Lisa's harrowed mind reviewed that she had never told her parents about 'the terrifying stalker pictures' because she didn't want to unnecessarily stress their minds. But now, the girl's emotional adversity was drastically affecting her own general sanity. The algebra apostate was afraid that if she divulged her outlandish theory about the Vermont Mountain murderer to her caring parents, then she might have to enter a state sanitarium for psychological rehabilitation for possibly manufacturing a colossal, false hoax.

One thing was for certain: the suspected murderer had been photographed by two different cameras; Lisa's old *Nikon* had been used in the *Green Mountains* shooting, and her new *Canon* had been expertly deployed at the "Boston Exposition Contest".

"The answer couldn't be in the type of camera," the jittery girl's brain suggested to herself before bed, as she was staring into the bathroom mirror situated above her all-too-revealing *vanity*. "Both cameras have accurately captured the deplorable rogue on film! That's an indisputable fact!"

The entire murder scenario was truly grossly uncanny, and Lisa Major felt that her remarkable camera encounters were analogous to psychic phenomena that coincidentally explore the unknown parameters of the paranormal universe. Moreover, 'the stalker/killer photographs' had basically alienated the very befuddled daughter from her devoted parents' unrequited love and pity.

'This is too shocking and too big to keep a secret any longer," the mentally disheveled daughter lectured to her image in the mirror. "I must tell my parents. I can't function properly at home or in school until my mind's pain is finally shared with Dad and Mom," the distraught daughter lowly uttered in almost a trance-like state.

* * * * * * * * * * * *

The following Friday evening, after the Majors had been out dining at an Italian restaurant, the family returned to their residence and immediately discovered that their dwelling had been broken into. The laundry room door had been smashed-open, and a clever burglar had surreptitiously made his escape before the local Springfield patrolmen had quickly responded to the home's silent alarm being received at the local police station.

A search of the premises revealed that a forced entry had also been made into the Majors' locked photo-printing room. Glossy snapshots were in total disarray upon the counter, and still others had been scattered about by an undesired intruder, with the items found randomly littered all over the black and white checkered tile floor.

Lisa showed the investigating officers the closet where she had kept her personal collection of proofs and instantly, the girl noticed something highly irregular; the container holding the pictures from the Vermont *Green Mountain* shoot had been pilfered. What was in those assorted pictures that might have been so valuable to a malicious trespasser? What was so valuable to a wanton murderer?

The concerned investigating officer then interrogated the Majors about the family's "Vermont shoot", and Jack immediately objected to their "elementary school questioning tactics." "You're treating us as if *we're* the criminals with all of your ridiculous, superficial demands! We're the innocent ones, Officer!"

"Sorry, Mr. Major," replied and apologized the second patrolman. "We're only gathering basic information and doing our jobs."

"Officer, we're all a little edgy right now," admitted Mrs. Major. "Having a complete stranger breaking into and entering our house when we were away at a restaurant is a rather terrifying experience. What would've happened if we had been at home?"

Regaining his composure, Jack informed the two investigating officers that he still possessed the negatives to the stolen Vermont photos on file and that he could print another set of the exact pictures. The police officers acceded to the idea and related to Mr. Major that the cops would return again when the new prints would be available to analyze.

"We'll try our best to catch your thief, Mr. Major," Sergeant Matthews promised. "Crime in the suburbs is on the rise. You would not believe how many felonious sickos are on drugs and have to steal from honest people in order to support their lousy addictions."

"I want to be part of the solution and not part of the problem," answered the very rattled homeowner in a more positive tone of voice. "I didn't mean to snap at you so disrespectfully!"

That night Jack diligently worked several hours in the Dark Room laboratory, and after much nerve-frayed waiting, Major finally finished developing all the duplicate Vermont prints. Meanwhile, Lisa's fragile mind had been incarcerated in a perpetual state of mild disorientation. She feared that the culprit who had broken into their beautifully furnished home was not a common thief who was trying to bankroll his nasty drug habit. Miss Major was terrorized in believing that 'the house burglar' was the same 'stalker' who had killed the first female hiker in the formerly tranquil *Green Mountains*. But if she were to tell her father about 'the Suspicious Set of Pictures', Lisa knew that her father would insist that they not take any more photographs at the fantastic Vermont setting, a location that the teenager truly loved so much. Lisa Major deeply dreaded that she might also be recommended for psychological counseling for fabricating a false witness testimony, and the jittery teenager certainly didn't want *that* negative repercussion to ever happen.

* * * * * * * * * * * *

Jack had made two copies of his stolen prints from the non-pilfered negatives and had locked one set in a utility room storage bin. The police arrived to pick-up the second produced set, and Major planned to transfer the extra set into slides to be later viewed on the large film laboratory screen. The private examination of the Vermont photos would reveal to Jack if the Springfield Police would be able to detect any relevant evidence gleaned from its received copies. Until then, the frustrated real estate mogul was instructed by the keepers of the peace to "keep all your doors and windows locked, and also have your silent alarm working."

"I feel like I'm a prisoner in my own house," Jack balked to Margie. "The trouble with America is that criminals have the same rights as decent, law-abiding citizens."

"The old 'Wild, Wild West' was a lot safer than this society is today," agreed the departing investigating police sergeant. "Let's see what the Vermont pictures might reveal."

Jack Major was so upset that the following day the wealthy capitalist had a more elaborate silent alarm system installed throughout his expansive mansion, and the homeowner immediately had the mechanism connected to the Springfield Police Department. The husband and wife now felt a degree safer, but in her heart, Lisa knew that no security system was an adequate deterrent to a depraved 'killer' persistently stalking her while on the prowl.

The opportunistic real estate developer was rather preoccupied between honoring his very busy office agenda and getting the new alarm system fully installed, and Jack regretted that he hadn't had the time to look in detail at the facsimile slides of his own 'stolen prints'. Mr. Major felt that 'the Burglar' had simply been 'a burglar' and that the new slide copies wouldn't reveal anything of noteworthy significance. Only Lisa was aware of the more sinister implications pertaining to the suspected 'murderer's encroachment. The confused daughter was tempted to study the new set of photos', but a latent fear about learning the perilous truth surfaced in her consciousness and completely negated her initial motivation.

During the next late Indian summer weeks, nothing unusual had occurred, and all of the routine family activities, including the traditional *Thanksgiving* dinner, were conducted in their normal fashion. The city police checked with the Majors from time to time and reported that the department's detectives were still intensively reviewing "the duplicate forest pictures". The Springfield sergeant would contact them if anything "connected" had been detected, but soon the pursuit of those particular material communications ceased.

"Have you any leads yet?" Jack Major inquired in his final call of frustration. "I'm a loyal city taxpayer and I demand results."

"No, Sir," diplomatically answered the suave police sergeant. "We're having so many house robberies lately that our computer system can't keep-up with the rash of larcenies."

"Sounds like my problem is only a small part of the general epidemic," attested Jack. "I think it's only the tip of the iceberg! But honestly, I don't want to be the next Titanic! You guys oughta' watch some old episodes of *Dragnet* on cable TV. You fellas might learn something meritorious from Sergeant Joe Friday!"

Lisa had not forgotten about the 'on-the-loose Vermont killer', for she felt very strongly that the missing young 'socialite hiker' had been viciously murdered by the unscrupulous 'prowler', who was now 'the rabid stalker', *her stalker*. The dejected daughter did not have the requisite daring or the needed resolve to closely analyze her father's additional proofs in the Dark Room, but the Major girl still had the original (and possible convicting) *Green Mountain* forest photos hidden and locked inside her personal diary.

On an early December Friday night, the teen's parents were going to the local supermarket to purchase much-needed groceries. Their absence from the home afforded Lisa the opportunity to again study in private 'the Pictures' that had been deliberately concealed inside her locked secret journal.

'I'll die of fright before the killer ever has a chance to murder me,' the frazzled girl defensively thought. 'Why couldn't this miserable trouble be happening to someone else? Yes, it should be happening to someone much tougher and braver than me?'

It was a cold, inhospitable Thursday night, a full week after *Thanksgiving*. Rain, thunder, and wild lightning dominated the foreboding, black New Moon sky. While opening the lock on her diary, Lisa's bedroom phone rang. Very restively, the girl gingerly lifted the receiver.

"Honey, it's Daddy," Jack announced. "Our *Infiniti* just got a stupid flat tire right after we left the supermarket parking lot," the father disgustedly disclosed. "We'll be delayed for a full half-hour or so until

Triple A arrives to fix the flat," complained Jack from his cell phone. "Stay safe until we arrive home."

"Don't worry, Daddy," Lisa bravely replied. "I'll keep all the doors locked until you and Mom can get back."

When the distressed daughter was finally ready to again view the mysterious 'prowler/stalker/killer's face half-shown in the Vermont foliage scene pictures, the phone again rang. It was the Springfield Police Department on the line. Lisa was informed that an Inspector who had been assigned to the recent series of house burglaries had just discovered some important evidence. Officers would be promptly dispatched to the Majors' house to further discuss the significant new revelations.

"Thank you, Sir. I'll be waiting for you," answered the relieved girl. "My parents will be home from shopping in about an hour."

Lisa put-down her bedroom phone into its cradle that was situated on the lamp table next to her bed, and then the young lady proceeded to thoroughly check the scary face partially hidden in the bushes of the all-too-familiar Vermont forest scenes. Then, her keen gaze specifically focused on the man's blue sapphire ring. Lisa peered more intently at the expensive piece of jewelry with the small magnifying glass, which she always conveniently kept inside her bedroom's desk drawer.

Suddenly, the front doorbell rang, but it seemed too soon for the police to have arrived. Lisa's fingers momentarily fumbled with the terrible photos', but then the daughter found the wherewithal to deposit the items back into her diary. The alarmed girl dashed briskly toward the home's front door and then slowly opened it. The algebra student courteously greeted the policeman, who had been impatiently waiting in the pouring rain. Lisa felt secure in the knowledge that an officer was on the property to protect her.

"Officer, where is the Inspector who has been assigned to the robbery case?" the daughter instinctively asked.

"Oh, he'll be along a little bit later," the policeman returned. "We're so busy at the station that we can't tell the weekdays from the weekends."

"Well, have you discovered who the local burglar is?" the girl anxiously inquired. "Is his face in your records?"

"As a matter of fact, I can't reveal *that* particular information," the elusive officer coyly stated. "The detectives know a lot more than us lowly patrolmen do."

Feeling secure, Lisa politely asked the policeman if he wished to assist her in scanning the photo-slide collection. For her own peace of mind, the teenager felt that the patrolman possibly could identify the clues from her pictures that the detectives had already located in their set of proofs that had been produced from the same negatives.

Lisa escorted the policeman down the hall directly to the printing room. In short time, the amateur photographer shrewdly projected the slides of her father's original photos onto the large screen in the laboratory so that her sharp eyes could safely observe the sequence of forest scenes with the visiting officer. Together the pair studied the telltale photos.

One after another the appropriate slides flashed upon the monitor. The daughter immediately recognized that the visiting Springfield patrolman had more than a casual interest in the Vermont *Green Mountain* forest pictorials.

The fierce storm outside was now raging to tempest proportions with violent lightning and thunder accentuating *Mother Nature's* belligerent mood. The procession of slides kept beaming onto the Dark Room screen, alternating intermittently with the lightning flashes coming from outside.

Suddenly, when the last slides of her father's *Green Mountain* photos had been reached, emanating from the trusty carousel projector, Lisa's knees instantaneously became weak. The general feebleness soon affected her entire anatomy. Miss Majors hands started trembling and her lips began quivering. One of her father's original pictures had captured a man and a woman fighting behind a camouflage of yellow and reddish leaves.

The next photo' clearly revealed the 'villainous male', who had brown hair and was wearing a leather jacket. A knife was firmly gripped in the attacker's right hand. The rotating screen pictures were in the exact sequence of the events that had actually occurred, almost as if the photos had been an uncanny newsreel of pertinent freeze frames.

A more revealing slide further portrayed the savage aggressor holding a long knife, and another one had the assaulter lunging at the defenseless young woman. That brutal attack was succeeded by a scene of a frantic struggle as illustrated in a subsequent, formerly discarded slide, which showed the knife luridly penetrating the victim's throat.

"This is positively horrifying!" Lisa ranted as her heart began palpitating. "What do you think, Officer?"

"The perpetuator probably thought that he had committed the perfect crime," concluded and articulated the all-too-passive uniformed Springfield patrolman. "That's precisely how emboldened psychopaths tend to operate!"

More convicting photos from Lisa's all-too-busy father's portfolio showed the 'ugly culprit' wielding the scarlet-hued knife peering in the direction of Jack's lens. Another snapshot caught the 'vile butcher' holding binoculars to his eyes, surveying the immediate homicide scene. Although Lisa was exceedingly terrified by the brutal documentation, her mind was mildly comforted being under the aegis of police authority.

The flustered girl then turned her head in the direction of the visiting defender of justice. Her eyes caught a glimpse of something peculiar just as a bolt of lightning crackled, causing an instant power failure. In the frightening darkness, the teen realized exactly what her eyes had seen. The cop was wearing the very familiar ring with the very expensive lustrous sapphire upon his fourth left ring finger.

"Ahhhhh!" the daughter screamed as she bolted-out of the dark printing laboratory. Lisa Major frantically felt her way down the wall of the lengthy pitch-black corridor, stumbling all the way to her bedroom, where she quicky entered and locked the door.

Fumbling in the black obscurity of the hallway (for the electrical power had gone out when the two had exited the Dark Room), the criminal (disguised as a policeman) could not exactly see where his targeted victim had gone. The cold-blooded killer wandered and searched around the unfamiliar black maze, and after a while, petrified Lisa couldn't hear any near or distant sounds originating outside her room's door. Everything in the mansion was as silent as the moon, except for the loud pounding rhythm of her frightened heart. The teenager's cerebrum was in an extreme panic; being only one step from delirium. The utterly still darkness only added a new level of awe and fright to the stunned girl's already great dread.

The policeman-disguised killer clumsily staggered down the long black corridor into the main sector of the enormous suburban residence. The desperate trespasser groped wildly, searching like a fanatical maniac in his foreign, rather confusing environment. But the crazed felon was totally hindered by the absence of light. The psycho's general ignorance of his uncertain surroundings, along with the time delay it caused, represented Lisa's only hope for survival.

The Major girl dared not stir a muscle. She could only shiver and quake as her left ear pressed against the locked door. Lisa prayed that the electric power would remain incapacitated, since she then theorized that a prolonged power-failure was her most reasonable chance for living through her present crisis.

The emotionally paralyzed intended victim stayed as quiet as a corpse, being alone inside what to her seemed an empty mortuary. After a short while, she falsely wondered what had happened to 'the investigating Inspector and the trustworthy Sergeant'. Soon, the neurotic young lady's ears discerned a loud thud, as the frustrated policeman/murderer tripped-over the living room ottoman during his frenetic blind search.

"Oh God! Please save me from this crazy psychopath!" Lisa gasped and prayed in the dark. "Please someone, save me!"

A minute later, the delirious girl slowly opened the curtains to look outside her bedroom window, hoping for a sign of the real police, or of her unwary parents' expected return. Coinciding with her window search, there was another terrible crack of lightning, which momentarily illuminated the dismal, cloudy night sky. Standing on the other side of the bedroom window during the sudden flash was the unscrupulous *policeman*. For a brief second, his evil, demonic eyes made contact with Lisa's.

The hysterical girl was absolutely horrified with her heart again having severe palpitations. She swiftly moved from the window back to her bedroom door, and without hesitating, the affected girl clumsily unlocked it, just as the ruthless felon impersonating a policeman crashed his body through the aforementioned bedroom window. The traumatized teen hustled madly down the dark hall heading toward the living room, where she also clumsily tripped and fell over the ottoman, and then the intended victim rushed towards the home's foyer.

Lisa heard the stalker's grunting and snorting, his legs approaching close behind her, as the determined pursuer was awkwardly maneuvering his irregular path in the total darkness. The frenzied girl managed to unlock and open the front door, just as the attacker grabbed her by the nape of the neck. An intense physical struggle ensued, and the assaulted victim was harshly thrown upon the tile floor. The enraged assailant ferociously gripped Lisa's throat and began relentlessly strangling his overpowered prey. The ongoing savage attack was both cruel and animalistic. The teen was on the verge of blacking-out and on the brink of succumbing and involuntarily entering the *Valley of Death*. The teen twisted her neck and coughed-out one last futile, ear-shattering shout.

Suddenly, a gunshot echoed off the walls of the dark foyer, and the crazed madman's body spontaneously slumped-down on top of Lisa. The semiconscious girl instantly sensed that the limp figure on top of her had been immobilized by the loud gun blast.

The Springfield Police Inspector stood in the front doorway, holding a pistol in his right hand along with a flashlight in his left, as pelting rain and wind swirled behind and around him. The detective had arrived on the scene with not a precious second to spare. His first task was to gingerly roll the unconscious strangler off of a still-dazed Lisa Major, and deposit the body onto the now-bloodstained adjacent white carpet. The Major girl could then be comforted from the awful shock of experiencing and surviving her incredible ordeal.

Five minutes later, Jack and Margie finally returned home from their misadventure in their dark blue *Infiniti* sedan. Just as the parents pulled into their tan brick driveway, the electric company had repaired the crackling transformer that had been hit by a bolt of lightning down the street, and residential customers again had power in their homes.

"My heavens Lisa, are you' all right?" cried-out the mother. "What on Earth has happened here?"

"Oh Mom, I came within a half-inch of dying," the girl frantically screamed. "It was the most horrible thing I've ever felt!"

"I'm so sorry we left you home all alone," Jack apologized while consoling his beloved daughter by caressing her tresses as Lisa continued to incessantly weep. "*The Triple A* mechanic told me that the right rear tire on my car had been slashed with a switchblade knife. I suspect that the dreg lying here on the floor had stalked us to the supermarket and had punctured a hole in the tire before coming back here to perform his insane wickedness!"

The pictures that the police had taken to the precinct station were identical to the slides that Lisa had astutely viewed inside the Dark Room laboratory. When matters finally calmed-down to normal, Jack had an appropriate question for the hero Police Inspector.

"How did you know that you were not shooting one of your own men?" Jack asked as the rich developer pointed to the disguised killer lying mortally wounded on the foyer floor.

The Inspector had to think for a second before responding to the curious citizen's intelligent interrogative. "Mr. Major, I believe that I had acted out of sheer instinct. I knew from my years of training that a uniformed officer would not be assaulting a helpless teenage girl from a good family on the home's living room floor," the sagacious Inspector concluded and confidentially related. The Springfield Chief Detective then admitted that the local police had just about abandoned all hope in their lengthy crusade to apprehend "the diabolical burglar", but now the case had been cracked-open and solved, thanks to Lisa Major's stubborn will to survive.

An ambulance soon arrived at the opulent residence, and paramedics lifted the immobile criminal onto a stretcher and then transported the critically wounded, almost-dead villain to a nearby hospital, before his presumed excursion to the facility's morgue.

Three days before *Christmas,* the courageous young woman survivor was awarded a *Certificate of Honor* by the Springfield Police Department for "Bravery, Integrity and being a Vigilant Citizen," and the special plaque would be a constant reminder of that frightful night's incredible adventure.

"You want to know something, Lisa," Jack indicated three weeks after the intruder/killer had been shot thrice in the back. "I feel ashamed of myself. I should've more perceptively studied those *Green Mountain* photos' I had taken from a distance with my telephoto lens. Your mental anguish during *that* terrible night might've been avoided if I could've spent more time doing my avocation in the Dark Room lab', rather than being distracted by my lucrative business enterprises."

"But why didn't you do that?" inquired the daughter. "Were you that wrapped-up in your business?"

"Because, Dear'," answered and interrupted Margie Major. "Your father was so worried about you not passing your algebra course that he wanted you to beat him in the *Boston Photography Exposition* in order to boost your overall sagging confidence. My husband figured that a contest win for you would bolster your faltering self-esteem. That's precisely why your father never really seriously analyzed his own original *Green Mountain* photos'."

* * * * * * * * * * * *

Epilogue

The stalker/would-be strangler miraculously recovered from the three pistol wounds and reluctantly confessed to the authorities that he had been the perpetrator who had murdered the daughter of the prominent socialite/politician, hiking and exercising in the Vermont woods. The mendacious villain re-created for the investigators the entire sequence of events leading-up to the barbaric forest killing. The victim had been the offspring of a very influential *Congressman* who had owed the "strangler" a substantial amount of money from past illicit drug dealings.

The stalker then surreptitiously lured the young victim to the *Green Mountain* murder site by promising her a reward of several bags of pure crack cocaine. The drug dealer and his addicted customer had parked their vehicles several-hundred-yards up the trail from where Jack Major had left his red *Ford Explorer*. Then, the killer and the victim trekked into the Vermont mountain forest to negotiate the terms of the transaction; a drug deal that went sour.

"Once in the woods, when the politician's kid did not give me the money her pop owed me from his last drug deal bonanza, we had a struggle. Then, I stabbed the lousy meth' and cocaine distributor's daughter," the heartless killer confessed, showing very little remorse.

"Why did you try to strangle young Lisa Major?" asked the Inspector. "It doesn't seem to make much sense."

"I would've gotten away with the perfect crime except for the many photos' the Majors had taken on their Vermont outing," the pernicious killer recounted. "I knew that if the pictures were discovered and looked at by the police crime lab', the cops would've had little trouble identifying me and swiftly solving the murder mystery. I do have a prior criminal record, and I wanted to keep all of you off my trail," the heartless criminal confessed. "I believe that my mugshot is already contained in your police computer records!"

"Premonitions"

The incredible experiences I am about to relate really did happen. The strange events being recollected can be attested to and authenticated by impartial individuals. I had told my wife Mary of several of my "peculiar dream premonitions," which oddly later "coincidentally" materialized as reality.

Many people are skeptical of this profound type of extrasensory perception that I'm identifying. I will not attempt to convince those cynics of the falsity of their *Diogenes*-style mind-sets. However, the pessimists and the sophists should keep an open mind to the possibility that clairvoyance may actually be an unexplored paradigm of the human cerebrum. Some things out there simply seem to transcend reason, defying both logic and science.

For those fortunate people who believe that the human mind is both a cosmic transmitter and receiver, the soon-to-be-mentioned "Premonition" manifestations should only reinforce their convictions about the validity of such exceptional-but-true phenomena. It is not my intent to generalize, to moralize, to editorialize, or to pontificate on the controversial subject. I'll leave *those* unpleasant chores to the plethora of pundits who daily practice newspaper journalism, or to random sensationalist *Hollywood* producers who organize science-fiction television documentaries.

My personal psychic experiences occur mostly in dreams, and many of my visits to *Morpheus* are usually quite lucid. My "Premonitions" are not the nondescript kind of psychic experiences that are soon forgotten after I awake. My three-dimensional color dreams literally leave me lying in a pool of perspiration, as if I had been realistically witnessing a forthcoming in-progress catastrophe.

* * * * * * * * * * * *

In mid-October, 1943, while serving in the *U.S. Air Force*, I had been stationed at Ellington Field, Houston, Texas, taking *Pre-Flight Training* courses before advancing to *Gunnery and Bombardier School*. While in Houston, I had envisioned several shocking future occurrences, which in the evolution of events ultimately spared my life. But honestly, I had no control over the paranormal sequence of inexplicable incidents.

One night, while I was sleeping in my barrack bed, I had a bizarre nightmare, one which was so real that I woke-up trembling. I had dreamed that my father had suddenly died. 'It was only a dream,' I kept thinking to myself as I expressed my determination to return to sleep.

An alien sensation made my disheveled mind interpret that the dreadful nightmare was going to wickedly transform into a terrible, heart-wrenching reality. The mental apprehension was haunting me for the remainder of my restive attempt at slumbering.

My father had never been sick for a day in his life. He had always been remarkably strong and healthy. There was never a hint that something might be drastically wrong with his health.

Saturday, October 30, 1943 was a day I will never forget. I rose that morning from my bunk with my soul trapped in a state of depression. It was the start of a weekend; a time when the trainees would excitedly travel into Houston to explore social adventures and seek the company of amorous, loose women. I did not have the right mental attitude to pursue the hedonistic pleasures that my ecstatic buddies were enthusiastically seeking. I kept thinking of the frightful, morbid prospect of my father's death that had the night before awakened me in a cold sweat.

That day after lunch, I finally did accompany some military friends into "town". I was invited to a college football game, but I had turned-down the request because I had felt uneasy and on edge. My restless mind really desired solitude from civilization more than anything else.

In the evening, the *USO* had sponsored a dance, and my friends and I attended the social event. It wasn't long before I realized that I did not feel like being as convivial as I normally would be. That evening, I had no evident tolerance for socializing or for dancing. My mental state was in a very melancholy mood, which was contrary to my normal humorous, fun-loving demeanor. I decided to leave my friends' company and the merriment of voluptuous Texas women, long before curfew time to return to my base.

I rode the army bus back to my barracks, my mind still in a quandary. As I approached the steps to enter the familiar building, two servicemen from my squadron were waiting for my arrival. The "Officer of the Day" indicated that he wished to consult with me. I couldn't imagine what he had wanted, but a nervous chill came over me as I hesitated before entering his office. The *OD* and two aides were sitting behind his desk.

I told the commander my identity, and the *OD* instantly replied that I should apply for an emergency furlough. I was startled and asked him for an explanation. The official informed me that someone in my immediate family was very ill, but didn't tell me whom. I was instructed to call Mrs. Blumberg (a friend of the family) in the morning to learn additional details.

I walked back to my barracks in a disconsolate and bewildered frame of mind. Naturally, I instinctively packed for my anticipated trip to Philadelphia the following day. Next, I climbed into bed and was awake all night, contemplating what "regrettable news" was in store. My negative thinking was expecting the worst; that is, the actualization of my ghastly premonition was soon to materialize.

The next morning, I phoned Mrs. Blumberg, whom I had been instructed to contact. The woman tersely advised me to "come home right away". When I asked the family acquaintance what had happened, she did not have the heart to tell me, urging that I should return to Philadelphia as quickly as possible. In my heart I knew that the bad news involved my father, but I wouldn't be able to confirm my suspicion until I would arrive in Philly'.

I was fortunate to catch a flight out of Houston on a small *Navy* plane to Pensacola, Florida. Then, I was again lucky to make a connection with a second military plane bound for Washington, DC. From there, I hastily boarded a train from Union Station to the *Quaker City,* where I was then met by members of my family. One quick look at my grieving mother revealed the essence of the whole personal tragedy.

My uncle escorted me inside a nearby restaurant and ordered me a "double" of potent rye whiskey. With tears in his eyes, my dad's brother proceeded to convey that my father had passed away suddenly on Saturday, October 30; the same day I had been enveloped with emotional depression. A weird coincidence, you might argue. Believe me, it is more than a mere coincidence when it happens to you.

That sad moment will always persistently haunt my psyche, not only because of my father's unexpected death, but also because of a series of extraordinary events that soon transpired afterwards. The unbelievable incidents would later alter the course of my life.

My commander in Houston had granted me a one-week furlough. I then asked my senior officer for a seven-day extension, and it was benevolently granted, so I have been extremely thankful ever since. If the additional seven days had been denied, then I would not be alive to record and report the following occurrences.

During the second week of my furlough, I had taken sick while in Atlantic City, New Jersey and was swiftly transported to the *England General Hospital*, which was an *Army* facility for *WWII* servicemen. I had a temperature of 104, and the doctors told me that I would have to be admitted and that I would have to stay as a reluctant patient until my in-jeopardy health had adequately recovered from my illness. "Len, you'll have to remain in our care until I decide to release you," the head physician maintained.

Right before I had been scheduled to be released to reunite with my squadron (which was still training in Houston), I accidentally broke a metacarpal in my left hand while lifting my little cousin into the air on the Atlantic City Boardwalk. It was a freak accident that I had trouble explaining to the authorities when I returned to the *England General Hospital.*

My new injury caused me to remain in the hospital until my splintered bone would be totally healed. During that unforeseen three-month delay in my training program, the remaining twenty-nine members of my squadron were being transported from Ellington Field in Houston to gunnery training in Kingman, Arizona. Regrettably, my eyes were never to see them again. Ever since that unexpected extended hospital time, I have had the strong impression that a guardian angel had been protecting and shielding me (for some inexplicable reason other than luck) from impending danger.

On the cold winter night of January 6, 1944, the twenty-nine members of my squadron were being driven in a military transport bus from the Kingman Airport to their barracks, after a hard day of intensive target practice. Two men from our squadron were missing on that bus. One was a lucky Cadet Lieutenant, who was riding in a jeep behind the doomed vehicle. The other fortunate individual was a fellow named Len Streitfeld, who was still recovering from his bone injury back in Atlantic City, New Jersey.

As the military bus approached a railroad crossing, it slowed down and stopped for a *Santa Fe* railroad train that was rapidly approaching the tracks' crossing at great speed.

When the freight train was about to pass through the intersection, the bus lurched forward in front of the speeding locomotive. There was a tremendously loud crash that soon resulted in a dense cloud of smoke. Screaming and crying filtered out of the bus's twisted metallic framework. In a short time, the pathetic cries transformed into pathetic moans, which soon converted into eerie silence. All twenty-eight of my squadron buddies seated inside the bus had been killed, along with the bus driver. The Cadet Lieutenant, who was riding behind in the jeep had been spared, but he had witnessed the entire tragedy unfold, and had to endure, and mentally rehash, the ultimate futility in seeing his best friends perish.

The Cadet Lieutenant verbally re-constructed the disaster to me several months later when we met again in England. He was shocked and astounded to see me, since he had assumed that I had been a fated passenger riding on the bus, and that I had been slaughtered in the impact, along with my fellow cadets. While recuperating from my finger injury in Atlantic City, I had experienced in my sleep a very surreal premonition that a major disaster was about to occur.

Four separate events had interceded to prevent me from dying in that lethal bus/train collision, along with the remainder of my squadron. Being a mere mortal, I had no control over any of those particular circumstances. My father had died in Philadelphia. I had been granted a one-week extension of my furlough. I had sustained a finger injury in Atlantic City while on the extended furlough. On doctor's orders, I had to stay in New Jersey away from my fellow trainees for an additional three months.

If all of the four unrelated events had not happened in that hard-to-fathom sequence, I would most certainly have been on the macabre military bus sitting with my doomed buddies. I would be as dead as Lincoln is right now. Someone *was* watching over me. Sometimes, I think I am a reincarnated *Old Testament* prophet. I see devastation coming, but my conscientious "Guardian Angel" always shelters me from the jaws of calamity.

* * * * * * * * * * * *

Before and after *WWII,* I have had numerous extra-sensory premonitions that have inexplicably come true. Several events in particular are outstanding and still vivid in my mind, and the incidents are indeed very unforgettable, gruesome recollections.

It was in late October 1958 when I experienced a frightening nightmare. I again awoke in a cold sweat because the dream was so intense and overwhelming that it had adversely affected my subconscious. I actually woke-up believing that I had been a helpless witness to a tragic accident.

I told my devoted wife of my strange phantasm at 3:00 in the morning, just to verbally document it. I dreamed that a young girl was about to be involved in a terrible car/trolley tragedy in Philadelphia, and although I (as an eyewitness in my sleep) had endeavored to stop her from imminent danger, my vain shouting appeared to be silent and ineffective, and the young lady never responded to my futile screams.

In my dream, I had rushed over to the accident scene and was horrified at the great carnage I observed. The girl, who I had been warning from a distance, had been beheaded. I could see that she had blonde hair, but her young face lying on the roadside still displayed opened eyes that seemed to penetrate right through my entire anatomy. In my premonition, I had been told by a distant anonymous voice that the girl would be Jewish and that she lived in the Wynnewood section of Philadelphia, not far from where I had resided in my youth.

In the morning, I reiterated to my wife the horrendous tragedy, and I gave Mary an exact description of the unfortunate girl. The remembrance of the premonition dwelled deep inside my psyche, and the 'dream event' cruelly attacked my spirit, so naturally, I couldn't remove the thought from my consciousness.

Before breakfast, I stepped outside to my front lawn to get the morning newspaper. I sat-down at the breakfast table, began sipping my usual second up of coffee, and I casually scanned the front-page headlines. I now recollect fearing that my "premonition chimera" would be reported as actual sensational news.

My roaming eyes found the reporter's dreaded, grotesque dispatch found near the bottom of the *Philadelphia Inquirer* front page. The scribe's eerie caption read, "Wynnewood Girl Decapitated in Freak Accident". I read the full account of what had transpired, and the graphic rendition went like this: The girl was standing on the curb at Broad and Arch Streets in Philadelphia, along with other pedestrians, who were waiting for the traffic signal to change. The light turned green, and the group started crossing the busy intersection. At the same time, a trolley car was advancing into the intersection from the opposite direction.

When the walkers were almost halfway across the thoroughfare, the crowd immediately recognized the trolley peril, and all except the ill-starred girl scattered. She kept walking ahead and was suddenly struck by a passing automobile, which knocked her under the wheels of the oncoming trolley. Horribly, her head had been severed from her blood-strewn neck.

The graphic newspaper account of how that accident had happened further explained why the young victim failed to get out of the way as had the other more alert pedestrians. The rapidly moving car, a taxi, was traveling on the street and couldn't stop for the red light because of brake failure. The cabdriver blew the horn, and everyone crossing instinctively scampered out of harm's way; all except the luckless, beautiful blonde-haired girl. She was hit and crushed by the speeding taxi, which then hurled her headfirst under the wheels of the approaching trolley. According to the newspaper article, the poor teenager had been *deaf* and couldn't hear the yellow vehicle's honking horn. In my distressful nightmare, I was shouting a fruitless litany of warnings at a deaf teenager.

The girl's picture shown in the *Inquirer* was the facsimile of the young female whom I had dreamt about the night before. According to the graphic newspaper account, the young lady was a Jewish blonde, and she lived in Wynnewood.

For a good number of years, that unsavory premonition, along with the ghastly incident, have been extremely disquieting to my mind's recollection. Its horrendous verification, however, is well-documented in the *Philadelphia Inquirer* local history files.

* * * * * * * * * * * *

Over the last twenty-years, I had experienced many uncanny premonitions that had converted from the mysterious spiritual state into actual material existence. From previous experience, I had expected the premonitions to transform into reality, and I did not demonstrate any arrogance or braggadocio when their real-life enactments had been realized.

In June of 1985, I had a "premonition" that still disturbs and plagues my memory to this very day. This mental uneasiness is because I had perceived that my physical presence had been present right there at the exact time when my subconscious mind had inexplicably manufactured the phenomenon. The dream-premonition went like this:

A girl was driving her car on a road near the bay in Somers Point, New Jersey. The weather was foggy and visibility was poor because of misty conditions. In the incident, the young lady had been lost during the inclement weather and kept driving around, searching for a familiar landmark. Upon coming to a deserted street that she had hypothesized was in the vicinity of her destination, the youthful driver veered directly into that road and progressed onward.

During the intense storm, the girl continued onward for about a block, but the misty, windy, wet haze prevented her from accurately surveying her immediate environment. That regrettable wrong turn was going to signal her last moment of life. In front of her approach was a fishing dock, and then thereafter, the unwelcoming cold bay. In my predictive dream, I vividly envisioned this whole tragic scenario developing, and obviously, my futile shouts were completely ignored by the fated victim.

My body was wildly twisting and turning in bed in a vain attempt to intervene, and somehow miraculously prevent the impending fatality. The disturbing nightmare continued, and suddenly, the dock was ominously looming directly in the car's course. The doomed driver made a frenetic attempt to stop her doomed vehicle; however, her destiny was ill-fated. In seconds, the driver's automobile hurtled over the small pier and then horribly splashed into the frigid bay. The vehicle sank to the bottom quickly, and twenty-five seconds of air bubbles were followed by absolute silence.

I was so startled in my subconscious duress the premonition that I was jarred awake with my body and pajamas soaking wet from perspiration. I sat-up in bed, and when my concerned wife asked me what was wrong, I described in detail *that* same very horrendous nightmare. Neither of us was able to fall asleep after that hellish midnight revelation. Before long, it was daybreak.

I shaved and then progressed to the kitchen to prepare my regular pot of coffee. While it was perking, I stepped out to my front lawn to retrieve the morning *Inquirer,* brought the publication inside and started perusing the front-page articles. I was very much relieved that the Somers Point dock and bay automobile disaster had not been reported in any of the publication's headlines.

My mind kept thinking of the similar Philadelphia trolley car nightmare my sleep had envisioned twenty-five years earlier, which I recalled I had sorrowfully read in the main city newspaper the day after the deaf girl's terrible demise.

The Somers Point automobile disaster dream had taken place on a Tuesday, and there were no media news accounts of any accident of that nature being reported during the next three days.

On Friday, my wife and I drove to eat dinner at the Point Pub, a favorite family restaurant located in Somers Point. As we were waiting for the hostess to escort us to our seats, I noticed the owner of the restaurant (and also a personal acquaintance) rushing towards us through the crowded dining room.

When the proprietor reached Mary and me, Mr. Collins vigorously shook our hands. I asked him how his health had been, and when the restauranteur attempted to answer, I could see that he was quite visibly upset. Just as Frank was about to again speak, a strange dread invaded my being, and suddenly, there appeared to be total silence in the restaurant. It was as if I myself had become deaf. I instinctively knew that the obviously disturbed proprietor was going to relate some woeful news. I stopped Frank and said, "Wait a minute. I'll describe in detail what had occurred."

I related in sequence the tragic news ending with, "The car with a girl in it went off an area dock in a heavy mist, crashing head-on into the bay, and she unfortunately drowned."

The restaurant owner looked bewildered and proceeded to ask me how I could have possibly known about the girl's untimely death, since he had just received a phone call that the accident had recently taken place a mile away from his establishment. The young female victim had been someone Frank had known very well, and that salient fact had made Mr. Collins feel exceptionally disconsolate.

Was it an example of psychic phenomena, or perhaps only a mere coincidence? I'll let the reader make the vital call.

* * * * * * * * * * * *

The following two events are separated by a half century, but both are absolutely true. There is a direct relationship between the incidents, which you shall soon discover.

During *WWII,* I had been a *B-17* Bombardier in the *398th Bomb Group* of the *8th Air Force.* It was the closing weeks of the brutal war in the *European Theater.* Our "Bomb Group" was assigned to obliterate an oil depot in the city of Derben, Germany. In the early morning hours of April 8, 1945, our various squadrons took to the air from our home Base in Nuthampstead, England.

I had been very psychic about many odd incidents that had occurred during the war. That day, I had been having 'bad vibes' and felt that our bombing mission was going to be in for an especially rough enemy encounter. I feared that the *398th* would lose some planes while participating-in and enacting the very dangerous raid.

The *B-17* attack squadrons rendezvoused over the south of England and adroitly aligned themselves in strategic formations for the execution of the challenging combat mission. The bomb-laden planes then turned onto a new heading over the *English Channel,* heading towards France, and then ultimately Germany. It was a beautiful, clear-blue, sunny sky while our planes were flying at our standard altitude of 25,000 feet.

Our squadron was to be the last of the Bomb Groups to savagely blast the designated Nazi target zone. As my plane approached Derben, I could plainly see that the mission-slated oil depot was already covered with thick black smoke, caused by the bombs of the preceding "Strike Groups".

The remaining planes dropped altitude down to 10,000 feet, so that the pilots and bombardiers could obtain better views of their assigned targets. On our second pass around the city, Derben was still covered with dense smoke, and so our squadron commander unwisely chose to make a third run to completely destroy the designated oil depot. Up to that time, our wing squadron had encountered no flak. That reality was about to transform into chaos.

Our bombs were swiftly dropped, and the projectiles descended toward their objectives with deadly accuracy. I was fortunate to have my motion picture camera on board and started taking film from the moment the ordnance had been released to the time when the bombs struck the remaining oil storage tanks. The munitions exploded with multiple red and white flashes, which could be seen (from my position above) as huge intense sparks wildly flitting through the black dense smoke.

When I sat back in my seat after taking the action film, I became aware that the plane immediately in front of ours had vanished from sight. Out of the corner of my eye, I detected a *B-17* that had been hit by heavy flak. It was tumbling-down in a death spiral with one flaming wing breaking-off. Lt. Bill Wells, a close friend, had been copiloting the nose-diving plane.

I watched Lt. Wells' *B-17* unbelievably plunging on its way down, rapidly descending into the thick smoke for a few seconds, which to me at *that* moment actually seemed like several minutes. One crew-member, Robert Templeton, somehow managed to bail out wearing a parachute, and the fortunate fellow was the only survivor. The *B-17* violently slammed into the ground and exploded instantly, killing everyone aboard.

The heavy flak around my *B-17* was horrendous. The loud bursts were so close that the crew could distinctly hear each shell exploding as our plane wildly rattled. All the remaining aircraft in my under-attack squadron were engaged in "evasive action", but such scrambling was hazardous, since there could be accidental mid-air collisions. Our plane was turbulently lurching from side to side, moving up and down, and I was almost thrown-out of my bombardier seat. Pieces of shrapnel hitting the plane could be clearly discerned. I felt and feared that our *B-17* would have a direct shell hit at any moment.

That unforgettable misadventure was the most nerve-shattering encounter I ever had on any of the perilous thirty-one bombing missions in which I had participated. The lead *B-17* had a direct hit on its rudder, which incidentally had killed the tail gunner, blasting him right out of the plane. Miraculously, the bomber's pilot and co-pilot had the wherewithal to make it safely back to its base in England. All of this aerial warfare occurred over fifty-years ago, but it is still indelibly burned into my memory, never to be forgotten.

Fifty-years later, a fantastic "coincidence" happened to me. The ironic event is directly related to the April 8th, 1945 *B-17* bombing mission over Derben.

In 1994, I had just completed writing a book titled *Hell from Heaven.* The autobiography was the product of a biographical diary I had meticulously kept, and the story represented an accurate account of my experiences as a veteran WWII *B-17* bombardier.

I had received the first copy of my new book just before I was on my way to a *398th Bomb Group* reunion in Tucson, Arizona. I was on the airplane heading west with my wife, who was occupying the seat next to the window. I had been seated in the middle, and no passenger was occupying the third seat next to the aisle. This additional space and free time allowed me an excellent opportunity to read *my* finished book for the first time in its final published form.

I had completed about one-third of the autobiography by the time the commercial jet had landed in Houston, where my wife and I had an hour stopover. Getting back onto the plane, everyone assumed his and her same seat, and I started to again enjoy reading my recently published hardcover book.

As several new passengers boarded the huge jet, the newcomers searched the aisle and eventually located their assigned seats. A very attractive woman sat next to me in the formerly unoccupied third seat. The female proceeded to open a novel and started reading, so initially no conversation took place between us.

Thirty-minutes later, the young woman leaned over and looked at my *398th Bomb Group* cap, which I was then wearing. The attractive lady suddenly exclaimed, "Oh Sir, I see we're both going to the same reunion!"

I stopped reading *my* book, putting my finger in the page that I had been scrutinizing. I felt obligated to answer her observation.

"That's quite a coincidence!" I politely remarked "Are you here with your husband?"

"No," she replied with a distinct blush showing on her cheeks.

"Then, you must be here with your father?" I awkwardly guessed.

"No, he was killed in World War II," the woman replied.

"I'm sorry to hear that," I sadly commented. "What was his name?"

"Bill Wells!" she replied in a melancholy voice.

I could have fallen out of my seat. I opened *my* book to the page I had been reading and showed the radiant woman the descriptive printed language. There was also a related photograph displayed on the page. I then asked the affable brunette, "Do you know this man?"

She stared amazingly at the picture and emphatically exclaimed, "Oh My God, that's my father!"

The singular chance of *that* rather particular "coincidence" happening in the ordinary course of events is incalculable. But quite apparently, the inevitable revelation was meant to be.

"The Combat Mission That Never Was"

On January 6, 1945, at the *American Air Base* at Bassingbourn, England, Commanding Officer Colonel Frank Walters was pacing back and forth inside the flight tower. The base commander was anxiously watching the overcast sky, waiting for the first sign of the *B-17* squadron returning from their very dangerous bombing mission over Cologne, Germany.

One by one, the planes of the battle-scarred *Bomber Group* broke through the low layer of dark clouds. The drone of distant engines was like sweet music to Colonel Frank Walters' receptive ears. No planes had been lost, German flak had been light, and no life-threatening injuries had yet been reported.

"Remarkable, Colonel," began Captain Evans. "A perfect mission has been accomplished. This is one for the record books!"

"God must be on our side," the elated base commander answered. "He most definitely must be, along with His angels!"

A Bombardier, Lt. Leonard Green, had experienced an agonizing mission during the Cologne raid. His *B-17* had been climbing towards the rendezvous location of the *Bomber Group,* and the plane had been ascending to the "designated drop altitude". Green could not clear his ears, and excruciating pressure was building inside his head. The afflicted *B-17* warrior had suffered for a full half-hour until his Eustachian tubes finally popped. After so-much serious pain, Lt. Leonard Green's torture had finally been relieved.

After the bombs had been released upon the *Nazi* marshaling yards, the squadrons took a new heading back towards the landmark White Cliffs of Dover. As the planes descended on their approach to Bassingbourn, Lt. Green again felt severe discomfort in his already-aching eardrums. The excruciating pain intensified to become much worse than it had been before. The severe torture was unbearable, lasting for an hour.

Suddenly, the long-awaited pop again alleviated the stabbing anguish. Lt. Green soon detected a warm stream trickling down the left side of his face. The gallant bombardier lifted his palm to his cheek and then noticed a handful of crimson. The bleeding had rolled-down his face all the way to his neck. Green's startling blood discovery continued until the bombers finally landed. Alert crewmen promptly escorted Lt. Leonard Green to the base's *Chief Flight Surgeon*, Captain Bruce Ryan.

The examination took place in Captain Ryan's medical Quonset hut. Lt. Green had survived a very close call.

"Len, you've broken several blood vessels in each of your ears," Captain Ryan determined and described. "This could become quite grave, possibly fatal, if it happens again!"

"When can I fly again?" Green asked. "I just gotta' fly!"

"You'll be grounded for at least a few days," the doctor disclosed. "Then, I'll do a re-evaluation and give you the news!"

Len Green notified his plane's pilot and co-pilot, Lieutenants Al Clark and Hank Berry. The flight crew would have to utilize the services of an assigned substitute bombardier for the next crucial mission over Hitler's Germany.

Len Green really intensely desired to once more be airborne. The soldier felt guilty that he was shirking his duty and letting his "in harm's way" buddies down. The Lieutenant's depression would haunt the sufferer until Len had the official approval to fly again from Capt. Ryan. Otherwise, if Green flew too soon, permanent damage, or a devastating life-threatening emergency, could result from irreversible internal injury. Then, loyal Lt. Green could be grounded for the remainder of his military career and risk the possibility of sustaining a permanent physical disability for the remainder of his life.

Twenty-four hours later, Len's *B-17* crew was awakened for another major precarious combat mission. The bombardier stirred and rose from his bunk, and after hopping-out with his feet on the wood-planked floor, the Lieutenant trekked-down to the briefing room where he sat and chatted with his crew. The *8th Air Force* was going to make a crucial "maximum effort raid" over Berlin. The date was January 8, 1945. All available squadrons would be flying.

Len was both frustrated and aggravated because the grounded fellow could not participate in the top-secret, critical mission. After the detailed briefing had been presented, the disappointed Lieutenant remained and conversed again with his sympathetic crew friends. A half-hour later, Leonard Green sadly watched the other guys change into their flight gear. Finally, the officer with the temporary disability witnessed his colleagues boarding an army truck that would transport them to their assigned *B-17*, "Beats My Queens".

"Too bad you can't make it this time," Lieutenant Clark commented to the disconsolate bombardier. "But I'm sure you'll be there in spirit."

"This is really bothering my conscience something terrible," confessed Len Green. "It's almost humiliating to be medically assessed as being disabled. I feel like I'm letting my buddies down over a trifling dual ear bleeding!"

"Don't let it bother you," replied Hank Berry. "The men all understand what happened to you and that it could've happened to any one of us. Everyone knows, Len, that you would definitely be up there with us if you hadn't caught this bad break. We'll definitely miss you and your admirable courage."

Lt. Green said his "good-byes" and wished the crewmembers of the *Beats My Queens* the best of 'poker luck". An hour later, Len watched the waves of squadrons roar down the two runways and the loaded bombers lifting-off one at a time into the legendary "Wild Blue Yonder". Soon, the attack-ready aircraft were all airborne and heading southeast towards Berlin. In five minutes, the *B-17s* were completely out of sight, but the grueling long wait for their return had already begun. The dial on Len Green's wristwatch verified that the time was exactly 6:00 a.m.

Around noon, Len tried getting some sleep, but all the dedicated bombardier could think of was his crew's hazardous mission and how guilty he would feel if something terrible had happened to any of them. The hours and minutes slowly dragged, and it seemed as if time had acquired amnesia and had forgotten how to advance.

Standing in the *Bassingbourn Base Tower,* Colonel Walters again ardently waited for the roar of the first returning wave of *B-17s*. It was after 4:00 p.m., and the formidable *American Bomber Groups* were nowhere in sight. What was the holdup?

"I'd try contacting their position, but I don't want any of our vital transmissions intercepted by the *Nazis,"* Colonel Walters confided to his fellow lower ranked officer. "I can't afford to jeopardize any of my men's lives! It's not worth the chance!"

"You're right," agreed Captain Evans. "We'll just have to sit tight and hope for the best."

The Colonel and the Captain were pacing back and forth as if the commanders were expectant fathers meandering outside a maternity ward delivery room. Len Green was also more than a little concerned about the tardy flight squadron, too. The *B-17s* should have returned by then from their most recent foray over Germany. It was almost 4:30 p.m. when the sound of the first *B-17s* could finally be discerned, approaching from the eastern horizon. Everyone standing on the tarmac at *Bassingbourn Air Base* was emotionally relieved and now ecstatic with heightened anticipation.

The roaring planes circled the field as if participating in a gigantic aerial parade. One by one the noble bombers landed and taxied to their respective service pads. Ground maintenance teams merrily greeted the surviving crewmen. Many of the newly-arrived battle-weary planes had been badly damaged by flak shrapnel.

Exactly forty-eight *B-17s* had majestically taken-off from the base, but in the final analysis, only forty-four had returned. Len kept eagerly looking for the legendary *Beats My Queens* to land. Soon, his worst fears were ultimately confirmed. A saddened airman reluctantly informed Lieutenant Green that German anti-aircraft guns had shot down *his* favorite *B-17*. The ill-fated plane had exploded in midair before anyone could bail out.

"I should've been on *that* plane. I deserve to be dead," Len sobbed with his shaking hands cupped-up to his eyes. "I can't endure this psychological punishment! I should've died with my pals!"

The sad news of his *B-17's* ugly fate had shattered Lieutenant Green's already flagging spirit. The grieving man was in tears and his sadness was visibly overwhelming. A quirk of destiny had spared Len from tragedy.

For Lt. Green, the next several days were absolutely miserable to cope with. The demoralized bombardier couldn't erase the horrible memory from his damaged psyche. 'How am I going to write to all of their families and explain what had happened?' Green mentally sorrowed. 'How can I ever explain why I wasn't also on board without *them* thinking that I'm a craven coward?' the Lieutenant remorsefully thought after waking-up from a frightening nightmare.

It required a few days for inconsolable Len Green to muster sufficient courage to write letters to his closest friends' aggrieved families. The bombardier's depression had evolved into what Dr. Ryan professionally described as "clinical melancholia".

Dr. Ryan advised Len that the feeling-guilty bombardier would be able to return to his normal air duties in approximately one week. The following Thursday, Lieutenant Green was finally scheduled to fly another important combat mission. Len knew that he had the wherewithal to make the *Nazis* pay for the deaths of his dearly-departed comrades who had been flying aboard the *Beats My Queens*, and also make military retribution for his irreparable mental duress. "I promise I'll get revenge in triplicate. I'll avenge the deaths of my good friends if it's the last thing I'll ever do," vowed Green's aggrieved heart to his lonely soul.

A last-minute notification assigned Lt. Green to the *B-17 Heaven Can Wait*. The on-a-mission bombardier assembled his gear at the crew staging area and was soon transported to the *B-17's* service pad. The sergeant driving the tarmac truck divulged to Len that the February 3, 1945 critical mission was "intensively going to again blast" Berlin industrial infrastructure.

"We're goin' to pound Hitler until his regime and its main city is completely obliterated," the garrulous sergeant asserted. "He'll get what the tyrant deserves. His minions will, too!"

"Sergeant, I feel sorry for the millions of German people who never wanted a damned world war in the first place," replied Green with great passion and empathy for victimized civilians. "War is worse than hell!"

It was 5:30 a.m. Darkness still governed the dark winter sky. The *Heaven Can Wait* crew was already nestled inside the *B-17*. As a result of the crammed quarters, Len Green had to enter the nose of the ship via the escape hatch. Because of his late arrival, the determined bombardier never got to see or meet the *B-17's* pilot or co-pilot. The reassigned Lieutenant was all alone, snuggled inside his tight cabin. Because of limited personnel being a problem, Green had the dual responsibilities of being both bombardier and navigator on that particular difficult mission.

After Len carefully spread his maps on the small "navigator's table" the airman next prepared all his navigational instruments in a thorough and efficient manner.

Suddenly, the bombardier/navigator became aware of an unusual stillness, almost as though he were isolated inside a soundproof room. The claustrophobic Lieutenant instantly thought that his ears had not sufficiently healed in time for his appointed participation in the essential urban bombing raid over Berlin. 'Maybe the haunting sensation will only be temporary,' the young officer hoped. The takeoff that was now being initiated could not be aborted. Len would have to cope with and endure his medical dilemma both to and from hostile Germany. The plane's vital mission across the English Channel and the crew's ultimate fate could not be altered by one individual's physical discomfort.

The pilot started the *B-17's* four engines and soon the propellers were all perfectly spinning, making their familiar loud rhythm. But Len Green was alarmed that his ears could not hear the normal thundering sound emanating from the craft's roaring engines. The wary Lieutenant suspected that he had somehow become deaf. Everything was as silent as if the *Heaven Can Wait* was gliding on the surface of the moon instead of speedily advancing down the airfield's runway.

"At least, I still have my vision," Green consoled himself' and kept repeating those truthful words to his lonesome heart. "My eyes will also be my ears until we finally return to base."

The squadron's planes smoothly took-off in their standard orderly one-by-one pattern. Dawn was quickly appearing on the eastern horizon. Before long, the *B-17s* got organized into their assigned battle formations. Berlin's Nazis would again feel the brunt of their mighty fury and ferocity.

The secret enemy mission went according-to-Hoyle, right at the commencement of the essential bombing run. An hour later, heavy flak soon surrounded the vulnerable *Heaven Can Wait*. The myriad puffs of smoke were very dense on both sides of the flying fortress. However, Len Green was experiencing another enemy besides the wicked German military. The bombardier's ears could not perceive any sensation of sound as enemy anti-aircraft shells were wildly exploding all around him.

The expected resonance of noisy flak bursts had been completely absent from the airman's auditory perception. To Lieutenant Green, there was a tomb-like silence prevalent inside the isolated bombardier cabin, seeming as if the ill-fated *Heaven Can Wait* had become a gigantic flying sepulcher. And it would still be several minutes before the *B-17's* powerful cache of bombs would be fully released over Berlin.

The Air Force squadrons rapidly proceeded towards their separate designated targets. Upon command, bomb bay doors were then opened under every potent *B-17* flying fortress. Just as the *Heaven Can Wait* ordnance was being released, a direct flak barrage hit and knocked-out Lieutenant Green's plane's number one and number two engines. Half of the left wing and part of the nose where Len had been sitting had been instantaneously blasted-away.

The bombardier frantically scrambled to get-out of the small, partially disintegrated cubicle. Green desperately made his way through the dark lurid smoke to where the pilot and co-pilot were futilely struggling to regain control of the severely-crippled aircraft. The half-demolished *B-17* was going-down and beginning its inevitable death spiral. The left wing was totally enveloped in flames. Centrifugal force was pinning everyone that had survived inside the plane against the walls, so no one aboard was able to bail out. The Earth's gravity pull was now the plane's master.

Len Green was still mercilessly terrified by his *deaf* death ride. The doomed officer was futilely screaming in a loud voice that he himself could not hear. Momentarily, the pilot and co-pilot slowly turned around in their twin cockpit seats. Their totally frightening facial features then fully came into terrified Lieutenant Leonard Green's instant view.

It was an absolutely exasperating moment for petrified Lt. Leonard Green. Al Clark and Hank Berry were both sitting there, grinning like two demented hungry sharks as the ill-fated *B-17* headed straight towards the ground.

"Hi, Len," greeted Hank. "We've been waiting for you to finally go down with us."

"*Heaven Can Wait* but Hell cannot," added Lieutenant Al Clark with a very sarcastic sneer ornamenting his macabre, skeleton-like countenance. "Welcome aboard, Len!"

"Or is this *B-17* really the *Beats My Queen* instead?" finished Lieutenant Hank Berry. "God only knows!"

At that very surreal moment, the death-bound *B-17* spectacularly exploded in midair, leaving only a monstrous black cloud along with a trace of dark smoke in its wake.

"The Skull"

Two years after I had graduated from Philadelphia's Overbrook High School in 1940, I began taking general liberal arts courses in preparation for later graduating college, and eventually becoming a licensed optometrist. But *WWII* was raging in Europe and also in the Pacific, so feeling a duty to practice genuine American patriotism, in 1942 I eagerly enlisted in Uncle Sam's United States military. After enduring the rigors of basic training, I became a proud bombardier in the Eighth Air Force, and soon thereafter, I quickly found myself participating in thirty-one hazardous combat missions over Nazi Germany and Eastern Europe.

Feeling fortunate to still be alive after I had received my honorable discharge papers, I felt that it was time for me to adjust to the normal habits and responsibilities of civilian life. I again entered a prominent Philly' University to continue my pursuit of becoming a respected Dr. of Optometry. I recollect roll call being read inside the huge auditorium, and when my name 'Len Davis' finally was phlegmatically announced, I instinctively raised my right hand.

Naturally, I had felt a trifle overconfident and much more mature than my greenhorn eighteen-year-old vernal counterparts, who were obediently sitting beside and around me. My mind was still fresh from me having many near death experiences, from having German flak shot-up at my *B-17,* and from witnessing first-hand other American bombers virtually obliterated by enemy shells, and then spiraling-down and crashing all-aflame onto the ground below. Since I was three-to-five years older than the other newly-enrolled students, *that* age advantage afforded me a measure of self-assurance, and that fact also conferred upon me a keen awareness of my overall growth in maturity.

Soon, I became chummy with Henry Barnett from Galveston, Texas, who incidentally shared with me valuable Air Force training background, for 'Hank' had been a skilled navigator on similar bombing expeditions over Germany. Our tours of duty mutually ended with the conclusion of the all-too-lethal *War,* and so upon settling-down at the University, Henry and I joined the same fraternity and remained best friends throughout our similar college educations.

"Three years of fighting Hitler has given us a real head-start over our adolescent competition," Henry objectively stated inside our dorm' room, before again sipping from a bottle of *Coca-Cola*. "Most of these untested eighteen-year-olds look pathetically naïve and unbearably idealistic to boot!"

"Perseverance and the will to survive are the qualities that in the long run will make us show ourselves as being a bit superior to them," I concurred. "Most of the gullible greenhorns don't even know what Storm Troopers, or the dreaded Luftwaffe were?"

"Right, Len. We've been through the rugged mill and these quixotic tenderfoots that'll be contending against us for Optometry Degrees don't even know what the adult mill looks like!"

One of the first courses that Hank and I were required to take was aptly titled "Human Anatomy". Unlike most academic subjects provided at our institution of higher learning (where the 'old man professors' stood erect behind sterile podiums and boringly lectured), 'H.A.' involved "hands-on experience" where the students had the opportunity to study cadavers inside a bona fide college lab'.

The corpses originated from various Philadelphia hospitals where the bodies were unclaimed for a period of time, and apparently, most of the "stiffs" were unfortunate homeless people before suffering their individual deaths. The cadavers were kept in separate morgue refrigerator compartments for several months until they eventually wound-up at the University, instead of being dishonorably deposited into mass paupers' graves at weed-infested city cemeteries.

Hank Barnett and I represented a pair of conscientious students who often collaborated on challenging assignments, and who also enjoyed performing joint research exploring certain designated Human Anatomy class projects. And despite our shared histories of witnessing a plethora of death and destruction in early 1940s Europe, the experience of dissecting bodies, muscles, internal organs, male and female brains, along with various elements of the nervous system and an assortment of skeletal bones, granted Henry and I a new kind of insight into what actually constitutes being gory and gruesome after being reinserted back into "civilized society".

However, everything was not serious book learning and dedicated laboratory experiments during *our* memorable sophomore year. Our fraternity was in the process of hazing freshman pledges, and the pertinent instructions were for each recruit to survive alone for fifteen-minutes inside the initially eerie and creepy "cadaver lab'." As a class rule, sturdy lids covered the half-dozen corpses that were accessibly situated upon the six cadaver tables; each dead body occupying a metal coffin-like container.

On the all-important academic initiation day, upperclassmen had surreptitiously opened the lids, thus exposing the immobile and macabre human remains inside. Unbeknownst to the unsuspecting and apprehensive pledges, one of the cadavers was actually a live fraternity senior lying motionless inside a selected container.

After each frat-sponsored freshman had been escorted into the brightly illuminated room and left to survive on his own, the steel door was swiftly closed behind him. The potential member had been previously directed to walk around the laboratory to individually inspect the assembled bodies. The scared ambler would soon pass the live cadaver, who then unexpectedly sat-up and took a very deep, gasping breath. The average paranoid freshman would then sprint to the heavy metal door, wildly open the portal and without hesitation, would hastily dash down the corridor and out to the street, screaming all-the-while like a very alarmed and neurotic banshee being pursued by the notorious vampire Count Dracula.

I recall that in mid-September my sagacious anatomy professor Dr. Connor sternly announced to his loyal subordinates that we were going to have our first formal course exam' on October 1st. Every night for a full week Hank and I assiduously crammed our noggins in order to master and absorb the necessary material that covered the first three textbook chapters. On the day of the major test, a wise guy in the class exercised a unique idea by coming to the academic seminar wearing an expensive black tuxedo.

"What is the meaning of your strange apparel?" Dr. Connor wondered and asked the audacious young comedian. "Did you just get married?"

"You told us we were having a *formal* exam' so I dressed appropriately for the special occasion!" the idiotic, callow fellow obnoxiously answered.

"Out! Out!" the dignified professor boisterously screamed while angrily pointing to the classroom's only exit, apparently not-too-amused with the nature of the mischievous freshman's insolent humor. In the meantime, Hank and I grabbed our throats and covered our mouths with our hands in an effort to avoid our dual urges to uncontrollably laugh out loud.

* * * * * * * * * * * * *

The following week, Hank suggested an intriguing idea to me while sitting inside the confines of our sheltered dormitory room. Although in my past I had always been fairly adventurous, I had not been expecting to hear the magnificent essence of Henry Barnett's rather crazy, bloodcurdling proposition.

"How about you and me creating a human skull by removing all of the scalp and facial tissues from a cadaver's head? What do ya' say, Len?"

"I say that's a lunatic plan that's sure to get us imbeciles quickly ejected from this prestigious institution!" I replied. "But I'm game if we can do it legally by getting permission from Dr. Riley, the head of the Anatomy Department!"

"I hope that our illustrious Dr. Riley doesn't interpret our clever brainstorm as being a case of academic *skull*duggery!" ornery Hank facetiously joked. "We don't need any bony skeletons hanging in our dorm's closet!"

After the esteemed educator Dr. Riley heard our fantastic project proposal inside his isolated office, Barnett and I were both surprised and elated when the eminent pedagogue gave us his exclusive approval by commenting, "I admit, I'm quite impressed with your remarkable audacity! But I'll allow my consent on one condition. You must make two skulls; one for yourselves and the other for a display model, which would constitute a novel teaching device for the lecture hall, if you will!"

Inside the musty anatomy lab', in the far-left corner, there was a large barrel with a screw-off lid, designed to keep contaminating outside air from penetrating inside. "Pick one to work on, and when you've satisfactorily finished your fascinating skull task, return to the lab' and choose another cadaver head for a school visual aid, after you've competently perfected your first skull procedure!" Dr. Riley firmly commanded us with a forced smile. "I'll make sure I confidentially speak with Dr. Connor so that you two stellar ambitious gentlemen can earn meritorious extra-credit grades after you officially present your imaginative skull donation to the school!"

Since Dr. Connor also acceded to our rather bizarre project scheme, the veteran instructor skillfully demonstrated to Hank and me exactly how to remove a human brain. The elderly savant sawed a six-inch-wide circular cut on top of a random cadaver head, thus exposing the brain for easy removal. The extracted cerebrum was then gingerly placed inside a thick glass container filled with formaldehyde, in order to reliably preserve the delicate nerves and tissues. The circumference lid was then replaced on top of the cadaver skull, and the removed brain (along with its enormous glass jar) was gingerly transported to the lecture hall to be a vital visual aid during a university professor's eloquent lecture.

The next Saturday brought along a terrible full-fledged rainstorm that deluged that entire drenched area around Walnut Street in West Philadelphia. Hank had taken the Elevated Train back to Frankford in North Philly' to spend the weekend with his family, so being positively bored, I intrepidly decided to initiate *our* academic skull project exclusively on my own. 'Most of the students will either be recovering from Friday night beer guzzling, or will be sobering-up in the library,' I hypothesized and concluded. 'This'll be the perfect time for me to obtain a human head and to begin modifying it into a perfect skull specimen.'

The side entrance door to the 'Anatomy Wing' had been kept unlocked to accommodate parcel post deliveries, and I was aware that no one of consequence would be roaming the halls except the low I.Q. weekend janitor. I knew if our paths should accidentally cross, I could probably talk my way out of the temporary crisis. I remember cautiously stepping into the lab' and then slowly closing the creaky metal door behind me. I then flicked-on the wall light switch and commenced enacting my strategic plan.

'It's a good thing I brought along this handy flashlight if an emergency power failure should occur,' I mentally evaluated. 'It'll suffice if I need it in a hurry!'

I meandered my way around and between the all-too-familiar cadaver examining tables, glad that each metal container had its lid closed and secure. I easily located the "head barrel" situated in the left corner and then anxiously unscrewed the tight lid. My heart was speedily pounding inside my chest when my shocked blinking eyes peered-down upon the terrifying and grotesque sight of a large drum full of decapitated human heads. 'Now to quickly select one, screw the lid back on and ambitiously get the hell out of here!' I easily persuaded myself.

Lifting-up a severed human head to generally inspect gave me a totally strange feeling that almost instantly overwhelmed my collective courage. For a moment, I felt like I had been the mythology hero Perseus victoriously holding the hideous head of the formidable monster Medusa the Gorgon.

Regaining my fleeting scruples, and with trembling palms, I realized that I had obtained a black woman's head, and next carefully set the morbid object upon the nearest dissecting table. Then, for the purpose of comparison, I raised a second head out of the cylinder, but at that exact moment my acute ears heard a tremendous crack of thunder, and suddenly, the lab's lights went out. During my frightening dilemma, the second cadaver head had rolled off the examining table, and the item then hit the underneath base support with a dull thud.

Immediately, I panicked and felt a paralyzing chill dominating my entire body. I then bravely managed to harness my disarrayed senses and subsequently reached into my pants' pocket for the trusty flashlight. After switching on the utilitarian device, and in my frenetic haste, I abruptly felt with my quivering hands when a series of myriad goose bumps appeared on my shivering arms.

While being on the verge of insanity, I still had the presence of mind to meticulously place the aforementioned cadaver head into a linen laundry bag that I had brought along, especially for the 'legal acquisition', and then after completing that most challenging phase of the furtive operation, I pointed the flashlight directly at the "corner head drum". And then, under more extreme duress, I carefully screwed the object's protective lid back on top.

I methodically approached the door with my prized bag in hand, flipped-off the non-functioning wall light switch, opened the lab' door, and proceeded to stealthily exit the eerie chamber. I happened to let-out a blood-curdling scream when a strong hand grabbed my shoulder and a deep male voice austerely demanded, "What are you doing here?"

My acute auditory perception readily recognized the source of the imperative-but-familiar masculine vocal tone, and I reflexively pointed the flashlight's beam at my vague acquaintance. Standing there was Raymond Stanton, the weekend custodian, a fellow who was heavyset, around age fifty, and a muscular guy who habitually wore commonplace, trademark horn-rimmed glasses.

"Mr. Stanton!" I exclaimed and gasped while physically shaking and staring at the janitor's signature thick gray hair. "I want you to know that I have full permission to be here! A friend and I convinced the administration that we could have a project where…"

"Oh, I know you now!" the burly maintenance man declared in a more relaxed tone of voice. "You're the young guy who was the B-17 bombardier! Sorry I scared the daylights out of you! It's a good thing you were carrying that lit flashlight, or else I might've given you a stiff uppercut to your jaw! I'm just glad I won't have to spend an hour writing-out a report describing some punk trespasser. Now kindly leave the premises so that I can lock-up this lab' door. But then I'll have to wait for the lights to come back-on to continue doing my regular duties!"

Using the already fading flashlight beam, I scurried out of the building and then rushed down the granite slate steps while clutching and carrying my prized linen bag in my right hand. Upon my entry into the dorm' room, my jangled nerves were comforted upon me noticing that my roommate Hank Barnett had returned from North Philly' early and was patiently awaiting my arrival.

"I had gone home to mow the lawn for my folks and then trim the rhododendron bushes on the side of my parents' house," Hank lethargically explained. "But because of the torrential rain, I came back to the dorm' to relax. Say Len, what's hidden in that linen bag sitting on the coffee table?"

"It's our extraordinary science enterprise!" I identified as I raised the black female head out of the white bag. "We'll begin stripping-off the hair and flesh right away if it's okay with you! That is, after we somehow locate a large, clean pot to boil the head in to soften the tissues. Then, my fine-feathered friend, just two ordinary scalpels will help us do the rest!"

Monday morning, Hank and I were among fifty bored students attentively listening to Dr. Connor's redundant rhetoric inside the main lecture hall when we heard an ear-piecing shriek originating from the dissecting lab' located down the corridor. 'I didn't have time to get into the lab' this morning to search for the dropped head!' I distinctly remember thinking and fearing.

As it turned-out, a first-year female student had fainted and was found unconscious lying on the beige tile floor. Immediately, my perceptive mind fathomed that she had probably reached underneath the dissecting table to deposit her pocketbook and had accidentally discovered the second misplaced decapitated head.

Later that day, I was called-down to the administrative office where I apologetically confessed to Dr. Connor and Dr. Riley exactly what had transpired, and after patiently listening to my rather sensational rendition, the pair of erudite lecturers reluctantly accepted the veracity of my oddball narrative.

"Despite your honesty, Len, I'll have to write-out a discipline card on you, and put the message in your Mickey Mouse file," Dr. Connor sadly reported. "It's no big deal! It's just standard procedure to cover the administration's *butt!*"

"We're not only cadaver dissectors," Dr. Riley mused and then laughed. "We also practice a little bit of rudimentary proctology around here, too!"

It took Henry Barnett and me two whole months to meticulously clean and clear the black women's head and face of its attached tissues and hair, so that the evolution of her cleansed skull could be expertly achieved. Hank then made a constructive comment that affirmatively gained my full endorsement.

"Len, that second head you had dropped on the lab' floor was a pretty close call! But let's not mention the other head we had promised to donate to the school, and perhaps Dr. Connor and Dr. Riley will have forgotten about it by the time we graduate! What do ya' say?"

"That might be the best idea you've had since I've known you!" I offered and chuckled. "You certainly know the best way to get *ahead* in this world!"

* * * * * * * * * * * *

Later that first college year, Hank and I had studied our important course materials quite diligently, both of us still being aspiring optometrists, but our immediate task at hand was to successfully make it through Fundamental Anatomy, 101. Back at our dorm' room, the black woman's head was slowly-but-surely making its transition into a presentable pearly white skull, but the female's skin complexion and distinguishing facial features both plagued and haunted my restive spirit as "the deteriorating head" was still kept wrapped-up inside our refrigerator's freezer compartment, so that the smell of decay would not permeate and odorize our rather modest dormitory quarters.

Our twin bed sleeping arrangement had a typical fish-tank that Hank had brought from home, and three glittering gold fish merrily swam around its perimeter, finning about in monotonous circles. The rectangular aquarium occupied a pertinent space upon a flat table, which had been conveniently positioned between our two beds. Hank and I had improvised a nightlight so that we could marvel at the sparkling goldfish maneuvering around at midnight, swimming inside the otherwise dark bedroom. Without question, the reflected green light being emitted had a mesmerizing, scary and almost-hypnotic effect upon the viewers' eyes.

At 3:00 a.m. the following morning, I woke-up in a heavy sweat and soon glanced over at the commonplace aquarium. The goldfish were still casually swimming about, but in the center of the illuminated tank I beheld the ghastly head of the black woman, but instead of a skull, her face and green eyes appeared exactly as the features had looked the first time I had fretfully observed her appearance in the lab'.

I exhaled several deep breaths to regain my sanity, and my alert ears heard Hank nastily snoring with his hairy back turned toward me. I stared again at the central fish-tank, and in less than a minute, the worrisome image mysteriously faded into obscurity. I closed my eyelids and uneasily dozed-off into a restive sleep.

At 7:00 a.m. Henry was strenuously shaking my shoulder to wake me up. "Hey Man, we have little time for breakfast. We gotta' be sitting inside the lecture hall before senile Professor Jensen arrives in order to maintain our almost impeccable attendance records, or else if we're tardy again, it'll be demerits for both you and me!"

Before I exited the dorm' room, I took a hard look at my bed. The sheets and blanket were all disheveled and still wet with sweat. 'I must've had a terrible nightmare; either that or a very troubling hallucination!' I reasoned in an effort to allay my concern. 'It's not easy around here making sense out of inexplicable nonsense!'

It is no exaggeration that the recurring vision of the deceased black woman's face had entered and plagued my fragile psyche on more than one occasion. Once, I believed to have seen the African lady window-shopping at a downtown Market Street department store, and another time, I was crossing 10th and Locust near Thomas Jefferson University Hospital and reckoned I witnessed the same female take-off from a red traffic light in a dark blue Ford sedan. What stood-out the most in my stark recollection was that the sightings, the subject's dark green eyes, facsimile to the one's once present upon the black female face that had been retrieved from the creepy cadaver room drum, were definitely not of *this* world!

By chance and coincidence, the following Saturday I casually strolled into a Chestnut Street pharmacy and was perusing the merchandise in the patent medicine section for a bottle of aspirins. Much to my utter astonishment, the green-eyed African American lady was impatiently waiting in line at the counter, evidently to obtain several already ordered prescriptions. I assessed the weird drugstore encounter as a special opportunity to introduce myself.

"I'm sorry to bother you but you look awfully familiar," I awkwardly began my stuttering salutation. "Do you live in the general vicinity?"

"No, Young Man. Truthfully, I haven't been in Philly' too long," the in-a-hurry woman remarked. "I arrived here from Montego Bay, Jamaica a month ago. My name is Hannah Bailey," she voluntarily conveyed, formally extending her right hand.

"I'm Len Davis, a sophomore at the *University of Penn*. Glad to make your acquaintance," I supplemented. "I had spent three years in the Air Force and was a bombardier on a *B-17!* I've recently returned to college to continue my education! Do you have a sister who resembles you?" I diplomatically inquired.

"As a matter of fact, I do!" Hannah confided with a wondering expression shown upon her face. "Her name is Julia, and she's my identical twin. She had mysteriously disappeared from the face of the Earth around two years ago without a single trace of her fate. That's why I'm here in Philly'; to learn exactly what had happened to dear Julia!"

"Was your sister employed? Was she a loner? Have you gone to the police?" I rattled-off in rapid detective-like succession.

"Julia worked as a receptionist in a doctor's office on Spruce Street," Hannah reluctantly informed. "She never had many friends, being somewhat shy, just like myself. And I've yet to contact the police to see if there's been any missing persons' investigation conducted. For you see, Julia was not the type of person to deliberately try and evade work responsibilities."

"Do you have any special hobbies?" I asked, clumsily attempting to change the subject to something that was more comfortable for us to discuss. "Sorry, I didn't mean to offend you!"

"Don't be too shocked!" Hannah Bailey answered as she moved to the position of second in line at the pharmacy's exchange counter. "I have enough money saved to stay in the city for three more months. In the meantime, you might be interested to know that I interpret Tarot cards and also perform Crystal Ball readings; that is, I do it by appointment only."

"Do your forecasts come true most of the time?" I foolishly asked, endeavoring to employ the Socratic Method of Reasoning, which I had conveniently learned five-years before in undergraduate Greek Philosophy Class.

"Yes, and here is my new business card," Hannah uttered and produced after digging and rummaging inside her cluttered purse. "My address and phone number are printed on the bottom. You can call me any time to schedule a reading."

'This woman's a psychic, and although I have my suspicions about *that* weird activity as neither being an art nor a science,' I objectively and scientifically speculated, 'I'm quite concerned that Hannah might already have known about the resemblance of the former black cadaver head to *her* identical contemporary facial features and emerald dark green eyes.'

Suddenly, the irritated patron that had been standing in front of Hannah Bailey finished her lengthy money transaction, and the very accommodating lady pharmacist signaled for the sensitive Jamaican woman to step forward to the purchasing counter. I politely waved to the dark-skinned woman, and quickly promised that I would contact her in the very near future.

* * * * * * * * * * * *

Just before the highly anticipated Christmas Break, Hank Barnett and I finally completed the transformation of the black woman's head into a stunning white human skull. All the while, my inspired mind contemplated whether the deceased 'ebony woman' might in reality be the missing person, Julia Bailey. Eventually, after much mental deliberation, my fragile ego garnered sufficient gumption to arrange a Tarot/Crystal Ball reading with Hannah, who presently resided in a small rooming house near 18th and Pine.

The unique doorbell ring produced a sequential sound of melodious wind-chimes, and within a minute's duration, the Jamaican woman appeared and graciously opened the door. Hannah was appropriately dressed for her rather unusual trade, wearing a purple robe covered with glittering sequins. Upon Ms. Bailey's head was an attractive jeweled tiara; definitely visual-pleasing apparel that was characteristic of, and truly consistent with, certain popular fortune-teller stereotypes.

"Come in, Leonard, or should I call you Len!" the door answerer requested. "You're quite punctual; right on time!"

I hesitated but then stepped into her small foyer, thinking all along that Jamaica was notorious for its practice and belief in such ludicrous things as primitive voodoo and black magic, but placing my credence in transcendent modern science, my advanced, ethnocentric mind had dismissed all aspects of me having a confrontation with sinister and dangerous arcane evil spirits. As I was escorted into the tiny Reading Room, my olfactory senses became acutely aware of an abundance of exotic jasmine incense heavily saturating the air.

As my eyes surveyed the overall 'eccentric' environment, my sharp perception noticed a deck of Tarot cards, accompanied by a shiny Chrystal Ball, that had both been strategically laid upon the wooden table's plain black cloth cover. My cluttered, erratic mind was desperately searching for just the right nomenclature to then orally deliver.

"This is my first exposure to a psychic reading," I cordially and candidly prefaced. "Excuse me if I seem a bit jittery."

"I assure you, there's nothing egregious here to be intimidated by. Now let's do the Tarot cards first, shall we?" Ms. Hannah Bailey authoritatively suggested. "The illustrations usually work well with nervous novices such as yourself."

The medieval-style cards had been confined to a silk pouch, apparently stored inside to protect their presumed power from external, detrimental, spiritual influences. I presumed that their concealment would ensure a more accurate reading for the visitor. Hannah took her time, carefully shuffling and then spreading the 'decontaminated cards' face-down upon the small table. I curiously sat in awe of what sort of outlandish phenomenon might be transpiring. "Now Len, tell me what question you want answered, and the deck will cooperatively respond to your deep desire."

"I'd like to know precisely what had happened to your missing sister, Julia?" I declared, fidgeting my entire erect posture upon the cushioned seat, which had been stationed directly opposite the throne chair that Hannah Bailey was occupying.

The reader then solemnly collected the assorted cards and with them once again being united into a deck, built three separate stacks with the last pile being placed in the middle. "Choose one of the three stacks," Hannah imperatively instructed like a martinet middle school disciplinarian. "Take your time, Len, and allow the spiritual magnetism to generate between your right hand's fingers and the pile to which they will be most attracted."

I chose the ten cards within the center stack, after which Hannah knowledgably stated, "The left stack pertains to the past, the right one to the future, and the one you have chosen corresponds to the present." But then, I noticed a puzzled and disturbed expression spontaneously appearing upon the woman's grim countenance.

"Is something wrong?" I wanted to know. "You seem to be bewildered or confused?"

"In all my years experimenting with the power of Tarot cards, I've never observed something so irregular. This inability of mine to intelligently understand your rare card combination leaves me with only one real alternative," the frustrated female interpreter extemporaneously indicated. "We must now digress to implementing the attributes of the dependable Chrystal Ball! For some obscure reason, the cards have strangely become impotent!"

My wits and sanity were on the brink of simultaneously becoming petrified as my eyes intensely studied Hannah's trance-like state. The scrupulous purveyor of the occult realm amazingly and mentally was communicating with the round object that her hands softly encompassed. The Jamaican woman articulated not a single word as a stream of tears began cascading down her puffy cheeks. Soon, the distraught reader suddenly snapped-out of her self-imposed, trance-like state.

"I'm sorry to tell you Leonard that I must now close-out this preliminary session of ours," Hannah softly declared. "This new-found twin anomalies that've transpired during our interpretation conference, well, I'm still trying to adequately comprehend, and to tell you the truth, the enigma had never occurred before. Mr. Davis, I've attempted to decipher what conflicting visualizations my brain has received through two separate sources of wave-vibration telepathy, but regrettably speaking, I'm having trouble decoding the transmitted garbled information. For the first time ever, neither the Tarot cards nor the mystical Crystal Ball could accurately communicate any distinct, relevant knowledge."

After I dejectedly departed the diminutive down floor apartment of the three-story rooming house, my knees almost were buckling. I considered and decided that I should not tell Henry Barnett of my exceptional Pine Street dealings with the fearsome Jamaican lady. Certainly, I truly needed my pal's guidance, assistance, and companionship for me to academically prepare for the State Board Examination of Optometrists, but first, Hank and I had to graduate from the University of Pennsylvania.

* * * * * * * * * * * *

One late March afternoon, two Philadelphia policemen arrived at my dormitory room's door and forcefully knocked. "Are you Len Davis?" the first officer asked.

"Yes, what is the matter?" I responded in a curious tone of voice. "I've already paid that parking ticket I had gotten with my old jalopy back in January. I settled the matter last month! In Plato's Republic," I defensively and foolishly equivocated, "while walking on the Piraeus Pier just south of Athens, the sophist Thrasymachus pontificated to the philosopher Socrates that the definition of an honest man is a dependable person who pays all his debts," I stupidly added to disguise my initial uneasiness. But all-the-while I had been demonstrating a miserably fake attempt at sounding sagacious to the visiting police officers.

"Nice try, Son, but we want you to come with us to the local precinct headquarters and answer a few elementary questions," the second patrolman imperatively directed. "Certain pertinent facts connected to an investigative case our detectives are examining need clarification. Now come along with us to be interrogated about the possibility of a serious crime being committed."

At the station, I was given a battery of oral questions for over a half-hour by the two on duty detectives, and I related to the investigators all I knew about the black woman's head being converted into a white skull. Then, I advised the precinct sleuths that they could contact Dr. Connor and Dr. Riley to confirm my candid testimony. "Okay, Len. We'll release you from our custody, but please don't leave town, because you'll be kept under police surveillance until further notice. Is that instruction clear?" the principal interrogator stated.

"Perfectly clear!" I gladly exclaimed with a sigh of relief. "I always want to stay on the good side of the law."

The police investigators did visit the college and spoke with the two very surprised law-abiding professors, who verified my extraordinary human skull story. So then to satisfy the cops' austere demand, that same afternoon, Hank and I had shrewdly brought-along the pure white skull to the precinct headquarters, with the unusual object being wrapped in a heavy white linen cloth. The mere sight of the grisly item had the pair of repulsed detectives lean back into their seats as I gently removed the anonymous black woman's skull, and set it upon the office's metal desk.

Then, much to my utter astonishment, Hannah Bailey was shown her way inside the dingy, nondescript police conference room, and upon her viewing the on-display jaw bones, and the accompanying cranium, the woman emotionally attested, "I'm certain that's my twin sister Julia. I can tell by the wide gap between her front teeth and by the four gold-cap molars, two on each side!" After comprehending the full gravity of the situation, Ms. Bailey began to sob and whimper. Then shortly thereafter, the Jamaican native cried incessantly, and the two astonished precinct detectives stood and tried to console her extreme grief.

"But how did Julia's head get to the Anatomy Wing and then put into the lab' barrel?" I objectively asked. "There're too many dots to this perplexing pattern that need to be joined!"

"Here's what we believe to be true," the first detective divulged. "Only two people had keys to gain entry to the cadaver lab'. One was Dr. Connor, a professor whose reputation is obviously beyond suspicion. So therefore, the professor, we believe, is completely exonerated. The only other individual having access to the dissecting laboratory is...."

"Raymond Stanton, the grouchy, grumpy janitor!" Henry Barnett automatically piped-up.

"Exactly!" the second detective abruptly concurred. "Now, hospitals usually keep bodies for about six-weeks, and if unclaimed by family or relatives, the corpse is either given to the University's Anatomy Department for dissection, or is buried in a mass paupers' grave. Congratulation Boys! You two young college students don't comprehend it yet," the second gumshoes related while specifically referring to Hank and me, "but if it weren't for your creative anatomy project," the stoic-faced cop paused and emphasized, "this truly baffling case would've still been floating around somewhere in Legal Limbo!"

Henry and I agreed to allow the police to keep the white skull as state's evidence in the prosecution of the empathetic-but not-too-bright building janitor. A day later, Raymond Stanton was picked-up by the local authorities and then extensively questioned for two grueling hours at the station. Asked to submit a written description of events, the flustered custodian offered the following elaboration in the form of a confession:

"One evening around 11:00 p.m., I saw a black woman staggering around the university campus, and I presumed that she was intoxicated. Feeling sympathy for the lady, I took her into the Anatomy Building Wing and sat her down in a chair. To my sudden shock, shortly thereafter, she collapsed onto the floor and had died. Thinking that I would be blamed for causing her death, I didn't know what to do.

My first impulse was to dispose of the body, believing that my ploy would evade discovery. I severed-off her head and placed in in a solution of formaldehyde overnight. Next, I entered the dissecting lab' early the following morning and deposited the head inside the almost-full, corner barrel. I then carried and transferred the rest of the body down to the basement crematorium.

All school cadavers are cremated down at the lower level after they have been thoroughly studied and dissected. No one would detect my furtive act, since I am entrusted by the faculty to dispose of all cadavers in a similar manner. The entire cremation process takes about three-hours to finally reduce the corpse to ashes. In the morning, when the woman's ashes had cooled, the remains were put into a cardboard container and later collected by city trashmen the next morning."

A week after Raymond Stanton's mind-boggling confession, my attention was then attracted to a *Philadelphia Inquirer* front-page, beneath-the-fold story. The comprehensive article immediately shook me into a state of self-induced delirium:

Woman Found Dead in Apartment

Yesterday, an area psychic was found dead inside her Pine Street apartment by a client who had arrived for a scheduled appointment. Hannah Bailey was discovered by Bernard Turner of Croydon with her head resting on the table where she often did Tarot card readings. "I tried reviving her, but it was to no avail. Her body was totally immobile. The lady was stone-cold dead by the time the city ambulance arrived!" the upset and saddened corpse finder told *the Inquirer*. Upon the table police found a note which read: "I can no longer live without my twin sister. I'm using an overdose of sleeping pills to be able to share eternity with my dear Julia!" For more information and details about this news story, read Hannah Bailey's obituary in tomorrow's early morning edition.

I sadly read the next day's alluded-to obituary, and hence, felt compelled to attend the Jamaican woman's viewing at a South

Philadelphia Broad Street funeral parlor. Upon entering the main chamber, I felt quite distressed when I observed only one mourner sitting stationary on a couch in the otherwise empty front row. I must admit that the entire scenario was singularly uncanny with me being the only other mourner present.

Esther Bailey introduced herself as Hannah and Julia's mother, and the family matriarch had flown-up to Philadelphia for her daughter's burial. I offered the elderly woman my sincere condolences and then approached the casket to respectfully view the body. My racing heart skipped several beats when I peered-down at dearly departed Hannah resting in peace with the material world, her corpse lying horizontally with her ebony hands holding a white skull exactly where rosary beads or a common prayer book would ordinarily be seen. Apparently, after hearing the entire case history from the precinct police, Esther had requested ownership of Julia's skull, and her peculiar request was compassionately granted.

As for Raymond Stanton, the devious Anatomy School janitor, the emotionally impaired, special needs custodian was eventually exonerated after a lengthy trial, his meager punishment being ten months of community service.

"Stained Glass"

"Your retirement party was great!" Donna Evans complimented as the woman drove her husband north from San Francisco across the picturesque *Golden Gate Bridge.*

"It was really nice, especially the memorable gifts my coworkers gave me," answered Ralph. "But the one gift I certainly plan to make use of is the nifty stained-glass kit."

Traffic was fairly light since it was 11:00 p.m. on a Friday night. Besides the very expensive stained-glass kit, the successful clothes' designer had also received a handsome gold watch along with a three-week all-expense-paid cruise for two to tropical Honolulu.

"When we return from our Hawaii voyage, you'll be able to spend many enjoyable hobby hours learning to construct stained glass windows," Ralph's wife suggested. "You needed an avocation, and now you've finally found one."

"Donna, I'm glad I've happily retired and can spend more time on what I *want* to do instead of worrying about what I *have* to do." Then, Ralph had a pertinent afterthought. "If I like working with stained glass, I'll have found a good part-time business to take the boredom out of my golden years."

"That's precisely what you need," Donna agreed while affirmatively nodding her head. "You need to work with your hands after spending so many challenging years worrying with your mind."

Donna and Ralph Evans lived in the serene community of Belvedere, California. The couple had moved from the East Coast in the late '60s and led very full and compatible marital lives as husband and wife. The pair resided in a beautiful stone rancher situated in a cul-de-sac near a deep blue lagoon. And Ralph Evans had a sailboat, which he would use regularly to take from the lagoon out to majestic *San Francisco Bay.* Sailing was definitely his favorite leisurely sport.

"If I were lucky enough to be Bob Sullivan, then I'd be hoisting the spinnaker on a huge yacht rather than the jib on my small boat," Ralph lamented and complained. "My only regret is that I spent most of my adult working life making other people rich; especially that corporate louse Robert Sullivan! That pathetic jerk's a totally abominable tyrant!"

It was no wonder that Ralph Evans greatly loathed his nemesis, Robert Todd Sullivan, the senior vice president of *Emerson Designs.* Ralph had suspected that Sullivan had stolen several of *his* original dress designs, and after making very slight modifications, had presented the adjusted styles to Mr. Milo Emerson, who then appreciatively promoted "despicable Mr. Bob" to his present eminent executive position.

"Now Ralph, that last comment sounds very much like sour grapes," Donna remarked in the form of rendering a small admonishment. "You've done very well on your own. You've absolutely nothing to be ashamed of."

"Donna, it's not just the money and the power," Evans replied in defense of his damaged, sensitive ego. "Robert T. Sullivan unethically pilfered my intellectual property; that's the main idea I'm communicating here. Sullivan is a black-hearted thief; an ambitious bold-faced liar, and a dangerous conniver who had made a practice of stealing little pieces of my mind, one theft at a time. That deplorable, slippery worm deprived me of my true place of honor in the firm!"

The wife sympathized with her unusually upset spouse. There was a moment of silence as Donna Evans changed lanes and maneuvered their white Mercedes to the left as the driver abruptly accelerated pass a slow-moving van.

"Ralph, I saw your face turn three shades of green when Bob presented you with the stained-glass kit," Donna reminded her already peeved passenger. "And it's impossible for you to prove that Bob has stolen your creative intellectual property. So, you really shouldn't waste your time seeking revenge or belated economic justice when it's too late to actually change anything."

A momentary pause ensued as the perturbed husband pondered organizing a rational reply to his wife's seemingly impeccable language. The distraught front-seat companion cleared his throat to disguise his mounting anger. "I assure you, Honey, I wasn't green with envy. I was green from disgust for me ever trusting that miserable rogue Robert Todd Sullivan!"

Ralph and Donna Evans were each in their late '50s, but the duo looked much younger than their ages suggested. The normally congenial pair kept their bodies trim and in very excellent physical condition. The Evans's backyard heated pool was religiously utilized for both daily exercise and recreational swimming.

Ralph was nearsighted and had to wear glasses ever since junior high school, and Donna also needed corrective bifocal specs for her favorite pastime, romance novel reading, which she avidly savored and relished.

In addition to being a women's apparel designer, Ralph was also a very accomplished amateur artist. Several of his paintings had won trophies in local competitions, and aspirational Evans was certain that his talents could now be effectively transferred from clothes designing and canvas painting to creative stained-glass expression. The husband viewed learning a new craft as a newfound quest.

Donna was the sole owner of a small jewelry store in a suburban San Francisco mall, and the wife was in no way dependent on her husband's employment for income. Mrs. Evans was very civic minded and was active in many community organizations and national charity causes. Dullness had never been a major factor complicating their childless marriage.

The suburban couple loved to travel and had experienced numerous vacation adventures around the world. Mr. Emerson's surprise "Hawaiian retirement cruise" appeared at *that* time to be the most appropriate gift that Ralph Evans could have received.

"Maybe we should bring Bob Sullivan along to spice-up our ocean voyage," Donna satirically jested.

"I think he'd be *cruisin'* for a bruisin'," the husband joked. "I'd like to stuff a red apple in the creep's mouth and rotate him above a fire while attached-to an enormous luau rotisserie."

"Look Ralph, as Milo Emerson would tell you, shape-up or ship out," laughed the giddy wife in reference to the Evans's upcoming Pacific cruise. "And let's not go overboard about your principal work enemy. Stop with all of the ugly animosity! Just be glad that nefarious Robert T. Sullivan is not *John L. Sullivan.* If you don't change and improve your attitude, I think I'll have to report you for retired anger management therapy."

Two days after Ralph's retirement dinner, the axe-to-grind fellow and Donna were seated with their packed luggage and riding inside a cab on their way to downtown San Francisco. Soon, the California duo was at *Pier 13,* and then were walking-up the long gangplank to the mammoth docked cruise ship. The couple was totally delighted that their well-appointed cabin featured an exquisite view of enchanting *San Francisco Bay.*

Two hours after the myriad passengers had boarded the luxurious tourist ship, the huge vessel pulled-away from its pier. A beautiful West Coast sunset accompanied the vessel's passage under the majestic *Golden Gate Bridge,* and it was a magical, festive moment and a fun time that was being enjoyed by all of the ecstatic vacationers, most of whom were already imbibing potent mixed drinks while meeting and mingling with new acquaintances. Four marvelous cruising days separated Ralph and Donna Evans from the exotic port of Honolulu.

On the third morning of their "Pacific odyssey", the clothes designer and his devoted wife amused themselves in the ship's game room by experimenting with an ancient-looking *Ouija Board.*

"Ralph, did you know that *Ouija* means '*yes*' twice; the first 'yes' is in French and the second one is in German," his wife academically informed. "I learned that esoteric fact watching a TV game show."

"No, Donna. I was unaware of that irrelevant piece of trivia," Ralph cynically and argumentatively replied. "You're a fountain of trite knowledge besides being a spring of vital inspiration!" Then, the sometimes-irreverent husband asked the enigmatic game board oracle several weighty questions that had haunted his delicate psyche for the past three decades. Ralph and Donna were amazed at the *Ouija Board's* direct answers to *his* specific inquiries.

"Did Bob Sullivan steal my designing ideas and then present them to Mr. Emerson as being his own?" Evans asked the board.

"Yes," the arcane board indicated and spelled-out with the couple's fingers softly resting upon the moving planchette.

"Tell us the full name of the person who got promoted using Ralph Evans' drawings," demanded the now-fascinated wife.

The observers were both astounded as the "Occult Oracle's" planchette interpreted the nervous vibrations generated from their trembling fingertips and promptly spelled-out the specific letters of the name, Robert T. Sullivan."

The couple's first week on Oahu was quite fulfilling for the two vacationers with many tourist attractions being visited such as patriotic *Pearl Harbor* and awesome Koko Head Volcano. Feeling inspired, Ralph spent a full day painting the enchanting *Diamond Head Mountain* on a canvas situated upon a rented easel.

While sightseeing in the malls opposite Waikiki Beach, Ralph and Donna entered a large, well-stocked hobby store, *The Devil's Workshop*, which coincidentally displayed a very extensive stained-glass sales section. Ralph had never before seen such a fabulous array of colors available for stained-glass arrangement, and so the intrigued customer eagerly ordered a vast supply of the exceptional product. A huge case would have to be shipped to their Belvedere home, and at that jubilant moment, expense was of no object to the extravagant purchaser.

"This store is no place for *idle minds*," jested the wife in reference to the craft emporium's *Devil's Workshop* name. "I just hope you do nothing demonic with your new hobby kit."

"Donna, I believe that this *Devil's Workshop* establishment has a bigger inventory than *hell patch a mile*," returned the very jovial husband in a play-on-words that was almost as imaginative as his wife's initial symbolic commentary.

The next two weeks in "tropical paradise" passed-by rapidly. Ralph's mind remained focused on his planned utilization of the stained-glass kit that the retired employee had received, and Evans was anxious to explore its sundry possibilities that would be adequately implemented once the supplemental stained-glass case would arrive in Belvedere from Hawaii. The formerly acrimonious clothes designer's robust imagination fantasized the magnitude of stellar wonders that his reputed artistic talent would soon produce. In a week, Ralph would be situated back home in sunny California, experimenting with the *two* new kits' properties.

"That was one of the best trips we were ever on!" admitted Donna with a noticeable sparkle in her eyes. "But it's always great getting back home again," she continued her evaluation as the returning cruise ship glided under the *Golden Gate Bridge*.

"I'll second that motion," agreed Ralph as the luxury liner was approaching its assigned San Francisco *Pier 13*. "I'll now look for Otis Redding sitting by the dock of the bay!"

The Evans' were naturally exhausted from experiencing their fabulous three-week hiatus and soon retired to bed to dream and relive their tropical paradise escape. Donna's thoughts were centered mostly on the delightful scenic cruise, but before Ralph fell asleep, he again contemplated his newfound fancy: the retirement stained-glass tool kit, along with the stunning variety of colorful glass that had been enthusiastically purchased at the *Devil's Workshop*.

Morning arrived, and the chirping of birds aroused the couple from their pleasant slumber. Rays of sunlight had marvelously filtered through the bedroom's sheer, mint-green drapes. The first morning hour was spent unpacking and sorting-out the couple's vacation clothes, and in a short while Ralph and Donna were ready for eggs and coffee on the veranda, which overlooked the nearby deep blue lagoon. The breakfast atmosphere was both peaceful and relaxing. The Hawaiian sojourners were both glad to be home.

"It's *great* to get away, but it's even *greater* to get back to San Francisco Bay," Ralph observed and claimed. "You really don't appreciate something until you miss it."

"Don't forget your new hobby," facetiously reminded his wife. "I know you can't wait to get started!"

Ralph stepped off the veranda and ambled over to a downstairs closet where he removed the watercolor paintings of *Diamond Head* that he had artistically drawn and finished on *Waikiki Beach*. Donna viewed and scrutinized the objects with critical eyes. The three canvas renditions were terrific in appearance, and were even sufficiently suitable to be prominently and proudly displayed upon the main living room wall.

As the husband was ready to hang the paintings and then thereafter ponder his gifted stained-glass kit, the kitchen telephone rang. Donna promptly answered the call.

"Hello!"

"Hi Donna; this is Rick Streit."

"Rick, it's so nice to hear from you," the woman of the house replied. "Ralph will be thrilled you called. I'll let you speak to him," Donna added as she summoned her husband to the phone. "Ralph, you'll never guess who's on the phone. It's your cousin's artist friend, Rick Streit," Donna directly communicated to her currently preoccupied husband.

Ralph abandoned his painting-hanging enterprise and briskly paced to the kitchen wall phone. "Rick, you couldn't have called at a more opportune time for me!" Evans politely informed. "Are you in town?"

"Yes, I was visiting some friends in Frisco' and was close by, so I thought I'd give you a buzz," Streit answered.

"Great! When can we expect you to visit?"

"How about me coming tomorrow?" the caller suggested. "I'm free all day."

"I'll have something that I've just received as a gift at my retirement party that I want to show you; and then maybe you can help me with some professional pointers," Ralph suggested. "I need your expertise and will be thrilled to consult your advice."

"Does it involve stained-glass?" Rick guessed and asked.

"Sure does."

"Then, I'll definitely see you tomorrow around 9 a.m.," Streit clarified, "if it's okay with you."

Rick Streit lived in Huntington Beach, just below *L.A.* and coincidentally was the proprietor of a prosperous stained-glass business called *Art Windows*. The shop-owner was a very talented artist in his own right and had developed a fine reputation for improvising outstanding original designs. The next morning, Mr. Rick Streit paid a promised visit to the Evans's residence and soon gave Ralph many workable ideas, showing the "cooperative student" basic crafting techniques, many of which the determined neophyte would possibly integrate into *his* own unique style.

Ralph was now ready to fully utilize the entire stained-glass kit, which had everything needed to manufacture small items that featured stained-glass designs. The kit would be used to practice the helpful methods demonstrated by "Johnny-on-the-Spot" Rick Streit, but Ralph's principal objective was much more ambitious than just that. The perfectionist's main desire was to create an original stained-glass window that would be worthy of professional admiration. Evans would definitely require more equipment, since it was evident that the tools and glass that had been supplied with the "introductory retirement kit" were insufficient to complete such a grandiose project that his brain had imagined.

* * * * * * * * * * * *

The next day, Ralph attempted synthesizing his first original endeavor, which was a small stained-glass panel to be hung on the living room wall, right next to the three distinct *Diamond Head* paintings. The "glass panel enterprise" required several hours of assiduous labor, but the on-a-mission apprentice was keenly aware that it would take extensive stoic patience to develop the essential skills prerequisite to creating something as intricate as a full-sized stained-glass window. 'Rick said it would take me at least a month of diligent experimenting to discover my 'true artistic personality',' Ralph sentimentally recalled. 'I'm all excited about making my first stained-glass statement.'

In the ensuing weeks, Ralph Evans made several more complicated items, and each time, the very deliberate learner demonstrated additional dexterity and notable savvy at pursuing his "new craft". The evolving artisan soon realized he would need a larger workroom, along with a bigger assemblage table to be able to skillfully manufacture a standard-sized stained-glass window.

Being a supportive spouse, Donna assisted her marital mate in converting the spare room into the desired new workplace. The "glass lab" was soon fully equipped, qualified, and ready for constructing glorious stained-glass windows. The various colors and associated patterns that had accompanied the retirement gift kit couldn't compare with the quality glass and stain colors Evans had later ordered from the fantastic Waikiki Beach *Devil's Workshop* store. Ralph however had a bothersome premonition about the soon-to-be arriving Hawaiian imported glass, even without consulting the aid of a prognosticating ocean cruise *Ouija Board*.

The following Friday morning, a bulky trunk arrived via *UPS* with the word "FRAGILE" heavily stamped upon it. Ralph immediately knew that the "special delivery" was the highly-anticipated stained-glass shipment from Hawaii. Parallel sturdy racks had already been built in the spare room to accommodate the glass color displays, and the shipped cartons were soon carefully opened.

Donna helped her husband in sorting-out and arranging the multicolored spectrum of wonderful stained-glass hues. Piece by piece, the couple gingerly placed each item into the vertical racks. The colors were gorgeous and intense, but some pieces were so unusual that they appeared absolutely unique within the sublime array that was on display. The next day, being inspired, Ralph would ambitiously initiate his first creation.

"Aren't these assorted specimens quite exquisite?" Donna marveled and declared. "Husband, I think you've finally found your true avocation."

"This looks like it's going to be much more exciting than canvas painting," replied the motivated husband. "My mind is definitely stimulated! I can't wait to get started."

While Ralph had been anxiously waiting all week for the stained-glass shipment to arrive, the artist-with-a-plan had made some preliminary window sketches. The sketched pencil illustrations were all of different designs. Some of the representations were of flowers, some were of buildings, some were of ships docked in port, and still others were of various people dressed in myriad attires. Ralph's natural ingenuity would certainly make each stained-glass "statement" an original work of art.

"Donna, what would you like my first exploratory endeavor to be? Think of something local."

"I believe you should do the first one featuring the ships in port," the wife aptly recommended. "I think *that* rendition would make a beautiful stained-glass design; one for a kitchen window."

"Fine and dandy, and thanks for offering your unbiased opinion. That's the one I'll do first," agreed her cooperative husband.

The pieces of glass which the artist selected were judged as being "perfect" for Ralph's first full-scale "window presentation". Aqua was chosen for the water, azure blue for the sky, and white and black for the two docked ships. Many other dazzling colors were chosen and used, and with meticulous precision, the preferred glass was carefully cut to the proper sizes as if each piece were an essential segment to a magnificent jigsaw puzzle. However, the tedious and arduous task absorbed the better part of the day. But Evans was a steadfast technician, and the determined fanatic managed to finish his ambitious goal by nightfall. Donna was quick to describe her husband's completed ship/port setting as "an incredible masterpiece".

The next evening, Ralph invited some neighborhood friends over to inspect and assess the newly-created stained-glass window. There were many "Oohs!" and "Ahhs!" exclaimed by the very impressed guests. The fascinated admirers couldn't believe the immense splendor represented in the craftsmanship of the recently produced window. Lagoon cul-de-sac neighbors Sam and Beth Epstein loved the art object so much that the couple offered to buy the product on the spot.

Ralph was agreeable to their generous proposition, and his first sale had been easily consummated.

Sam and Beth had the ship and port window installed, and the stained-glass item instantly became the gossip of the neighborhood. Almost every visitor to Sam and Beth's abode immediately transformed into a new stained-glass client, who then prodded Ralph into creating a novel, unique masterpiece "exclusively customized" for him or for her. One newly acquired customer was quite impressed with the preliminary sketch of two heavenly angels that Ralph had been designing for a Roman Catholic priest's rectory. Working late into the night, Evans' facsimile "dual angel" window had been expeditiously completed in a mere three weeks.

But the fortunate resident who had procured the "angelic window" was *not* often regarded in the housing development as a very friendly person. Many area residents disliked the obnoxious, arrogant, pugnacious individual bearing the dreaded name Robert T. Sullivan. Everyone in the neighborhood was sorry Sullivan had purchased Ralph's carbon-copy rendition of "Two Angels", haughtily bidding the highest price at Ralph's impromptu auction.

The stained-glass seraphim, both angels facing each other like the pair exhibited on the Old Testament Arc of the Covenant, were individually portrayed blowing into heavenly golden horns. Ralph had been reluctant to sell the elaborate design to his former antagonist and corporate rival, but the winning bid price was right, and Evans did not want "Todd" to know that *he* had deeply resented his despised adversary over the past three decades. "Let bygones be bygones," Ralph lamented to his understanding wife. "But Donna, I would've preferred selling that special design to someone possessing more morality and humanity than evil Robert Todd Sullivan!"

"You don't suppose that those pristine angels were signaling and summoning Bob Sullivan to Heaven?" the female jewelry-store-owner remarked and laughed. "That would be a remarkable irony."

"Don't be silly, Donna," her contrarian husband chastised in defense of his frail, fragile psyche. "The angels were blowing their trumpets to warn Bob that he'll wind-up in hell if he doesn't soon make amends for his countless misdeeds," Ralph chuckled. "I think the dual archangels represent a sort of prophecy!"

"Didn't Father Burns want that second window for his rectory?"

"Yes, Donna. And now because of Bob Sullivan's greedy nature, I'll have to think of a new, original religious theme for the Padre's rectory window," protested the husband. "Perhaps I can do Moses religiously holding the two famous Ten Commandment tablets on Mt. Sanai."

In the next six months, many sophisticated windows were competently and efficiently produced and quickly sold, and suddenly, Ralph Evans' former hobby/avocation was becoming a lucrative business enterprise. Each and every new rendering soon wonderfully evolved into a very special and expensive original. However, the most treasured and praised stained glass masterpiece was still the elaborate configuration of the two celestial angels prophetically sounding their trumpets (that had unfortunately been purchased at auction by Robert T. Sullivan).

* * * * * * * * * * * *

One Wednesday morning, when Donna was casually reading the *San Francisco Chronicle,* the wife was shocked by a frightening news headline. "Ralph, listen to this. Last night the suburban lagoon home of Robert Sullivan has been robbed and ransacked. The police claim that a destructive vandal had broken-in through a stained-glass window and had maliciously shattered it. The third-page article further states that Robert Sullivan is nowhere to be found. The police suspect that his disappearance is foul play."

"Unbelievable!" exclaimed Ralph. "Let me see *that* newspaper article! I can think of fifty people that would like to do harm to 'boisterous Bob'."

The phone rang just at that exact moment, and the now-unsettled artist slowly answered the call. The accomplished stain-glass window designer was staggered and speechless when the recipient learned the caller's identity.

"Ralph, this is Grace Sullivan," the caller stated in a melancholy tone of voice. "I guess you've already read about my husband. Our home was broken into last night. The punks, I assume there was more than one, came in through the stained-glass window, and it's been shattered into numerous pieces. Bob went downstairs to investigate a noise and now he's missing. The police are searching for him all over the *Bay Area.*"

"Gee, I'm very sorry to hear that, Grace," Ralph genuinely stated. "I was stunned when I learned about it from Donna just a minute ago. Is there anything I can do for you?"

"Yes, Ralph. The reason I called is to ask you if there is any way that the stained-glass window can be fixed," Grace Sullivan sobbed over the telephone. "I would feel much safer if the window could be repaired and reconditioned back into its original state!"

"I'll come right over and take a look at it. I'll see what I can do," Evans assured Grace Sullivan.

Ralph immediately trekked the quarter mile to Bob and Grace's opulent mansion situated on the opposite side of the scenic blue lagoon, and upon arriving, scrutinized and evaluated the extensive damage. Evans was happy to report some positive information to the very upset wife.

"Grace, fortunately the window had been shattered at the seams where it had been sealed with lead. Only several larger pieces of glass were actually broken-off, maybe a half dozen. I'll be able to repair it in a jiffy. But I believe the newspaper report was wrong," Ralph asserted. "I think the vandals must've broken into your home through another window or door and simply broke the window from inside just to be destructive. This whole thing looks like a case of malicious vandalism to me!"

The window frame was methodically removed and then carefully conveyed to Evans's home "workshop lab", where the necessary replacement pieces were very meticulously laid-out upon the spare room assembly table. The still-intact individual articles were then selectively inserted together inside the empty frame until the admirable dual angel window design had been fully re-created.

Before evening, the stained-glass replica had been brought back to the posh Sullivan residence. By the time Ralph had finished adroitly installing the new window frame, twilight had descended on Northern California.

"Thank you so much Ralph for your prompt consideration. It is greatly appreciated and quite comforting," Grace Sullivan gratefully acknowledged. "My mind is so out-of-sync about my husband's disappearance," the distressed wife added, bursting into tears. "Do you think that poor Bob has been kidnapped?"

"I only hope he shows-up in the area unharmed," intimated Ralph as the stained-glass artist attempted concealing his abundant vindictiveness for Robert T. Sullivan, all the while weakly hugging and consoling Sullivan's grieving spouse. "I'm sure your husband will turn-up somewhere! I'm certain the authorities will find him!"

Ralph Evans left the spacious Sullivan palace with a very rare guilty conscience. In the meantime, Mrs. Sullivan was about to flick-on the foyer lights to examine and amply appreciate the newly-installed stained-glass window.

Suddenly, Grace's living room landline telephone rang. "Mrs. Sullivan, this is Webster Daniels, the proud proprietor of the *Devil's Workshop Hobby and Craft Store*. How do you like your new window? Isn't it exquisite?"

A nerve-shattering, piercing scream was emitted from the throat of Mrs. Grace Sullivan. Ralph rushed back inside the rich man's castle to learn exactly what terror had caused the woman's hysterical shriek. Grace Sullivan had fainted from absolute fright, and the overwhelmed lady was lying prone on the living room's Oriental rug, her shock being caused after viewing her husband's facial image mystically appearing inside the stained-glass window.

At that haunting moment, Ralph's eyes got a good look at the repaired window, and what his pupils perceived positively terrified his psyche. A new image materializing inside the window had Robert Todd Sullivan very slowly transforming into a vague blur. Soon, the depiction projected from the stained-glass refocused; the window's new theme freezing into a rather more horrid appearance.

Instead of the two heavenly angels blowing into their long golden trumpets, there was exhibited an almost life-size image of Robert Todd Sullivan with heavy manacles encumbering his wrists and cumbersome chains shown around his chest and waist.

The other morbid figure that had just appeared in place of the second incomparable angel was that of horrific Lucifer, who displayed a cruel and satanic smile, which ornamented his grotesque-looking dark red face.

As Ralph's gaze remained transfixed at the image of Sullivan and his diabolical, hellish companion manifested inside the stained-glass window, the now-petrified eyewitness became aware of a scary new phenomenon. Whichever angle Evans' viewed his former chief corporate rival, Sullivan's stained-glass eyes followed him as the incredulous retired apparel designer stepped back and forth across the room to verify the 'supernatural visual hallucination'.

Ralph was even more aghast when the horrified spectator detected actual tears flowing from the remorseful eyes of the shackled, incarcerated stained-glass victim. Robert T. Sullivan's enslaved soul was fully aware of its hopeless eternity, mercilessly trapped inside an un-heavenly stained-glass window, as if the eternal victim were Jacob Marley reincarnated.

"The Image"

The end table's clock radio activated, and *Tommy Dorsey's* big band music awoke Robert and Alice Hartmann from their sound sleep. It was still steadily raining outside, and after the husband rose and rubbed his bleary eyes, Robert peered-out the bedroom window and instantly became disappointed, thinking that his scuba diving club would probably cancel the day's scheduled ocean outing. Despite the non-cooperation of *Mother Nature,* two-hours later Bob Hartmann and his best friend and diving buddy Leon Harper would still stubbornly arrive at the club's marina boat dock in the hope that the foul weather might eventually clear-up.

The thirty-six-year-old diving enthusiast worked as a purchasing agent for a large national bookstore chain. Bob's Mays Landing, New Jersey place of employment was not far from the defunct *Atlantic City Race Track* and the popular *Hamilton Mall*. Hartmann was tall, had black hair, and was extremely handsome. A dimple highlighted his left cheek, and it generally accompanied a captivating smile.

Alice Hartmann was an attractive brunette possessing a beautiful hourglass figure. The voluptuous wife was a wonderful cook who preferred preparing the day's ocean catch to laboring over the stove heating common, mundane supermarket food. But unlike her adventurous, athletic husband, Alice did not enjoy the excitement associated with scuba diving.

Bob had recently read a book obtained at one of his firm's area store's that dealt with psychic phenomena. The occult had always fascinated the active diving enthusiast. Since Hartmann's place of employment afforded the avid reader access to many selections in the *New Age* genre, the husband had become a devout student of the arcane, and was truly becoming quite knowledgeable in the subject.

Robert Charles Hartmann considered himself a novice scuba diver, having only one year's experience. But Bob always felt secure when underwater with intrepid Leon Harper, a very skilled underwater veteran. Leon was a tall dark-skinned confirmed bachelor, who sported a perfect suntan from numerous deep-sea fishing excursions, which accentuated and complemented his muscular Adonis-like physique. Leon was also a rugged outdoorsman, capable of calmly handling himself in virtually any given emergency. Bob felt very comfortable venturing-out on intriguing diving expeditions with Leon Harper acting as his trustworthy partner.

"Bob, do you think you'll be able to go out into the *Atlantic* today?" Alice asked. "It's really pretty miserable outside!"

"I just called Leon on the phone and my diving partner says there's a fifty-fifty chance that we'll be able to go out," her husband answered. "I gotta' admit that Mother Nature is fairly erratic today."

Bob Hartmann soon found himself in his *Ford Expedition* accompanied by all his coveted diving equipment: mask, scuba wetsuit, air tanks, underwater watch, knife, weights, fins, *May West* vest and snorkel. Hartmann was anticipating another successful club mini-expedition, if "the fickle atmospheric elements" would only extend some genuine cooperation. The adventurous man's diving squad rarely canceled a "summer drop", mostly because the members considered themselves dye-in-the-wool underwater explorers.

Hartmann drove his navy-blue *SUV* to Leon's small white stucco rancher in Pomona, picked-up his trusty companion, and next the affable pals were on their way to the mouth of New Jersey's *Mullica River,* where the club's diving ship was docked.

The persistent summer rain was finally letting-up, and as dawn filled the eastern horizon, both men observed that it was going to be a misty, foggy August morning. Fortunately, the river (and the bay into which it flowed) was relatively tranquil, despite the persistent early morning downpour.

"A few storm clouds can't deter our club from its objective," Leon typically bragged. "We'd bravely go-out into the ocean in a fierce northeastern if we had to!"

"You know it!" Harper aptly agreed. "The guys in our group aren't wimps. We would go underwater in a typhoon if need be."

The other scuba club members were waiting for the new arrivals inside the Chestnut Neck Marina's "nautical décor" restaurant. Coffee and doughnuts were always devoured for "good luck purposes" before the garrulous entourage would decide exactly where the club should conduct their next dive. An abundance of sunken shipwrecks dotted the *Atlantic's* continental shelf from Brigantine down to Cape May. Three-hundred-years of nasty "nor'easters", along with a number of violent torrential hurricanes have sent scores of vulnerable vessels sinking-down to visit *Davy Jones Locker.*

A number of ships had been sunk on the characteristic ever-drifting shoals situated near the New Jersey shoreline. Treasure hunters often risked life and limb descending the briny depths in quest of finding precious lost cargo. The strong *Gulf Stream* currents had battered the sunken hulls through the years, and in time most of the underwater wooden shells had eventually disintegrated. Poor under-ocean visibility had always hampered the steadfast efforts of scores of local amateur divers.

Every so often, ship debris or rare cargo relics from underwater wrecks would be washed ashore and deposited upon the sandy beaches, especially several weeks after a ferocious coastal tempest. Local maritime museums often displayed the memorabilia, along with a brief history of the discovered items' value, the name of the ship, the type of treasured cargo the vessel had been carrying, and a list of the lost seamen's names that the downed boat had aboard. Most coastal wrecks have been identified and classified, but not all are presently known. Occasionally, a new "ship bottom" is discovered in the nearby *Atlantic* by sheer accident; hence, the origin of the name of the nearby coastal town, Ship Bottom.

"Let's go inside the restaurant and talk some basic scuttlebutt with the boys," Bob Harper amiably suggested. "The guys look like they're all primed and ready for some serious action."

"Bob, some day you and me are gonna' make a great discovery," Leon predicted. "You and me are gonna' make *Atlantic City* and Chestnut Neck famous for something other than casino gambling and beer chugging."

A familiar huge map was displayed on a back wall inside the office of the popular marina's boat rental department. The chart accurately pinpointed the locations of all known offshore wrecks. Over four-hundred-and-fifty sunken hulls have been documented off the South Jersey coast, and different colored pins marked which century and decade each wrecked ship had once navigated the *Atlantic.*

Red pins indicated the seventeenth century, blue pins represented the eighteenth, orange pins the nineteenth and yellow pins signified the twentieth century. The various wrecks had been discovered anywhere from a few hundred yards offshore to a distance of over twenty-miles from the mainland. As a rule, Bob and Leon's diving club usually frequented skeleton hulls that were from six to ten miles out to sea. The usual depths were from ten to twenty fathoms (60 to 120 feet). Lobster and tog fish inhabited the newly formed sunken reefs, and the vulnerable sea creatures were often doomed easy targets for Leon's "lethal spear gun".

Bob Hartmann was more interested in ship artifacts than in Leon's favorite nautical pursuit, underwater hunting. However, the two made a compatible team, with each diver doing what he preferred while being a reliable sentinel for his trusted companion.

"Someday Robert," Leon facetiously began inside the Chestnut Neck Marina Restaurant, "I'm goin' to be the first human around these parts to have underwater hunting safaris. I'll pioneer a totally new industry!"

"If I ever find one of *Blue Beard's* legendary treasure ships, I'll use the booty to finance your first deep sea sightseeing expedition," Bob declared and laughed. "But if anyone can pull-off your wild and crazy dream, I predict it's gonna' be you!"

Every club member showing-up on that wet August morning finally boarded the sea-worthy diving ship. Before long the engines were started, and soon the reliable vessel was free of its mooring. That morning the lower atmosphere was very foggy and visibility remained poor. It was still drizzling as the boisterous local mariners' boat crossed the bay north of Smithville, heading in the direction of *Harrah's Casino* on Atlantic City's northern inlet. Fifteen-miles separated the club's current position from the alluring ocean. There was sufficient time to enjoy viewing the nearby Jersey coastline while heading south before the fifteen chatty crew members were to don their diving gear.

"Scuba diving is what I live for," Bob confessed to Leon. "It's definitely one of the finer joys of living, and it sure beats hustling silly romance novels up and down the East Coast."

"You said a mouthful and a half," agreed Hartmann's loyal partner. "Your avocation is actually my fantasy vocation."

The diving club's new objective was a known wreck situated twenty miles off the coast of Cape May. The men had never investigated that particular area before so, because of unfamiliarity, their expedition would be a novel encounter that suggested more than routine caution. The ship was equipped with "loran", which made their quest a relatively easy task to successfully locate a sunken vessel.

The fog and early mist were gradually lifting, and the determined "treasure pirates" were encouraged that their in-progress excursion would not be performed in vain. Ten-miles out to sea Bob was sitting in a chair next to the craft's knowledgeable captain. Hartmann and the old salt were preoccupied, conversing trivia while casually studying the fish-finder's readings. Since the scheduled mission was exclusively earmarked as a "wreck dive", it mattered little if the group located a school of hungry bluefish or meandering ocean shad.

The on-a-mission diving ship had to motor another thirty-five miles south of Atlantic City to finally approach their designated heading coordinates situated off the Cape May shore. Then, it would be twenty additional miles out to sea before the divers would finally rendezvous with their intended destination. Leon pulled-up a chair and sat next to Bob and the captain.

"Let's leave fishing for the fishermen," Hartmann suggested. "I just want to plunge to the sandy bottom and investigate what's there."

"But the rules automatically change if I spot a lobster," laughed Leon Harper as he intentionally showed-off by lifting and holding his fearsome spear gun into the air. "I might even shoot a white marlin or a wayward tuna if the opportunity happens to arise!"

Ninety-minutes later, while relaxing on "the bridge", Bob's keen perception soon noticed a dark fleeting 'image' being revealed on the dependable fish-finder screen. The lackadaisical captain had been momentarily preoccupied watching other dials and gauges on the "Out to Sea's" main console, and so the ship's navigator was not privy to Hartmann's most interesting observation.

The object Bob had glimpsed certainly was not a sea animal, and before Hartman could alert Leon about 'the image', all three men's attention had been momentarily diverted by the passing of a playful school of arching porpoises. The addled bookstore chain purchasing agent had a sudden strange feeling. Instinctively, Bob Hartmann diverted his eyes toward the same spot in the dark blue waves where he believed his pupils had seen the 'phantom screen image', or 'the mysterious shadow of a unique image on the fish-finder screen.'

Hartmann kept peering-down at the monitor, but the amateur aquanaut could not discern at *that* moment any distinct outline showing below the dark blue ocean. The chilling sensation that something enchanting had been remotely beckoning his attention remained in Bob's recollection throughout the balance of the day.

The designated, charted, sunken wreck was finally reached fifteen minutes later. The divers meticulously prepared their separate apparatus in order to commence a routine "ocean jump". The boat's depth-finder indicated that the water was one-hundred-and-ten-feet down to the sandy bottom, and even though there was still a sprinkle of rain, once in the water, atmospheric conditions no longer mattered.

When everything was decided as "go", Bob and Leon flipped backward over the port side and splashed-down into the seventy-degree salt water. The surface waves were clearer than usual, and as the two divers submerged, the ocean suddenly became colder, darker and certainly much more alien. Hartmann and Harper slowly and mechanically followed the taut metal anchor chain all the way down, and eventually their feet and flippers made contact with the ocean bottom. Twenty-minutes of precious oxygen could be consumed before each diver would have to surface.

The eerie outline of the wreck's anatomy was barely visible in the murky seawater. The unfortunate hulk of rust and metal was once a large European cargo ship that had encountered its demise in a wicked 1948 coastal hurricane. A half-century of thick seaweed growth clung to the sunken ship's gunwales, indicating that the remaining skeleton had become a good habitat for colonies of feeding fish. The little nooks and crannies of the newly-formed reef were excellent safe havens into which lobsters and crabs could safely nestle, their forms deftly hidden from the surveillance of hungry, on-the-prowl sea predators.

Several of the divers came prepared to capture seafood specimens, and those individuals eagerly searched for delectable shellfish prey and before long, many adult lobsters had been snatched and imprisoned in handy "capture bags". Leon had a rather challenging exploit which he was about to accomplish; that goal was pursuing and then capturing a fantastic twenty-seven-pound lobster, which was later voted by the club as the "coveted catch of the day". Bob had been Harper's assistant on the "off subject animal hunt", and while Leon was struggling with overpowering, lifting, and conveying the massive lobster, Hartmann's oxygen supply began running low, forcing him to surface.

Minutes later, Leon broke through the water's surface with each hand holding a large claw of the enormous sea creature. It wasn't long before "the monster" was placed in the holding tank with the other smaller crustaceans that had been gleaned from the ocean's bounty. The two friends were each imagining the sumptuous feast that the explorers and Alice Hartmann would merrily share that evening. Dining ecstasy was now guaranteed to be theirs for the taking.

Despite the capture of the mammoth lobster, Bob was still recalling the anomalous screen 'image', and his mind distinctly remembered the haunting feeling he had consciously perceived upon originally noticing the screen sighting. Soon, the diving ship hoisted its huge anchor, and the excited men departed to inspect another known wreck, which was located closer to shore.

"Bob, did you find any treasure down there while I was grappling with the giant lobster?" Harper asked his fellow diver. "Any gold doubloons or silver pieces of eight!"

"Just a few small trinkets that weren't worth salvaging," Bob sadly replied. "I was too engrossed watching your mammoth struggle with that monster lobster that I was fully distracted from *my* real reason for being down there."

"Well," returned Leon with a contented smile. "I finally managed to catch the lobster of all lobsters while I was actually searching for tasty crabs. At least I caught us a fine supper!"

The club's custom was to go on a deeper dive first, and then the members would practice a second descent into more favorable water closer to shore. A shallow dive preceding a deeper one could result in "the bends", where nitrogen bubbles could dangerously clutter and ultimately congest one's bloodstream and lungs.

The prospective second known wreck was much closer to the Cape May shore, and the sunken ship was located in the opposite direction from where Bob had witnessed 'the obscure image' on the captain's reliable fish-finder screen. Hartmann felt that no one except Leon Harper could or should be trusted with "the image story", because no one else onboard (except maybe the captain) would ever place serious credence in *his* fanciful claim.

"You can't always trust your five senses," opined and commented Leon. "Things can get distorted underwater; that's for sure!"

"You're right about that," Hartmann agreed and answered. "And that goes for above water, too! I guess it's time for a belated visit to the optometrist's office for the both of us!"

Bob and Leon spotted the familiar *Cape May-Lewes* ferry crossing *Delaware Bay* off in the distance; the transport was conducting summer tourists from one beach resort area to another. A half-hour later, the diving ship dropped anchor near the second wreck's charted position. Its depth was only ten fathoms.

The crewmen who were planning to participate in the dive noticed and commented that the water was "murky". The sunken hulk was that of a small "clammer" that had gone-down in a March storm during the first *Clinton Administration,* and its presence didn't really arouse or stir Hartmann's curiosity. Bob decided not to become involved in the group's "simple plunge" overboard. Instead, the distracted fellow desired scrutinizing the captain's map to pinpoint the exact coordinates where *he* had spotted 'the elusive image'. Leon's comrade soon carefully made a mental note of the precise coordinates identifying the object's general location.

The rain had now completely stopped, and the dark clouds had gradually separated, allowing shafts of glorious sunlight to beam-down upon South Jersey. The ocean was still somewhat passive, and the still-active scuba divers accomplished another successful foray. The expedition again spied and seized several dozen average-sized lobsters, along with a variety of edible fish. One lucky member caught a rare monkfish, commonly known as "all mouth", since the creature possessed such a huge and impressive set of jaws. The ugly sea denizen is very good eating, and the weird-looking fish is often referred to as the "poor man's lobster".

The conscientious divers all mustered on deck for an official head count, removed their gear, and soon the hunt club was heading back north along the coast to the *Mullica River*. The harvested lobsters and fish were democratically divvied-up and of course, Bob and Leon confiscated the prized gargantuan lobster, which later would be gingerly broiled to their palates' delight by Alice. Leon had always relished the savory meals that his "chef wife" carefully prepared, so to complement the upcoming supper to perfection, Harper intended to bring along a case of cold imported beer; the expert diner knowing full well that good brew and great lobster always made a most satisfactory combination for the trio's easy to satisfy appetites.

As the diving ship motored its way past the Atlantic City shoreline, the two congenial friends conversed about the day's splendid "surprise lobster catch", and then Bob and Leon conversed and reviewed the fun and camaraderie the pair genuinely shared while seriously working as a well-synchronized team.

On the walk from "the expedition boat dock" to the home marina's asphalt parking lot, Bob confidentially mentioned to his pal the dark "image" he had briefly spotted upon the diving ship's fish-finder. The two friends briefly discussed possible explanations.

Later that evening, after Hartmann and Harper had filled their stomachs with Alice's delectable gourmet meal, the tired explorers put a lid on the day. Leon left the Hartmann's residence and drove his red *Corvette* back to his isolated bachelor bungalow.

That night, Mr. Robert H. budgeted a few private minutes to further contemplate 'the image'. Its persisting mystery really bothered his avid curiosity. Hartmann knew that he would have to solve its puzzle to be at complete peace with himself. Perhaps Leon would accompany him on a singular investigative diving mission and assist in alleviating the odd enigma puzzling his mind, once and for all. Then, Bob certainly would feel more secure being in his dependable colleague's underwater company during 'the image's ocean investigation'. Quickly surrendering to exhaustion, Hartmann's consciousness gradually wandered-off into deep slumber-land.

* * * * * * * * * * * *

The following morning, occupational duty called. Robert Hartmann had to return to the rat-race work arena, but the diving enthusiast never complained one iota, since volumes of fascinating books would be surrounding him the entire day.

Another shipment of fiction was due for delivery to the busy Mays Landing "mother bookstore". Along with the fresh literature supply, a special collection of very old volumes had been purchased from an extensive, recently-dissolved, private library, and all of the new additions had to be systematically catalogued into the retail store's computer system. Many entries obtained from the liquidated estate dealt with metaphysics; an arcane subject that greatly intrigued

162

Hartmann. Bob removed several books having paranormal themes from the store's newly-acquired inventory, and secretly placed and kept the pilfered volumes inside his office safe, earmarking the literature for future leisure reading at home.

When the book authority's tedious-but-propitious office travails had been completed, it was already mall closing time. Hartmann opened his office safe, gathered-up the half dozen occult books he had borrowed, and then neatly arranged the literature in his black briefcase. While venturing home from Mays Landing, the driver's obsessed mind again contemplated 'the fascinating cryptic image aberration', which had sinisterly appeared on the ship's reliable fish-finding screen. The determined fellow was certain that he and Leon would return to the exact site. But it would require a calm, clear day, along with a gentle *Atlantic* current, before a fruitful revisit to the alluring Cape May sea canyon would be feasible.

The next three days Bob had been engrossed, reading the half-dozen *New Age* 'esoteric knowledge lit' books'. The researcher's susceptible mind had strangely been drawn into an obscure world that readily transcended his rather mundane, Monday-through-Friday 'boring job reality'. Hartmann's obsessed mind was now convinced that some remote supernatural influence had been luring him closer to the alien power of 'the enigmatic image', and his feeble will found the foreign phantom force to be almost indomitable. Bob's soul had also become magnetized to the obscure themes abounding in the new arcane literature, which obviously had solidly impacted and affected his overall judgment.

As aforementioned, Leon Harper was the only diver Hartmann could fully trust to accompany him on his frivolous diving quest, so the motivated pair made arrangements to engage in a joint dive the following weekend. Their clandestine sea enterprise would be conducted independent of the other club divers' knowledge, mostly because Bob knew that he would be the object of myriad jokes and abundant jesting about 'the ridiculous imaginary image'.

Alice had learned from Leon about the "sea manifestation" and confided to Bob that she also was very curious about identifying "the image", which her husband then adamantly maintained he had seen, and so Robert reluctantly consented to her requested permission to "tag along for the ride". Hartmann's wife offered that she would pack the lunches, and then Alice pleaded to her devoted spouse that she could also be of some practical assistance on Leon's popular fishing boat, "The Wreck of the Hesperus". Both men agreed with honoring Alice's proposal during a cellphone conversation. "Besides you Leon," Bob confided, "I wholeheartedly trust Alice more than any other human being on the planet."

"I'm really glad you said that," replied Harper. "Chauvinism has been on the decline since the 1960s. I wouldn't want your wife suing me for gender discrimination."

The mid-August date of the trio's scheduled expedition had arrived, and the fickle coastal weather again was less than satisfactory. The early morning downpour was worse than the previous Saturday's drizzle, when the diving club had intrepidly voyaged-out to the remote Cape May ocean trench. After sunrise, the mercurial air was warm, humid, and foggy. The water's sixty-five-degree temperature was much colder than the land's more tolerable reading of eighty-six. This new thermal air and water mix had created fog rising-up from the *Mullica River's* surface, which soon resulted in a rather gloomy, ghostly-type atmospheric sight.

The only observable good omen was the serene river water. Although Robert H. had originally promised himself that the clandestine expedition would only be initiated on a perfect summer day, his stubborn emotions prevailed over and transcended his normally sound logic. Hartmann's tremendous enthusiasm absolutely dominated his mind's weaker reason. The 'image quest' was going to be "a go" in spite of the bleak weather pattern.

Leon's seaworthy Wreck of the Hesperus was well-equipped to be equal to the rigors and demands of the well-conceived exploratory venture. The white boat's dual-motor inboards made it an extremely swift craft, and the powerful ocean cruiser was adequately appointed with a cabin, three bunks, a commode, and a stove. Now in late August, the noteworthy vessel was also sporting the presence of an ambitious three-person crew.

Dawn had finally shown her rosy face through an open patch in the overcast eastern horizon when the industrious triumvirate energetically boarded Leon's small cabin cruiser. Soon, the on-a-mission trio had briskly embarked on their clandestine boat passage across the meadowlands' bay heading toward the vast *Atlantic*. A few small dinghies were already bobbing out in the distant bay; the "early-bird fishermen" and accompanying crab trappers were cleverly taking full advantage of the incoming tide.

Bob kept checking the charts and monitoring the weather forecasts to smoothly expedite the ninety-minute voyage south to the Cape May Trench. Along the way, Hartmann's mind imagined that he was a contemporary *Amerigo Vespucci,* busily pinpointing and assessing virgin underwater territory. The passenger approximated that the general area of "the image sighting" was twelve and a half miles offshore, lying southeast of the historic Cape May lighthouse and the nearby Delaware Bay.

"Wouldn't it be more intelligent if we chased rainbows or packs of wild gooses?" Leon affably joked to his two alert companions. "How about looking for needles in haystacks? Or better yet, haystacks inside the eye of a needle!"

"Do you think I saw an optical illusion?" answered Bob, acting a bit offended by his buddy's facetious and skeptical remark.

"Bob, next time we vacation in Las Vegas, make sure we stay at *The Mirage*," acutely quipped Alice. "You seem to be big on spotting illusions and elusive phantoms."

Alice Hartmann faithfully heated a pot of coffee in the small below-deck galley, and then the three self-appointed mariners enjoyed refreshing cups of delicious java while soberly discussing the particular aspects of the dive's principal game plan. First, their initial task was to locate the exact same "elusive illusive spot". When Leon's expensive *Fiberglas* fishing boat finally approached the designated "Red Zone", Bob kept his eyes focused upon the trusty fish-finder readings. His preliminary study observed nothing irregular (or of any significance) as the somewhat-disappointed ocean mystery searcher impatiently sipped his third cup of coffee.

Leon kept the speedy boat skimming over the waves through the light fog, running at a conservative fifteen-knot pace. The skilled pilot adroitly avoided a few pieces of errant debris that had been floating in the *Atlantic* directly off the Ventnor shore. A length of flotsam could easily puncture a hole in the *Fiberglas* hull, or if hit, the propeller blades could get knocked out of alignment. Leon was a very competent captain (even in the early morning fog), and Bob and Alice felt almost invincible and completely safe under the illusion of Captain Harper's reputed navigational expertise.

The persistent, annoying, patchy fog continued to make visibility very poor. Although the air had cooled-off, the ocean environment was still inhospitably dismal and drizzling. Indeed, the general conditions certainly weren't the most desirable to allow for an opportunistic deep-sea dive. All the while, Bob kept his eyes shifting between the navigation chart, the fog, the reliable fish-finder, and the endless dark blue sea. Every two-minutes or so, Leon would blast the boat's horn to alert possible other craft in the vicinity of their presence.

The next three-quarters of an hour passed-by fairly quickly, and the *Wreck of the Hesperus* was slowly approaching the Ocean City offshore area. Leon informed his mates that the normal hour-and-a-half boat trip would now take three hours because of the unfavorable atmospheric conditions.

After passing by Wildwood, an hour later, the threesome hoped that a momentary bleep would appear on Leon's cabin cruiser's instrument reading, just as it had done on the diving ship's accurate fish-finder. The *Wreck of the Hesperus* slowly propelled through the targeted search zone, and the three persistent mariners kept their anxious pupils focused on the ultra-sensitive sonar equipment. But much to their dismay, nothing extraordinary was visible, and the realistic shadow of discouragement was rapidly invading Bob's diminishing spirit. Perhaps there was "no substance" to the cryptic shadow's existence, and Hartmann was beginning to doubt his own credibility.

"Maybe we should return home," Bob stated to his faithful companions. "This whole fiasco might be an ugly false alarm I've caused you two to participate in."

"Nonsense, dear Robert!" Leon objected. "You wave the white surrender flag too readily! If Columbus had felt the way that you do right now, the audacious Italian would've never made it past the *Rock of Gibraltar,*" answered the boat's supportive never-say-die captain. "Show me some good old-fashioned American perseverance."

"We're having a great time, even if nothing unusual happens," chimed-in Alice. "I still think that this search is pretty darned exciting! And I'm loyally supportive of Captain Leon's constructive opinion one hundred percent."

Another hour had elapsed with no positive signs of "the image". The trio poured another pot of perked coffee into their mugs, and the cruiser kept repeating its persistent circling of the suspected "image site". This time Leon took a wider turn in order to circumference a greater diameter. Ten-minutes later, Bob notified the others that he had seen something very interesting flashing onto the screen.

"I see it. I see it! Leon, stop the engines!" Hartmann ecstatically exclaimed. "There's *the image* sitting right before our very eyes!"

The boat roughly rocked and swayed back and forth upon the choppy water, its presence being directly over "the spot". The dark image dominated the monitor, and much to the wonderment of the three astonished passengers, the shady impression remained stationary on the screen. Bob, Leon, and Alice were absolutely astounded because the huge never-before-documented object was estimated being several hundred feet long. Whatever it was, the three would soon know its exact composition: "animal, vegetable, mineral, or strange thing".

Leon maneuvered his dependable craft, and then shut-off the dual engines about fifty-feet from and above the extraordinary, immense enigma. The two scuba divers were immediately inspired to descend and conduct their preliminary investigation, but the duo both felt a degree of apprehension about the mystery of whatever they might discover. Bob and Leon were happy that Alice had come along because she would stay topside and navigate the *Wreck of the Hesperus* in case dire emergency procedures would be needed.

The ocean bottom wreck, if it was indeed a wreck, had never been mapped or charted. Hartmann and Harper were elated when each Jacques Cousteau wannabe' imagined that *he* might be making a significant contribution to New Jersey maritime history by reporting and documenting *their* important ocean discovery.

What was awaiting the two adventurers at the sea's bottom? The men's intense desire to investigate the unknown soon superseded the natural fears that concurrently filled the daring aquanauts' hearts.

* * * * * * * * * * * *

Leon's stationary ocean cruiser incessantly bobbed up and down in the choppy waves. bouncing above the recently-found location of "the image". Hartmann and Harper were very animated as the enthused pair entered their wetsuits. Underwater flashlights would be essential tools, and the practical need for the indispensable devices had become paramount in each man's thrilled mind. Leon was always prepared for any diving emergency, and because of *his* partner's stellar reputation, Bob implicitly trusted Harper's underwater judgment. Wife Alice was glad that her less-experienced husband was accompanying such an accomplished underwater partner.

The anchor and its chain were dropped to simultaneously serve as a metal rope and a helpful guide. The exploratory search party had brought along eight oxygen tanks, so that the daring divers could repeat and complete their euphoric dual submergences. The supplemental tanks would allow the pair to thoroughly survey the bottom if two consecutive fifty-minute dives would be necessary. Each diver would require two canisters, and when one tank would be empty, the user could then easily switch over to his auxiliary air supply. Leon thought the entire search mission could be achieved in two dives.

"Well, *Jacques Cousteau,*" began Bob, "are you ready? The fog's clearing but it really doesn't matter under water!"

"As ready and as a focused as a horny buck during mating season," Leon smartly replied. "Let's start rutting!"Both sea adventurers spontaneously fell backwards over the side of the sleek cruiser and ecstatically plunged into the vast *Atlantic's* dark blue depth. Leon submerged into the deep with Bob obediently following.

The anchor rope was the men's utilitarian guide as the pair nervously tugged themselves nearer and nearer toward the bottom. Visibility was not as optimal as each would have liked. Halfway down the anchor chain, and still, each diver could only see no more than twenty-feet in all directions. The nebulous sea was almost as obscure as "the image enigma" that had now captured the determined friends' wild imaginations.

When the bold searchers reached the hundred-foot-deep sandy bottom, the sea wanderers saw nothing unusual. The twosome then swam around in a semi-circle in quest of locating the unknown captivating mass. The men's hearts were wildly pounding with anticipation as the divers moved their frog flippers quicker, advancing southwest, and vigorously swimming closer toward their suspected objective. Suddenly, Leon perceived the outline of an enormous silhouette lying in the distance, and as Harper and Hartmann cautiously swam closer to the huge hulk, Bob imagined that a plump sperm whale had been taking a nap on the ocean floor.

Leon and his entranced diving companion momentarily paused to gain a better perspective of their quarry. The perceived object was so colossal in size that the astonished observers had to emotionally assess its true identity before gaining the courage to swim any closer. The inquisitive aquanauts then warily swam alongside the dark, ominous, metallic form until the amazed friends had finally fully circled it.

The mammoth structure had certainly been man-made because "the image" had a symmetrical cucumber shape. The divers weren't sure of its origin or composition until the scuba searchers gazed upon a large but barely distinguishable marking that had been painted on the sunken vessel's right side. The symbol was a *Swastika,* and the frightening representation verified the existence of a sunken German submarine, an authentic *WWII* U boat.

During the destructive *War,* Nazi submarines had regularly visited the proximity of U.S. shores. The subs often stalked cargo ships and tankers, and often deliberately followed their intended prey onto the slope of the continental shelf. When a merchant ship was detected by sonar, a treacherous *U-boat* would surface, and the sub's captain would then up the vessel's periscope, and next the German crewmembers would violently torpedo the unwary target. Hundreds of innocent lives were lost in such swift, devastating Atlantic Ocean surprise attacks. The local stretch of beaches in the early *1940s* were frequently deluged with grease and oil, and eventually, the bodies of merchant marine nautical victims would wash ashore. Such was the wicked consequence of many innocent commerce vessels, along with their ill-fated crews, in that historic and destructive 1940s decade.

A number of concrete observation towers had been constructed along the New Jersey and Delaware coasts, but the elusive German submarines were rarely detected as the stealthy vessels conducted clever underwater surveillance so close to shore. The wily Nazi captains had developed some very sly methods to avoid detection. One shrewd tactic was to lay in wait on the sandy bottom and furtively position the sub' next to one of the hundreds of sunken wrecks. This wily practice made identifying the presence of a German submarine extremely difficult for the *Coast Guard* and for reconnaissance blimps being flown out of upstate Lakehurst. 'Remember the Hindenburg', Hartmann though as he swam very near the sunken German sub.

Bob and Leon were still quite awed at discovering an uncharted German *U-boat*. Over fifty-years had elapsed since the submarine had buried itself in its obscure watery grave. Mass colonies of barnacles had naturally attached to the sub's exterior, and seaweed and marine vegetation also instinctively utilized the newfound, splendid convenience, the recently created artificial reef.

Bob and Leon had already been submerged along the ocean floor for twenty-five minutes, so it was then time to flip the switches to activate their essential auxiliary oxygen tanks. After completing that perfunctory task, the euphoric divers were now guaranteed another twenty to twenty-five minutes of curiosity-seeking, during their extended, fantastic underwater investigation.

As the two "human fish" keenly scrutinized the massive hull, there appeared to be little evidence of external physical damage. The absence of any gaping holes negated the possibility of any internal torpedo or engine explosion. The sub's overall composition appeared to be completely intact, so following his basic impulse, Leon garnered enough fortitude to touch the side of the sub'. The metallic surface was slimy from its long tenure resting beneath the salty sea.

The awed adventurers next began slowly swimming along the top of the ominous-looking *Nazi* sub'. Luckily, an entrance hatch was soon located, but the access portal was still shut tight as a drum, encrusted in a thick layer of green and orange rust. A blowtorch would be needed to effectively loosen and free the hinged lid.

Both men anxiously desired gaining entrance for the purpose of inspecting the sub's interior, but *that* wishful goal could not be attempted on *that* particular dive. The enthralled divers had exhausted their valuable forty-five minutes of precious oxygen, and even if the adamant aquanauts had miraculously opened the stubborn rust-encrusted hatch, there would not have been sufficient time to even partially examine the ship's alluring compartments.

The out-of-oxygen men decided to surface, rest, and then make an all-important second dive as soon as they could. Since the sub was at a depth of one-hundred-feet, it was critical that the two wait several hours to allow accumulated nitrogen bubbles to escape their fragile blood streams. Then, another exploratory dive could be safely tried.

After the temporarily fatigued ocean sleuths had ascended and climbed onto the boat, Alice curiously interrogated them about what special phenomenon had been discovered. The woman was quite elated after listening to the ensuing discussion. Leon's Second Mate could not control her very animated exuberance.

"Bob, are you sure of what you saw down there?" the wife asked. "This sounds like an historic find!"

"Alice, I'm as sure about seeing a Nazi sub' as I'm certain I'm talking with you this very moment," Hartmann panted with conviction. "My eyes didn't hallucinate or deceive me. And neither did Leon's!"

It was now after 11:30 a.m. and as Leon and Bob were taking-off their depleted oxygen tanks, Alice had recovered from her temporary stupor and was setting some lunch sandwiches, hot soup, and steaming coffee on the tiny table inside the small galley. The trio soon reviewed the incredible find and how the lucky divers would manage conducting their prospective second dangerous search of the mystery submarine's internal chambers. Leon had taken a variety of useful tools that could be functional during the greatly anticipated second diving caper. An underwater blowtorch, which Harper occasionally used for strategic repairs, was then cautiously removed from a side storage cabinet.

The sub's unknown past promoted a great deal of speculation that naturally influenced the general upbeat tone of the threesome's fluid conversation. Hartmann and Harper conjectured that gruesome human skeletal remains were possibly still floating-around inside what constituted a cold, aquatic, metallic cemetery. During the ongoing dialogue, the cruiser's twin speakers emitted low, easy-listening background music, but the suave rhythms could not alleviate the trio's heightened apprehensions pertaining to their recent major discovery. No radio station lyrics could relax their jangled nerves and their reinvigorated spirits.

A *Coast Guard* weather alert reported that two swift-moving storms were converging on the *Baltimore Canyon* coastal area, just southeast of Cape May. Wind gusts would cause excessive, rough sea waves, and small-craft-warnings would soon be in effect. Such summer flash precipitations were a common occurrence along the famous Jersey shore, and being a discerning sailor, Leon knew that the ocean-worthy *Wreck of the Hesperus's* crewmembers would have to immediately react with dispatch.

Only three short hours remained before the encroaching western/southern gusts would unleash their merciless fury on *that* aforementioned, vulnerable section of the *Atlantic*. Little time would be available for important academic investigation, so desiring to be on the safe side of caution, reasonable Captain Harper unilaterally decided that the next *extended* dive would have to be delayed and safely conducted at a later date.

But another cursory dive was still possible. The new sets of dual tanks were swiftly strapped-on, and the second alluring ocean descent was now imminent. Leon carried the blowtorch and other vital tools needed to execute the team's second phase of operation. Bob held and carried additional utilitarian tools; a pair of flashlights and two salvage bags brought-along to hold various *WWII* vintage artifacts that might be found. The very ordinary smaller bag would contribute its worth as being an important property on the second daring dive, but Bob Hartmann's imagination never speculated exactly how significant the smaller salvage bag would actually become.

* * * * * * * * * * * *

It was now about 2:00 p.m. when Leon and Bob donned their diving masks to bravely attempt their second dive. The approaching storm gales were paramount in the men's stubborn minds, but the pair was motivated by their parallel obsessions to enter and assess the guts of the extraordinary sunken *Nazi* sub'.

"Do you have your crowbar and blow-torch?" Bob asked his veteran diving partner. "But don't' expect me to use them!"

"Sure do. What about your big and small salvage bags?" Leon inquired. 'They might come in handy."

"I have them right here," Hartmann indicated with his head nodding towards his hands.

"Are you ready to pay a visit to old King Neptune, alias Emperor Poseidon?" Leon asked his diving companion. "He's supposed to be down there somewhere with his trident."

"If he's home, I hope the sea-god gives you a gentle poke in the rear end with his sharp, three-pronged fork!" replied Hartmann in an effort to alleviate the very apparent tension the two men felt. 'That encounter should represent your own personal *Poseidon Adventure!*"

Then, the amused divers simultaneously inserted their mouthpieces and together again tumbled backward into the navy blue *Atlantic*. Leon and Bob cautiously followed the taut guideline down to the anchor that was still firmly embedded in the ocean floor. Not wasting a precious second, the pair swam in the direction of the sunken sub', and moments later, visually and vaguely ascertained its exact position. After locating and verifying their bearings on Leon's wrist compass, the treasure-hunters very deliberately flipped their feet and propelled their way toward the encrusted entry hatch.

The blowtorch was quickly lit, and Leon expertly heated the hatch's rim. Meanwhile, Bob used a large wrench to forcefully bang on the crust-laden handle, and then the mission assistant strongly pounded upon the metal object several times with his hammer. The portal entrance didn't budge an inch as the external disturbance caused an excess of brine and rust to drift upward. Leon continued to heat the implacable object with the scorching blow-torch, and Bob was persistent in repeating his continuous hammer slamming.

Eventually, the handle moved ever so slightly, and after a few more severe jolts had been administered by Bob's mallet, the hatch offered the interlopers only a little more resistance. Using all the strength their bodies could muster, Harper and Hartmann were able to slowly rotate the corroded handle.

Leon knew that the hatch rim still had to be heated a tad more, and soon the hinged lid could be successfully pried-open, deftly employing the useful crowbar. From previous research about obsolete submarines, Harper knew that the aperture would lead to a tight holding area that would be sealed-off from the sub's interior. The hatch (like all its counterparts) had been an emergency escape route for the German crewmen if its utilization were ever needed. Certainly, the lid would be used if the harried seamen had to quickly abandon their underwater vessel, and naturally, only a single sailor could slip through the narrow, cylindrical, vertical tunnel one at a time.

Leon methodically swam into the narrow enclosure, and then Bob imitated his friend's audacious example. Five-minutes later, the second hatch leading to the inside compartment was finally forced open, and Leon slowly and warily entered the accessed freed space. Once fully inside the sub', Harper, waving his flashlight, tacitly signaled Bob to tail his path closely behind.

The center of the sub' was already filled with corrosive salt water, so the two American visitors could easily swim from section to section with little difficulty. Bob rejoined Leon, approaching from the rear, and the bright beams from their powerful flashlights illuminated the German sub's formerly secret interior.

Since the *U-boat* had not been extensively damaged, its hull had remained mostly intact; the Nazi vessel had taken months (and maybe years) for the seawater to seep inside, and then gradually flood the innermost recesses. Some air pockets were still trapped inside the upper extremity of several compartments, which were now in the process of being comprehensively investigated. Neither trespasser had ever before been inside a sub', and both Leon and Bob were unaccustomed to maneuvering inside the very cramped quarters, which initially hampered their general mobility.

Space economy was 'a necessary given' in *WWII* naval submarine accommodations. The main compartment soon was discovered near the sub's center, and using beams from their flashlights as guiding beacons, the dauntless explorers paddled their way toward the vessel's periscope area. Upon shining their respective searchlights around the immediate perimeter, the apprehensive intruders were terrified and shocked by what their disbelieving eyes witnessed.

Several macabre skeletons wearing tattered German naval uniforms were eerily floating around above the metallic floor. The investigating divers had to overcome their instinctive horror, and it required several minutes for the two valiant encroachers to catch their breaths and realistically adjust to the new morbid reality.

After the interlopers recovered from the terror of the all-too-gruesome sight, Harper and Hartmann very deliberately began intensely surveying what their eyes and bodies had just accessed. The divers expected to observe more of the same morbidity as their undaunted expedition continued onward into the remaining chambers of the silent, cadaverous underwater mortuary.

Continuing forward to another more remote section, the fearsome twosome found a portal that then led to a smaller compartment, which had been the *Nazi* sub's radio room. Leon proceeded to explore the fallen-upon section until Bob was able to swim into the radio room's narrow opening to join his mate. Inside, the divers noticed additional uniformed skeletons of *Nazi* officers and associated subordinate sailors. One particular corpse was eerily still sitting in front of his communications' panel. His bony hands appeared to be arranged in what Leon interpreted as 'a futile last prayer formation'.

Bob hastily scanned the macabre room utilizing his powerful flashlight. The diver then pivoted and exited the enclosure and hastily swam down the narrow corridor to further investigate some other ancillary compartments. Hartmann nervously made his way down the dark, sinister passageway when a foreign feeling instantaneously enveloped his thought processes. Some inexplicable alien influence was strongly drawing his emotional awareness back toward the funereal radio room.

Hartmann recollected the *New Age* paranormal books he had been curiously reading, so his fertile, rampant imagination began to overwhelm his normally objective temperament. Bob carefully veered around, and his frogman form obediently followed his flashlight beam, again proceeding in the direction of the still-spooky radio room. The attracted diver was becoming increasingly neurotic about reentering the former *Nazi* communications' sanctuary, which was now a horribly detestable spectral grave, ominously situated inside a totally ghastly, underwater Nazi morgue.

Bob shined the light around the ghostly enclosure, and nothing appeared to be out of the ordinary except for the frightening skeleton still sitting stationary behind the metallic communications' desk. Leon had already evacuated the radio room, and Hartmann was temporarily left all-alone to search for valuable plunder. A large gold and silver cross had been observed dangling around what remained of the former human being's neck. The diver decided to remove and confiscate the rare jewelry piece to keep as a coveted souvenir.

The frightening figure's bony hands were then gently separated in a very prudent manner. That activity by Hartmann unveiled a sealed cigarette case, which had been concealed under the grim-looking corpse's meshed fingers and hands. Bob, then under duress, collected both items into the diver's small salvage bag.

As the still-stunned "frogman" further surveyed the creepy radio room, his astute eyes focused on a small safe that had still been locked after five decades of underwater tranquility. Hartmann's curiosity greatly intensified his desire to search the safe's compartment for possible important identification documents. Several hard hits with his hammer sprung open the latch to the waterproof safe. Inside was a well-preserved leather wallet. The salvager marveled that the item had survived intact for a full half-century, and that the pouch still remained in near-excellent condition.

The wallet, too, was carefully placed into the small collection bag, along with the golden cross and the exquisite cigarette case. Bob was now thoroughly elated in that Hartmann speculated that the waterproof safe might also contain documents that would provide relevant information about the history of the intriguing sub', including its ill-fated crew. A sealed parcel was expeditiously removed from the safe, and the alert diver cautiously slid the new sample into the larger salvage bag.

Leon soon rejoined his totally-awed companion, and Harper motioned for Bob to trail *his* route through other undetected segments of the remarkable, well-preserved German sub'. Every compartment revealed frightening skeletons with uniform ranks ranging from *Seaman* to *Captain*. The divers' high-grade flashlights had revealed over sixty crewmembers that were counted in all, eight of whom were identified as officers.

The two gallant explorers in unison switched-over to their auxiliary oxygen tanks. The pair would only be able to stay submerged another twenty-five minutes. Each diver collected dog tags from around the skeletal necks of several unfortunate long-dead crewmembers. These personal effects were transferred into Bob's larger retention bag to accompany the sealed leather parcel that had already been pilfered from the safe.

Several pistols were also found, and Hartmann imagined that each weapon would make a great collectors' item. The handguns were quickly confiscated and then entered into the front of the larger retention bag, which by that time had become crammed and quite heavy, even under water.

Bob gestured to Leon that it was time to transport the acquired memorabilia up to the surface because their indispensable oxygen supplies were running low. The sub' was starting to creak and shift slightly on its sandy base, and the movement caused the divers to incidentally collide inside the tight chamber; the slow shift being a sure sign that the turbulent ocean storm was then announcing its rude appearance up on the surface.

The divers, through hand gestures, decided that their mission could return to 'the great find' when their future exploration would be less hampered by the threat of nature's violence. Bob tightly clutched the small salvage bag containing the wallet, cigarette case, and cross, and his left hand signaled to Harper his intent to hurriedly evacuate the sinister sub'.

Bob Hartmann exited the sunken *U-boat* first, and his exit was trailed by Leon, who seconds later closed the outside hatch so that ocean sharks or area octopuses wouldn't penetrate inside. One by one the men commenced their slow ascents to the surface. The sea's currents were quite erratic, and when the divers' heads finally broke through the choppy salt water, *their* nostrils were in great anticipation of again breathing fresh air.

The nasty summer storm was beginning to show its mounting rage. The exhausted duo experienced great difficulty swimming the short twenty feet back to Alice and the bobbing cabin cruiser.

At that moment, Alice Hartmann was in a state of near panic. The wife had feared that the recreational fishing boat's constant gyrating had the force to dislodge the rocking craft's anchor from the ocean's sandy bottom. Leon's cruiser was then turbulently rocking up and down, and the wife couldn't wait until the immediate motion crisis would be resolved. Her anxiety would not be allayed until both her husband and Leon were again safely aboard the *Wreck of the Hesperus*.

When the divers' reached the swaying boat, the duo didn't hesitate to awkwardly clamber-up the side steps and clumsily plop aboard. The anchor was immediately lifted, and the dual engines started. Before long, the three fortune hunters were on their homebound heading, traveling north along the coast, back to the welcoming mouth of the *Mullica,* but first the swift boat had to navigate past the barrier tourist islands of Wildwood, Ocean City, and Atlantic City.

The nasty August storm exhibited wind gusts of over fifty miles an hour, and being an experienced licensed sea captain, Leon was able to deftly pilot the *Wreck of the Hesperus* safely back to its familiar Chestnut Neck port. With the wild winds swirling, Harper had some trouble maneuvering the cabin cruiser into its assigned marina slip, but as soon as he succeeded, Bob and Alice tied the boat's ropes securely to the sturdy moorings. Mrs. Hartmann had gotten seasick during the rocky excursion back to Chestnut Neck Marina, and she (like her companions) was thoroughly soaked from enduring the pelting rain. All three survivors then leaped one at a time off the cabin cruiser onto the marina pier. The trio was indeed relieved to be back once more walking on good old terra-firma.

The very daring dives had been a massive achievement, but the treasure hunters knew that an additional expedition would be necessary to fully accomplish their main objectives. In his awkward haste, Bob had inadvertently left behind the larger rescue bag containing the dog tags, the pistols, and the parcel, and possibly also containing *Nazi* identification papers, all left either inside or in the underwater vicinity of the sunken submarine. Hartmann regretted that he had panicked and had reactively dropped the bigger recovery bag when the sub' had unexpectedly shifted on the ocean floor, the sudden movement caused by the strong storm currents occurring above.

When Bob and Leon had collided, the two had become temporarily tangled, and Hartmann had accidentally released the bigger salvage bag from his grip. The sack would possibly be vital in determining the true identities of the deceased German sailors that had been trapped for decades inside the doomed sub'. The friends promised to each other that the *U.S. Government* would not be notified until after *they* had finally retrieved their very relevant larger salvage bag booty from the sunken metallic cemetery.

"We'll contact the *Pentagon* after we've had first dibs," Bob stated on the storm-ridden drive back to the Hartmann's home. "Alice, you are my witness!"

"I endorse your position wholeheartedly," agreed Leon. "The Feds' will take over the whole operation and just send us a standard form thank you memo' through the mail."

"Next time we go out, I want to don a wetsuit, too," laughed a totally drenched Mrs. Alice Hartmann. "I nearly died from fright when the storm was wildly raging, and you two absurd clowns were moronically searching for trivial trinkets. Truthfully, Guys, I think I'd rather die from drowning than to die from fright!"

The cigarette case, the wallet and the golden cross from the small recovery bag were soon to play an extraordinary part in changing Bob Hartmann's formerly-monotonous life, but the novice historian never once suspected for a single moment that the three special items would have any serious, dramatic consequences.

* * * * * * * * * * * *

Bob and Leon had truly endured a very grueling underwater adventure, so Hartmann got on the horn and called his company boss and informed the chief executive that he intended to use his final week of allotted vacation time for much-needed rest and relaxation. Later that day, the incentivized divers agreed via telephone that the following morning would be the ideal time to closely examine (with clear minds) the leather wallet, the charming cigarette case, and the beautiful golden cross. Itinerant Leon Harper promised to be present at the Hartmanns' abode for an early dinner. After supper, the diving colleagues and curious Alice would open the smaller bag and together evaluate the confiscated contents.

"Make sure you don't peek beforehand," Leon facetiously commanded his interested comrades. "Curiosity is what killed the cat, and his brothers and sisters too, ya' know!"

"The suspense will be killing me, but I promise I won't be murdered," Bob cutely answered with a smile. "But Leon, there's only so much procrastination that I can tolerate!"

Alice Hartmann always had an entrepreneurial spirit, ever since she had graduated from nearby *Hammonton High School*. The Honor Roll student had owned a prosperous dress shop inside the *Trump Taj Mahal Hotel Casino* on the Atlantic City Boardwalk, but Bob's wife later sold that thriving enterprise to a wealthy buyer for a huge profit. The energetic businesswoman then had rented space for a large "Contemporary Boutique" in the nearby Mays Landing *Hamilton Mall*. But it was Alice's newfound sense of romantic adventure that effectively tore her away from her flourishing retail clothing establishment to again desire voyaging on the notorious *Wreck of the Hesperus* into the deep ocean off of Victorian Cape May.

"I can't wait to return to Cape May Point again," prefaced the wife at the dinner table. "And just the thought of that German sub' is more exciting than winning the *Pick 6 Lottery*."

"You mean more exciting than winning the big lottery three fantastic times in a row," Alice's husband gleefully clarified. "Money somehow loses my interest and pales when compared to pursuing *our* major secret discovery."

Mrs. Hartmann had prepared her favorite dinner of thick pork chops, nutritious vegetables, and then baked apple pie for a sumptuous dessert. The two deep-sea prospectors and Alice Hartmann were pretending to be very relaxed, but all three were nervously awaiting the examination of the golden cross and the by now dry contents of the wallet, along with the German cigarette case.

The large, green, velvet tablecloth had been cleared, and the three diners entered into the Hartmanns' cozy den. The recently found artifacts were gently removed from the small salvage bag and carefully deposited upon the den's main table. The cigarette case had a mother-of-pearl lid, which still remained snapped shut. The back of the case was inscribed in German: "To Karl, with love always, from Ruth— April 25, 1944." Bob then cautiously opened the elegant case.

"This is sort of like opening *King Tut's* tomb," Leon marveled and opined. "I wonder what's inside?"

"Let's hope it's not cursed like that Egyptian Pharaoh's crypt was," Bob cutely answered. "And please make sure there's no hieroglyphic scribbling that might represent some kind of heinous, taboo curse!"

The three amateur "historical archeologists" were surprised to find no disintegrated cigarette remains inside the airtight case. Only a zodiac medallion and two amazingly still-dry photographs were kept inside. The neck medallion was made of authentic gold with a "ram" engraved on one side. On the reverse side was the accompanying word *Aries,* and the inscribed birth date indicated as April 19, 1924.

The cigarette case's first small photograph was that of a German Naval officer. It had been taken at a *Bremen Naval Academy* graduation, with the main building of the institution being shown in the background. The very personal pictures made the three viewers simultaneously gasp. Astoundingly, the seaman's *image* depicted in the photo' looked exactly like Alice's husband. The resemblance was so remarkable that the German sailor and Bob Hartmann could have been identical twins living in different decades.

"This bizarre coincidence is totally incomprehensible!" Alice incredulously exclaimed. "Bob, are you the reincarnation of this German sailor who lived and died over a half century ago? Is this conspicuous picture some sort of anachronism?"

"Our similarities have got to be stranger than fiction," Hartmann affirmed and verified. "It's way beyond paranormal. To tell you the honest-to-God truth, I don't know exactly what to call it!"

The second small snapshot was that of the sailor's wife standing alongside three small children, two of whom were boys. The comely woman had attractive light-shaded hair, which in black and white film was presumed to be blonde.

Bob intensely studied the second black and white photo' and then again contemplated the first picture for a few seconds. "The poor woman had never seen her sailor husband again," Hartmann concluded and shared. "*The German Naval Department* must've notified the wife that her husband had been missing at sea and was believed to be dead." Bob then paused for a moment to further gather his random thoughts. "I guess that the lady would probably now be in her middle to late seventies," Hartmann conjectured to his wife and friend. "She might still be alive!"

"Or maybe she's also dead," declared Leon to balance optimism with pessimism as was his natural habit, being a staunch Libra.

Two additional smaller pictures were also nestled inside the compact cigarette case, but an accompanying notecard descriptively revealed the names of the wife and children. Bob made note of the obtained data, jotting the pertinent information onto a journal's spiral pad, and then the writer returned the shocking *images* back inside the attractive case having the mother-of-pearl lid. In addition to the photos' and small hand-written card, Hartmann also inserted the golden *Aries Medallion,* dated April 19, 1924.

The dark-brown grain wallet was the next focus of attention set for examination. Hartmann was very deliberate in opening the billfold, since the expensive leather was over fifty-years old and could easily crack with ordinary handling. Inside was contained four folded *German Marks,* still existing in excellent condition. Some personal credentials were also found. The official *Nazi ID* card indicated that the man had been a "*Seaman First Class*" and was certified as a qualified radio operator. The latter *ID* had been signed by *Admiral Karl Doenitz,* but the *Seaman's* name listed upon the document had faded, and unfortunately was illegible.

However, a second identification card found inside the wallet disclosed the name Karl Kraus, who had lived in Saarbrucken. Kraus's blood type was listed as "O negative". Bob then prudently and delicately tucked everything back inside the retrieved *WWII* era billfold. Hartmann next placed the "leather parcel" back into the small salvage bag alongside the cigarette case containing the German photographs and the lustrous *Aries Medallion.* Next, the trio examined the last of the retrieved items.

"Look at this stunning gold and silver cross. It must be worth a mint!" Alice Hartmann observed and verbally concluded. "It's absolutely magnificent!"

"Yes; that cross is the most beautiful of its kind I've ever seen," Leon added. "You're right, Alice. It's quite magnificent, that's for darned sure."

The outstanding relics obtained from the *Nazi* submarine had stimulated the three history buffs to want to again revisit the site of the sunken *U-Boat*. Bob strongly desired to retrieve the *large* salvage bag, which held the pistols, dog tags and the large sealed parcel that had been purloined from the vessel's safe. The three submarine scouts also agreed that they would contact the *U.S. Government* right after two members of "the triumvirate" would make and complete one last exhilarating dive down to the sunken German submarine.

* * * * * * * * * * * *

While waiting for the next clear day, Bob Hartmann visited the *Oyster Creek Marine Shop* to purchase a new valve for his "lucky" archaic oxygen tank. The more advanced "time economy valve" would have a novel feature, which would add a valuable three-minute reserve to the main air supply. A simple pull up on the lever would activate the "new unit attachment", and Robert Charles Hartmann planned to use the special device on the next crucial dive where three more vital minutes could mean the essential difference between life and death.

By Wednesday, the overcast clouds had finally dispersed, and radiant sunshine was again filtering-down through the clear blue sky. Alice excitedly accompanied her husband and Leon onto the *Wreck of the Hesperus*. It was established that the second mate would stay on board and control the ocean cruiser while the divers pursued and hopefully completed their next fascinating mission. Soon, the appropriate gear had been promptly loaded onto the boat's deck.

Leon started the dual engines, and soon thereafter, Harper piloted his pride and joy out of the *Chestnut Neck Marina* and then eased into the serene *Mullica,* and within minutes, the splendid craft was entering *Great Bay.* While the mentally-focused trio was zipping across the channel, the three observed the new skyline of Atlantic City; each separate tower indicating a brand-new popular casino-hotel.

The bay transit took twenty-minutes, which gave Bob ample time to attach the new "time extension valve" to his "lucky" archaic oxygen tank. Hartmann was planning to only use one tank, since his goal was that he simply had to retrieve the *large* storage bag, which he had accidentally dropped and left behind. The resolute diver also wanted to test the new valve with its three extra minutes of oxygen to non-scientifically conduct his own "personal academic experiment." The "air economy valve" was a little different in appearance than the

180

original "ancient one", but the self-confident assembler was certain that he had connected it properly.

"Is that valve patented?" Leon wondered and inquired. "I don't want to see you using some quack invention developed by an area *crackpot* professor doped-up on either crack or pot."

"I don't know. Marty over at *Oyster Creek Marine* claimed it's guaranteed to work, or I'll have my money back, if I should die."

Soon, the speedy *Wreck of the Hesperus* had crossed the meadowlands bay, and after skirting several low water areas identified by channel markers, the jubilant explorers were approaching a familiar landmark, the old fish factory, which for years had processed fertilizer and also distributed bait to area fishing supply outlets. Next on the local itinerary was the familiar *Coast Guard Station,* where the fresh water bay inlet and the salty *Atlantic* met. The channel buoys were closely followed into deeper water as Leon changed the boat's course to a southern heading.

The Brigantine shoals were then passed, and many unfortunate ships had grounded or had sunk around *that* hazard during severe shore thunderstorms. The *Wreck of the Hesperus* swiftly and safely passed the shallow, dangerous area, which was then followed by passing *Gardner's Basin Marina* and soon the string of high-rise casinos stretching along the northern coast of Atlantic City, which made impressive picture postcard scenery. However, neither sightseeing nor gambling happened to be the principal objective of the day's more serious ocean excursion.

"Honey, if your new mall 'Boutique' ever goes bankrupt, you could get a decent job as an '*Anchor*' woman on the local TV news," Bob boisterously jested and laughed. 'I believe you most certainly now have adequate anchor experience."

"Don't worry! My new store will never go out of business as long as I'm *at the helm,*" Alice playfully joked back.

"I can't at all *fathom* the gist of this absurd conversation," inserted and humored Leon as the captain navigated the sleek *Wreck of the Hesperus* past the northern end of the world-famous *Atlantic City Boardwalk* and the city's historic *Steel Pier*.

"Do you know exactly what you're doing on this voyage?" Harper loudly yelled to his first mate.

"Sure do, Leon. I've been dreamin' about this sort of terrific chance all my life," Hartmann nobly answered. "No direct insult intended to the Mamas and the Pappas, but I'm New Jersey Dreamin', and not California Dreamin'."

"Don't forget to breathe slowly while you're hyperventilating down there," coyly joked Hartmann's good-natured wife, who awkwardly tried disguising her nervousness with glib humor.

Within two hours, the three sea trekkers had passed Ocean City, Sea Isle City, Avalon, Stone Harbor, and tourist-oriented Wildwood. The exact course that Leon was on had a destination heading for the *Baltimore Canyon,* where the two men had gone *White Marlin* fishing the previous year. However, this was not a sport-fishing venture, and within the hour, Sea Captain Harper had found the precise coordinates and had promptly anchored the cabin cruiser at the designated sub' site, several miles off the Cape May coast.

"I believe that I dropped the bag into the sub' when *we* collided," Hartmann recalled and reminded Harper, "so Leon, I feel it's my duty to go down into the submarine and get it!"

"All right," Leon diplomatically agreed. "I'll let you volunteer for the dangerous gig, but please, by all means, stay out of trouble, even though you *are* trouble to begin with."

In little more than a flash, Bob and his exuberant companion were flipping backwards overboard, and one-by-one, tugging their way down the taut anchor chain. In short time, their flippers had made contact with the sandy ocean floor.

The self-assured divers then hand-paddled toward the briny German sub', and soon the swimmers were approaching the by-now-familiar hatch. Bob would enter with his underwater flashlight to retrieve the larger salvage bag that *he* had unintentionally deposited, while Leon would stand sentinel at the portal and vigilantly wait for his partner's expected return. With his new oxygen tank valve apparatus, SCUBA novice Robert Hartmann had less than twenty-five minutes to complete the rudimentary task.

This time the rust-encrusted hatch was more easily opened. Bob slowly swam into the narrow vertical cavity. Then, not seeing the sought-after bag, Hartmann opened the inner hatch without struggle or incident, and seconds later, was swimming inside the ancient sub's central section.

The earnest searcher wasted little time in enacting his "compensation mission". Hartmann swam directly into the radio room when he fortunately recalled dropping the larger bag containing the dog tags, the sealed parcel, and the spectacular German handguns. The diver was encouraged upon recognizing that the sack was lying on the metal floor, exactly where he had lost it. Employing his flashlight, the amateur frogman marveled to himself how simple his treasure quest was proceeding without any troublesome snags, obstacles, or irritating interruptions. Hartmann fantasized that soon he would be triumphantly standing up on the *Wreck of the Hesperus deck,* exhibiting his wonderful plunder, and receiving lavish compliments from Leon and Alice. Bob routinely checked the supplemental air valve, and the attachment appeared to still be in its proper position. The readout indicated that three essential minutes of oxygen still remained after the singular main tank would become empty.

The large plastic bag articles' retriever had to resist a compulsive urge to experiment and prematurely employ the new second valve. The overconfident rookie diver logically knew that it wouldn't be operable until the main tank's air would expire. Hartmann kept periodically referring to his watch to verify the exact time in which he had left before the oxygen/valve transfer would be initiated. Exactly two vital minutes remained before the reserve would be tapped. The heavy salvage bag was gently lifted from the sub's floor and next, the satisfied retriever lazily swam and made his slow path to the sub's entry hatch.

The "aqua man" entered the second hatch, and after exiting the narrow vertical tunnel, the diver effectively closed the rusty portal behind him. The SCUBA enthusiast again peered at his watch. Bob had been down for over twenty-minutes, so in about sixty-seconds, the main tank would be out of air. Then, the new-valve-owner would have the opportunity to utilize the extra three-minutes of vital oxygen during his anticipated glorious ascent.

Bob tried his best to avoid deep respiration and was surprised to notice that he was still breathing from the main tank. He briskly passed through the outside hatch, after thankfully abandoning the metallic tomb. Hartmann then carefully closed the hull's non-convenient entryway. Leon saw that his friend was okay, and the watchful partner signaled that he would start his vertical return to the boat.

Just as the second diver was about to also rise, Bob realized that he could no longer breathe. He was aware that his main tank had just expired all of its depleted oxygen supply. The alarmed diver desperately pulled the lever to the down position for the critical additional three-minutes of oxygen to activate, but nothing happened. The suddenly panicked man still couldn't inhale life-giving air. Hartmann violently pulled the lever again, but still no new air was released to enter his lungs. Bob started becoming hysterical because Leon was nowhere in the immediate vicinity to render much-needed critical assistance.

The beleaguered diver was now isolated and in peril at a depth of twenty fathoms. Bob Hartmann couldn't ascend any faster than one foot a second, a necessary rise that would require two eternal minutes. The imminent threat of getting the bends or puncturing a lung was all too real. One hundred and twenty seconds separated the endangered book-purchasing agent from the surface's life-providing atmosphere. The frantic swimmer very deliberately continued his treacherous ascension, but in his neurotic state-of-mind and frenetic haste, the large salvage bag slipped from his grip, and there was no spare time to expend vital energy to recover it.

Momentarily looking down, the half-dazed man viewed the plastic bag drifting downward and settling on top of the barnacle-laden sub'. In desperation, the disoriented diver then paddled upward rather furiously, and in his mania, advanced too quickly towards the life-saving surface. Hartmann's instinct for self-preservation and his fear of drowning had now eclipsed his essential need for caution.

The diver's crazed struggle seemed like an hour's emotional agony. Hartmann imagined that he was being suffocated alive, and his sensibilities doubted whether he could hold his precious breath a second longer. The anguished sea-sufferer kept incessantly rotating his arms and his feet to no avail. Bob knew that his will-to-live was his only hope to reach the surface and to wonderfully inhale fresh air: fresh air meant survival, meant life, meant love, and meant all else that makes human existence worthwhile.

'I must suffer and endure this excruciating pain or I'll surely die. I *will* suffer and endure this pain,' the aggrieved victim decisively thought. 'I must survive!'

The shade of the water above was finally turning to a lighter blue. Bob's fuzzy mind concluded that he would at any moment certainly collapse into unconsciousness from sheer exhaustion. But still, the struggling fellow nobly fought death and his will to live persevered. Without any trace of oxygen left, the diver's vision besides his disrupted thought patterns were becoming both incoherent and dramatically impaired. Hartmann was nearing the limits that a human's body and mind could cope-with and tolerate.

The encumbered man had only precious seconds before he would lapse into total delirium. With a final surge of instinctive paddling, Bob shot-up out of the water like a dolphin, yanked out his mouthpiece, and gulped the life-sustaining fresh air. After ten desperate breaths, the grateful survivor had the wherewithal to insert the snorkel into his mouth, blow-out the water, and then settling-down and floating on his back, all the while, still managing to heavily pant and breathe. Hartmann had escaped the jaws of death with not one second to spare. The snorkel was his amazing insurance policy against drowning.

Seeing his best friend in dire need of immediate help, Leon leaped back into the *Atlantic* to render warranted assistance. Harper latched onto Bob's right waist, and the two comrades in concert slowly kicked their flippers the full fifty-feet to the side of the bobbing cabin cruiser. Fortunately, a loyal woman was standing there ready to assist.

Alice mustered enough stamina to pull her husband's arms while Leon strenuously pushed Bob's buttocks aboard. After fully regaining command of his vital signs, the quivering-but-thankful diver informed his colleagues the details of his terrible, life-threatening ordeal. It was no doubt miraculous that Bob had found the primitive physical and mental strength to prodigiously survive his totally incredible two-minute trauma.

"What happened to the salvage bag?" Alice asked as calmly as she could. "Where is it?"

"I panicked and dropped it when I noticed that I was out of oxygen!" her still-gasping spouse related to his concerned listeners. "I should've handed it to Leon before he went up!"

"Who would have ever thought that the extra emergency valve would be faulty?" Leon questioned. "Don't talk Sir Robert, and in fifteen-minutes you should be back to normal."

An hour later, when Bob and Leon finally examined the newly purchased "safety valve", it became apparent exactly what had actually occurred. The attached valve was not defective at all. Inadvertently, in his excitement, Robert Hartmann had accidentally installed the valve upside-down. In very small letters on the underside of the device read the instructive words: "THIS SIDE UP". As a result, Hartmann unknowingly could not have used the additional three-minutes of *then* non-accessible oxygen when he had pulled-down the reserve air lever.

"How stupid it was of me to have anxiously installed the valve upside-down!" the rescued diver gasped while negatively shaking his head. "And we were so cocky coming way out here that we didn't bring along any extra oxygen tanks should they ever had been needed. Now, we have to again return to the marina empty-handed."

The three "young salts" soon alternated cranking-up the anchor and slowly evacuated the by-now-familiar location of "the image", without having possession of the larger, seemingly more important retrieval bag. The trio was truly disappointed to the brink of frustration, but also after reevaluating the entire futile situation, the crestfallen trio acknowledged that they had been very lucky about Bob's mind-boggling "near death ordeal". A major tragedy had been averted, *and* that particular close encounter with the Grim Reaper was to be Alice's husband's final ocean dive.

On Thursday morning, Bob Hartmann honored his patriotic responsibility and made a phone inquiry to the *United States Department of the Navy*. The caller informed the authorities that he had discovered a sunken German *U-boat,* and a high-ranking *Navy* administrator advised that a detachment of investigative officers would soon arrive in Mays Landing by the end of the week. Hartmann was instructed not to reveal his discovery to anyone, and not to return to the sub' to conduct personal private detective work. The failed second exploration was a mutual discouragement to both Bob and Leon, since the long-time friends really coveted the idea of having exclusive possession of the rare German pistols.

That Friday in early September, a team of three Naval Officers paid a visit to the Hartmann residence. Bob summarized the general story, but the narrator purposely omitted the mentioning of the wallet, the cigarette case, the ram medallion, and the gold and silver cross. The items' acquirer decided to keep those specific treasures as cherished mementos of his great underwater adventure.

"Thank you for your fine contribution to the *Naval Archives*," stated the head officer, a *Rear Admiral*. "Your government appreciates your historic discovery."

"Anything for God and for country," patriotically replied Robert Hartmann. "I felt it was my civil duty."

"You say you left a recovery bag that had landed directly on top of the sub?" the *Rear Admiral* asked. "Are you sure that *that* comment is still applicable?"

"Yes, Sir," Hartmann candidly and almost-apologetically answered. "When my oxygen supply ran-out, I went bonkers!"

The Navy divers assigned to the recovery were extremely anxious to obtain precise measurements of the sunken submarine, but their bureaucratic superiors insisted on conducting a strict military search without any interfering sidebar searches. All the accumulated evidence would then be forwarded, according to standard handbook regulations, to *Naval Headquarters* in Washington, D.C.

The next morning, Leon and Bob guided the visiting Navy brass to the Cape May ocean site, riding to the scene in a dispatched *Coast Guard Cutter*. Three minor Naval Officers came equipped with their own SCUBA gear. The subsequent dive went smoothly, and the Navy Seals easily found the large retrieval bag (that Bob had dropped) still lying directly beside the anonymous German sub'. The recovered papers, the pistols, and the Nazi dog tags would be thoroughly examined by the bureaucratic Washington authorities.

The *Senior Officer* gratefully thanked Bob and Leon for patriotically reporting "the magnificent find". The *Rear Admiral* promised the two New Jersey "heroes" that they would receive earned recognition from the *Pentagon* for making and reporting the historic discovery. Surprisingly, the Naval Officers then gave Leon and Bob two of the six salvaged "lugers" as coveted souvenir rewards for participating in *their* arduous ordeal.

During the following weeks, Robert Hartmann kept thinking about the two, small black and white photos' that belonged to the deceased German seaman, and the tarnished pictures depicting *his* wife, along with their children, all of which had been contained inside the secretly kept cigarette case. The wondering book merchant, still on vacation, also pondered the general address where the Nazi sailor had lived with his family in Saarbrucken, Germany. The more Bob reflected on the captivating matter, the more Hartmann had a burning desire to locate the German widow and her fatherless offspring, if any of them were still alive. The occasional desire soon evolved into what constituted an intense obsession. Nothing else seemed to matter. Bob's boring job', his love of diving, and the myriad problems of the convoluted world all paled in comparison to his compulsive need to find-out the whole truth, and nothing but the truth.

* * * * * * * * * * * *

The summer was on the wane, and the late September leaves were starting to change from green to yellow and brown hues. Early fall was Bob Hartmann's favorite time of the year, and the "nature addict" was happy that he had chosen *that* particular season for his much-anticipated "across the pond" trip to Germany. The night before his next morning departure for Europe, Hartmann had packed Karl Kraus's photographs, *ID,* and the address of the seaman's widowed wife inside his carry-on luggage. The prospective traveler also decided to take along the gold and silver cross, the *Aries* medallion, and the associated cigarette case. A half-century was a long-time interval; Karl's wife was probably dead, or perhaps a resident in an elderly care facility. 'If I can't locate the woman or find-out that she died, I'll stay for a week and enjoy the many sights of Germany.'

The week before his slated European trip, the book-purchasing agent had studied a map of Germany, and had eagerly searched for the secondary city of Saarbrucken. His perfunctory research discovered that its location was in southwest Germany on the *Saar River,* very near the French border.,

Bob had a good friend, Colonel John Martin, who was stationed at *Ramstein Military Airfield* (an American Air Base), not far from Saarbrucken. The self-appointed South Jersey genealogy investigator subsequently contacted his high school acquaintance by long distance phone, and John was able to pull a few military strings, arranging a flight on a *C-130* cargo plane that would land Hartmann at *Ramstein.*

The amateur deep-sea diver was looking forward to visiting Colonel Martin and his personable wife Ronnie.

"Are you sure you want to do this?" Alice pleaded. "Why can't I tag along? I've never been to Germany!"

"I won't rest until my curiosity about the articles found in the sub' is fully satisfied," her husband stubbornly confessed. "And you've been neglecting your mall store for at least a month, and it's already time for you to purchase winter and spring inventory."

"Are you certain you don't want me to tag along?" the wife asked. "I have a very capable manager who can adequately substitute for me for a week or more."

"No, Alice," Bob adamantly insisted. "Stay here in Jersey and take care of your profitable boutique. I'll be back in the States in a couple of weeks, and I promise I'll escort you to Las Vegas when I take my January vacation. We'll stay at *the Mirage*."

A week later, after a good night's sleep and a leisurely late morning breakfast, Bob kissed Alice "goodbye", and that early afternoon was driven by his best buddy to *McGuire Air Base* for a scheduled 6:00 p.m. plane departure. On the short drive up *Highway 206,* a peculiar sensation suddenly affected Leon's meditating *Corvette* passenger. 'Maybe I shouldn't be going to Germany in quest of a ghost's wife,' Bob imagined. 'Maybe I should leave the past *in* the past.' Hartmann had never before journeyed anywhere without Alice, so those very disturbing thoughts haunted Robert's faltering psyche the entire excursion up *Route 206.*

Leon and Bob shook hands on the *McGuire Air Base* tarmac. "I'll see you in a couple of weeks, good buddy," Leon sincerely said in a rare moment of frank emotion. "Don't do anything I wouldn't do! And don't eat too many meaty frankfurters in Frankford or big hamburgers in Hamburg!"

"I'll see you as soon as I get back," Bob candidly replied. "And make sure you don't bury the speedometer drag-racing your *'Vette* against a mean State Trooper on the Garden State Parkway!"

While seated on the military transport, an *Air Force General* started conversing with Bob, and shortly, Hartmann felt a trifle better about his long trip to Germany for the purpose of historical research into the perplexing 'submarine mystery'. The new acquaintances sat together for the entire *C-130* flight, and after a few whiskey drinks had been drunk, which the cordial General had smuggled onto the plane, the personable passengers became weary and downright drowsy. In another hour, the two European-bound passengers were both sound asleep. Despite being in cramped positions, General Boyle and his

New Jersey "SCUBA friend" managed to rest rather comfortably for the remainder of the flight.

Sunrise appeared on the eastern horizon, and the *C-130* was ready to land at *Ramstein Air Base*. It was 5:00 a.m. Germany time, and after awakening, Bob had to reset his watch, which was keeping time in error by six whole hours.

When the two American travelers disembarked from the huge transport plane, Bob heard several people calling his name from the boarding and exiting gate. The yelling voices belonged to familiar acquaintances John and Ronnie Martin. It was a joyful reunion, and naturally, the three Oakcrest High School friends had plenty of shared experiences to reminisce. Soon, Bob was seated in the front passenger seat of a black *Buick Skylark,* and the "old amigos" were motoring to the Martins' handsome ranch home, not far from the airfield.

"Well Bob, welcome to Germany. I'm sure you'll enjoy your stay here," assured Ronnie Martin from the rear driver's side seat. "The base is almost like living in the USA."

"How ya' been all these years, good buddy?" John Martin asked his traveling passenger. "Long time no see!"

"I've been great, Colonel! I've missed your funny company the past few decades," Hartmann admitted. "As a result, I've had to pal around with a crazy rascal named Leon Harper!"

When Colonel John Martin asked why Bob had specifically come to *Ramstein,* the wanderer had little trouble divulging the tale of the sunken German sub', of the tarnished photos', and then discussing Karl Kraus's local address. *World War II* was very distant from the present computer age, and John and Ronnie strongly doubted that the sailor's widowed wife would still be alive.

Martin had made arrangements for Bob to be escorted in a military jeep to Saarbrucken, where the touring U.S. visitor would initiate his challenging search. Just after consuming a very delicious breakfast, Hartmann left the Martins' attractive ranch home, accompanied by an assigned off-duty *MP*. The jeep's destination would be the regional tourist center, where Robert figured he could obtain pertinent advice about how he might continue his strange odyssey in locating Karl Kraus's aged wife.

"Thanks for the lift," Bob acknowledged to the by-the-rules driver. "You've been most helpful."

"Think nothin' of it, Mr Hartmann. Any friend of Colonel Martin is a friend of mine," the loyal driver declared, enunciating in a deep Brooklyn accent.

After doing some assiduous research, the English-speaking regional tourist center guides were able to locate the in-question

German woman's reported address on a Saarbrucken street map. Bob politely thanked the center's personnel for their courteous assistance. The now-refocused traveler then hailed a passing taxi, and took it to *that* remote section of town.

The driver had some difficulty isolating the aged woman's house, so Hartmann instructed the cabby to stop and ask specific directions at a nearby corner grocery store, where the elderly proprietors were very cooperative. Bob's inquiry was an incidental stroke of luck, since the elderly woman in question often shopped at the mom and pop establishment, and amazingly, still lived in the vicinity at the exact same address, only two blocks away.

Bob couldn't believe his good fortune. After paying and generously tipping the cabby, the tenacious researcher entered a neighborhood florist shop to buy Mrs. Karl Kraus a gorgeous bouquet of red roses. 'That noteworthy gift will be an appropriate way to formally introduce myself,' Hartmann pragmatically thought.

The visitor had to then cross a busy thoroughfare to reach the elderly lady's home, but Bob's mind was so preoccupied with meeting Mrs. Karl Kraus that he dashed-out onto the highway and into the path of an oncoming car. There was a screeching of tires as the auto's right front fender smashed into the pedestrian, and upon impact, the bouquet of fresh red roses had flown high into the air. The ill-starred pedestrian was seriously injured, and the American visitor had instantly fallen unconscious from the fierce street collision.

An ambulance was summoned, and Robert Hartmann was rushed to a nearby Saarbrucken hospital. His clothes had been badly soiled and torn, and the victim's shirt and trousers were totally bloodstained, not to mention crimson stains on his large suitcase and accompanying travel case. The victim's clothing had to delicately be removed before urgent surgery could be performed on the newest O.R. patient.

The wallet in Bob's tattered trousers was devoid of passport, credit cards, and identification, because an alert city thief had stolen those important items in the general confusion that had immediately followed the terrible street accident.

The paramedics had salvaged Bob's ripped jacket, which he had been carrying that warm morning after exiting the floral shop. One of the jacket's pockets had the pictures of the *WWII* German sailor, and of his family. The individuals' names were also provided on the backsides. In another jacket pocket were a gold and silver cross, a gold ram medallion, and an exquisite 1940s cigarette case. All of the personal effects had been placed in a container to be stored in a hospital safe until Hartmann was ever well-enough to recover and continue his incredible journey.

The unfortunate victim was still lying unconscious inside the operating room, and it was apparent to the staff' doctors that Bob's battered body would need immediate surgery in order to repair extensive internal bleeding originating from a severed vein. Otherwise, the American's life would be in serious jeopardy.

Robert Hartmann's identity remained anonymous to the hospital personnel, and the German family photographs were the unconscious man's only current links to reality. Every surgeon and nurse in the operating room assumed that the man in the picture and the man on the operating table to be one and the same individual, since Bob Hartmann was a carbon copy of deceased Karl Kraus, right down to the dimple on his left cheek.

* * * * * * * * * * * *

The hospital operator tried contacting Mrs. Karl Kraus because the staff had surmised that *she* was either Bob's wife or mother. The receptionist was finally able to reach the elderly woman by phone an hour later. The decrepit-looking Saarbrucken resident answered and was asked if her name was Ruth Kraus. She responded, "Ja".

"Mrs. Kraus, we have some rather bad news for you," the hospital operator sadly reported. "Your husband or your son has been badly injured in a car accident."

"You must have the wrong person because my husband was killed in the war over 50 years ago," the shocked listener replied. "What you are saying can't be true!"

"But we have a photograph of your husband and family as well as cards with your names and address on the back. His name is Karl Kraus, isn't it?" the now-confused operator impetuously asked.

With *that* question being heard, the elderly widow felt weak in the knees. "Are there any dates on the picture?" the staggered, gray-haired woman inquired.

"No. They do appear to be quite old, though."

The bewildered Saarbrucken apartment dweller thanked the candid operator and informed her that she would visit the hospital to clarify the misunderstanding. Mrs. Karl Kraus collected her thoughts and then took a local transit bus to the regional medical facility, which was only a mile away. The widow proceeded to the front desk as fast as her rickety legs could carry her.

"Do you have a patient here by the name of Karl Kraus?" Ruth politely asked the receptionist seated at the main desk.

"Yes, but he's recovering from major surgery, and I believe he's still unconscious," replied the young lady. "The doctors are going to operate some more on him, perhaps tomorrow. He cannot have visitors right now. Not even close family."

Just then the chief surgeon in charge of the *O.R.* paced down the long hall to the front desk where the physician had overheard the tail end of the formal conversation.

"Are you Mrs. Kraus?" the doctor asked. "The hospital needs this very important information."

"Yes," answered the distraught and confused feeble woman.

The German M.D. respectfully spoke to the aged lady, who obviously appeared several generations older than the young man that was unconscious lying horizontally upon the operating table. But all the vital details seemed to fit, including the same names on the card, the several 1940ish photos', along with the same identical addresses.

The concerned surgeon then informed puzzled Mrs. Kraus that he would allow an exception to hospital's policy. "Your husband is now semiconscious. You can go in to see him, but you'll be permitted to stay for only a few minutes."

The patient's arms and legs were heavily bandaged, but his face was not. A deep wound however was quite prominently evident on the right side of the accident victim's forehead. Mrs. Kraus stared at the occupant lying upon a recovery room gurney, and her eyes couldn't believe the shocking sight that they beheld. It indeed was her husband's face. The woman's knees suddenly buckled, and the elderly visitor felt compelled to grab the side of the gurney.

Just then the injured patient opened his eyes and directly peered at Mrs. Karl Kraus. He smiled and said, "Guten tag, Ruth; wie geht es ihnen?" in a thick German accent.

Upon hearing those absolutely incredible words, Mrs. Ruth Kraus immediately held her right hand to her heart and collapsed onto the tile floor. Three nurses transported the stricken lady out of the recovery room and into the O.R. suite for immediate medical attention. The weak, palled-face man lying in the intensive care unit's operating room lapsed back into listless unconsciousness as his anemic and damaged memory sank deep into the past.

When Ruth Kraus eventually revived from her emotional trauma, a compassionate nurse calmly spoke to her. "We have some cherished belongings of your husband," the R.N. suavely indicated. "They were removed from his jacket, and we would like to show them to you."

The items had been stored in a metal container, and the nurse presented them to Ruth one by one. The appearance of the gold and silver cross soon made Mrs. Kraus lose her breath, since it had been the exact cross that Karl had always worn. Next, the baffled woman was given the incomparable cigarette case, which she instantly remembered because of the distinguished mother-of-pearl lid. Without turning it over, Ruth had memorized the inscription etched on the back, which appropriately read in German, "To Karl with love always, from Ruth- April 25, 1943."

When the astonished nurse turned the case over, she read the exact same language as Mrs. Kraus had just verbally recited. Ruth's emotions soon overwhelmed her heart, and the aged widow began crying uncontrollably. Ten minutes elapsed on the room's wall clock, and after somewhat regaining her sense of reason, the awed German lady was next shown the golden ram medallion that had her husband's birth date engraved, April 19, 1925.

"Karl was of the zodiac sign *Aries,*" Ruth Kraus sobbed to the supportive nurse. "He absolutely loved this horoscope medallion showing his birth sign."

The last thing Mrs. Kraus was handed was the wrinkled leather wallet with the two pictures that hospital personnel had placed inside the container box after the billfold had been removed from Robert Hartmann's tattered trousers. The family photo' with Karl, Ruth and the children triggered another lengthy crying spell from Mrs. Kraus. Ruth finally believed (as being valid evidence) all of the presented articles as being authentic, which she had honestly witnessed and then verified as being nostalgic family possessions. The distressed lady now believed that the young man lying in the recovery room was somehow actually her beloved husband Karl.

The three subsequent operations performed on the strong-willed accident victim were successful, and then the patient's head was heavily bandaged from receiving the latest medical incision. The new wrappings shrouded the recuperating man's face, and Bob was not allowed visitors for forty-eight hours. After three days of healing, the bandages were finally removed.

Ruth Kraus revisited the *Saarbrucken Hospital* to further fathom and explore the peculiar mystery of her long-lost husband. She still could not ascertain what had recently happened, but when the befuddled woman and the strange man lying in the hospital bed began exchanging conversation in German, the alert patient asked about their three children, Rene, Karin, and Alex. The bedridden American also inquired about Ruth's long-deceased mother, Klärchen. The hospital patient's awesome acumen about Ruth Kraus's private past life was positively astonishing.

The awe-inspiring, peculiar dialogue tested the boundaries of believability. Ruth finally believed that she had Karl back after nearly six lonely decades of prolific sadness and despair. The arcane occasion at hand was indeed a happy ending to Mrs. Kraus's half-century of perpetual sorrow.

As Ruth closely stared in awe at 'Karl's' scarred face, the woman noticed that his general appearance seemed much older than he had during her initial hospital visit. 'His aging is disguised with a heavy gray beard,' she plausibly concluded, 'since he has not been shaved since his hospital admission.'

The couple continued conversing with each other in German, and the speakers were able to recollect events that they had shared before *he* had entered the *Nazi* naval service. The present moment was being communicated as if Karl Kraus had never departed *WWII* Germany.

Several weeks elapsed and the hospital patient gradually had been healed from his multiple injuries, but now the accident victim's withered facial features became even more wrinkled and haggard-looking. When the recuperating accident victim was ready to be released from the Saarbrucken hospital, he looked like a tired, weak, debilitated fellow graciously enduring life's miseries in his late seventies. The thick, fully-grown gray beard looked rather appropriate, matching the apparent decline of his general physique. Despite those observable difficulties, Karl and Ruth made a loving couple, and the Saarbrucken Kraus family was together once more.

Back in the United States, Alice Hartmann never again heard from Bob, or ever discovered anything relevant about his surreal fate as rejuvenated Karl Kraus, living in Germany. No one could explain the outlandish riddle of Ruth's husband's sudden disappearance into oblivion. It was as if Bob's existence had completely vanished without a trace from the face of the earth. An intensive search was conducted in Germany, but it was to no avail. Neither a hint nor a clue of Bob Hartmann's whereabouts was ever found.

Eventually, Leon and Alice's shared sorrow and loss led to the start of a budding romantic relationship. Since Bob had been missing for a decade, it was believed that the U.S. citizen had met with foul play with soulless dangerous criminals somewhere in Germany. Hartmann was presumed dead, and so the former close New Jersey friends eventually married, and afterwards, Leon and Alice had their gala wedding reception inside the main ballroom at Atlantic City's *Resorts Casino Hotel*. The cheerful couple then merrily honeymooned in Las Vegas at *the Mirage*.

The *Department of the Navy* never informed Alice and Leon Harper of any subsequent information that had been recovered from the World War II documents found inside the *Nazi* submarine's safe. The military records included the confidential list, later to be officially quaranteed, was of deployed German sailors who had fatefully died aboard the sunken Nazi *U-boat.*

All retrieved data had been carefully filed-away and labeled by the United States Goverrment as classified material to be kept in confidential folders inside the *Building of Naval Records.* One of the dog-tag names appearing on the list of deceased German submarine sailors belonged to one Robert Hartmann, *Seaman First Class, Submarine Radio Operator.*

"An Incense Burner"

In 1916, the United States was on the threshold of participating in *World War I*. Jason Newman was a bright six-year-old who lived with his parents and younger brother, Jack. The curly blond-haired boy's father Jake was a hard-working tailor whose shop was located just below the family's tenement apartment in the low-rent *Bowery* section of New York City. Manhattan's lower end bustled with an amalgam of often-exploited European immigrants seeking refuge from famine, escape from rampant poverty, and isolation from man's cruel political inhumanity to man.

Woodrow Wilson was the U.S. President, and most of the "civilized" world was at war. Ships from foreign countries docked at bustling New York piers to unload cargoes and to restock supplies for their return voyages. Sailors of all nationalities came ashore to do sightseeing of famous landmarks, or to visit sleazy *Bowery* bars searching for "easy women", or if the mariners had money, finding cheap prostitutes. That seedy cosmopolitan district of New York teemed with modest hotels and inelegant restaurants, which the land-starved sailors enthusiastically and wholeheartedly patronized.

Many seamen frequented Jake Newman's humble tailor shop to obtain alterations to their uniforms. Jake became well-known among transient mariners, and the honorable gentleman was one of the busiest tailors working in the East Side ghettos. A good reputation usually meant and guaranteed more hard work in lower Manhattan.

Little Jason Newman was always "a fixture" inside the humble tailor shop, and the roving sailors often favored the lad with small gifts and tokens. Foreign coins and unique souvenirs from distant quadrants of the globe were generously offered to the delighted-but-meek youth. Jason eagerly saved the various gift items inside a cherished metal box, and from practicing his hobby, the wide-eyed lad was able to learn much about world geography while studying the many nations from which the various collectibles had originated.

Over the years, the boy's coin assortment grew to several thousand pieces, and about fifty cigar boxes had to be utilized to keep the articles stored inside. As Jason Newman matured, the ambitious adolescent diligently studied (in his modest room) the true value of his accumulated shekels, rubies, and Spanish reals. The plethora of information that had been gleaned about the lad's hobby was obtained from certain popular published coin books.

"Jason, my son. I believe that the definition of a lucky man is one whose job is his childhood dream," Jake Newman had often told his older offspring. "But I think that you should learn to be a realist instead of remaining an idle dreamer."

"Papa, I'll remember those words for the rest of my life," replied the appreciative boy to his frugal, good-natured father. "But I just like being the age that I am."

One particular item that fascinated Jason was a miniature incense burner. The novel object had been given to him by a seafarer whose ship had just arrived in port from New Orleans. The unique burner had three legs, was made of a copper/tin alloy, and the resilient bronze object had over the years oxidized into a beautiful turquoise patina. The odd-looking incense burner had a singular perforated lid with a half-moon welded onto it.

After the initial novelty of the very different-in-appearance souvenir had worn-off, Jason Newman's incense burner had been stored-away without being used. The "strange thing" remained in Jason's collection, and the young teen soon forgot about the unusual object as his hobby expanded to include other more exotic articles. At the time, "Jay" never once suspected that the unique keepsake would someday dramatically impact his life.

As a curious academically-oriented teenager, Jason Newman became very knowledgeable about the world's various monetary systems. Rare coin valuations became the adolescent's principal interest and avocation. The ambitious-but-shy teen coin accumulator was an excellent public-school student, and when he graduated high school, Jason had a distinct desire to visit the exotic countries he had voraciously studied in library reference books. 'I've never told Papa, but I have no desire being an ordinary Bowery tailor. I really wish to do something else with my future.'

But first Jason Newman had to establish a viable business that would earn the necessary money to fulfill his lofty travel aspirations. The fledgling's rather sophisticated knowledge concerning basic international numismatics afforded Jay the opportunity to easily gain employment in a Lower Manhattan company that traded in coins and stamps for lucrative profits.

"I'm glad to have found a young man with such a keen mind," said Mr. Ed Saunders, the owner of the well-established firm. "Welcome to Saunders and Finch."

"If I weren't working for you, Sir," Jason humbly stated, "I'd be an unhappy tailor slaving-away in the Bowery like my poor father. I love coins and stamps Mr. Saunders, so as you can plainly see, my pleasure will be my work, and my work will be my pleasure."

It wasn't long before the astute and enterprising Jason Newman realized that the coin business was a very excellent money-making activity, especially for the store's owners. The greenhorn employee knew right then and there that becoming a successful coin entrepreneur was definitely to be his future occupation. Living frugally, within three short years the young man saved enough money to open his own coin shop, along with his younger brother Jack as his partner. The newly found business thrived, and soon Jason and Jack's "Canal Street Coin Shop" had a noteworthy reputation that amazingly attracted some of the wealthiest American East Coast collectors.

Parlaying their initial success, Jason and Jack next opened a branch store several blocks away, just off of busy *Broadway,* and as that second establishment became prosperous, the enterprising brothers christened a chain of duplicate operations in Philadelphia, Chicago, and Los Angeles. In a matter of ten years, the ever-expanding coin trading company had proliferated into twenty-two outlets coast-to-coast. Jason Newman and his brother Jack became very rich coin and stamp moguls within a mere decade.

"How much money do *you* need to live?" asked Jack. "Isn't a million bucks a year enough for you to live comfortably?"

"We're opening new stores because of the challenge, not because of financial gain," Jason cleverly replied. "I'm telling you, Jack; the money is just a natural consequence of *our* challenge," intelligently answered the older brother. "Do you want to die a pauper like our poor father did?"

The following September, Jason married his childhood sweetheart Julia Stein, and the happy couple was blessed with two children, Robin and Seth. By his teen years, Seth took an avid interest in the family coin business, much to the satisfaction of Jason, who still considered himself very fortunate to have his childhood aspiration evolve into a truly wonderful career.

Feeling extravagant, Jason built a magnificent mansion north of the city that was situated on a majestic palisade overlooking the *Hudson River*. There in Yonkers, the coin tycoon merrily entertained his affluent clients, many of whom had amassed their fortunes before the introduction of federal income tax in 1913. The New York City based trading guru had satisfactorily reached his financial goals and was now earning sufficient "geld" to easily afford the finest luxuries and living accommodations.

Jason Newman's architectural Hudson River mansion had a massive den, which featured a museum's display of splendid collectibles that, over the years, the coin baron had very diligently accumulated. A special wall-length mahogany cabinet held some of the more coveted pieces, including the treasured-but-unused "good luck incense burner" that Jason Newman had kept ever since his sheltered youth. That special rare item, although by far not the most expensive in his prized possession, had indeed become Jason's favorite among the hundreds of noteworthy valuables exhibited in his fabulous personal "Gallery". The very proud coin and stamp tycoon considered the strange-looking incense burner gift his personal "magical good luck piece".

* * * * * * * * * * * *

While the nation languished in the aftermath of the *Great Depression,* Jason Newman was preoccupied developing and growing his lucrative transcontinental coin and stamp empire. The industrious businessman also acquired a flair for antiques in the mid-1930s, which was an era of tight money. Whenever the coin wheeler-dealer had the opportunity, the aggressive merchant would browse antique shops, looking for profitable scarce collectibles. Invariably, Jay Newman would purchase volumes of out-of-print books, and also antiquated rare catalogues. The coin and stamp expert also evolved into an authority on the value of Chinese artifacts and foreign curios.

Either Jason or Jack would travel to metropolitan areas across the country to keep track of the ever-growing chain of coin outlets, for many smart, opportunistic businessmen (like the Newman brothers) had become wealthy, while millions of struggling Americans had to live from day to day in the very daunting *"Post-Depression* years".

A decade later, *World War II* performed its ugly act upon history's stage, and later, with the arrival of the 1950s, a new wave of post-war prosperity hit capitalistic America. Fast and easy profits could be made as more money became available to the buying public, and in 1957, on-a-mission Jason Newman audaciously engineered an enviable "store expansion program".

"Jack, I'm going to have to arrange a meeting in New Orleans with the manager of our latest coin emporium," Jason explained to his not-as-motivated younger brother. "I'll be leaving New York tomorrow and will be gone for a week."

"Now Jay, don't go buying every antique you see displayed along the *Mississippi,"* facetiously jested the younger sibling. "You'll need a bigger den to store them, and the one you already have is almost the size of a football field!"

"And Jack, don't join the army," Jason advised his main antagonist, tongue-in-cheek. "The Russians are expanding the *Cold War* in Europe, and there's plenty of conversation of the U.S. getting involved in the ugly mess."

"Don't worry one iota, Jay," the lazier brother laughed. "We're both too old to be drafted!"

Jack Newman had always been a tad jealous of his older brother's success ever since childhood. Jason was more affable, more likeable, more successful, and more handsome than his younger brother. Also, Jack Newman had dated Julia Stein several times in high school, but after the younger sibling had introduced the attractive girl to Jason on a ferry ride en-route to the *Statue of Liberty,* the pretty, petite lady was instantly swept off her feet by Jay's more dynamic, rather charming, congenial disposition.

* * * * * * * * * * * *

The following morning, entrepreneurial Jason Newman boarded a plane for New Orleans that flew out of *Newark International Airport.* After the rocky three-hour flight, Jay obtained his suitcase from the airline's luggage carousel conveyor, hailed a taxi outside the main terminal, and then proceeded to a popular Crescent City Hotel, where the coin and stamp guru would rest before meeting his newly hired store manager. In his plush hotel room, Newman scanned through a tourist magazine that listed the many activities to be seen and done in "America's most interesting City".

A section of the periodical dealt with the reader's principal loves, antiques and coins. Another magazine segment introduced the fascinated reader to certain occult superstitions that were practiced by Creole and African Louisiana descendants. The totally impressed hotel guest perused several additional informative articles and eventually read the magazine's offbeat literature section that described the performance of certain black magic rituals. The esoteric subject was a field of interest that immediately intrigued eager-to-learn Jason Newman, and since the coin authority had conquered the "natural" world of coin economics in his propitious business enterprises, the "supernatural" world seemed to be the next logical step to triumph over along the path of human adventure.

"The first spare minute I have in New Orleans I'll detour off Esplanade Avenue and visit some of these unusual places I've just read about," Newman mumbled to himself as he thumb-nailed through the remainder of the intriguing forbidden arts' periodical. "The bizarre and the uncanny have always attracted my attention."

Jerry McCoy was the new manager of the *French Quarter,* Jason and Jack's most recent coin outlet, and the visiting major company stockowner was very satisfied with the store's displays and with its initial sales reports. A few suggestions in regard to merchandising and display arrangements were orally provided by the visiting coin expert, and then after closing the new establishment at 7 p.m., the two men had dinner at an exclusive restaurant that specialized in preparing spicy Cajun Country food.

"How did you manage to make an admirable fortune during the *Great Depression?"* asked the new store's very curious employee. "My father told me things were exceptionally tough back then."

"That's very simple, Jerry," Jason replied before sipping his dry merlot wine. "When everyone was losing their shirts in stocks and bonds, gold and silver prices skyrocketed. And when paper assets declined in value, commodities like gold and silver went through the roof. Valuable coins just happen to be minted in precious metals."

Then, the restaurant table conversation switched from luck in business to the arcane influence of the occult. Soon, Jason made a specific inquiry to his new manager. "Jerry, what do you know about black magic?" the coin genius wanted to know. "I'm very enamored with a magazine article I had read this afternoon in my hotel room."

"Mr. Newman, I would steer clear of the local practice of African taboos and voodoo if I were you," Jerry McCoy confidentially advised and warned. "One person that I know quite well got involved with it, and then he mysteriously disappeared without a trace. As you might be aware, New Orleans has a large felony crime rate, and the superstitious natives claim that many outlandish homicides that you read about in the newspapers are really of a supernatural origin. You really have to be careful with your local choices."

The millionaire's curiosity peaked upon listening-to the store manager's stern warning. In Jason's logical mind, the prospect of interacting with the mystical invisible world transcended the very mundane process of making large sums of money as a prosperous independent coin merchant.

"Doesn't sound too good," responded Jason for the sake of casually maintaining the amiable conversation. "There's no harm if I just look inside some of the antique and junk stores while I'm randomly strolling around Bourbon and Canal Streets, is there? I may even find something special that catches my fancy."

"Just be careful," Jerry cautioned and recommended. "Some wicked things happen in this rather extraordinary city that never make sensational news headlines!"

"I only fear dangers that I can see," laughed the haughty self-made coin mogul before gulping-down more tasty wine. "The invisible world is full of invisible things that in actuality, have no material existence. How can something immaterial harm me in any way, Jerry? It's all such a silly, superstitious notion!"

The two chatty diners separated after enjoying their delicious meals, and then Jason Newman trekked back to the reputable hotel for a good night's sleep. The New Orleans visitor was seriously weighing the stark warning that Jerry McCoy had just given him. The more Newman's aggressive mind dwelled on the arcane subject of black magic, the more determined the obdurate tycoon became about exploring *its* forbidden dimensions.

'I really think Jerry was exaggerating with all of this trumped-up voodoo nonsense,' assessed the skeptical visitor to the city of levees and bayous. "I don't think *Jerry's* ideas are the real *McCoy,*" laughed Jason to himself inside his luxury hotel room, as the jolly guest was overcome by merlot giddiness and by general fatigue.

The next morning, Jason Newman hired a cab and took a quick tour of Metairie Cemetery, where the tombs rested above ground because of the underground water table being so near the surface. The knowledge-hungry tourist was next driven to Bourbon Street where a multitude of various gift and antique shopkeepers hawked exotic and outrageous wares. Showing his gratitude, the itinerant coin entrepreneur handed the garrulous cabby/guide a handsome fifty-dollar tip for his patience and amicable cooperation.

The very interested traveler soon entered an attractive tourist trap and his vigilant eyes browsed around the crowded aisles. However, nothing extraordinary initially caught Jay's keen attention. Then, the swarthy-skinned proprietor approached the prospective customer and initiated a pleasant conversation.

"Can I help you, Sir?" the merchant politely asked.

"Yes. I'm interested in finding something rather unusual," Jason responded with a forced smile. "I haven't yet noticed anything I would consider to be remarkable. Could you perhaps suggest a shop that deals with the occult?"

The short, chunky shop owner immediately thought of a relative's establishment, and the Canal Street proprietor's avaricious mind instantly speculated the handsome finder-fee commission that he would receive from his greedy brother-in-law for *him* successfully recommending a sizable transaction.

"It just so happens I know of such a place as you've described, but its location is in a section of town where few tourists venture," the dark-skinned shop-owner divulged. "If you decide to risk traveling there, the name of the store is *The Devil's Den*. It's located just off St. Claude Avenue. But I must warn you, Sir. Please be very careful, and watch your back at all times."

"Thank you. I most certainly will heed your sage advice," declared Jason, just before the rare coin baron left the premises with a sardonic smile upon his face that reflected a basic lack of respect for the city's notorious supernatural realm.

* * * * * * * * * * * *

The cynical-but-wealthy pedestrian from Manhattan flagged the first empty taxi that approached his active street corner. "Take me to *The Devil's Den*. It's a shop just off St. Claude opposite the French Quarter," the in-a-hurry passenger insisted as the new passenger quickly opened the cab's back door. "Driver, do you know anything about *The Devil's Den?*" the inquisitive backseat traveler asked.

Ironically, the New Orleans tourist soon realized that he had hailed the same cabby who had given him a very comprehensive education about Metairie Cemetery, the historic Mississippi Delta, and "the most European city in all America". Jason promptly recognized the talkative cabby by the tone of the driver's voice and by his singular body language as the fount-of-information characteristically gestured with his right hand as his left palm skillfully steered the cab.

"Yes, Sir," replied the very likeable and accommodating taxi pilot. "You're the first person in months who has asked to be taken there. Not many people know about *that* weird shop," added the cabby, who claimed not to be a Creole but a Mestizo, whose ancestry was a combination of Aztec and Spanish cultures. "Sir, the products they sell in that taboo place have the reputation of being extremely dangerous, if the objects are not properly used. I suggest that you be very careful because I've always had bad vibes about that odd store," cautioned the meter monitor as the chatty driver deftly swerved his yellow machine to the curb, directly in front of the infamous remote tourist trap.

Jason stepped-out of the yellow vehicle, thanking the driver for his candor, paid his fare, and gave the happy driver another very generous tip. "I love this exotic city. It's loaded with pessimistic and fearful people," the former passenger declared to his grateful guide. "But from my observations, dollars seem to work around here a lot better than black magic does."

The *Devil's Den* curiosity shop was shabby and dimly lit with cheap candles glowing upon display tables, and inexpensive, nondescript tiffany lamps that were hanging from the ceiling were providing supplemental dull light. The aroma of incense permeated the stagnant air, and the fully entranced newcomer nervously browsed-around, nonchalantly examining several weird-looking items on display. Newman immediately recognized that the peculiar-looking retail articles were definitely outside the well-defined parameters of his vast inventory of world knowledge and personal experience.

204

As Jason Newman scrutinized the extensive exhibits of rather strange-and-undesirable merchandise, the sales-hungry proprietor approached his prospective gullible customer. The stocky man was middle-aged and wore a bulky wool vermilion sweater. A thick full white beard matched his bushy gray hair, but the shop-owner's horrendous breath abundantly smelled of garlic. Immediately, Jason's wild imagination fancied that the 'excessive herbal usage' was an appropriate antidote for deterring local vampires.

"What can I do for you, kind Sir?" the unkempt proprietor asked as the queer-looking merchant slowly and suspiciously encountered the bewildered shopper. Newman had to bite his tongue, for the browser was still chuckling from imagining *his* fairly humorous garlic/vampire mental association.

"I'm in the market for something special and unique. There're so many off-the-wall things in your establishment that I can hardly identify most of them by name," Jason indirectly complimented. "Maybe you can suggest something that would be an exquisite collector's item for me to take back to New York."

"Unless you're familiar with the occult and black magic, I don't know what to suggest to someone of only trivial exposure to the forbidden arts," the eccentric shopkeeper elucidated and explained. "I would first recommend you looking at our treasure trove of library books; you may then get some good ideas."

"I'll do just that!" Newman amiably agreed. "Give me a few minutes to decide."

Newman slowly wandered to the book display inside the store's rear section, and in the dim artificial light the New Orleans visitor briskly leafed through several ancient-looking, leather-bound volumes. Soon, an old tarnished manual captured the tourist's full attention. The old frayed edition had a distinct musty odor that emanated from its four hundred faded pages. The obscure treatise had been published in 1920 and featured many photographs and illustrations of strange instruments often used to perform African black magic rituals.

The spellbound visitor sat-down in an antiquated, cushioned, velvet chair and intently inspected the newfound source of information quite thoroughly. Near the book's appendix, Jason Newman observed a picture of an object that surprisingly appeared more than vaguely familiar. A photograph of an extraordinary incense burner revealed a startling replica of the smaller one that the coin merchant had treasured inside the revered cabinet shelf of his splendid extravagant den overlooking the *Hudson*.

The captivated customer read and comprehended the object's history with a mad passion. A general description disclosed that the unusual burner had been commonly utilized in the early 1900s' and had invoked myriad black magic rituals. Text passages depicted in the magazine claimed that many Louisiana inhabitants' deaths had been attributed to the demonic incense burner; the unfortunate souls experiencing fatal exposure to its sinister, lethal implementation.

The magazine article also stated that in 1916 a fearful New Orleans judge finally banned and confiscated the two existing incense burners in an effort to quell possible mass hysteria. The local magistrate had felt compelled to yield to societal pressure that had been exercised by alarmed area residents. The dreaded objects were then brought to a parish police station for safekeeping, but the smaller demonic incense burner had become mysteriously missing the next morning, and the accursed object was never found, or ever seen again. A local near-scandal arose as the associated police officers were accused of enacting the theft, but not one patrolman had been convicted because of a lack of relevant evidence. The other larger incense burner pictured in the faded photograph was immediately destroyed to avoid any further regional controversy.

After Jason finished reading the imaginative article, the recently converted occult connoisseur gladly purchased the expensive out-of-print book, which quite clearly outlined appropriate procedures for effectively practicing African black magic. The coin store CEO was obsessed with learning esoteric paranormal laws and taboos that seemed to arrogantly defy the standard axioms of familiar sciences, such as physics, biology and chemistry.

"Is there such an animal as white magic?" Jason innocently asked the shop proprietor in a jovial tone of voice.

"Yes, but it's not nearly as powerful as black magic," the Mestizo storeowner very seriously asserted. "The owner of the missing smaller incense burner should have mastered *that* fact by now!"

Before Jason Newman reluctantly departed *The Devil's Den,* the newfound black arts' patron purchased a box of incense from the happy owner who, after his customer's departure, made a hasty phone call to his brother-in-law in order to inform him of a very substantial finders-fee commission.

* * * * * * * * * * * *

On Saturday morning, Jason exited the ornate French Quarter hotel and proceeded by taxi to *Moisant Airport*. The coin executive was soon sitting in a first-class seat aboard a four-engine prop, the flight destination being *Idlewild Airport*. The passenger had three airborne hours to further avidly read and comprehend the 'voodoo theories' comprehensively advanced and described in the rare book Newman had procured at the gloomy and foreboding *Devil's Den*.

Certain outlandish paragraphs revealed in the dusty book defined in detail the particular preparations and procedures required to effectively command and control the arcane forces of "the invisible world". Newman made a personal vow that he would never divulge to anyone his acute interest in primitive Old World African black magic rites, not even to ultra-cynical, Jack. The acquired text would be hidden within Jason's fabulous den, and the book's esoteric rituals would be secretly practiced when the Newman family members were preoccupied off the family estate. Jason's uneventful flight arrived on schedule at *Idlewild,* and ever-faithful Julia was waiting with open arms as the itinerant businessman disembarked the plane and then deliberately entered the main airport terminal.

"How was your trip?" the still-pretty wife asked. "Did you meet your new store manager?"

"It was very constructive. I believe the New Orleans shop will do very well," Jason reckoned and shared. "Jerry, the hired store manager, seems knowledgeable enough. Jack had personally trained the guy over the winter in our Chicago operation. We'll have to wait and see how the rest of the business year goes. Then, I'll pay the coin shop another visit, maybe around *Mardi Gras* time."

"That would be nice, Jay, and I would love to join you. I've never been to New Orleans!" Julia Newman exclaimed.

"You're more than welcome. I was going to surprise you with the slated Louisiana trip in February," Jason confessed and then paused. "Now that *you* know about it, we can look forward to traveling down South together. We'll have great fun while eating prawns and Cajun chicken, right up to midnight on Shrove Tuesday," predicted the ecstatic husband. "I think you'll like the city, especially the *Mardi Gra,* very much."

That evening, the pair enjoyed dinner in their favorite Manhattan restaurant, *Sardi's*. Later that night, Newman realized that it had been a rather grueling day for the CEO chain coin-store millionaire, so the fatigued traveler decided to retire to bed by eleven. But in a short while, the recently-returned New Orleans visitor was still tossing and turning. The fidgety fellow was suffering a terrible, uncharacteristic, restive sleep as Newman's mind kept rehashing the purchased voodoo book's unorthodox principles, along with the strange native cults that eagerly performed the ante-medieval rituals.

Even in his light sleep, the obsessed man was anxious to experience and master the essential elements of his newfound avocation. 'No one will know about my clandestine activities, not even Julia,' the nervous, sweating plotter confided to himself. 'My friends at the club are only interested in polo, golf, whiskey and tennis. My stubborn brother is focused on retirement and entertainment. My wife's major concern is how to squander my fortune by perchasing extravagant clothes and expensive jewelry. My children are quite spoiled by the corruptive evils of leisure and materialism.'

Weariness finally overcame the light-sleeper's apprehensions, and Newman eventually surrendered to his body's need to replenish its lost vitality. Dawn would herald-in a different new day.

At 7 a.m. Julia had breakfast ready on the elevated patio, which lorded over the sparkling *Hudson*. Harriet, the loyal and laconic family maid, served the pair pancakes with scrambled eggs, while Julia and Jason blandly discussed their separate agendas for the day. The wife expressed that she would shop the emporiums on *Fifth Avenue,* but her wily husband claimed to be still exhausted from his rigorous Louisiana excursion. "Honey, this morning I can't seem to attempt anything more arduous than breathing!" the scheming husband falsely claimed and exclaimed. "I think I'll pass on visiting Tiffany's."

Harriet had the afternoon off, Reginald the chauffeur was with Julia, Seth was in Bermuda, Robin was in St. Louis, and Jack was cutting the ribbon at a new coin store in Phoenix. It was a very opportune time for Jason to be alone, and to experiment with "the invisible world".

"There must be more to life than greed, money, success, work, and business, and I plan to discover and savor it all," whispered Jason to his pallid face image being reflected in the living room mirror.

Unfortunately, midnight was the prescribed time to enact the mystic black magic rituals and to chant the needed actions' accompanying incantations. The wealthy "new generation self-made aristocrat" was temporarily frustrated by the lengthy time delay until the strike of twelve. Newman focused his entire attention on the small incense burner, which he had clandestinely kept as a lucky keepsake from childhood. But up until now, Jason had never really studied the item closely, but the Hudson River resident was positive that his possession was truly the sister burner to the one that had reportedly been destroyed back in New Orleans.

Conducting a simple comparison, the inspired coin merchant noticed that the bronze object held in his hands was identical in design to the larger one graphically described in his "dark side" manual. Jason was now wholly convinced of the generous mariner's 1916 gift's authenticity. 'I'm convinced that this burner is definitely the missing entity that had been lost. After the *Crescent City* police had confiscated the burners, *that* event was the last time anyone in New Orleans ever touched this important bronze object,' Jason plausibly concluded. In his hands was indeed the last of its kind. Jason Newman could no longer control his mounting psychological anxiety, along with his ascending curiosity any longer.

The first experiment to be conducted would be a mild practice run, closely following the basic directions specifically stipulated in 'the book'. Votive candles and artificial, dim red light would be utilized just as the instructions' manual had explicitly outlined. Newman stubbornly ambled into the luxurious den and quickly located (in the familiar locked drawer) the pack of potent incense he had purchased at *The Devil's Den*.

The purple window drapes overlooking the *Hudson* were then drawn shut, as general darkness prevailed in the quiet room. The sole-surviving burner was carefully placed upon a pecan-wood table. The dull red light emitted from the burning votive vaguely illuminated the immediate dark area, and the faint glow added a very eerie and suspenseful appearance to that particular section of the Yonkers manor's spacious room.

The incense was carefully arranged inside the burner in order to ensure that the most optimal conditions prevailed for the initiation of the all-important recitation. The dense smoke wafting-up from the coveted pot's confined incense billowed-out, and slowly-but-surely rose, profoundly clouding the immense room from the solid oak-planked floor all the way up to the majestic cedar-beamed ceiling. The enchanting eddy gradually joined invisible ethereal forces apparently associated with the small candle's dim red flickers.

Jason suddenly felt queasy during the enactment's commencement, but the experimenter was quite resolute in his intent to identify black magic as being either fact or fiction. According to the 'black magic' book's instructions, the entire voodoo doll process would require a full hour to undertake and complete.

Newman expected nothing exceptional to result from performing the ancient ritual, and his skepticism received nothing in return. Jason wasn't totally discouraged, despite the fact that nothing peculiar or observable had yet transpired. The rushed voodoo apostate attributed the 'demonstration's failure' to the time-of-day not being precisely midnight. The disappointed fellow returned each involved property to its proper den drawer or shelf, and then in a disconsolate frame of mind, the mansion dweller awaited Julia's exuberant arrival from shopping *Fifth Avenue*. Naturally, Newman would show his normal synthetic interest in asking what ostentatious merchandise his wife had purchased on her whirlwind *Cartier* and *Saks* buying spree.

Mrs. Newman arrived at the family domicile, and after Jason showered his spouse with a litany of false compliments, the couple spent a quiet evening watching TV. The WPIX eleven o'clock news soon appeared upon the massive wall screen, and the bored duo kept their eyelids open just long enough to learn of a major robbery that had occurred at the First National Bank of New York. Photos' of the holdup's suspected culprit had been taken by the bank's latest technological innovation, a 3-D closed circuit TV camera. The pictures had been enlarged and were very detailed, and the television news anchorman reported that the desperate bandit had escaped the depository's vault with several thousand stolen dollars. The following morning, the robber's face was prominently exhibited on every New York City newspaper's front page.

* * * * * * * * * * * *

As Jason conducted his morning transactions inside his downtown Manhattan coin and stamp office, the entrepreneur couldn't disengage his mind from his preliminary failure while experimenting with the "African black arts". The compulsive fellow figured that he would have to employ an alternative system when Julia, Seth, Robin, and the four grandchildren would be on their planned month-long European hiatus. That time period would be the most propitious chance to investigate his imaginative exploration into the black magic realm in perfect seclusion, without the inconvenience of having annoying and bothersome interruptions. And it all would be surreptitiously conducted without distraction, precisely at midnight.

Whenever Jason enjoyed an hour of treasured privacy, the Yonkers resident would practice his new addiction by secretly reading about the dynamics of the astral universe that had been hypothetically defined within the forbidden 'black un-hallowed text'. Exact ceremonies were thoroughly discussed, and each ritual was specifically designed to accomplish a particular objective. Three general categories were individually represented: "Love Magic", "Hate Magic", and "Amulets and Talismans". A lengthy, informative dissertation indicated the precise materials and the exact rune, rhyme, and meter that would effectively instigate the devil's potent sorcery being implemented.

The coin executive avariciously read the book until Newman felt he could articulate and recite each preface and every conjuration to perfection. The enthralled and ardent reader soon believed that he was fully qualified to either objectively verify or disprove the unearthly book's veracity.

210

The day finally arrived when Jason Newman's family journeyed-off to their scheduled summer European vacation, and Jay couldn't wait to see his beloved family board their *TWA* intercontinental plane.

"Take good care of yourself, Jason, and also the family coin business," Julia implored. "It's too bad you aren't joining us for this marvelous European tour," the wife melodramatically stated before she kissed her wealthy husband on the cheek. "You'll be missing London, Paris, and Rome."

Newman paused for a second, feigning unhappiness and melancholy. "I guess I'll be okay walking treacherous fifth Avenue in the meantime!" the coin sultan pessimistically answered. "There's so much work I have to get done with the new shops opening in Boston and Richmond. It would've been impossible for me to fully enjoy London, Paris, and Rome right now with my mind fully concentrating on my company's future financial growth. Julia, it's all very simple," Jason concluded and declared. "I have to make more money for you and the kids to spend-like-water all over the world. Just have a good time and think of me while you're gone."

"Jay, take care of yourself and also the family fortune!" Julia cautioned. "I do believe that you live life a little too seriously!"

Jason then mechanically kissed his wife goodbye to further confirm his marital loyalty and sincerity. As Julia was about to board the huge jet plane, Newman made one last pretentious comment. "Enjoy yourself and don't worry about me. Have fun. I'll be all right. And don't do anything I wouldn't do!" the facetious spouse implored, using certain words he had once heard in a motion picture scene. "And say 'hi' to the rest of the family that's already across the pond, relishing the historic sights of Europe!"

After the *TWA's* departure for "the Old World", Newman drove *his* black *Lincoln* to his original coin shop, where he had first occupied himself taking care of *his* "infant business". The workday seemed extremely monotonous because the only real "important matter" that the sluggish coin collector could somberly contemplate was a second more "competent midnight attempt" at invoking black magic spirits, according to the voodoo manual's directions.

"Everything has to be *black*. My businesses are all in the black, my car is black, and I want my magic to be black, too," the coin czar chuckled to his image being reflected in his *Lincoln's* rear-view mirror. "God, I'll never make it home from the store if this lousy center city traffic congestion doesn't break-up!"

The new devil's disciple parked his black *Lincoln* in the brick-paved front driveway and then briskly stepped inside his mansion's mammoth foyer. Jason then entered his spacious den and finally being alone, conscientiously preparing the necessary items to conduct his 'first uninterrupted, skilled, voodoo venture' into the obscure occult world. Newman planned to stick pins into a 'voodoo doll' to summon the assistance of 'energized supernatural forces'. The Yonkers shaman considered that the voodoo doll would represent the non-captured villain who had audaciously just held-up the venerable First National Bank of New York.

"I'll not practice evil, so I'll especially use black magic to achieve honorable goals. That brazen grand larceny criminal belongs behind bars, and if this little method of mine works, that's exactly where you'll be," mumbled and emphasized Newman to the inanimate male voodoo doll representing the anonymous thief.

The voodoo experimenter had an enlarged newspaper photo' of the pernicious fugitive-from-justice that had been taken by one of the bank's surveillance cameras, and 'the invoker' would now attempt to borrow the snapshot's characteristics and incorporate them into the lifeless doll's existence, causing a 'magically contrived, spiritual-symbiotic relationship'. The police had not made any noteworthy progress in their seemingly stalled investigation, except for the series of pictures that had been obtained from the bank's closed-circuit security camera, so Newman desired to personally intervene and aid law enforcement in capturing the on-the-loose bank villain.

The incantation that the amateur wizard uttered beckoned for the male doll to magically absorb the felon's true identity and personality. That invoked supernatural integration would then immediately transfer the designated evil curse from the afflicted male voodoo doll directly into the exact human body that had been scrupulously targeted.

The gloomy hour of midnight finally arrived and was shown on and chimes from the den's solid oak grandfather clock. The dull, red votive light was dim, the respective candles and incense were lit, and soon the perfumed smoke spiraled upward from the turquoise-stained incense burner. The male voodoo doll was then slowly placed upon the room's mahogany card table. Next, the scoundrel's newspaper photo' was meticulously pinned onto the doll's face, just as the uncanny directions specified. The chosen doll figure was authentically dressed like a little man wearing a brown leather jacket to resemble (in miniature form) the malignant thief pictured in the *New York Times* snapshot.

The weird ceremony officially commenced, exactly at the stroke of midnight. Jason did not intend to symbolically murder the crook; instead, using the miniature voodoo doll, the patriotic American desired to have the transgressor experience excessive physical agony, which eventually would prompt the afflicted criminal to enter a hospital and then make a full confession to the notified authorities.

Following precise directions, the pins were tempered in the candle's flame until the piercing objects became red-hot. Each projectile was then very deliberately plunged into the doll's stomach, and the following mantra words were enunciated and chanted twelve times: "Suffer evil thief until you feel obligated to turn yourself in."

Jason felt stupid and foolish executing the 'silly enactment', speculating all the while that he had been engaged in another 'moronic, ridiculous, fruitless experiment'. But Newman felt he had to again attempt the 'preposterous procedure' to ascertain once-and-for-all either the truth or the falsity of "African Hexology".

The brief chanting ceremony quickly ended, and the junior sorcerer would have to wait for any tangible results of his initiated whammy. Days slipped by and nothing of consequence was reported in the media, either on the local television news, or in the metropolitan newspapers. Two additional weeks elapsed, and still no evidence of the wrongdoer's remorse had surfaced. Surrendering to a passing whim, Jason curiously examined the under-frame of the incense burner, and his incidental inspection detected six small raised *hex*agon designs, all of which had been seen-but-ignored on previous perfunctory examinations. In the past, Newman had accepted the common gargoyle figures as being mere common and meaningless decorative symbols.

As the mesmerized incense-burner owner ran his fingers over the grooved lines, suddenly a panel on the base of the object accidentally flipped open. Inside was a small pouch, and the on-a-mission investigator slowly removed it from its holding bracket. To Newman's great astonishment, inside the sack were several supplemental sticks of incense, which when ignited, would emit a much more pungent aroma than the ones existing inside the pack that Jay had purchased at *The Devil's Den*. The ecstatic discoverer easily distinguished and then mentally described the strong odor as 'jasmine'.

Being crestfallen without obtaining any tangible results pertaining to the brazen bank robber, the next evening, again at the stroke of midnight, Jason Newman reenacted the aforementioned "black arts ceremony". This time the voodoo greenhorn instead intended to burn the newly-discovered, more potent-smelling jasmine in place of the weaker incense sticks.

The by now familiar procedure was confidently repeated. Just as the gigantic grandfather clock was about to strike twelve, the red votive's light was again dim, the auxiliary candles were lit, and the more potent "jasmine incense" was beautifully burning. The male voodoo doll was carefully positioned lying face-up upon the mahogany card table. Jason very gingerly removed the old set of ineffective pins that had remained intact from the prior rite. When each clock in the house chimed midnight, an owl hooted outside the room, and Newman cautiously removed a hot pin from inside the incense burner and then forcefully plunged the heated projectile into the stomach of the motionless voodoo doll. Several more red-hot needles soon followed with Newman almost maniacally utilizing the exact same bizarre insertion procedure.

The smoke filtering-up from the strong-smelling incense rose in a mushroom-shaped cloud, but then the blue fog remained stationary, not completely dissipating throughout the room. Instead, the man-made cumulus hauntingly hovered over the enigmatic incense burner. The azure haze appeared as if it were a ghostly specter, which then gracefully moved and wafted down towards the punctured male doll. Then, the accumulated mist mystically gravitated to where the pins had penetrated the victimized doll's stomach and abdomen. Finally, in one rather exceptional downward zoom, the mysterious vapor disappeared and became swiftly absorbed into the male doll's midriff.

The witnessing of the spectacular phenomenon caused Jason's spine to suffer a series of unnerving chills. The demonic liturgy lasted precisely an hour, and then the strong-smelling incense inside the burner automatically sparked-out. The coincidence of the exact time and the exact occurrence was truly amazing. Jason had a sudden premonition that the aftermath of his second 'solicitation of the black spirits' would definitely register a more efficacious effect.

* * * * * * * * * * * *

In the ensuing day, neither the newspapers nor the TV news had reported any outstanding story concerning the on-the-loose elusive bank robber. Jason characterized his second contact with the universe's metaphysical dark forces as another 'wasteful, futile mistake and subsequent failure'. The fourth day following the 'futile voodoo mistake and failure' a *New York Times* third-page article stated that the evasive bank robber had been captured and taken into custody after admitting himself into *St. Vincent's Hospital* while the suspect was enduring severe stomach and abdominal pains. An alert hospital staff member quickly identified the bandit from printed photographs that the local police precincts had circulated.

In custody, the crook told the attending hospital surgeons that the intolerable agony had begun precisely at midnight, four days before. His extreme distress had increased steadily until the accumulative pain became unbearable. The official emergency room diagnosis was aptly described and recorded as, "Abdominal pain of unknown origin". Just

214

after the wily rogue had been arrested, the stabbing torture inside the bandit's stomach had inexplicably subsided.

"Now *that* unsavory fellow knows how it feels to be a *victim,"* snickered the dark-side black arts' dabbler as Jason Newman finished reading the very revealing third-page column. "The evildoer now has experienced some egregious effects and didn't like the excruciating agony I had administered one bit!"

Jason Newman was thoroughly elated about the crucial secret role he had played in bringing the slick bank thief to justice, but on his skeptical side, the black magic administrator reasoned that the entire coincidence could have been a fluke development, or simply a peculiar parallelism, or an uncanny coincidence. Possessing a very tenacious disposition, the "dark arts" practitioner wanted to 'integrate' another voodoo doll's spiritual penetration on some other devious individual, so the 'black arts vigilante' scanned the media for news of anyone who had committed a particularly heinous felony. 'Focusing on a murderer should be no special problem with twelve-million people living in metropolitan *Gotham,"* Newman theorized and mused.

It didn't take Jason long to discover a dishonorable person who had masterminded a brutal murder. According to area tabloid accounts, the black-hearted killer had entered a restaurant and began firing a handgun, killing a prominent citizen and seriously wounding several other vulnerable diners. An attempt by waiters to thwart the culprit's escape was fruitless, and after a brief struggle with an off-duty policeman, the perpetrator broke-away from the cop's clutches. The desperate killer wildly dashed-out of the chaotic restaurant, but the malicious gun carrier did leave several material clues behind. A button off of his jacket and a few drops of blood were the only remnants of the gruesome homicide that the vile escapee had left behind for police detectives to analyze.

"I'll target this ruthless butcher as my next project. I'll use my black magic power for the ultimate good of society," the New Age Sheriff-at-Large vowed.

Jason hypothesized that black magic worked best while employing the use of an article of clothing draped upon the voodoo doll as a personal link connecting a 'reality symbol' to the guilty assailant. The coin-store genius was determined to acquire some personal possession or token that had once belonged to the heinous killer, but how?

The self-proclaimed enforcer of justice ambled across *Times Square* and sauntered into the crime-scene restaurant in an impromptu manner. Newman conversed with the addled owner, an old-time friend and mutual coin collector. The restaurateur showed his distinguished guest the exact spot where the crook's scuffle with the off-duty policeman had occurred.

"The villain banged his head here, and there's a spot of blood on the rug that the cops have already taken a sample and analyzed it," the upset owner revealed.

Jason asked permission to scrape-up a small blood specimen for his own secret evidence probe, and then the amateur Dick Tracy deposited the tiny speck into a 4" x 4" metallic container. Newman thanked the bewildered owner for his general cooperation, and hurriedly left the exclusive high-end eating establishment.

'Inspector Newman' was highly piqued about reaching his stately mansion, and his keen mind was focused upon repeating his second successful black magic ceremony. 'Would it work once more?' the incense burner fanatic wondered.

Everything was set-up in the den according to the book's explicit directions, and precisely at midnight, Jason gently placed the same male doll upon the same mahogany table, and methodically smeared a trace of the dried blood sample below the voodoo doll's right eyebrow. This time the doll was garbed in a dark blue business suit as had been documented in several New York City newspaper articles. Newman then heated the accompanying pin until the needle tip became red-hot, and next, the voodoo student forcefully inserted the sharp object into the doll's right eye.

"Suffer the way you made others suffer until you're finally caught and prosecuted," the black arts' witch-doctor repeated several times. 'It's now time for you to be disparaged and tortured!"

Like before, the odd ceremony lasted exactly an hour, and all of the requisite paraphernalia was then furtively put away in the den cabinets. The next morning, Jason nervously anticipated the results of his "supernatural conspiracy", perceiving himself' as a fearsome medium whose awesome power was commuting between the physical and the metaphysical worlds. The zealous-but-fatigued black magic advocate went to bed, and shortly thereafter, fell asleep, wondering what sort of surprise the next day's news might yield.

The morning papers presented the same routine catalogue of fires, robberies, and the old, hackneyed, candy-coated tabloid celebrity gossip, but the media outlets failed to report any allusion to Newman's ruthless killer suspect. Later on, the evening news featured a special story on the crafty "murderer", who had escaped on foot from the popular high-end restaurant.

The following morning, the *New York Times* reported that the 'restaurant killer' had suffered intense pain in his right eye, and out of necessity, had gone to an ophthalmologist for immediate treatment and to obtain vital medication. The eye doctor could not determine the cause of the discomfort, but then sent his new patient to a pharmacy to pirchase a strong pain prescription. The pharmacist was an alert citizen who had recognized the first-time customer (from media accounts) as the crazed triggerman who had discharged the handgun inside the center-city restaurant. The vile 'revenge killer' was swiftly located and apprehended, arraigned, and instantly incarcerated.

After reading the relevant news article, Jason imagined himself to be a valiant crusader fighting against crime; a bona fide flesh and blood modern super hero. If the honest-to-goodness defender of justice could continue his personal war against iniquity, urban violence could be drastically reduced. The ecstatic coin dealer still had several more magical sticks of the 'marvelous jasmine incense', and Newman would soon repeat his dedicated campaign against other warped, reckless, law and order violators, all being vile adversaries of human morality.

"The ends justify the means and the means justify the ends," moralized the proud, contemporary, self-appointed, masquerading police detective. "Criminal scumbags deserve the consequences of black arts' revenge. Now, to select my next targeted victim!"

The black arts' manipulator wanted to try his esoteric witchcraft on a wicked acquaintance other than a wanton criminal, but Jason wished to practice his spell ability on someone who nevertheless possessed unethical, detrimental standards.

Rosco Scola was a loud-mouthed, wholly deplorable, arrogant, antagonistic individual who happened to be President of the exclusive *East Coast Numismatics Consortium*. Rosco was not only belligerent and acrimonious at club meetings, but the insufferable bully also threatened many board members who had contradicted or opposed the psychopath's past policy positions. As was his obnoxious habit, Scola rudely confronted and mocked innocent organization members, who disagreed with his dictatorial personality, and the nasty harasser frequently challenged each dissenter to "step outside" to engage in a bare-knuckled fistfight.

Rosco Scola was especially unruly, gruff, and uncontrollable; the fanatic was a fierce-tempered Sicilian, who was the bane of existence for many respectable *Consortium* members, including Jason Newman. 'The Mafia Don's' innumerable enemies would love to have the flippant instigator silenced by an act of God,' Newman reasoned.

Jason often sat next to Rosco's black swivel chair at scheduled meetings, and one afternoon, the coin merchant nourished an idea in his fertile mind that would permanently neutralize Mr. Scola. Rosco would always take notes at discussion sessions that he later used to fuel his constant vitriolic tirades, and then the ill-tempered offender would predictably discard his temporary records into the under-the-desk trashcan, right after the coin meeting had adjourned. That night, Rosco had maliciously and publicly accused Newman of complicity in an organizational conspiracy designed to malign *his* integrity.

The voodoo vigilante was mortified that he had been humiliated, scorned, insulted, and embarrassed by the crude, callous bully at the coin society's latest formal meeting. A heated argument soon erupted, which immediately destroyed any dignity the club's decision-making session had originally generated. When the verbal donnybrook finally ended, Jason remained behind inside the conference chamber to cunningly collect the torn scraps of paper that argumentative Rosco Scola had angrily ripped-up and then hostilely thrown into the nearby metal trashcan.

That night was the perfect time for voodoo priest Jason Newman to perform another clandestine "dark rite ceremony". The coin guru's heart was now motivated by extreme, almost-visceral vengeance, all because Rosco Scola had savagely intimidated his rival before the assembled board members, one time too many.

At 11:55 p.m., the New Age black magic medium cautiously prepared the 'spiritual-laboratory operational card table', the very essential incense burner, the vital red votive candles, and the male voodoo doll, that was then dressed in similar white shirt and black pants. The figure's costume was similar to just what Jason's principal adversary had been wearing the night before at the confrontational coin club meeting. Jay Newman carefully spread Rosco Scola's former note scraps over the male voodoo doll's clothed body. The insidious, loudmouthed Coin Organization President had never conceived or realized that he had made an immense blunder by inadvertently leaving behind the hand-shredded written notes, with his indecipherable, crude handwriting scribbled upon the thoroughly ripped paper.

When the den's grandfather clock pendulum signaled the stroke of midnight, Jason snickered as the black arts' prestidigitator began performing his supernatural 'other world methodology'. The devil's new metaphysical priest then roughly thrust the red-hot pin into the doll's throat, and next, the hex practitioner meanly and spitefully twisted the pin back and forth several times to dramatically emphasize his great enmity for his spiteful avowed enemy. Four more pins were soon also viciously inserted, a representative separate needle being shoved into each of the doll's arms and legs.

The incense burner was at that critical moment wildly smoking-out dense fumes and puffy billows, and a moment later, a ghost-like cloud rose and wafted, and next, the dark gaseous mass hovered above the inert form lying upon the den's voodoo operating card table. The fog

218

formation slowly drifted towards the targeted doll, and when the fumes encountered the lying figure's throat, the thick, hazy mass mystically zoomed into the doll's voice box, and then, the visible gas phenomenon suddenly disappeared from visual existence.

The unearthly ceremony was over at precisely 1:00 a.m., and the vital items that had been used for the "spiritual retribution communication" were again stealthily placed and concealed inside their respective den storage hiding compartments. However, the five malignant pins still remained implanted in the doll's anatomy.

"Languish in your anguish," laughed the contemporary warlock to the tiny doll representation of antagonistic Rosco Scola. "Your pain is my gain!" Jason Newman very intentionally and humorously rhymed. "Let's see what happens to your throat and to your four doomed appendages. Ha, ha, ha!"

The self-learned black arts' witchdoctor could not wait to read in the newspapers, or see on TV, the inevitable negative news story about the ugly fate of his chief adversary. A few days passed by without any sign of incident or malice. The next Wednesday morning, while having breakfast on the riverside patio overlooking the majestic Hudson, Jay Newman's kitchen phone rang. The exasperated caller was Wally Bennett, the newly-elected president of the *Numismatics Organization of American Dealers*.

"Jason, have you heard about Rosco Scola?" Wally rhetorically asked. "The pathetic creep had a terrible stroke several hours after the stormy meeting ended last night. He's lying in the hospital in very bad shape," Bennett loudly reported. "Rosco's reported to be paralyzed from his throat to his toes, and his voice-box cannot speak a blessed syllable. The jerk, or should I say 'the guy', can't even move an arm or a leg. The doctors say there's little hope of recovery from his horrible paralysis. If he lives," Wally Bennett qualified and then cleared his raspy throat, "poor Scola will be confined to a wheelchair the rest of his life."

Jason listened intently to Wally's 'good news', and it was certain now that current President Bennett would be selected to succeed Rosco Scola as the *Consortium CEO* by the prestigious organization's powerful executive board committee.

"Gee, Wally. I'm really very sorry to hear about that terrible development," the call recipient replied, adroitly feigning concern, grief, and sorrow. There was a broad smile of sadistic satisfaction forming on the devil advocate's face as Jason Newman gently hung-up the kitchen phone. The coin and stamp executive's chief nemesis had been permanently silenced and neutralized.

* * * * * * * * * * * *

Jason's family had returned the following week from their month-long European vacation, just three days after Rosco Scola's dramatic stroke misfortune, which Newman had creatively classified as 'a well-deserved *stroke* of revenge'.

"Too bad that *that* reprehensible heckler didn't burst all of the blood vessels in his disgusting throat," denoted and stated Julia, who also despised the impetuously rude Sicilian loudmouth. "It's hard to feel any remorse or compassion for a contemptible brute like him!"

"Now, Honey, the Golden Rule suggests that we should love our enemies as we love ourselves," the wily coin mogul prevaricated. "Let's try to show a little *Hudson River* empathy!"

The novice sorcerer soon performed a subsequent black arts' demonstration that yielded astonishing results, since Jason had been feeling a trifle guilty because his harsh punishment that had been dispensed to Rosco Scola had been too blatantly severe.

The next evening, just before midnight, Newman ventured from the master bedroom downstairs to his secret laboratory/den. Upon opening a locked cabinet, the feeling-guilty mogul located the abused Rosco Scola voodoo doll and then proceeded to gently remove four of the five pins, leaving intact only the one penetrating into the figure's voice-box. That last throat pin was then pulled half-way out, and without any further special black magic techniques being employed, Newman returned the abused specimen to its den cabinet, and soon, the mansion resident re-locked the door. 'I'll see if my adjustments will make any improved changes to Rosco's incapacitated condition.'

Three days elapsed, and the coin-store baron answered the living room phone inside his stately palisade home. The excited caller was new *CEO* Wally Bennett.

"Jason, you'll never believe this story in a million years!"

"What's got you senses so out-of-kilter, Wally?" the call recipient exclaimed. "Did you hit the Pick-6 Lottery?"

"It's Rosco Scola. The detestable braggart made almost a full recovery and can actually move and control his arms and his legs," Bennett loudly related. "The dumbfounded hospital doctors are calling the phenomenon a miracle!"

"Wally, did you say that *that* bellicose nutcase has made a full recovery?" Newman asked, pretending to be shocked.

"Well, Jason, the nasty instigator *almost* did just that," Wally Bennett qualified and answered. "Even though Rosco's no longer an invalid confined to a wheelchair, for some remote reason, the sarcastic Sicilian still can't speak a word of English normally."

"Thanks for the info' update, Wally," Jason matter-of-factly responded. "Keep me posted on old Rosco's physical condition. The world's much better-off if that belligerent loudmouth never speaks a syllable in any language, ever again! Even now, I believe that Rosco Scola is an *invalid invalid!* Ha, ha, ha!"

Several cold months passed by, and the February calendar date of the annual *Mardi Gras* celebration was rapidly approaching. Julia was thrilled about attending the raucous event for the first time, and the enthralled wife couldn't wait to pack her bags for New Orleans. She and Jason had special costumes, custom-made by their favorite New York City tailor, and the super-exhilarated husband and wife were anticipating their participation in the gaudy Bourbon Street parade, and then later, being present at the tremendous gala hotel party occurring immediately after the downtown festivities.

"Oh Jason, I can't wait to go. I've always wanted to see the gorgeous Garden District and also visit Basin Street!" the pretty middle-aged wife communicated. "Truthfully, Jay. I wasn't half this excited about journeying first-class on my recent European vacation!"

"I can understand what you're all *jazzed* up about," giddily laughed her semi-comedic spouse, who was overly enamored at uttering his own rather ludicrous New Orleans pun.

Reservations had been secured in advance (by the family travel agent), and Giles, the substitute family chauffeur, drove the couple across the *East River* to *Idlewild Airport*. Jason and Julia merrily flew to the *Crescent City* via a *United Airlines* four-engine prop', which touched-down at their fun-filled destination in the early afternoon. By 5 p.m., the Newmans were comfortably resting inside their *French Quarter* hotel luxury suite.

"Jay, while you were in the lobby buying your newspaper Jack had called," Julia informed her affluent marital mate. "He's flying into New Orleans from Denver. Your brother says he'll meet us at the hotel right after the *Mardi Gras* celebration."

"Is he gonna' be in the parade?" her husband asked. "Jack was a fanatical wannabe' mummer every New Year's Day when he lived in Philly'! The *Mardi Gras* fiasco ought to have my exhibitionist brother flying sky high!"

"No, don't be silly. You know how Jack is," Julia mildly criticized with a contrived frown showing on her face. "He hates drunken crowds and loud repugnant noise."

Jason Newman reflected for a moment, imagining that he would share a small secret with his spendthrift wife. "You know, Julia. I became a tad jealous when you were slow-dancing with my little brother at the last company *Christmas* party. I guess I still have a bit of sibling rivalry ingrained inside my envious heart."

"Jay, to tell the truth," Julia blushed, "Jack is the only other boy I ever *liked* in high school."

"You say you really *liked* Jack?" Jason testily asked. "He's always resented my success!"

"Yes, but I *loved* you then, and still do now. I fell for you right on the spot when Jack introduced us on that memorable ferry ride out to the Statue of Liberty."

"Julia, I believe you with all my heart. I'll never forget your kind words," Jason remarked. "Let's bury the past and enjoy the present. Now, it's almost party time!"

After examining their clothes and transferring the items from their suitcases to the room's dresser drawers and side bureau, the couple hung their formal suits and dresses, along with their garish silver and black *Mardi Gras* costumes, near the room's closet entrance. The husband suggested that the two should pay a surprise unannounced visit to his company's *French Quarter Coin Emporium*.

After a five-minute taxi ride to the corporate store, Jerry McCoy was introduced to Julia, and the trio casually discussed general business at the *Emporium*. The husband inquired how business was doing with the advent of numerous the pre-Lent parties.

"It's tripled so far during *Mardi Gras* week," confided Jerry. Indeed, all facets of the store's business seemed to be going well without any serious hitches or snags."

After their short chat with Jerry McCoy, the company owners left the coin and stamp establishment for their hotel in order to rest-up for the next day's extensive carnival week festivities. The colorful costume parade was to commemorate *Shrove Tuesday* and also the religious advent of *Ash Wednesday*. The Newmans enjoyed a quick meal served at the hotel's fabulous Southern Buffet, and soon were comfortably relaxing in their elegant suite.

The next morning, Jason and Julia had a late brunch, and thereafter, spent the afternoon lounging inside their splendid hotel room, preparing for an exciting, festive evening. About 5:30, the New York couple entered their theme costumes, because the famous annual carnival parade was scheduled to start at 6:00 p.m. sharp.

The husband was disguised as the monster *Frankenstein,* and Julia was costumed as Elizabeth, the beautiful bride of the mad scientist Victor Frankenstein. Jason's frightening mask added the descriptive adjective *"gruesome"* to complement the common noun *"twosome"*. The Newmans entered into a random marching formation, and assumed their line position within the rowdy parade assemblage, with

Julia standing next to a flamboyant-but-colorfully-costumed clown on her left, and with a boisterous masked circus ringmaster in attendance, being adjacent to Jason's right.

Thousands of eager spectators lined the crowded sidewalks, and the colorful marching bands were playing stirring *Mardi Gras* festival jazz music at various parade intersections. It was a jovial, celebratory time for all the thousands of enthusiastic participants.

The clamorous procession meandered through the *French Quarter* district, and when the formal pageantry gradually ended a few hours later, Jason and Julia merrily returned to their plush hotel to review and discuss their individual marching performances. In a short while, more heightened revelry awaited the New York visitors at the hotel's wild *Grand Saturnalia Gala.*

"Julia, I'm going down to the lobby and wait for you. I want to sample a double shot of Southern Comfort."

"Okay, Jay. I'll need about ten-minutes to powder my nose and freshen-up," the wife verbally indicated. "Don't get lost staggering around in the maddening crowd!"

The gigantic party was to be celebrated inside an enormous hotel convention meeting room. Newman waited impatiently for his tardy wife, but after twenty difficult minutes of mingling and jostling with inebriated strangers, Victor Frankenstein's bride still had been absent from the noise-laden lobby. 'Where's Julia? I'm beginning to worry. It's now been a full half-hour?' the anxious husband wondered and contemplated. 'I'll give her another ten-minutes. If she isn't here by then, I'll go up to the room and see what's delaying her besides wearing her super-tight bra and girdle,' Jason amusingly thought before swallowing-down his potent second round of Southern Comfort on the rocks. "One more glass of this potent whiskey and I think I'll be just as intoxicated as the rest of these hotel revelers!"

Ten-minutes later, the concerned coin merchant took a lobby elevator to the couple's third-floor suite and soon knocked on the door, but there was no answer. The nervous hotel guest then used his room key and suspiciously entered. Newman was positively horrified at what his half-inebriated eyes beheld.

The entire room was in complete disarray. Drawers had been pulled-out, clothes had been strewn-about all over the floor. and Julia was not visible anywhere in the bedroom. Jason searched the marble-tiled bathroom and much to his shock, his wife was lying upon the black and white checkered floor with her clothes torn-off, and her garments were scattered all about. Blood streamed from the naked woman's open mouth, and red streams also trickled from her nostrils. Julia Newman had evidently been savagely attacked and beaten, and the brutalized woman was mumbling indiscernible words while in a semi-conscious daze.

Jason lifted and then carried his injured wife to the adjoining room and tenderly lowered her limp body onto the large, king-size bed. The distraught husband next notified the hotel's security department of the savage criminal assault. As Julia started regaining her sensibilities, the partially incoherent wife intimated in a low whisper, "I've been raped, Jason. I've been raped."

"What! Who did it? Who did it?" Newman angrily demanded. "I'll violently strangle the wretched culprit to death when I find out!"

"The Clown!" the wife gasped in horror. "The circus clown that was marching next to us in the downtown parade," the wife pathetically moaned, and then drifted-off back into unconsciousness.

Hotel security personnel rushed into the ritzy luxury suite and seeing what deplorable malice had occurred, the head official immediately called for an ambulance. Then, after regaining their professional composure, the security personnel thoroughly inspected the neighboring rooms to obtain any visible telltale clues. Several valuable items had been stolen, including Julia's prized diamond earrings and her cherished favorite gold bracelet. Also, Jason's good luck St. Gaudens $20.00 gold coin had been pilfered.

Newman met his brother Jack later that evening inside the crowded lobby of the exclusive *French Quarter* hotel. Both men were wearing dark blue business suits.

"Jay, you look fairly pale and weak. What's the matter?" Jack asked his only sibling. "You look like you've seen both Caesar's and Cleopatra's ghosts!"

"Jack, you'll never believe it in a million years. Julia was raped earlier tonight inside our suite when I was waiting for her down in the lobby. The despicable crime has been the most horrible, atrocious, and devastating experience of our married lives!" the elder brother disclosed before sniffing twice.

"Who would do such a terrible thing?" Jack asked. "Especially with it occurring during a joyful *Mardi Gras* celebration."

Jason was almost in a trance as the beleaguered bearer of bad news stared dumbfounded at his brother's florid face. Newman's voice was broken, and his eyes were now producing large tears. "Jack, I just don't know. I haven't a trace of a clue," the fazed coin distributor dejectedly replied. "The police told me that everyone in New Orleans is a suspect. What a crock of horse manure *that* asinine statement was! Tell me, what time did you get into town?"

"My plane arrived from Denver at five," Jack Newman recalled and related. "I then checked into my hotel down the street at seven. I showered, took a brief nap, and finally walked over here."

"Well, Jack, the crime was committed a little over two-hours ago," Jason commented while carefully phrasing his slurring words. "And according to the police's broad definition, even *you* and *me* happen to be eligible suspects."

Jason Newman then paused again to gauge his younger brother's reaction to the disgusting news. Then, the older brother noticed a deep gash showing on Jack's left cheek.

"Jack, how did you get that nasty facial cut? It looks pretty deep and the gash might get infected!"

"I was ready to start shaving in my hotel room in Denver. I was standing on a wet bathroom towel and as I stepped to grab my shaving cream can, which was positioned on top of the toilet tank lid. When I reached, I slipped and fell on the floor," Jack Newman explained. "Unfortunately, I was holding my razor in my hand. I'm afraid that in my haste, I accidentally slit myself really good."

Julia Newman was hospitalized for a week before the rape victim was emotionally healthy enough to be released. The New Orleans police never caught the heinous rapist, but the fiendish rogue had left something tangible behind. His facial skin had been embedded under Julia's long fingernails, and that skin transfer had happened when Jason's wife had scratched her attacker in self-defense during the grotesque and barbaric act.

The Newmans left for New York a week after Julia's more than traumatic *Mardi Gras* experience and the wife's subsequent hospital recuperation. But still, angry Jason had a vengeful plan to handily punish the anonymous, diabolical perpetrator.

* * * * * * * * * * * *

Julia was not feeling well when she had returned to the family's stately mansion overlooking the regal *Hudson* and the very scenic New Jersey palisades. Using strong persuasion, Jason convinced his traumatized spouse to voluntarily enter a city hospital and undergo a complete mental and physical examination. Money was no object. Mrs. Newman was swiftly admitted into the *Einstein Medical Center,* and her prescribed convalescence would require a full week of absolute rest and tranquility.

"I'll be back for you in a week, Honey. I promise. Then, you'll be as good as new," the husband pledged to his beloved spouse. "Listen to my advice. You need this important hospital stay as much as you need precious oxygen."

"I hope so," Julia softly answered. "Please try your best to visit me every day. My damaged self-confidence needs to be bolstered!"

The infuriated voodoo practitioner departed the premises in a very vindictive frame of mind. The revenge-seeker entered a *Greenwich Village* organic health store, shopped very scrupulously, and soon purchased special herbs: yarrow and vermillion. Newman also bought a batch of ironwood and a small black metal caldron, which the alert clerk labeled as "a seldom-used novelty item". Newman's final black magic ceremony would be different than any others that the voodoo incense burner artist had previously performed. The man's heart was overflowing with an abundance of rancor and disdain. His sole purpose was resolute; the protagonist would not procrastinate. It was all plain and simple. Julia's evil rapist must die.

"The attacker will wish he were rotting-away in hell before I get through with him," the enraged husband muttered as the self-appointed law-enforcement deputy drove his black *Lincoln* home from the uptown hospital, all-the-while mentally plotting his elaborate scheme. The assaulter's facial skin scrapings had been kept isolated in an airtight jar inside the master bathroom's medicine cabinet. Those salvaged vital evidence vestiges Newman had purposely obtained from underneath Julia's fingernails the very night of the terrible New Orleans rape.

That evening during a full moon, Jason Newman's face had the look of a demented maniac. The surreptitious schemer cunningly heated the black metal caldron on the kitchen range. Then. the sly ingredient-mixer reduced the hardwood chips, yarrow and vermillion with a penknife, and next Newman furtively burned the debris into ashes, which were soon cautiously added to a specially scented oil compound. The concocted formula was then deftly poured into a glass beaker. To that satanic mixture the crazed madman very systematically added the skin scrapings obtained from the vile rapist's face, and which later had been astutely removed from under Julia's fingernails.

The symbolic male voodoo doll had been dressed for the occasion as the hideous circus clown who had marched next to Julia in the *Mardi Gras* parade. Again, the red candle light was dimmed, auxiliary votive candles were lit, and the oxidized, turquoise incense burner was respectfully placed onto the mahogany den card table. It was a very eerie scene, especially with the layer of patina crusted on the incense burner strangely glowing bright emerald. The functional candles flickered, and the emitted flames swayed upon their separate wicks in the midst of the dimly lit, rose-colored atmosphere. Undoubtedly, the in-progress death experiment had reached the point of no return.

'Oh my God,' assessed the New Age alchemist. 'This evil clown being represented by the doll had marched beside Julia in the *Mardi Gras* parade. Yes, dear Bozo. Get ready to join hell's perverted circus, you anonymous lowlife.'

The possessed sorcerer had only one more piece of incense left from the antique burner's secret panel, and the sought-after stick was still lodged inside the underneath compartment. Newman tugged and removed it, and then wrathfully pushed its entire length directly into the center of the metallic incense burner. The selected bronze, astral communicator was then satisfactorily lit.

At the precise stroke of midnight, the Black Arts Apothecary anointed the clown figure with the demonic soot that had been rubbed from the black metal caldron. As Jason hypnotically performed *that* secret enactment, Newman uttered the black magical words, "Xapa, Xitha, Xandry, Zapith, Zapera, Zika."

The smoke from the burning incense rose in a puffy billow and gently fluttered above the burner's circumference. Suddenly, a ghostly image appeared, and the haunting phantasm looked like the classic portrayal of Devil Lucifer. The horrid-but-palpable apparition floated towards the circus clown model, and as the specter hovered above the symbolic representation of the rapist, the demon's vaporous outline swished directly into the diminutive voodoo doll, and amazingly, instantaneously disappeared. The awesome reprisal ceremony was over. Its extraordinary results would leave Jason breathless.

* * * * * * * * * * * *

Several weeks passed and the black magic conjurer surmised that his latest ritual had regrettably resulted in a complete failure. Jason speculated that his personal animosity for the doll's human counterpart had somehow interfered with the hellish curse's direct effectiveness. Newman was both depressed and melancholy, since the obstinate enchanter had used the last stick of the special incense, and *that* rod's feeble impact suggested that 'the black magic tool' had been either defective or impotent.

The final Monday in late March, just after lunch, the husband drove Julia to *St. Vincent Hospital* for her next scheduled physical checkup. Shortly thereafter, Newman felt an irresistible urge to rush home to hide the exposed incense burner still positioned upon the den card table, and to next survey the early edition of the daily newspaper. After reading the morning press, the thwarted black magic pharmacist again stepped outside, this time to retrieve the afternoon mail.

In his haste, the mentally distracted walker tripped over a small box that had been mysteriously placed outside the mansion's front doorstep. There weren't any mailing labels or postage stamps evident anywhere on the delivered 'incognito package'. The befuddled resident brought the nameless parcel inside and carried it into the enormous den.

Being curious by the unexpected delivery, Jay ripped-off the brown paper wrapping, and the startled recipient instantly experienced a nervous sensation, just as the desk telephone rang. The caller *was* Julia, informing her preoccupied spouse that her checkup had been completed and that the wife needed a ride home from the lower *Manhattan* hospital, because it was Reginald's and Giles' day off.

Jason reluctantly put-off finishing his opening of the unsolicited package, and in a bad mood, drove his black *Lincoln Continental* through the theater and garment districts, finally reaching Grenwich Village's *St. Vincent Hospital*. Julia was picked-up near the valet parking area, and Newman learned in their homeward-bound conversation that the doctors' evaluation of her total condition was "satisfactory". The couple celebrated the good news by stopping at *Sardi's* and partaking in an excellent lunch. The ambiance was pleasant and wonderfully cordial, and thereafter, the Newmans returned to their cherished destination, their opulent Yonkers mansion overlooking the placid *Hudson*.

Upon arriving home, Julia declared, "Jason, I don't need a tranquilizer. I'm so tired that I'm going right to bed."

"I'll be up there to join you in a short while," her husband half-heartedly replied. "But first I must finish doing something."

The man of the house finally was able to step to the den and complete his prying-open the unknown-origin, recently-delivered mystery box. The baffled recipient carefully removed the external brown wrapping paper. Much to the receiver's utter consternation, inside the container was nestled a voodoo doll dressed in a ridiculous-looking circus clown's costume. Newman nervously removed the small mask covering the clown's face and was instantly so horrified that the millionaire coin merchant nearly fainted to the floor with overwhelming fright. Jason's eyes gazed upon the mummified, shriveled face of Jerry McCoy, the formerly trusted manager of the *New Orleans Coin Emporium*.

Clutched in one little hand was Jason's valuable St. Gaudens twenty-dollar Golden Eagle good luck piece, and in the other bony palm was Julia's large diamond ear-rings. The wife's golden bracelet was also present, the jewelry piece adorning the doll skeleton's tiny right wrist. A closer inspection of the male doll's withered face revealed the scratches that Julia had frantically inflicted upon Jerry McCoy during the vulgar hotel room rape.

The frightful mummified doll was then locked-up with trembling hands inside a bottom compartment of the plush den's wall-length cabinet. 'No human being will ever see the miniature macabre cadaver as long as I still live,' the vengeful voodoo witchdoctor mentally decreed and vowed.

Jason Newman knew that the next morning's obituary page of the *New Orleans Picayune* would list the unexpected and suspicious death of one scurrilous human being, Jerry McCoy. The profound question that rattled around inside Jason Newman's troubled mind was, 'Exactly who had sent the tiny doll clown coffin to his stately mansion overlooking the *Hudson?*'

"The Dye Is Cast"

Howard Steel was age thirty-five and his 6' 3" frame housed a well-conditioned, enviable muscular physique. The dark-haired, brown-eyed Adonis was extremely popular with status-seeking members of the opposite gender. The bachelor/optometrist owned a very successful lens manufacturing firm in Northridge, several miles above downtown Dayton, Ohio. Besides gorgeous single females, Steel's next favorite hobby was aviation.

Howard's best friend Bill Martino was an excellent optician who was also Steel's very reliable business associate. The pair made a good team in socializing with 'swinging jet set clubs' around the famous mid-western city where the *Miami,* the *Stillwater,* and the *Mad River* geographically converge.

In terms of U.S. invention history, Dayton, Ohio was the setting where creative Orville and Wilbur Wright had designed (in their bicycle shop's workroom) the first man-carrying powered airplane. Howard Steel believed that the two founders of modern flight were so fascinating that *he* had become the area's foremost authority on the two early *Twentieth Century* aviation pioneers' biographies. The eager optometrist was totally enamored with studying the entire background of aircraft history, from the Wrights maiden flight at Kitty Hawk, North Carolina on December 17, 1903, up to the marvels of today's lethal stealth bombers.

The *United States Air Force Museum* at Dayton's *Wright-Patterson Base* was virtually regarded as a shrine by Howard Steel, and ever since his youth, the enterprising eye doctor dreamed of earning a small plane pilot's license. And after a year of intense flying lessons, the flight enthusiast finally received his single engine certification in March of 1995.

As an elementary school student, Howard Steel had avidly read about the early air battles fought over Europe, and the young academic pupil later became very knowledgeable about the various planes flown by the American, German, British, and French early pilots. Steel's fondest dream was to one day own and fly a vintage biplane similar to the ones that had dotted the battle skies over France and Germany during *World War I.*

Popular Aviation Magazine had been carrying advertisements sponsored by a French company, which had been manufacturing replicas of classic aircraft for the expressed use of modern-day collectors and aviation enthusiasts. The first plane the ambitious aviation history buff planned to acquire was a biplane reproduction of his *WWI* dream machine: a *Spad.*

Howard placed an order for the expensive novelty with the French manufacturer, and Steel and Bill Martino planned to take an *Air France 747* to Paris in the spring, when the weather pattern would be more conducive for piloting small one-engine airplanes.

"I've never been on the other side of the Pond," honestly admitted an Bill Martino. "Is it true that the French are jealous and antagonistic of self-motivated Americans?"

"William, I think you'll like the way French women kiss," Howard Steel jested to his often-facetious business partner. "Could you believe it? Our upcoming Parisian adventure will be much better than eating French fries smeared with *Heintz* ketchup."

"Howie, I'll chalk that one up as one of your best classic tongue-in-cheek remarks ever," Martino answered with a wry smile. "But really, you're pretty funny for an optometrist who thinks that *pupils* are students in school! I'll bet that the amorous French girls will probably call you Howie kisses!"

* * * * * * * * * * * * *

The close friends had been invited to a festive *New Year's Eve* party that would officially welcome-in 1997. Extrovert Lucy Brookes was a long-time acquaintance of the sought-after bachelors, and the party hostess had commissioned a reputable psychic who could accurately and authoritatively read the guests' Tarot cards. Howard and Bill were looking forward to attending "the happening", since Lucy's parties always included the most vivacious and available women in and around Dayton.

"What time do we have to be at the get-together, Bill?" Howard asked his favorite drinking companion. "I'd like to get there early to mix and mingle."

"We should be at Lucy's pad by 9:00 p.m. I'm sure that our gal will have a nifty food and beverage spread as she always does," Bill Martino elaborated. "And her shindigs are notorious for providing plenty of fun and originality. Confidentially, I've never had a Tarot reading before, so I'm really going to immensely enjoy the swift departure of the year 1996 from my office wall calendar," the garrulous optician added. "Your wheels or mine?" William Martino inquired in regard to the mode of transportation to and from the slated super *New Year's Eve* celebration.

"Bill, I'll pick you up at 8:30," Howard genially replied. "That should give us ample time to imbibe some tasty whiskey before the *Times Square* crystal ball stuff starts showing on television."

Later that afternoon, Howard pursued exercising his regular daily weightlifting routine in his private basement gym, and after the stud finished his upper body workout, the suave bachelor spent several seconds admiring his well-defined biceps in a full-length wall mirror. And then after showering, the *Spad* fanatic carefully dressed for the much-anticipated gala *New Year's Eve* revelry at Lucy Brooke's place. The handsome physical specimen quickly stepped out the door, locked the portal behind him, and was soon sitting at the wheel of his immaculate white *Mercedes*.

Bill Martino was picked-up five minutes later at his condo', and the frivolous companions conversed about the prospect of reuniting with several "hot" females whose names were on the popular hostess's extensive guest list. Feeling refreshed and ready to party on that cold starless December 31st evening, Howie drove the sleek *Mercedes* in the direction of the city's eastern suburbs.

Lucy's palatial home was spacious and the abode featured a vast combination open-den and kitchen area. The recreation space had been especially designed to accommodate "Our Miss Brookes" free-spirited lifestyle, and her massive den flaunted a magnificent red cedar-wood cathedral ceiling and a solid oak-planked floor.

"Our Miss Brookes" was the proprietor of a swanky jewelry store situated in an exclusive suburban mall, and the effervescent doll had become very successful in operating her flourishing retail endeavor, as evidenced by her red *Ferrari* and by her coveted European *Club Med* membership card. Lucy's valet Stephen Furgione was clad in a black tuxedo, and had been serving as the party's bartender.

The manor's doorbell rang and the very curvaceous, flamboyant hostess answered. "Welcome Howie! Come on in! I'm so glad that you and Bill could make it. I'll introduce you to everyone you might not know," Lucy Brookes promised. "Are you dynamic guys looking forward to your special Tarot card readings?"

"You bet, Lucy," Howard Steel readily agreed. "I wouldn't have missed it for the world. It's a really terrific novel idea, and it should be lots of fun doing the metaphysical thing."

"I'll be okay as long as I don't have to suffer through a tea leaf seance while gazing at nasty animal entrails!" Bill Martino amply laughed. "I don't know exactly why, but out-of-the-ordinary oddball things always tend to fascinate me!"

"Don't worry, Bill," returned Lucy Brookes. "Tarot cards are much more sophisticated than those other more primitive methods of divination you always see advertised all the time on TV."

It wasn't long before the two male specimens were beneficially socializing with attractive women who could have easily been contestants in the *Miss Universe Pageant*. The taped background music featured a variety of Madonna and Steve Miller Band hits, and everyone present was-fast dancing to the feverish rhythms.

The mansion's bar area was also very active, and after "cutting a rug" with two "knockout" models from Akron, Howard and Bill each imbibed several eggnogs that had been powerfully laced with rum. Everyone making merry at the party was forgetting his or her personal problems and abandoning his or her inhibitions, while the fun-loving guests mingled, danced, and amiably joked. Throughout the ongoing merriment, a hired caterer and his staff were serving a buffet of hot and cold hors d'oeuvres, along with delicious hamburger sliders. Being *New Year's Eve* hungry gluttons was quite acceptable for everyone attending Lucy's annual big soiree.

"Howie, Lucy really knows how to throw a great happening," Martino related to his best buddy. "She's absolute nitro' and also plenty of fun."

"You know it, dear William. There's a rather charming lady standing over there in the far corner that I'm dying to make some time with," Howie Steel confided and whispered. "Another ounce of courage and I'll be ready to make my big move," predicted the optometrist to the optician before indulgently chugging-down the remainder of the potent alcoholic mixture.

Lucy Brookes lowered the music volume and then shouted loudly to gain everyone's attention. Then, the stunning, dark-haired hostess made her important announcement. The Tarot reader was ready to practice her mystical art in the adjacent "sewing room".

"My amazing lady prophet will be glad to do a personal Tarot reading for anyone here, so please sign-up and she'll try to schedule everyone interested," Lucy loudly informed her numerous receptive guests. "My special prognosticator will attempt to predict what the future has in store for all of you in regard to money, jobs, travel, but most importantly, in regard to love."

Most of the assembled celebrants were excited about the prospect of an individual card reading, so the more-daring partygoers stood in line to print or write their respective names onto the Tarot reader's ledger. Howard Steel and Bill Martino patiently conversed and waited their turns, because the basic notion of a reputable fortune-teller attending a New Year's Eve party had garnered a great deal of support from most of the very curious guests.

"Howard, what gimmick do you suppose Lucy will think of next?" Bill asked. "Possibly she'll have a Hindu group meditation, or perhaps an outrageous African safari seminar?"

234

"Next year, she'll probably have *Nostradamus*, if dear Lucy can either reincarnate or resurrect the medieval psychic," Howard Steel wittily answered. "I hope we're invited again next year, no matter what the theme venue might be!"

Lucy's grand revelry was now going full swing. Howard was preoccupied speaking with a voluptuous auburn-haired magazine model exhibiting a rich tan and flaunting long, gorgeous "*Rockette* legs", who looked like her gams belonged high-kicking on the *Radio City Music Hall* stage. Carla was just as attracted to Steel as he had instantly been magnetized toward her. The former beauty queen's handsome new acquaintance (who had introduced himself' as "*H.S.*") proved to be an excellent dancer, and Carla was having the time of her life. Soon, Howard and his newfound lady friend returned to the crowded bar.

"Here, Carla. Take these *glasses* from the optometrist," jokingly suggested Steel as the eye-doctor gingerly handed his party girl a pair of whiskey sours. "I told Steve to put a little extra high octane into the mix. He does a great job behind the bar at all of Lucy's shindigs."

"You're as clever as you are cute," the knockout beauty with the professional stage dancer's perfectly shaped legs declared. "Howie, your last name wouldn't be 'kisses', would it?" Carla awkwardly joked. "Do you have a sweet brother named Hershey?"

Names were being called at fifteen-minute intervals for the individual private Tarot card readings. Meanwhile, a splendid smorgasbord had been set-up in Lucy's elegant dining room. The enamored guests served themselves "buffet style" as the thrilled "party animals" rotated around the long oval table, casually exchanging pleasantries and touchy-feely affections. Succulent meat dishes such as roast beef', turkey, corned beef sandwiches, and spicy shrimp along with salads and a neat selection of delicious cake and pie desserts satisfied everyone's palate.

The catered buffet selections were conveniently replenished every half-hour by the hired, well-paid local chef, and the "finger food" was politely served by *his* accommodating employees. The mixed rock & roll and disco background music was continuously played, and was seemingly contagious to either dance or listen to. Howard and Carla demonstrated great dexterity and mobility on the open living room floor; that is, when the lovebirds weren't at the bar mesmerizing each other with their charismatic personalities.

"You dance great, Carla," Steel sincerely complimented. "Have you ever had lessons at *Arthur Murray's?*"

"No, silly. I've learned my more difficult steps at several exclusive clubs in downtown Chicago," the dazzling female ingenuously answered. "Everything from jazz to tango moves!"

Midnight quickly arrived, and simultaneously, the familiar *Times Square* ball descended on the huge TV wall screen, and all the party guests traded brief kisses while wishing each other a very glorious and boisterous 'Happy New Year'!

About 1:00 a.m., Howard finally heard his name announced for obtaining his confidential Tarot seance. The cooperative party guest entered the designated "sewing room" and slowly closed the door behind him. A stern-looking gypsy woman sat erect at a folding table, with her hands mechanically shuffling her colorful deck of mystical cards. Howard was tempted to ask the austere woman if her birth name was *Claire Voyant,* but Steel's better judgment prevailed, and the audacious jokester demonstrated rare discretion and refrained from verbally doing so.

"My name is Audrey," the serious-sounding lady card interpreter revealed. "Please provide me with your identity."

Howard thought of being fresh and asking the psychic why the reader needed to know his name if indeed the woman already knew it, because the reader was supposed to be an accomplished soothsayer. Instead, the now-mannerly party guest elected to take the diplomatic non-confrontational route. "Howard, Howard Steel," the visitor clearly enunciated. "I'm looking forward to this reading. I've never had this done before. How accurate is it?"

"Quite revealing," bluntly replied Audrey, as the take-charge woman continued to skillfully shuffle her deck. "And if you don't believe the cards' reliability now, you certainly will a year from now."

Audrey handed her skeptical client a piece of common notebook paper and instructed Steel to jot-down a pertinent question to which he desired an appropriate answer. The no-nonsense psychic then handed Howard back the sheet with a clear message jotted on it. Steel immediately glanced at the memo' and crumpled it up, discarding the note into a nearby wastebasket.

"Howard, I just needed a sample of your handwriting so that I could tune-into your divine soul and have your mortal spirit synchronize to the exact frequency of the omnipotent universe," Audrey cryptically explained. "Do you now understand my motive?"

"I think I'm a little *tuned* already," the visitor quipped as he foolishly referred to his slightly inebriated state. 'Is there a special technique you wish to implement?"

"Okay, I want you to shuffle these cards and make three equal stacks," Audrey directed. "If you drop a card, you're required to begin the process over again. You need to transfer your spiritual energy vibrations into the cards with your fingertips. Then, leave the rest to my intuition. Is that perfectly clear?"

Howard nodded and loyally followed the oracle's simplistic directions. The three stacks were retrieved in a different order than which they had been sorted and displayed. The fascinated-but-dubious party guest then confidently handed the selected rearranged pile back to the grim-faced medium.

"Now please, Howard," Audrey proceeded with her imperative command instructions, "you must be solemn and sincere while I prepare myself mentally to squarely decipher events that are destined to happen in your immediate future."

Audrey then performed a brief rhythmic chant that seemingly summoned the omnipotent forces of the infinite universe to the dimly lit sewing room. The chosen cards were next carefully placed face-down upon the green-felt table, one at a time, again represented in three distinct columns.

"Are you ready to have your spiritual self' united with the forces of the cosmic universe?" Audrey very emphatically asked.

"Yes," replied Howard, rather restively. "I'm ready."

As each new card from the first pile was turned-over revealed, the rigid-minded *Delphian* rendered her authoritarian evaluation. As Audrey carefully proceeded with her bizarre analysis, the grim forecaster appeared very baffled by the confusing messages of the unusual sequence of card symbols that were showing-up.

"I've never seen a display quite like this one," the contemporary *Cassandra* solemnly confessed. "It's very labyrinth-like and difficult to decipher, almost too contradictory to precisely decode. What I believe I've observed is this. Howard, you're going to have a series of adventures unlike any that have ever been experienced by any other human being," the predicter ominously declared. "Your encounters will be quite terrifying, but conversely, also extremely enlightening. Your exploits will never be completely understood by you while the separate episodes are happening. Individually, at first, they'll have no plausible explanation to your basic comprehension. But collectively, they'll exhibit some common theme that you'll eventually fathom. Howard, I'm afraid I cannot tell you any more salient details about your seemingly complicated future," the stoic-faced reader apologized. "This arrangement of cards you've currently provided is so incredibly extraordinary, I'm sorry, but the intricate pattern transcends my competency level."

"Thank you, Audrey," Steel rather anxiously remarked. "You've given me something quite demanding to think about, and honesty, my sometimes-dormant curiosity has certainly been aroused," Howard Steel stated and confided. After reflecting for a moment, the confused optometrist guest rendered his final impression. "I've found this strange reading to be extremely entertaining."

"You'll discover shortly that this impromptu conference will far exceed your rather mundane world of commonplace human *entertainment,*" casually admonished the very somber seer. "You shall experience its obscure meaning, and then you shall learn to believe its essential truth!"

Howard Steel exited the strange consultation to receive the waiting arms of Carla. A certain look of distress mirrored from his facial features. The incomparable doll immediately sensed that her new beau was not the same affable guy who had easily charmed her fancy a brief half-hour before. The gorgeous model's newfound soulmate seemed preoccupied in deep thought, and suddenly, was not romantically catering to her abundant whims and wishes. The pair quietly again ambled over to the crowded den's bar, and Howard nervously mixed Carla another whiskey sour. Then, the addled guest concocted a double-shot screwdriver for himself.

"I need a double jigger of vodka after that crazy seance session, or whatever it's called," Steel disclosed to his eye-appealing gal. "It was pretty unnerving to say the least."

"Howard, you don't take that preposterous superstitious stuff seriously, now do you?" the beautiful doll articulated and laughed. "I thought you were a man of science?"

"I'm not so sure anymore," Steel candidly confessed. "I have a weird feeling about it, that's for certain. Carla, I must admit a deep secret of mine. I might just take you along on one of my future escapades. I travel all over the world as a hobby. The jet-setting journeys deliver me a welcomed escape from mediocre day-to-day boredom, you know."

"If you stop being so serious and stop sending me all these mixed signals, I'd probably go with you anywhere," the all-too-alluring Miss Ohio State University revealed. "But truthfully, I liked you a lot better when you were loose and amusing just a half-hour ago."

Howard was getting a tad tipsy and also a little light-headed, so the somewhat groggy eye doctor suggested that *they* should leave the in-progress revelry to get to know each other in a calmer, more private physical environment. Carla instantly concurred, even though the flirtatious beauty queen was a trifle disappointed of her most recent mental appraisal of her newly-discovered beau. Realizing that her Tarot time slot reading would have to be relinquished to some other more-fortunate waiting guest, Carla told Lucy to postpone *her* slated psychic conference to a future "cosmic get-together".

Soon, the Dayton sweethearts were sitting inside the impeccable white *Mercedes*. As Howard was slowly pulling-out of the mansion's mammoth U-shaped driveway, the driver caught a glimpse of Bill Martino leaving the premises with a fantastic-looking redhead, and the merry couple then entered the young lady's sleek blue *Jaguar*. Martino's keen pupils spotted Steel and Carla, and Howard's red-haired girlfriend offered the pair an energetic wave. The on-the-prowl bachelors would not have the opportunity to compare notes and exchange anecdotes about their fresh female dates until the following business day.

The *Mercedes* entered the brown brick-paver driveway leading to Howard's isolated castle, situated like a mighty fortress upon a knoll overlooking the *Miami River*. Steel was still a tad fuzzy-minded as the talkative pair entered the handsome residence's foyer. That was the last recollection of *that* somewhat-memorable *New Year's Eve* "swaray" that Howard Steel would remember.

The next morning, the rested optometrist awakened to the aroma of fresh-brewed coffee. That wonderful java stimulant was just what Howard Steel needed to revive his ordinarily perfect perception of reality. The still-groggy eye-doctor sauntered into the kitchen nook and there was marvelous Carla, dressed in one of *his* bathrobes, preparing a splendid breakfast. The annual Philadelphia *Mummers Parade* was being telecast on a small color TV that had been stationed on a side ceramic tile countertop, and conservative-minded Howard Steel was not particularly interested in objectively TV viewing *that* 'totally obnoxious, ridiculous activity'.

"Good morning, Handsome," greeted the cheerful doll, who still looked like an American Venus in spite of the absence of makeup. "I stayed over and worried about your welfare, since after midnight, you were in no condition to drive me home. You had conked-out in the master bedroom as soon as we arrived. For your information, I used the guest room to spend the night."

Howard vigorously scratched his head in pure disgust, which was a contrived mannerism disguised as total disbelief. The health addict was both baffled and embarrassed by his sudden demonstration of January 1st party fatigue. "I can't remember a damned thing," the ranch-home owner admitted with a degree of mortification. "It must've been the vodka in that last drink I consumed. Sorry about that," the guilty gentleman apologetically replied.

"Howard, now I know why the Russian czars were so *intoxicated* with power," Carla cutely chuckled. "We'll definitely have to see each other again when we're both more sober."

"Next time, I promise to take you home without drinking any wicked *vodka* concoctions," Steel smartly pontificated before giving the beautiful vixen a heavy smooch on her adorable lips.

The kitchen wall phone rang, and the affectionate optometrist answered by saying "Hello!"

"Howie, it's me, Bill! Arlene and I are coming right over to your place for breakfast. I've just confirmed that she and Carla are real good friends. We'll be there in a few minutes," announced the fun-loving friend from Arlene's home phone.

Howard had just enough time to shower before greeting the new arrivals at the front door. "Come on it; the food will be terrific!"

"Well, Dr. Steel. How did you enjoy the great New Year's Eve party last night?" Bill Martino asked. "I noticed that you were a little incoherent towards the end!"

"I thought it was a little too rambunctious, but I think that *that* last powerful screwdriver did me in," Steel awkwardly expressed. "I was asleep before my head ever had a chance to hit the pillow. Carla was a true lifesaver and heated-up the coffee before the morning roosters ever started crowing. Yes, Bill. The powerful aroma woke me up."

The compatible couples chatted over bacon, eggs, and bagels as the morning hours rushed by quickly and pleasantly. After noon, the pair of stunning females left with Arlene driving Carla away in her expensive steel-blue *Jaguar.* Plans for a romantic reunion had just been made among the four optimistic revelers. A "definite rain date" had been firmly established.

* * * * * * * * * * * *

The cold winter months passed-by quickly, and soon frigid Jack Frost surrendered power to the beauty of Sister Spring. In early May, Howard was notified by the French Manufacturing Company that the *Spad* biplane he had ordered was ready for prompt delivery. The following week, Mr. Steel and Mr. Martino were on their merry way, enthusiastically jetting-off to Paris, the city where the classic-model plane factory was located.

"Bill, we're going to visit some French *insects,*" Howard stated in a jovial tone of voice.

"What the heck are you talking about?" Martino volleyed back. "Stop being so facetious!"

"I'm goin' to show you some *Paris-sites* like the *Eiffel Tower* and the *Louvre,*" laughed the aspiring aviator. "And you'll be absolutrly 'insane' when you get to see the city's river!"

The sportive friends settled-in at the *Washington Hotel,* conveniently situated near the famous *Paris Opera House*. The music venue was a popular retreat for many American tourists. The entire first day in France was spent sightseeing, since Howard had scheduled an introductory appointment to comprehensively inspect the *Spad* the following morning.

The American duo was picked-up at their downtown hotel by the multi-lingual plane company representative, and then driven to a remote airport on the outskirts of Paris. The excursion's destination was certainly an exciting moment for Howard Steel. When the black *Lexus* arrived at the off-the-beaten track suburban airfield, the President of the *Replica Vintage Biplane Company* cordially greeted the two Dayton, Ohio visitors.

"Good morning, Gentlemen," the company executive greeted. "My name is Jacques Norman. Now Mr. Steel, I have your new aircraft here for your examination, and I must admit, it's a splendid machine indeed. The replica is the first one of its kind manufactured right off the assembly line," the very distinguished-looking, gray-haired, company executive emphasized. "It's an actual facsimile in every detail to the original *WWI Spad*. Naturally," Jacques Norman elucidated, "the motor, along with the biplane's instrument panel, have obviously both been vastly improved since the early 1900s original production. Our new sophisticated edition can achieve much more horsepower than the early engine could ever generate, and it also comes equipped with the latest communications and navigation gear."

Howard couldn't wait to fly the modernized edition of the historic machine. The biplane's color was olive green, and the intriguing object had similar markings as the revered fighting *Spads* that had been operational in 1917.

"It's a real nice rendition!" Steel marveled and exclaimed. "I'm glad I've earned a flying license back in Ohio so that I can take this baby up into the wild blue yonder!"

"It's truly an investment in history you're making," convincingly replied Jacques Norman, the French company's president.

That afternoon, Howard eagerly climbed into the replica cockpit and started-up the modified engine (when a company worker spun the propeller blade). The motor instantly purred, and slowly-but-surely, the classic biplane taxied to the runway and in mere moments, Howard had the authentic-looking *Spad* droning high above the Parisian suburbs. Steel was euphoric, realizing that his childhood dream was actually being achieved.

The *Spad* floated through drifting low clouds like a feather and as the flying machine gradually ascended to a more-lofty elevation, Howard couldn't contain himself. The pilot showed-off by rapidly descending and buzzing the airfield, waving at the startled spectators who were standing near the small airport's terminal. However, the sun's glare penetrating inside the open cockpit really was bothering Howard's unprotected eyes.

'No problem,' the always prepared pilot logically thought. 'Bill had made me a nifty pair of sunglasses. I'll wear the goggles the next time I take this baby up.'

The elated flyer angled the plane back down to the runway and easily accomplished a perfect landing. The *WWI* reproduction model taxied to the assigned hangar, and then the operator joyfully clambered out of the rather confining cockpit.

"How was your maiden flight?" asked the company President.

"Perfect, Jacques! Very exhilarating!" the *Spad* pilot gleefully shouted. "In fact, it couldn't have been better." Then, a certain idea flashed through the American's ever-alert mind. "Bill, I think I'll need that special pair of sunglasses you made for me before we left the *States*. The glare is brutal up there inside an open cockpit. Did you bring them along?"

"It's as sure as the trees and rose bushes blossom in the spring," aptly stated Steel's loyal associate. "You'll have the visual aides available tomorrow, but by all means, please don't make a *spectacle* out of yourself!"

After having a bite to eat inside the airport's quaint restaurant, the pair of Ohio adventurers were chauffeured back to their Paris hotel in the same black *Lexus*. Bill entered his suite's bedroom and retrieved the aforementioned tinted sunglasses that Howie would wear on his second trial flight. The lenses had been shaded with a new glare-limiting experimental dye.

But when William Martino had handcrafted the tinted glasses back in Dayton, something mildly unorthodox had happened. At the time, the skilled optician had thought that the minor aberration was insignificant, and the craftsman paid little attention to the minute deviation. The lenses had somehow tinted a grayish-green, which regrettably did not appear dark enough to address Howard's preferential need. Bill then made an adjustment and darkened that particular tint with a second dye, which had been stored-away for years inside a seldom-used office cabinet.

In his office, Martino had difficulty locating the second nearly-obsolete dye, but the optician eventually found an ancient bottle that he had misplaced a decade before, stored inside his laboratory's neglected crammed side cabinet. Upon unscrewing the tight cap, the bottle had slipped-out of his hand, and several drops splashed into the new formula he had been preparing. The old dye bottle appeared rather murky, and William decided not to use it, but his professional instincts did not at the time seem to matter. By accident, a foreign laboratory ingredient had been incidentally introduced into the now-complicated chemical dye composition.

When Martino finally finished preparing his alien dye mixture, the tinted lenses looked unlike any Bill had ever seen before. However, Howard's partner was stubbornly confident that the new lenses would work satisfactorily with Steel cheerfully flying above Paris on his second French flight. Bill was too vain to ever admit making any error in his very deliberate preparation, so the secretive Dayton native never divulged the trivial dye irregularity to his fussy and demanding business partner.

The next spring morning, Howard and Bill were again transported to the suburban airport in the airplane company's black *Lexus*. After exchanging polite small talk with a bevy of high-ranking corporate officials, Howard Steel again piloted the vintage *Spad* up into the partially cloudy sky. However, the existing overcast conditions did not warrant the need for the recently-manufactured tinted sunglasses. The replica *Spad* cruised along smoothly at a low altitude and, Howard fantasized that he was zooming along with Eddie Rickenbacker and his "Flying Circus" in a glorified *World War I* aerial parade. The totally thrilled American was without a doubt fully enjoying *his* wonderful vicarious experience.

The amateur aviator was in his absolute glory as Howard navigated the *Spad* over Paris and soon adroitly had circled above the *Eiffel Tower, Notre Dame Cathedral,* and the incomparable *Champs Elysees.* After gliding over the *Arc de Triomphe,* aviator Steel followed the *Seine River's* west bank until the pilot spotted the magnificent *Versailles Palace,* and then "Captain Howie" proceeded onward to distant Le Chesnay airport, where the Ohio native brought the *Spad* in for second perfect landing.

* * * * * * * * * * * *

The following morning was quite different, with the clear blue sky being sunny and bright. The emboldened pilot planned to zip over the sites of several exciting *WWI* air battles that had been fought between archaic American and German biplanes. Howard's novel flight itinerary would take adventurous Steel over Reims, Metz, St. Avold, and Nancy.

The company black *Lexus* was unavailable the following morning, so Howard and Bill hired a taxi to transport the duo to the suburban airport at Le Chesnay. The *Spad* was swiftly rolled-out of the large hangar, and the anxious, exuberant pilot clambered into the rather tight cockpit. The gas gauge on the instrument panel indicated that the *Spad's* tank was full.

The plane's engine was started, and Howard Steel soon taxied the biplane from the apron to the concrete runway. In a matter of a minute, the Dayton daredevil was cleared for takeoff. After Steel humorously responded over the radio with an emphatic "Oui!", the *WWI* facsimile roared down the runway and was soon majestically airborne.

The exceedingly proud American casually monitored the electronic instrument panel as the museum-quality biplane gracefully ascended to eight-thousand-feet. Altitude was only one consideration, for the risk-taking pilot sitting at the controls wanted his third flight endeavor to encompass a greater geographic circumference. The sun's glare was getting quite bothersome as "Captain Steel" swung the *Spad* in the direction of the eastern horizon.

Feeling like the master of his environment, the ecstatic pilot first pretended that he was Charles Lindbergh cruising over Paris in the historic *Spirit of St. Louis*. Next, imaginative Howard Steel began fantasizing about the legendary "Flying Circus" and its prominent military commander, Eddie Rickenbacker.

As the infatuated dreamer cruised along at his steady altitude, Howard noticed that the sunglasses Bill had made completely reduced the intense glare, but something rather sensational was noticeably different. The physical characteristics of the eastern Parisian suburbs appeared to be altered. Where were the paved roads? Where were the new super-highways along the regular bumper-to-bumper traffic? Where were the large towns that were vividly portrayed on the flyer's modern area map? Where were the myriad colonies of suburban housing developments?

The now-confused aviator continued flying eastward, his puzzled eyes surveying the strangely modified, less-populated landscape that was being perceived through his newly-acquired tinted sunglasses. Howard's *Spad* was approaching the German/French border, just above Saarbrucken. Suddenly, the *WWI* devotee became aware of a distant plane formation existing the cloud cluster just off to the far east. As the half-dozen aerial objects became more visible, the befuddled

American had to rapidly blink his eyes and pinch his legs. Howard couldn't believe what his pupils were visualizing.

A squadron of six German *World War I* vintage biplanes was flying in a tight wing formation in Howard's direction. Their bold markings became more distinguishable as the half-dozen objects headed straight toward the astonished American. "My God in Heaven!" Steel gasped and exclaimed in total exasperation. "I think I need a shrink! German biplanes with distinct cross markings, and they're apparently reacting to my encroachment into German air space."

The neat formation's leader was flying a red Fokker triplane, a twin to the one that had been expertly maneuvered by notorious Manfred Richtofen, the infamous *World War I* "Red Baron". The Fokker peeled-off as if to challenge the olive green *Spad* to a brutal aerial combat. Howard veered to his right and quickly discerned that the Fokker's machine guns were spitting a volley of bullets at his recently manufactured aerial machine. The emotionally bewildered American couldn't believe his incredible time/space predicament, nor did the baffled flying optometrist have the luxury time span to contemplate the total magnitude of the whole anachronism.

'My childhood dream has transformed into an ugly nightmare,' Howard pondered. 'What the hell is going on here? I always wanted to be involved in a *WWI* dogfight! But now I regret ever having that fanciful desire. Steel incredulously acknowledged. 'Right now, I want completely out of my silly childhood wish!'

A round of bullets suddenly pierced the *Spad's* fuselage as Howard desperately attempted escaping the adamant German predator's wrath. Next, the other five *WWI* German wing planes commenced their methodical attack firing their blazing, outdated machine guns. Bullets violently ripped into the *Spad's* center and tail sections. Was Steel's mind dreaming a horrible nightmare? 'This can't be happening!' Howard neurotically determined and concluded. The petrified pilot sitting at the controls quickly looked at his hands. The pain was real. Blood was spurting out of Howard's left wrist.

The targeted *Spad's* damaged engine was now emitting a quantity of dense smoke. Sparks were randomly shooting-out from the biplane's sputtering engine. Captain Steel impulsively put the *Spad* into a severe nosedive, instinctively initiating a futile last-ditch attempt to creatively extinguish the numerous flaring flames, which were uncontrollably shooting-out from the coughing engine.

The German Fokkers raced downward in hot pursuit, and the attacked *Spad* was on a downward spiral collision course with the ground. Anticipating an imminent crash, the attacking Fokkers deftly peeled away, regrouped into their winged formation, and the formation speedily headed on maintaining a westward course.

At the crucial last second, Pilot Steel was able to level the *Spad's* wings, and in so doing, removed his blood-smeared dirty sunglasses, and miraculously, the recent external engine inferno was non-existent. Howard incredulously scrutinized the instrument panel's compass, remembered his precise heading coordinates, gained sufficient altitude, and then established his appropriate course heading in the direction of the suburban Le Chesnay Airport.

How could the visiting American ever explain his nerve-racking misadventure to Bill? To Jacques Norman? To anyone? The harried and befuddled pilot landed his beloved *Spad,* and soon the biplane erratically taxied down the recently paved runway. Steel looked-down at his clean sunglasses and immediately recognized that they were no longer thickly smeared with blood and dust. The biplane's engine was sounding normal, but for safety's sake, it was quickly shut-off in front of the craft's designated hangar.

The flying optometrist frantically leaped from the cockpit as if he was a frightened bat zooming out of *Hades.* The paranoid pilot couldn't believe his recollection of paranormal combat events. There was not a single evidence of damage visible on the plane's exterior; no bullet holes, and no actual verification of his astonishing time travel encounter; not even a trace of crimson existed, either on his white scarf, or smeared upon his pallid face. It was as though nothing out of the ordinary had ever occurred.

Feeling disillusioned, Howie again examined his special tinted sunglasses. The specs appeared perfectly clean and brand new. Not even a scintilla of dust marred the dark plastic surface.

"What happened? Are you alright?" Bill Martino inquired in a concerned tone of voice. "You appear a bit stressed-out!"

"I don't know; I think I had some sort of queer hallucination," Steel panted. "Yes, my mind strangely suffered some sort of wild, crazy, delusional manifestation!"

Just out of curiosity, Howard impulsively put the sunglasses back on. Amazingly, the *Spad* plane appeared a total wreck. Bullet holes had punctured the wings and fuselage. The ancient engine was still smoking. The pilot's scarf and hands were now smeared with blood. Taking the glasses off, everything in his modern environment was somehow returned to normal.

'No one should know about this strange occurrence, not even my best friend, Bill,' Howard secretly thought. Steel had no inkling that this extraordinary episode predicted by Audrey's Tarot cards was going to be the genesis of other even more fantastic events.

"Are you sure you don't need some French medical attention?" Bill constructively asked his usually poised business partner. "You seem to be thoroughly perplexed and radically flustered."

"Bill, I'm okay now," the still-alarmed pilot falsely attested. Then, the distressed aviator thought about the most incredible exploit for a second. 'I must find-out the secret of these remarkable sunglasses,' the optometrist considered and evaluated. 'When I figure it all out, maybe I'll share my newfound knowledge.' "Look Bill," Steel imperatively stated. "I'm telling you for the last time; I'm perfectly all right!"

* * * * * * * * * * * *

Howard Steel and Bill Martin were later relaxing in their Paris hotel room, discussing their options about transporting the purchased *Spad* back to the USA. Jacques Norman suggested expeditiously shipping the plane by ocean freighter to New York. The trans-Atlantic delivery would take approximately six weeks, and then the marvelous biplane would be flown by major transport from the bustling *Big Apple,* westward to Dayton.

Howard agreed with Jacques' practical recommendation, and the appropriate delivery arrangements were soon made. After the visitors ticket reservations were confirmed at the *Charles De Gaulle Airport's United Airlines* counter, confirming the pals return flight to America, the vacationing business confederates decided to visit several Parisian nightclubs for some well-deserved, farewell, French recreation.

The following morning, the on-the-go tourists took a taxi to the international airport terminal, and later, just before noon, boarded a *United Intercontinental 747* back to the States. Then, a smaller *United 737* flew the weary Ohio residents from New York's *Kennedy International* to the all-too-familiar *Dayton Airport.*

After arriving home, the dual returnees were both "pumped-up" to be back in the good old USA, especially Howard Steel. His nerve-racking aerial encounter with the *WWI* German squadron was far more shocking than any virtual reality battle being played on any boardwalk or mall arcade video game screen.

"Bill, now that we're alone in our office, I want to ask you about the special dye you had used to darken my new sunglasses," Howard insisted. "How did you ever get that unusual color? Honestly, I've never seen anything like it before!"

Martino was reluctant to reveal to his closest friend the minor accident that Bill had made while conscientiously preparing the unique mixture. Steel was notorious for occasionally exhibiting sudden temper tantrums, and Bill Martino didn't want to say anything unsettling that would inadvertently disturb his sometimes-mercurial friend and business associate.

"Howard, I must tell you something strange, but believe me, I didn't think anything of it at the time," Bill defensively prefaced. "I was searching for an old dye to make your sunglasses a shade darker. While rummaging through our storage cabinets, I incidentally came across an old bottle I had ordered back in 1985. It had been misplaced and forgotten about for over a decade," Martino continued his guilty explanation, "and I never found it until that day I had been preparing your shades. I tried to open the tight cap, but the sticky bottle slipped-out of my hands. I had haphazardly spilled some of the liquid, which had splashed onto the counter, and I noticed that a couple of drops had entered the dye that I was darkening," Bill elaborated, as sweat beads began forming upon his forehead. "The remainder of the old dye looked a bit murky, so I decided not to use it again. I next found a more up-to-date dye for the purpose of adding needed darkness to the original formula."

Howard listened to Bill's strange admission very carefully and immediately comprehended that the accidental inclusion of the 1985 dye seemed the only logical explanation to rationally account for the extraordinary aerial adventure *he* had singularly experienced while flying over eastern France.

"Well, is there anything else you might want to divulge?" Howard wanted to know.

"After I tinted your lenses with the new combination dye," Bill proceeded with his explanatory narrative, "Much to my satisfaction, the prepared color appeared darker. The unique tint was different than anything I had ever seen before. I felt that the new formula was adequate, and that it had done the trick. But Howard, why did you ask about the dye? Is there a problem of some kind?"

The mum listener felt that he could not even trust himself with the supernatural-like sunglasses' story, let alone another human being hearing his bizarre testimony. But Bill had been perfectly honest and sincere in his depiction, and Martino had always been Howard's exclusive confidante. Now, it was time for the *Spad* owner to spill his soul to his best friend.

"Bill, I wish you had told me about the dye formula accident when it had happened. Something really strange had occurred when I put on the sunglasses at six-thousand-feet," Steel confidentially related. "Now, either I was hallucinating, or the tinted sunglasses put me into a time warp of sorts, and to the best of my recollection, I was suddenly transported back to *WWI* flying a real *Spad*. The whole oddball thing has me completely baffled and frustrated."

Howard went on to describe in detail his phenomenal aerial escapade with the anachronistic German Fokkers, as Bill sat wide-eyed on a stool with his mouth agape. When the persuasive pilot/optometrist finished recalling and sharing his spectacular story, Bill sat motionless on his laboratory stool, quite reticent and fascinated, listening intently to his colleague's extraordinary off-the-wall testimony, with his mind in a state of emotional shock.

"Howie, I would suggest we don't ever tell anyone about this!" Martino insisted. "We'll comprehensively study the magic dye and the effect the compound has on lenses when applied in different concentrations. I'll even try duplicating the exact compound. Actually, my simple laboratory mistake might be making a major contribution to science, if not to science fiction!"

"Bill, I suggest we first do some experimenting with the remainder of the 1985 dye," Steel persuasively vociferated to his confidante. "That remarkable substance seems to be the key to solving *our* enigmatic time travel enigma."

The partners remained deep in thought about their outlandish hypothesis. An hour later, the fatigued optician dozed-off, still sitting upon his familiar lab' stool, dreaming about the fantastic possibilities that the incredible 1985 dye actually represented. Howard removed the magical sunglasses from the inside pocket of his sport jacket and stared incredulously at the dyed olive-green lenses for a pregnant moment. Steel dared not put the specs on his ears inside their joint office, fearing the unknown consequences of such behavior; a disastrous, lethal reaction that might dangerously materialize. 'Who knows what might happen in a confined space?' Howard conjectured. 'I might find myself riding on a horse in medieval England, fighting either Sir Lancelot or King Arthur!"

The mystery embedded in the new set of spectacles had completely captured both men's fleeting imaginations. The next morning, the two bleary-eyed friends arranged to cancel all patient appointments and meet for a lengthy strategic conference at their shared office. After entering the lab', Bill showed Howard both the old and the new dye bottles and asked for Steel to render an opinion.

"Bill, I think we should first try one drop in another fresh container of dye," Steel strongly advised. "We'll use the blue blocker dye first, and make a light tint."

"Good idea, Howard," the junior partner commended. "It should be interesting, seeing what effect it'll have."

The dye was mixed, heated and then new clear plastic lenses were shaped to fit the desired frame. Then, the plastic lenses were skillfully dipped into the concocted "secret solution". It would take two-minutes for the tint to evenly distribute and satisfactorily color the experimental lenses n a controlled environment.

When *that* time interval expired, the newly-formed lenses were then slowly removed from the mixing basin, dried for an hour, and finally gently washed. The new introduced color was a spectrum compromise, existing between dull red and orange shades. The lenses were then expertly inserted into their respective frames. Next, the quiet partners stepped outside the office, and Howard bravely put the new sunglasses over his eyes.

"My God, you won't believe this phenomenon, Bill! Try them on!" Howie loudly directed. "This insane experience is positively way beyond the pale!"

The optician complied with his companion's hasty request. "Wow! Howard, this is really unbelievable. It looks like I've stepped out of 1997 and time-traveled right into the 1950s!" Bill exclaimed. "The cars are uncanny, and the people's clothes are like those worn on *American Bandstand,* or on *Ozzie and Harriet* cable reruns."

"William" removed the tinted specs and was just as astounded as his flabbergasted colleague, and Martino acknowledged to Steel that his reactive fascination was indeed justified. "Howard, everything is now back to normal and back to modern-day Dayton again. This discovery of ours is absolutely some type of fantastic anomaly. I wonder if we could get a patent!"

"Now, Bill," Howard cautiously stated. "I want you to try looking into the original pair I had worn in Paris."

Martino placed the first set of magical sunglasses that he had manufactured for Howard onto the bridge of his nose and was absolutely stunned when startled Bill made a quick time voyage into turn-of-the-century early 1900s' Dayton.

"Howard, the men I see all have handlebar mustaches and derby hats; the kids are all wearing knickers, and the women all have long cumbersome dresses, and the ladies are holding parasols over their heads. *Model-A Fords* are everywhere."

"Billy, we have much more experimenting to do before we can determine the enormous economic possibilities of our incredible discovery," the senior business associate suggested. "But we can't function together unless we share the same reality. We'll have to make two identical pairs of sunglasses for us to wear together, so that we'll be able to collaborate our mutual time-travel activities."

"You're right, Howard," Martino reflexively agreed. "One of your ancestors must've been *Einstein* or *Sir Isaac Newton!*"

"Bill, let's add a few more magical drops to the mixture. We'll make several tanks of this recipe in different chemical proportions," Howard maintained. "We don't want to mix the formulas up. So, we'll carefully label each one."

The enamored experimenters pondered and then discussed another quirky idea. "Bill, if the Time Traveler knew about our fabulous secret, the guy never would've had to spend two-years inventing and building the time machine in that fanciful sci-fi novel by *H. G. Wells*. Our terrific grandiose discovery was by sheer accident! His time machine creation was by design!"

Several tanks of the mystical dye were very delicately prepared. Each successive "ordinary sunglass batch" contained a greater amount of "miracle 1985 dye", and each more "potent batch" permitted the lenses and their wearers to travel further and further back in time. Since one drop of the 1985 "old dye" was equivalent to approximately fifty years, it was simply a matter of mathematical calculation to accurately estimate that six drops would constitute a time-journey of around three hundred-years into the past.

"Do you want to witness the signing of the *Declaration of Independence?*" William Martino seriously asked his delighted co-conspirator. "We can go back and meet George Washington and Ben Franklin. Come to think of it, I always wished that I had been alive back in 1776 to participate as a patriot in the *Revolutionary War!* Now, I could have the opportunity!"

"Bill, whatever happens to be there wherever we should land, we will surely witness some outstanding aspect of U.S. history," Howard Steel surmised and orally concluded. "Just think for a minute. Everybody else in our present reality is limited to the three dimensions of space: length, width, and height."

"That's right, Howie!" Bill marveled and commented. "We now have the power to readily and conveniently access different periods in time; yes, the incredible fourth dimension."

The novel "reverse time travel laboratory experiments" were soon completed, and dual sets of magical sunglasses had been carefully manufactured for the two avid possessors; the fantastic utilitarian equipment has been created from the newly formulated dye.

"Bill, I have a wild idea. We have very competent help and a dependable manager," Howard reminded his eye care center colleague. "The office staff can run things without us for at least a month. Now, here's my ingenious plan. It'll take at least six weeks for the *Spad* to arrive in the U.S. from France," Steel intelligently lectured. "How about if we' take Carla and Arlene on a really cool trip to the tropical Virgin Islands? Maybe St. Thomas?"

Martino considered Howard's most interesting, plausible, and sagacious suggestion and then verbally responded with a contrite endorsement of Steel's "extremely outstanding opinion". "Sure, Howard. We can rent a sailboat and then cruise the Caribbean for a few weeks of idle leisure. The girls will be thrilled with our clever scheme, and we don't have to tell them about our sunglasses secret. I only hope that we can keep our fantastic secret to ourselves!"

The *Spad* enthusiast, who was also an ardent woman enthusiast, had now evolved into an avid sunglasses' time-travel enthusiast. "Bill, but whatever you do, never tell the girls about our special specs'. Just because we love the dolls doesn't necessarily mean we can trust the chicks with our historic discovery!"

"I'm game, Chief. You're the boss calling the shots in this crazy turkey shoot," William Martino submissively assented. "We can tell our beautiful dates about the impending Caribbean trip tonight at dinner. Nothin' else, right?"

Howard was always two-steps ahead of his less mentally gifted affiliate, and trustworthy subordinate, junior partner Bill Martino had always admired his comrade's Promethean shrewdness and Odysseus-style daring.

"I have a surprise for you, good buddy," Howard announced. "I've already made reservations at *Chili's Grill and Bar* over on Fairfield Road in Beaver Creek. And Carla and Arlene have already been notified by telephone. We'll spring the vacation idea on the enchanting babes while dining at the restaurant," Steel informed Martino rather nonchalantly. "The rest will be romantic history!"

The dynamite girls were picked-up in Howard's white *Mercedes* and at seven o'clock sharp, the foursome was being comfortably seated at an exquisite VIP booth inside the Mexican-style restaurant. The knockout babes both sipped on whiskey sours, and each glamour queen was nibbling delectable fried mushroom hors d'oeuvres like there was no tomorrow. The scheming business partners sipped large vodka and orange juice concoctions like the rascal pair didn't care one iota about either today or yesterday.

"Now, tell us about your trip to France and all about that crazy *Spad* thing you bought," asked Carla. "It all sounds rather adventurous as opposed to being romantic!"

"The plane is a beauty and flies like a dream," Howard claimed and boasted before again sipping his potent mixed drink. "And Bill and I saw all the important sites in Paris that you usually see on TV. But before we get carried away on *that* sidebar topic, we have something important to ask both of you gorgeous dolls."

"What is it?" questioned Arlene Burns, who appeared very intrigued with exploring the mystery subject.

"Bill and I promised the two of you on *New Year's Eve* that we'd take you both on one of our next big trips," Howard reminded the voluptuous babes. "How would you two lovely princesses like to join us on an exotic Caribbean sailboat cruise?"

The girls shrieked with joy at the extravagant invitation, getting the attention of the more conservative diners, randomly seated and hearing in nearby booths.

"What a tremendous surprise!" Carla giggled. "I simply love the idea! I've never been to the Caribbean! And I'd truly love to visit St. Thomas!"

"Does St. Thomas live in the Caribbean?" Howie jested.

Carla and Arlene ignored Steels' preposterous joke. "When do we leave?" the enchanted girls simultaneously together yelled, and then simultaneously laughed.

"Yes, Dolls; there's nothing like a little fun in the sun," Howard remarked. "I'll have my travel agent make the necessary reservations tomorrow. How about if we'll leave three Saturday mornings from now," informed the enthused optometrist with a sparkle showing in each of his eyes. "Is that enough time for you gals to get ready? This exotic trip is goin' to be a blast and a half!"

There was no hesitation coming from the jubilant females. "No problem!" Carla gleefully consented and approved. "The two of us will be ready, willing, and able."

Howard gave Bill a wink, and Bill raised his mixed drink, indicating that a formal salute was in order.

"May this upcoming Caribbean hiatus be the greatest adventure of our formerly dull lives," Howard toasted as the four energized restaurant patrons mutually clicked their glasses above the center of their VIP table.

The third Saturday morning of the month arrived rather quickly. The girls were waiting at Carla's front door when the white *Mercedes* pulled into the asphalt driveway. The spacious trunk accommodated the four additional pieces of luggage, and quickly, the expectant couples got seated inside the luxury sedan. Howard hit the accelerator and the expensive vehicle sped toward the *Dayton Airport* "in record time", and within the space of two-hours, the four passengers were sitting in first-class leather seats anticipating their smooth jet flight to semi-tropical San Juan.

"We'll arrive in Puerto Rico after a brief stopover in Atlanta," Howard informed the others as the foursome awaited the jet's takeoff. "We'll rent the sailboat that my travel agent Linda Johnson has especially reserved for us. Tonight, we'll stay in the Crown Prince

Plaza Hotel and Tropical Casino in San Juan," Howard finished. "I think a bit of gambling might be on the agenda!"

"It's got the reputation of being a first-class place," added Bill. "We'll have dinner at the hotel's gourmet restaurant, and afterwards, we can try our luck with a little friendly blackjack and poker at the casino tables."

The enthralled Dayton girls were most appreciative of the boys' apparent generosity. "Howard, we're really going first-class all the way, and I want you to know that Arlene and I cannot contain our high excitement. This'll certainly be a tremendous vacation for us all to remember," Carla Simpson acknowledged.

"I can't wait to roll a *pair of dice* in *Paradise,*" Bill Martino bantered, amusing himself. "I'm sorry, but right now even my itchy feet are *corny!*"

The *737* departing from Atlanta arrived in Puerto Rico right on schedule, and the lovebirds checked-in early at their ritzy hotel. While the girls changed into more leisure attire, Howard called the marina where the twin-mast sailboat had been docked. Steel learned that the sleek schooner was all set and rigged for immediate charter. At five-thirty, the happy quartet sauntered into the hotel's restaurant for an early lobster and crab dinner.

After enjoying their sumptuous meals and relishing each other's stellar company, the Dayton visitors hired a cab to the marina to inspect the jibs and the foresail on the rented schooner. Bill was as thrilled as anyone, since the nautical buff was very familiar with the art of sailing, and knew virtually every aspect of the skill from the mainsail to the mast staysail. Martino was more than qualified to be the "elected captain" on their imminent voyage, and of course, Howard Steel had the nautical expertise to be the first mate.

The streamlined vessel was securely moored at the dock, and the well-appointed craft was ready for immediate voyaging. The schooner was more magnificent than either Howard or Bill had expected. The boat was forty-five-feet-long, and its two sturdy masts and white linen-like sails complemented its ultra-modern design. The rented vessel came with eight cozy bunks, and sported a more-than-adequate galley. The mint green boat's exterior and exterior were spotless, and the captain's panel featured advanced navigational and communications' equipment, which included a sophisticated depth-finder. The ocean worthy vessel even had two sets of powerful binoculars onboard, and the craft was appropriately named *Paradise*.

Howard informally conversed with Miguel Gonzalez, the owner of the upscale marina, and also the prime investor in the state-of-the-art schooner. "Mr. Gonzalez, we'll be leaving at eight o'clock in the morning. What's the local weather forecast for tomorrow?"

"Perfectly clear and little wind, with calm seas," the cigar-smoking, greedy entrepreneur assured his latest credit-worthy client. "The weather's just like any other magnificent day here in the tropical Caribbean. This month is probably the best time of year for you to go sailing! I predict that you and your fun-loving friends will have a marvelous time out at sea!"

"Good, I don't want any seasick people ailing aboard on this trip," Howard whimsically replied. 'I'm not a licensed medical doctor, you know! But I do know a little bit of first aid!"

The waiting taxi then transported the quartet from the dock area back to the hotel/casino for the foursome to enjoy an evening of active entertainment. The giggling girls played the assorted slot machines, and the guys dabbled in blackjack, roulette, and craps. Carla lost a hundred dollars in coins, and Arlene didn't fare much better. The dolls then watched their gambling vacation dates exhibit exceptional skills in the exclusive baccarat lounge, where the eyeglass specialists each won over a thousand dollars.

"We've more than made-up for what the girls have lost," laughed Bill. "Life's definitely more fun when you have the luxury of excess money to wager!"

"Yeah, but we both would've come up losers if we didn't have two beautiful lady lucks standing at our sides," finished Howard, as the lucky gambler casually winked over at Carla and Arlene, each date comfortably seated at a roulette table.

* * * * * * * * * * * *

Dawn soon penetrated the darkness of night and after a well-rounded light breakfast, the four vacation travelers hired a taxi to transport them to the aforementioned dock where the *Paradise* was moored. Their heavy luggage was loaded onto the sailing vessel, and after Howard revealed to his shipmates the various assignments of onboard duties, along with other "housekeeping particulars", the four Americans waved goodbye to avaricious Miguel Gonzalez, and soon the well-appointed schooner quietly drifted away from its slip into the neighboring harbor.

A slight breeze inspired Bill to deploy the main sails, so Martino silenced the inboard engine. Everyone helped raise the mast sails, and in a short while, the canvas sheets were catching the force of the friendly Caribbean winds. The splendid sailboat portrayed a regal appearance as the *Paradise* glided-out of the emerald-green harbor into the shimmering sea.

"Bill, our heading will have us landing in Charlotte Amalie, the capital of St. Thomas," Howard uttered and noticed as the first mate gazed upon the boat's compass. According to this graphic map, St. Thomas is only forty-five nautical miles from San Juan."

The temperature was well into the eighties, and with the benign "old Sol" sharing its abundant warm and benevolent companionship with the Tropic of Cancer, Carla and Arlene figured that it was time to engage in some serious sunbathing.

"Guys, we're going to try on our new bikini bathing suits," Howard's revered lady companion informed. "We'll get some vital tanning in before the sun gets too hot. Arlene and I use the best brand of sun-blocker so that we won't burn or sizzle."

"Great idea!" Howard pleasantly answered with more than mild interest. "Hope you both brought along your own sunglasses. Bill's and mine are special prescriptions, so we can't share them with you."

It wasn't long before the girls, boasting hourglass figures, came-out from below deck, wearing their alluring, skimpy bikinis. The two dolls, superb health-club Aphrodites, were enough of an attraction to make the amateur male sailors presently standing at the helm drool with lustful visions of romance.

Five minutes later, the first mate was reading a tacked-on wall chart where Bill learned about the numerous barren islands that populated the general vicinity of St. Thomas. Fifty uninhabited islets dotted the area geography in and around the eye-pleasing Virgin Islands. Captain Howard's watchful pupils would have to monitor the shallow waters with a set of the schooner's reliable binoculars. Some of the tiny sandy beach islets around St. John and St. Thomas could become shrouded with only a thin veil of water, the shifting shoals being visibly evident only at high tide.

The illustrious fun-loving expedition was going rather terrifically, and at noon, it was unanimously agreed upon to drop anchor and have lunch. The bikini-clad girls prepared ham and cheese sandwiches, and the "young salts" sat and ate ravenously like famished mates, amusing themselves inside the all-too-convenient galley. All four passengers were immensely enjoying the inspirational pleasure cruise to the absolute fullest degree.

"Truthfully, Guys. This is the best fun Arlene and I have ever had," Carla Simpson attested. "I hope we can do it again next year."

"Carla, I think there's a strong possibility that *that* reality will surely happen," Captain Bill echoed, with First Mate Howard affirmatively nodding his head in tacit approval.

256

"Who wouldn't want to go on another trip like this with two fabulous Dayton chicks like you girls? This boat was given a perfect name: *Paradise*," Howard praised with a genuine glisten in his eye.

The sailing party was now only one-half hour from St. Thomas. As the resplendent schooner approached the welcoming dock at Charlotte Amalie, Bill Martino was ready to attach the sturdy tie rope to the appropriate piling as nominated Captain Howie adroitly guided the craft into its appointed mooring. Two thick ropes were then needed to fully tether the *Paradise;* one at the bow, and the other at its stern.

Everyone aboard disembarked and stretched their legs, and it didn't take Carla Simpson, Arlene Burns, Howard Steel, and William Martino long to recognize that St. Thomas was indeed a glorious tropical island to both sightsee and explore.

"I've already made reservations to dine at the *Bottoms-Up Bar and Restaurant* at the port's marina. I was told it has a casual atmosphere, and that the seafood is out of this world," Howard exaggerated to his famished three-member audience. "Remember girls, on this trip, money is no object!"

"Let's browse around the town first and see what the shops have to offer," expressed Carla. "I love to browse for bargains, and Arlene does, too!"

"Fine with us," Howard very amenably agreed as the astute Captain scrutinized and admired his woman's fantastic hourglass figure.

The four sailboat visitors strolled through Charlotte Amalie's narrow streets and botanical-style alleys, and next, the couples casually surveyed the inventories on display in several tourist-trap jewelry stores. Many of the proprietors were Arabs, which greatly surprised the new arrivals, for the Dayton visitors thought that well-to-do American and European merchants would own most of the exclusive Virgin Island stores.

Negotiating a reduced price was a necessary verbal art traditionally practiced on the main street, and Howard took command and effectively haggled, buying the girls matching golden bracelets for a compromised cost that was less than half the originally quoted retail price. In their shopping travels, the young ladies also bought matching casual lounging clothes to wear while walking-about the deck on the *Paradise.* Next on the generosity docket, Howard and Bill surprised their dates with two fine hand-crafted turquoise rings.

"I think we should get back to the *Paradise* and change for dinner," a very hungry Bill advised. "I'm totally starved!"

"Your erudite culinary proposal has my vote," Howard answered, as the comedic captain sounded like a Washington Congressman seconding a flamboyant motion in the *House of Representatives.*

The four shipmates all endorsed the rather inviting dinner proposal and commenced strolling back from the Charlotte Amalie waterfront to the *Bottoms-Up Bar and Restaurant*.

"Hey, that's Hassel Island over there," pointed-out Captain Steel. "Just like the map shows, the landmark partially closes-off the harbor."

The four trekkers stepped into the popular eatery and ordered grilled steaks, shrimp, salad and fries. *Bud Lite* was the beer of choice.

"This place is not especially fancy, but it's basically really good cuisine," Alternate Captain Bill assessed. "But we sure don't have restaurants with tropical scenery like this in Dayton."

"I'd recommend this island bistro to anyone. It's down to Earth, allows casual dress, and the drink prices are actually reasonable," Howard chimed-in. Maybe Captain Billy and I can buy this place and have it shipped back to Ohio."

"Carla, tomorrow Bill and I would like to take the *Paradise* out alone and do some personal exploring," first mate "Commodore Steel" informed their luscious dates. "You and Arlene can spend the entire day merchandise shopping at *our* expense. We'll meet in the late afternoon for dinner."

"That suits us to a T. Tomorrow Arlene and I will do a little sightseeing and also use the afternoon to buy a few trinkets and souvenirs," Carla revealed. "And Arlene and I need a little free time to ourselves for some gossipy girl talk."

"Just point us in the directions of *Frenchman's Reef* and *Bluebeard's Castle*; then we'll eventually meet again for supper," Arlene Burns humorously added. "As long as there's gift money to spend, Carla and I will find a way to spend it."

"Okay with me," Howard confirmed with a broad grin. "Just go around those cruise ships anchored to your left, and you'll find *Frenchman's Reef. Bluebeard's Castle* is situated on *that* hill up to your left, and don't forget to also take a gander at Magens Bay."

After exiting the super-fine *Bottoms-Up Bar and Restaurant,* Howard Steel picked-up an informative brochure about St. Thomas and its natives inside an off-the-beaten path novelty shop. The self-appointed tour-guide brought the acquired literature along to casually study aboard the moored *Paradise.* Later that night, the coy optometrist reclined in his bunk and then perused the pamphlet.

One of the brochure's side-panel articles dealt with the notorious pirate Blackbeard. The description aptly stated in the pamphlet: "This pirate, also known as Bluebeard, was one of history's most famous swashbucklers. Edward Teach was nicknamed *Blackbeard,* and the formidable sea rover was first described as a heinous pirate in 1716. The following year, the enterprising buccaneer converted a French

258

merchant ship into a forty-gun warship, named *Queen Anne's Revenge*, and the outlawed rogue soon became an infamous renegade marauder, terrorizing sea coast towns and villages along the Virginia and Carolina coasts, and also later, engaging in illegal sea activity all throughout the Caribbean."

More descriptive information about the infamous pirate was then gleaned on the colorful publication's back sleeve. "Blackbeard robbed ships of their gold and silver treasures upon the high seas," Howard read to Bill from the informative four-sided document. "The ruthless marauder and his treacherous crew were the scourge of every respectable sea captain that dared sail the perilous waters between Bermuda, Cuba and the southern tip of Florida. The evasive scoundrel was both feared and abhorred for his hideous reputation involving cruelty." The brief article further reported and summarized Blackbeard's mythical "satanic ability", which was reputed to emit red death rays in the form of "fiery heat exploding from his eyes."

Howard knew from legend and from history that the villainous Edward Teach had operated within the area of the fearful *Bermuda Triangle*. According to local lore, Pirate Teach had buried a fabulous treasure somewhere in the Caribbean, and its exact location has remained a long-lost mystery.

"Over two-hundred inexplicable incidents have occurred inside the fearful *Devil's Triangle;* ships have disappeared, planes have crashed into the sea, and unfortunate mariners have involuntarily become ghosts," the interesting brochure further stated. "Was it all possible? Or was the pirate's evil deeds all a colonial era mass media hoax?" the last paragraph stated.

Howard was especially fascinated by the *Bermuda Triangle* disaster theory, and by the renowned Blackbeard legend. The St. Thomas seafarer wondered if there was any significant connection between the two separate and seemingly disparate Caribbean "myths".

When Howard Steel had finished reading the captivating article to a vaguely attentive Bill Martino, the other two schooner passengers were already fast asleep in their bunks. Howard-dozed off to visit Mr. Sandman, and soon thereafter, Bill also drifted off into dreamland.

The next morning the clear, mild, cloudless sky was just as beautiful as the calm azure sea. The *Paradise* gracefully swayed ever so slightly at its Charlotte Amalie mooring, gently rocking amidst the bland waves approaching the shoreline from the crystal-like placid harbor.

"Up and at 'em," Howard commanded the three other "barnacles" aboard. "It's time to wipe the heavy sleep out of your eyes."

Everyone stirred and soon Bill put a pot of coffee on the galley stove's front burner. Carla prepared a Spartan breakfast of cereal, bacon, and scrambled eggs. It was almost time for Steel and Martino to depart on their preplanned Virgin Island secret expedition.

"Have a good time shopping, Girls. We'll see you later-on this evening for supper," predicted Howard as the sailboat separated from the marina dock. "Bon Voyage!"

"Bill, I hope you remembered to take the two pairs of sunglasses that I had entrusted you with?" Howard confided as both guys waved to their respective babes on shore. "They're the most indispensable things on this trip, besides Carla and Arlene!"

"Would I ever forget them? This is the real reason we're both here," Bill blandly chastised. "The girls are really nice company, but the dye-cast time-travel sunglasses are even nicer!"

Martino held the seaman's chart and carefully examined the more pertinent details. The fifty uninhabited islets were represented on the map by individual, miniature dots. It would become a very perfidious situation if their schooner scraped bottom in the shallows, so plausibly, the depth-finder on the *Paradise's* instrument panel would have to be assiduously monitored. The craft's mast sails were full from winds that prevailed in an easterly manner, originating from the trade latitudes. The Virgin Island shoreline soon disappeared into the eastern horizon, while the water depth registered a safe one-hundred-feet.

"Bill, I think it's now time for us to wear the specs. Let's put 'em on," Howard pertinently urged. "According to the mixing formula, I estimate we'll be navigating back into the past around three-hundred-years; I speculate us wandering somewhere around the Caribbean in the late 1600s. Maybe some generous blind buccaneers will pass by in a rowboat and hand us a full bucket of shiny gold doubloons."

"I'll settle for some less valuable silver pieces of eight," modest First Mate Bill replied. "And I'd hate to say it, but I think the only real *Pirates* around today are playing baseball in Pittsburgh."

"You're right on that count," laughed Alternate Captain Howard. "And the only real *Buccaneers* are haplessly meandering-around playing pro football in Tampa Bay."

Twenty-miles west/northwest of St. Thomas, a dense fog began engulfing that sector of the *Bermuda Triangle.* Suddenly, the depth-finder was accurately reading seventy-five feet, and the indicator numbers on the device were apparently dropping fast. In five short minutes, the readout was showing an extremely shallow depth of twenty-feet. The schooner's rudder was turned so that the *Paradise* would parallel the vaguely outlined western St. Thomas shoreline seen in the far distance The sight of the island was about to vanish over the horizon, ever through the men's powerful binoculars. Soon, Sentry Bill was able to spot, through an opening in the enveloping mist, a deserted, sand-laden, palm-covered islet.

The encroaching dense fog began hindering Martino's visual perception, so the amateur mariners promptly anchored the *Paradise* in the all-too-quiet shallows. The stalled crewmen then lowered the schooner's small rowboat, hopped inside, and steadfastly began oaring their way toward the tiny nearby body of land. The thickening fog grossly hampered their visibility, but their initial visual survey detected nothing but palm trees, thick scrub bushes, and some large rocks lying on the desolate islet's beach.

For adventure's sake, the arriving rowers kept their sunglasses on, for to take them off would dispel any late 1600s' effect that the amazing past spectacles would be creating. The fog was getting heavier and visibility was becoming poorer. The fervent explorers decided to wait for the thick fog to lift, fully knowing that the small island hadn't changed too much in the past four centuries, so wearing the time-travel sunglasses really didn't matter. It was still early afternoon, and the sea drifters were hoping that the atmospheric hindrance would dissipate before nocturnal darkness would set in. Steel and Martino sat still and orally commiserated in their diminutive boat.

"Bill, the fog's as thick as canned soup. Say, did you hear something. Listen? It sounds like distant human voices!"

"I think we're both becoming paranoid," Martino confirmed and responded. "Instead of interacting with Caribbean ghosts, I hope we can someday live to return to Dayton to see your replica *Spad*."

"Damn the *Spad!* Bill, there it is again! I'm sure I heard voices somewhere in the distance," Howard whispered. "Don't even make a tiny sound, Bill. We'll soon see where the noise is coming from."

The thrill-seeking twosome stealthily beached the small rowboat and quietly crawled-in towards the islet's center. The gruff alien conversations became louder, and the two American spies knew that they had moved much closer to the sounds' source. Through the dense mist, the forms of several unsavory-looking colonial-era thugs dressed in ragged, tattered, seventeenth-century apparel became faintly visible. The crude-looking characters were grunting and carrying a rather burdensome wooden chest. Recognizable words were now being exchanged and distinctly heard.

"Tell us, Blackbeard. Where do ye' want to bury this here treasure box?" the taller pirate asked his mean-looking superior.

"Between the two large rocks next to the angled coconut tree," Blackbeard specified. "Dig down five-feet. We'll bury the booty right here. This tiny island is so remote that nobody will ever be able to find the king's missing gold in at least three-hundred-years," the savage-looking villain uttered and cackled.

Howard and Bill astoundingly watched and eavesdropped the dialogue behind a wild bush cluster. The lower atmosphere's vapor was beginning to lift, and the shocked spies could now faintly discern the abominable form of the dreadful pirate: dangerous, nefarious Blackbeard. It didn't take long for the brawny crewmen to inter and bury-over the heavy wooden treasure chest.

Soon, the band of lawless sea rovers trekked-off to the right, got into a four-passenger dingy, and rowed-off toward a ship's ghostly, nebulous outline that was barely perceptible in the distance. The fog was still dense enough that the unsuspecting pirates never noticed the presence of Howard or Bill, *their* little beached rowboat, or the modern twentieth-century distant sailboat, which had been securely anchored out of sight on the opposite side of the secluded islet.

The ruthless renegades were then heard rambunctiously boarding their notorious gunboat. The designation "*Queen Anne's Revenge*" was now vaguely discernible to the eyes of the petrified hiding Americans, still lingering behind several thorny scrub bushes; the rookie sailors were extremely afraid to even gallivant around the desolate Caribbean islet where the huge wooden treasure chest had been deposited, six-feet-deep under the golden sand.

When all the pirate anarchists were finally aboard what Howard had erroneously termed the "Jolly Roger", the *Queen Anne's Revenge* slipped-away north into the obscurity of the jeopardous *Bermuda Triangle*. Howard and Bill remained stooped-down until the duo finally garnered sufficient courage to locate their tiny beached rowboat, and then rapidly venture back to the awaiting safety of the wave-rolling *Paradise*. At last, the paranoid pair felt intrepid enough to attempt their daring escape.

The time-travel sunglasses were removed, and the wearers were stunned to notice that the weather was now absolutely clear without an overhead array of cottony clouds being visible. The relieved schooner mates could still see the islet and its cactus-like vegetation being very evident. The general landscape, however, was not exactly the same as it had appeared while the Dayton, Ohio intruders were wearing their specialized back-to-the-past sunglasses.

After strenuously rowing back to safety and next climbing aboard the *Paradise,* Steel and Martino observed that the islet's two large volcanic rocks could still be hazily observed with binoculars. The men mathematically charted the exact coordinates of the "treasure island" on their ship's wall map, and the exhausted explorers calculated its precise position within specified longitude and latitude quadrants. All of the essential, strategic information had been very accurately documented, and it was soon time to raise anchor.

"Howard, I can't believe what we just witnessed with our science-defying time-journey sunglasses."

"Bill, I can't either!" Steel concurred, still a bit out of breath. "This whole unpredictable scenario is just too crazy to ever believe!"

"Howie, what should we tell the girls?" inquired the still-amazed optician. "They'll want to know everything we've done."

"Well, Bill, we'll simply tell the babes we have someplace special to take them. Don't tell the beauty queens about the magical sunglasses, though," Howard advised. "Even though we really *like* Carla and Arlene, I still don't know if we can completely *trust* their selfish motives if we divulge our fantastic secret."

* * * * * * * * * * * *

The contemporary treasure searchers arrived safely at the Charlotte Amalie Marina within three-hours, right after dusk, and also, just in time for supper. The gossiping girls were chatting and waiting at the dock, both clad in their newly-acquired Caribbean-fashion outfits.

"How was your high-seas trip, Howard?" Carla asked. "Did you go swimming or snorkeling?

"No, we didn't. But the word 'unbelievable' is the only worthy adjective that comes to mind," the still-rattled Caribbean sailor replied. "It's all certainly worth of seeing and experiencing again."

"Can we come along with you two very handsome musclemen tomorrow?" Arlene bellowed with her hands cupped around her mouth to form a mini-megaphone. "Carla and I can wear our skimpy red bikinis and do some swimming in shallow water!"

"Tomorrow will definitely change your mediocre lives forever, I absolutely guarantee it," Howard smartly yelled-down from the boat's deck. "But both you dolls will have to wait until then, that is, before Bill and I can show you our mind-boggling discovery. Be prepared for the ultimate adventure of your life," Alternate Captain Howard haughtily and confidently predicted.

On Friday morning, Mariner Howard and First Mate Bill awoke early before the local roosters ever remembered how to crow. "We have to buy two sturdy shovels," Steel remembered and reminded. "Bill, you go into town and find a hardware store. I'll stay aboard with the girls and guard the magic sunglasses while they're busy making breakfast," instructed the schooner's commander to his closest friend.

Martino was gone from the *Paradise* for about an hour and happily brought back the required shovels, along with an artistic treasure map of the area. The digging tools were stored in a wall cabinet aboard the schooner, before the inquisitive girls could ever spot the spades and ask any curious female-type questions.

The four *Paradise* passengers enjoyed a hardy fruit and toast breakfast, and during the early morning feast, the girls were trying to pry out of their favorite males exactly what was in store for them in the line of seafaring adventure.

"Don't worry," promised Bill. "I guarantee that you two princesses won't be disappointed. In fact, I double-promise it!"

"But what's with the treasure map hanging out of Bill's back pocket?" Arlene observed and questioned. "Don't think that Carla and I are foolish enough to go digging for fools-gold' treasure!"

"Don't get all bent out of shape. I bought the stupid map from a begging kid on the beach for five bucks. The pipsqueak said it's destined to find a hidden buried treasure chest," Howard laughed and equivocated. 'I just felt sorry for the barefooted kid, that's all!"

The enviable sailboat smoothly slipped-out of its mooring and glided-out of serene Charlotte Amalie harbor. The clear day's sky portended many fine hours of clear sailing. The men's versatile tinted sunglasses would not be needed, for they had already served their essential purpose the day before at the seemingly commonplace islet. The glasses were left onboard and placed inside a galley drawer.

Everything had been reliably calculated and recorded on the schooner's local wall chart. The *Paradise's* direction and bearing were the same as the precise readings that had been mathematically determined the day before. Only a two and a half' hour cruise separated the sailing quartet from what Howard described as "un-taxable *IRS* proof' gainful riches".

The dauntless navigator and his first mate faithfully monitored the depth-finder, while the unsuspecting dolls sunbathed on the deck in their bright, tight-fitting red bikinis. "One-hundred-feet and holding," Bill objectively announced. However, the electronic readout was soon about to radically change.

"Bill! Look! The depth is now fifty-feet, and the water's getting shallower just like before!" Howard spontaneously pointed to the readout and yelled. "Now it's only twenty-feet."

Bill corrected the *Paradise's* course, and his positioning soon paralleled the by-now-familiar St. Thomas western coastline, barely seen in the distance. It wasn't long before the novice mariners duplicated the exact coordinates where the neophyte island pioneers had spied the pirate's islet, which had appeared nebulous in the dense mist, just the day before. The daring helmsmen made their gradual approach as the giddy girls laughed and sunbathed upon the large sailboat's front deck.

The dependable anchor was dropped, and the useful rowboat was very deliberately lowered. The sun dolls were summoned, and in a minute, the foursome climbed inside "the dinghy". Howard luckily remembered to take the pair of shovels, along with the aforementioned "fake treasure map".

"What's that map for?" Carla Simpson asked, pointing at the colorful illustration depicted.

"We're going treasure hunting," teased Howard. "And we're going without the professional services of Jim Hawkins, Long John Silver, and Robert Louis Stevenson."

"With a silly cheap, phony map you had bought from a kid huckster on the beach?" Arlene nobly challenged and guffawed. "Tell us the truth now! What's really up?"

"Yeah. Shiver me timbers, and the intrepid lad told me his name really was Jim Hawkins," Will Martino laughed while alluding to young character in a famous pirate novel.

The jovial, boisterous quartet eventually reached the islet's sandy beach, and then singularly hopped-out of their rudimentary, nautical mode of transportation.

"Now what?" Carla Simpson wondered and asked her laconic companion guide. "Where have we gone to in this flimsy boat? You two guys better get us off this island safely, or else Arlene and I won't ever get to see that incomparable *Spad* flying machine you're always talking about!"

"You're both in for a magnificent, huge surprise. Follow my lead, mates," Howard explicitly ordered. "You'll be immensely rewarded; that fact I'm certain."

"Look to the left! There're the two volcanic rocks!" exclaimed Bill as the cfontemporary Starbuck pointed and steered the cynical girls' attention in *that* direction. The four islet trespassers pulled their small boat ashore, and soon beached the dingy in proximity to the twin landmark volcanic rocks, just as a light mist started enveloping their quixotic expedition.

Howard and Bill began strenuously excavating like obsessed gravediggers, and within ten-minutes, laboriously achieved a five-foot-deep cavity. Suddenly, Bill's shovel made contact with a hard surface. The digger quickly dropped his shovel and rearranged with both hands the surrounding loose sand, and shortly thereafter, the bracketed lid of a somewhat-decayed wooden box appeared.

Howard assisted his muscular colleague in completing the arduous endeavor, and with their dual due-diligence being exercised, the entire lid of a splintered wooden chest had successfully been exposed. The enthralled girls watched in awe as the male discoverers tenaciously tugged and pulled their buried trove above ground, together functioning like crazed maniacs.

After five more suspenseful minutes of intense toil, the heavy chest had been mutually raised from the three-hundred-year-old hole, being lifted-up to ground level. Carla and Arlene, affected by the overall sight of the phenomenal treasure chest, voluntarily pitched-in and assisted in the tug. Soon, the four American interlopers had the heavy wooden object fully extracted from its three-or-four-century-old grave.

The ever-thickening fog was getting much worse by the minute, and the accompanying chilly breeze, causing sudden dampness in the air, felt quite emotionally foreboding and ominous. But the four very zealous treasure-hunters were now entirely overwhelmed by greed. The money-hungry diggers couldn't contain themselves any longer, and finally, after ferociously struggling with the chest's extremely rusted hinges, the obsessed, searchers managed to pry-open the long-lost wooden container.

"Oh my God! Just look at the invaluable precious jewels and lustrous gold coins!" Carla euphorically shouted. "This could be the greatest treasure find of the century!"

"It's completely loaded and brimming-over with priceless gems! This blessed plunder must be worth millions, maybe billions!" Arlene exuberantly confirmed.

"I can't believe it," Bill deliriously verified. "These gold coins are worth a king's double-ransom!"

The elated foursome repeatedly sang "16 men on a dead man's chest, yo-ho, ho and a bottle of rum." Then, the festive booty hunters leaped about and danced, totally oblivious to any potential threat or looming danger. Their raucous merriment and unbridled revelry were almost a defiant act of selfish contempt directed toward the rapidly approaching *Bermuda Triangle* fog.

A gargantuan, antiquated gunboat had quietly dropped its anchor a quarter-mile offshore. Rowing to the islet in two landing boats was a crew of eight reprehensible, mangy-looking, uncouth felons, led by the mean-spirited and very licentious swashbuckler, *Blackbeard*.

The self-absorbed treasure hunters were totally unaware of the contingent of detrimental, fugitive-from-justice scoundrels, who were stealthily and gradually encroaching. It was too late to evade the head pirate's wicked wrath as the maniacal crewmembers aggressively surrounded the very surprised victims, and after a minute of intense screaming from the shocked girls' throats, and after the very rough wrestling to the ground of Howard and Bill, the four astounded vacationers were roughly tied-up, conducted to the first dispatched landing boat, and soon cruelly hauled-off to the prison-hull of the inimitable *Queen Anne's Revenge*. Ironically, the alien high seas' floating anachronism had the infamous *Jolly Roger* flag gently waving in the breeze, swaying atop the ship's main mast.

Next, the four-hundred-year-old chest was easily retrieved, and then the four remaining marauders all together rejoiced and celebrated. Onboard the fearsome pirate ship, Blackbeard felt compelled to threaten and intimidate his oddly-dressed captives. "You'll surely all pay for your insolence, quite dearly," the pernicious pirate bellowed as the four woeful, crestfallen, chained prisoners were led down rickety stairs to the dingy, dismal brig.

The *Queen Anne's Revenge's* anchor was heard below deck, being cranked and elevated-up from the eternal light blue sea, and then the sinister pirate gunboat moved like an unearthly phantom deeper into an even denser layer of tropical fog.

The four greedy slave/hostages managed to tug their wrist manacles from the grimy, below-deck stench-laden wall, and their bleary eyes peered-out of two of the smelly brig's three small windows. Their appalled pupils instantly beheld a most terrifying sight. Beside a long, wooden on-deck plank stood a grotesque-looking pirate having destructive red heat-beams being emitted (like a flurry of sparks) from diabolical Blackbeard's evil eyes.

"Arabesque"

In his younger days, Malik Kannan was a precocious child who lived in the Middle East near a small village on the outskirts of AZ-Zarqa, Jordan. Malik was a playful-but-inquisitive youngster who had one very dear companion and favorite bosom buddy, a friendly well-mannered boy named Tariq Safar. When both lads were twelve years old, the duo spent many happy moments together, toiling in Malik's father's fertile fields while simultaneously enjoying each other's jovial personalities. But much to the external effect of heretofore future developments, the Arab boys' contemporary fond occasions would actually someday become severely tested.

Malik's hard-working parents, Hamil and Kamil Kannan were by no means wealthy landowners; the husband and wife operating a quaint rural subsistence farm, while insisting all along that the ever-dreaming Malik should voluntarily assist them in performing the difficult daily chores. "Son, you must diligently work planting and harvesting the vegetables before you can ever once consider playing!" Hamil often politely chastised Malik. "Work should always come before play! Play must be earned!"

Occasionally, Malik's same-age neighbor Tariq would arrive and engage in helping his friend with growing the traditional, predictable, annual crops, and finally, succeeding in getting the excess produce ready to ship to commercial markets in AZ-Zarqa and Amman. Naturally, a close, compatible bond had developed over the years between cheerful Malik and cooperative Tariq.

One spring morning, while the standard crop seeds were being planted, Malik had to vigorously employ his hoe to separate well-entrenched weeds from a patch of productive soil. While casually reaching into his deep waist pouch to search for more seeds, the quixotic young man discovered several dirty-but-interesting archaic trinkets (along with a rather shiny white object) lying just beneath the surface sand. Young Malik Kannan knew that nearby farmers had discovered several fascinating ancient artifacts in the past, but during this seemingly nondescript event, one strange, small white stone instantly attracted Malik's attention.

While friend Tariq was preoccupied with his face turned as the lad was enacting his own laborious hoe digging, Malik paused and closely examined the violet veins that were evident on both sides of the very unique white stone. Young Kannan secretly placed his peculiar find inside his left pants' pocket, stealthily keeping its visual existence apart from Tariq's scrutiny.

Later that spring day, while being alone in the family's tiny stone house, Malik carefully washed and cleansed the white stone until the object finally reflected a smooth, polished surface. 'Not even Tariq will know about this rather curious-looking rock,' Malik decided. 'Some things a person must keep all to himself! Who knows what century this weird-looking stone is from? Perhaps it belongs as an important exhibit from antiquity inside the famous Amman Museum! Oh, dear me. My imagination is running wild!'

Throughout his brief educational career, Malik Kannan had been a very studious, academically-oriented student, and the self-motivated pupil suddenly recalled reading an ancient book titled *Arabesque* that supposedly contained long-lost magical knowledge, dating back from medieval times. *That* specific title was seldom read by anyone else in the school, but the intriguing volume provided "Malik-the-Dreamer" with an abundance of rather pertinent information about such arcane and esoteric subjects as "The Philosopher's Stone", "Aladdin's Lamp", "Legendary Alibaba," and finally, "Middle Ages Alchemy Secrets", which contained a vital, captivating chapter describing the use of "The Awesome Talismans".

'After I had found the major White Stone Talisman with the radiant purple veins on both sides,' young Malik Kannan recollected from his relevant book reading, 'all that the lucky discoverer has to then do is utter the magic word 'Arabesque' three times, and soon the remaining Talismans will gloriously appear in his midst!'

Late that afternoon, Malik's parents had ventured into town to sell some of their surplus spring vegetable crops to certain vendors doing business inside the village marketplace, and so being comfortably alone, the twelve-year-old boy held the White Talisman Stone with the purple veins in his right palm and then solemnly repeated the words "Arabesque" three consecutive times. Amazingly, and to Malik's total consternation, Jade, Onyx, and lustrous Ruby Talismans all physically appeared in his right hand to prodigiously accompany the unique White Stone, possessing the colorful purple veins.

With his heart frenetically pumping and his mind swimming in sheer ecstasy, Malik carefully placed the presumably four magical objects inside a "Secret Treasure Box" that the fanciful Dreamer had always kept stashed beneath his bed; his mother and father believed that the small chest was merely a harmless play thing, designed to delight the fantasies of their loyal, well-behaved, naive son's rather extensive imagination.

'I'll lock the four neat stones inside, but first I want to make a special wish for my family's sake!' the euphoric boy considered. 'I wish that I could become especially rich and spare my poor parents the responsibility of paying for my future college education. Is *that* wish asking too much?'

And after praying those wonderful words with the White Stone still firmly grasped in his right hand, the youthful Keeper of Truth gently placed the small white mineral into the box, locating it alongside the other three very different-in-appearance Talismans. Malik next locked the 'Toy Container', slid the special item beneath his ancient bed, put the cheap Box Key inside his pants pocket, and five-minutes later, the callow curator dozed-off upon his mattress into fantasyland, dreaming that his wishes would come true.

The following Sunday, with little farm work to be performed, Malik was allowed to travel and visit AZ-Zarqa with his parents Hamil and Kamil. As Mr. Kannan drove the old rusty Toyota truck towards the city, the mother and father discussed how Malik had been saving money to purchase a radio for his bedroom. The son remained rather reticent during the short trip.

Upon arriving in downtown AZ-Zarqa, the excited boy asked his parents' permission to enter an electronics store to examine available radios that were for sale. After obtaining trusting approval, the anxious lad left his elders' presence and soon engaged in enacting totally bizarre and uncharacteristic conduct. Using a silver coin of a decent value that the boy had been saving, Malik audaciously bribed a drunken, feeble mendicant to purchase a Lottery Ticket, which the youngster regarded as an 'experimental investment' to accurately test the validity and power of the White Purple-veined Talisman. A brief conversation ensued.

"Thank you, Sir," the lad courteously stated as the grateful old lush accepted the silver coin in exchange for the much lesser valued lottery ticket. "I'm far too young to legally gamble, but I'll give this ticket of chance to my father as a small gift! I'm sure he'll appreciate my lucky token if it wins!"

The next day, right before supper, Malik listened intently in the modest living room to the radio broadcast, while his industrious mother was preoccupied preparing the dinner meal, and his father was busy washing his hands after a hard day's labor in the fields. When the winning lottery number was eventually announced, Malik's emotions were brimming with dramatic jubilance.

'Praise be to Allah!' the ecstatic youth enthusiastically thought. 'I shall give this huge fortune to my parents, so that they won't have to sacrifice with hard manual labor for the rest of their boring existence. This rather simple piece of paper truly represents the happiest day of my life! I'll tell my father and mother about the lucky lottery ticket, but not Tariq. Knowing *his* impulsive nature, the hothead might become jealous of my good fortune!'

"Son, this time I shall forgive you for bribing the old man and then gambling with some of your hard-earned savings," Hamil gently admonished. "But please don't make a habit out of taking other foolish risks. Please be wise and prudent in the future. I shall deposit your colossal winnings into a safe bank account, and I assure you, your education will be paid for in full. Thank you, Malik, for generously contributing to our family's prosperity! I'm sure that your dear mother will be most surprised!"

* * * * * * * * * * * *

Gossip abounded throughout the crowded village marketplace about Malik's recent good fortune, and the associated scuttlebutt and typical envy seemed like a terrible curse to both Hamil and Kamil. Many former friends and acquaintances deliberately avoided the family, and so, on the brief truck trip home, Malik, Hamil, and Kamil agreed that a much-needed humanitarian plan regarding "charity action" had to be aggressively set into motion.

That evening, after engaging in a lengthy dinner table discussion, the concerned father determined that he would endeavor rectifying the new difficult social conflict situation by deploying some of the money that his son had amassed for the expressed purpose of improving the local community. Soon, philanthropic sums were discreetly donated and intelligently designated to assist the less fortunate townspeople, and in short time, with the lottery bonanza promoting the general financial improvement of the village's lower class residents, local attitudes toward the now-envied Kannan family were rapidly changing for the better.

"The Kannans are using a good portion of their Lottery Ticket profits to aid us!" people gleefully concluded and shared. "The boy's deviant bribing and gambling can be forgiven! The Kannans and their lucky son are decent human beings after all! Praise be to Allah! Praise be to Allah!"

In *that* abbreviated time frame, Malik came to realize that the mysterious Talismans could amazingly protect him from evil spirits, could cause either torrential rain or radiant sunshine, could dispel melancholy, depression, and sadness, and when used all together, the objects could easily control all of *those* essential matters, in addition to creating mammoth personal wealth, along with huge monetary profits from sound investments.

And as Malik's teen years continued to advance into adulthood, the "Kannan Village Welfare Fund" continued uplifting many local residents from poverty-to-mediocrity-to-Middle Class Life, and so the established rural family was again respected, honored, and revered within the small town, and also its lackluster outskirts.

Eight-years had passed since the sensational Lottery Ticket good fortune, and a minor rift had now developed between Malik and Tariq; the latter friend had believed that his former close companion had deceived him by not originally disclosing the true source of the Kannan family Lottery ticket bonanza.

Malik soon enrolled at Amman's prestigious *Jordan University,* studying modern farming methods in the School of Agriculture, and over his remaining adolescent years, the now-mature young man had learned additional significant details about the dynamic properties and supernatural powers, of regular Black Onyx, of Jade, and of Ruby Red Carnelian stones.

'A mediocre Jade Stone can provide a conscientious Agricultural Student like myself with a miraculous 'Green Thumb,' Malik logically recognized, 'and commonplace Black Onyx can cause a grudge-wish on someone, and negatively cause that mendacious person extremely unlucky circumstances. And an ordinary Carnelian Red Stone can either protect a wish recipient from the hot sun, or, if held firmly in the palm of the left hand, it can cast an evil spell upon a wicked enemy. Only a benign Mother of Pearl can neutralize a Red Stone's strong curse, all of which is generated with the left hand gripping the Carnelian Talisman when the object mystically changes from a dull shade color to bright ruby red.'

* * * * * * * * * * * *

Mohammed Bahar was a destitute farmer living between AZ-Zarqa and the now upwardly-mobile village where the Kannan family resided close by. Because of many frustrating years of constant agrarian failure, Mohammed felt exceedingly inferior when comparing his decades-long-dilemma to the various successes of other area growers. Malik heard about Bahar's pathetic plight, visited the disconsolate farmer, and during their lengthy conversation, the college sophomore silently prayed for Mohammed's benefit, while tightly gripping the wonderful Green Jade Charm. 'You shall no longer feel *jaded* and ostracized,' Malik sincerely imagined. 'In fact, Mohammed Bahar, others will be green with envy of you a full year hence. I predict that you shall enjoy a plethora of benefits! Your economic fate shall rise above your life being destitute!'

Amazingly, the powerful Jade Talisman Stone managed to produce tremendous economic results for formerly despondent Mohammed Bahar. His crops that summer and also that fall were the most bountiful harvests in the entire region, and Bahar's fellow farmers now held the rags-to-riches grower in very high esteem. 'It all transformed right after I had invited that pleasant student from Jordan University into my humble home,' Mohammed gratefully acknowledged to himself. 'And I hope the young man returns someday, so that I could personally render my genuine gratitude. Now, thanks to Allah, I have the nicest home in the vicinity, also a very beautiful wife, and I can afford to maintain the most impressive botanical garden found anywhere in this remote part of Jordan!'

* * * * * * * * * * * *

During the always-welcome academic Spring Break, which that year heralded the termination of Malik's junior year, the conscientious college student received an unexpected letter from his now-envious childhood friend, Tariq Safar, who had never gone to college, and was currently working as a meager, unimportant laborer on a distant farm. In the sad missive, disheartened Tariq sorrowfully revealed, "I strongly love my precious wife Rasha, but she refuses to have children, thinking that the kids would become too much of a burden upon my truly deficient wages. Malik, over the years, you've evolved into a very wise, respected, and eminent man! Conversely, my whole life is an accursed debacle. What do you suggest I do?"

Malik stopped eating his me bland breakfast inside the university cafeteria, paced to his dormitory room, and promptly and confidently reciprocated Tariq's surprise inquiry with a sympathetic letter. "I will hereby wish you a satisfactory arrangement with your wife, Rasha," Malik's missive compassionately indicated, his words sounding almost like those of an accomplished veteran attorney. "Positive thinking has always effectively worked for me. I place maximum credence in the notion that my blessing will bring a new favorable compromise to exist between you and Rasha! I guarantee, Tariq, that if you loyally follow my sound directions, your current, aggravating family problems will certainly be alleviated!"

Malik was fully cognizant that the Dull Red Carnelian Stone had the astounding capacity to revitalize marital love, while effectively altering a person's counter-productive negative thinking. So tightly grasping the magical 'Ruby Stone' in his *right* hand, the young magician prayed that obstinate Rasha would gradually come to a beneficial verbal settlement with worried Tariq about the prospect of prolifically having many wonderful offspring. 'Ruby Stone, please don't fail me! Make Rasha understand her role as a mother! Praise be to Allah!'

A year and a half later, another surprise letter addressed to Malik coming from Tariq was received. Young Kannan was thrilled when reading and comprehending the message's sincere content:

Dearest Friend Malik,

I'm delighted to finally hear from you again. And I'm quite glad to report that I've indeed reinstated you as my true best friend. I must admit that plenty of marvelous things have strangely occurred since my first letter to you was sent. At the time, I had seriously wished and prayed that Rasha would change her stubborn mind and heart about us having children, and incredibly, within the span of several months, my obstinate wife did just that. Much to my utter joy, last week we became the proud parents of twin baby boys.

Please forgive me, Malik, for being so haughty, selfish and arrogant to you over this last turbulent decade of our difficult relationship. I no longer am jealous of your immense achievements, and I now have the confidence to pursue gainful investments of my own. I currently have an excellent job acting as a field manager on a very large estate, the property having two-hundred loyal employees working under my direct supervision. And I am very happy to report to you that the estate's owner is quite satisfied with my service.

Thank you so much, Malik, for converting me to endorsing the awesome powers of Positive Thinking. Rasha and I are deeply indebted to your most singular wisdom, and to your very practical advice. In all honesty, Malik, it's been abundantly fortunate for me to have such a fabulous friend over all these last, very critical ten years!

Your old friend,

Tariq

'The Talismans can indeed transmit strong energy over great distances,' Malik comprehended and concluded. 'I'm now going to test the potency of the Black Onyx Stone on a nefarious person who's pretending to be a benign force in AZ-Zarqa. And I think that the unassuming tyrant is non-other than Farrah Antar, the treasurer of the City Trust Fund, to which I am presently a junior member. Farrah's an absolute phony, an arrogant impostor faking to be philanthropic while suspected by many citizens to be siphoning money out of the club treasury for the nefarious thief's own personal gain! I'll begin my daunting quest by innocently insisting that a full comprehensive audit be performed on the organization's financial records. I am sure that wicked Farrah Antar is guilty of committing embezzlement!'

At the following late June club meeting, Farrah Antar was greatly disturbed by his young rival's bold recommendation for an audit to be performed, but then the wily crook verbally acceded to the request out of fear of his illicit activity being detected, while coincidentally, the obnoxious rogue had been making a boisterous and vehement public protest scene against his young nemesis. By late July, the official accounting had been completed, and the final evaluations were soon publicly revealed.

"Thousands upon thousands of securities have been funneled out of our treasury, and the principal suspect undoubtedly is our fiendish Treasurer, the Dishonorable Farrah Antar. Thanks to our intrepid junior board member Malik Kannan," the Club Chairman cited during a well-attended dinner speech, "this ethical issue has been efficiently resolved. Will the Sergeant-at-Arms please escort disgraced Mr. Antar out of the boardroom, and kindly turn the vile scoundrel over to the proper authorities for legal prosecution!"

Malik was fantastically satisfied that the Black Onyx Stone had worked to perfection, causing the unscrupulous embezzler Farrah Antar to eventually have an abrupt rendezvous with community justice. 'The nasty, grumpy criminal has met his fate,' club junior member Malik Kannan assessed and determined. 'Now, I again have renewed faith in the supernatural magic power of the omnipotent Talisman Stones. Thank you again for your intercession, my dear Arabesque! May Almighty Allah be praised!'

Malik soon discovered that the Black Onyx Stone was extremely versatile and possessed additional supernatural powers, one of which would enable the object's possessor to read minds and also perceive the evil thoughts that mean-spirited people often harbor. The Black Onyx Talisman could also make its owner know either the targeted villains externally projected false piety, or the person's tremendous hate. 'I've learned that when the veins inside the Black Stone turn deep red, then that person being analyzed is lying, or has cruel and malicious intentions. I must now utilize the stone to isolate an individual contemplating murder, and then act quickly to shrewdly prevent the heinous crime from happening.'

While attending a Jordanian Archeological Excavation as an elective course assignment to complete a University Geology Seminar, Malik perceptively noticed two belligerent brothers arguing and yelling profanities at one another. Soon, ugly rhetoric erupted into imminent violence, which soon escalated into a terrible.

Using the Black Onyx Stone to effectively perform special mental telepathy, Malik immediately perceived that Abdul and Omar were of the same argumentative ilk; the combative brothers always engaged in enacting sundry forms of aggressive sibling rivalry. Malik's gifted 'sixth sense' informed young Kannan that Abdul had once committed murder, but had cleverly escaped being convicted for his hideous crime when his corrupt lawyer invoked a technicality that got the diabolical culprit off the proverbial legal hook.

'Abdul wants to have Omar killed, but the wily villain doesn't desire to physically perform the sinful misdeed with a weapon,' Malik competently interpreted, while obtaining mental transmissions from the inimitable Onyx Stone. 'The deplorable thug has deliberately filed-down the fifth rung from the top of *that* tall ladder, which is anchored down inside the pit below. When corpulent Omar puts his entire weight on that tampered-with rung,' Malik shrewdly rationalized, 'he'll swiftly plummet sixteen-feet to his demise, probably breaking his chubby neck. I'll just concentrate deeply and mentally have Abdul's sturdy ladder switched with Omar's defective one! It'll be my distinct pleasure shrewdly witnessing that contemptible thug Abdul plunging to his unanticipated and most ironic death!'

The frightful episode unfolded exactly as sagacious Malik had ingeniously planned, and Abdul's black soul was soon on its eternal destiny to meet awaiting Lucifer face-to-face. During the uncanny sequence of incredible events, Malik's heart experienced little sorrow, but instead, intentionally savored the altered 'accidental death'. In the final analysis, young Kannan felt extremely guiltless and fully vindicated by his rather clever implementation of the seemingly indispensable Black Onyx Talisman.

* * * * * * * * * * * *

The week before his well-earned graduation from the Jordan University's School of Agriculture, Malik Kannan closely examined his handsome countenance in his dormitory room's wall mirror. 'My shaved face is appearing to be wrinkled and haggard! I look more like a terribly fatigued middle-aged beggar and not at all like an energetic, graduating senior! I think that the Powers That Be are trying to clearly tell me something symbolic; perhaps a certain act which I need to perform concerning my potent Talisman collection!' Malik Kannan plausibly theorized. 'I'm more inclined to view the baneful aspects of people than I am to keenly measure their better qualities and attributes. Perhaps my interfering into having Abdul instead of Omar killed while both brothers were climbing-up the dual ladders has been discerned by Almighty Allah as me furtively committing a very reprehensible, inexcusable, unforgivable sin!'

While somberly weighing the good and the evil elements of the amazing Talisman Stones, Malik judiciously decided to rid himself of the objects' influences in order to live a normal, ordinary, happy life devoid of apparent premature aging. The young sorcerer purchased a bus ticket and journeyed from Jordan to neighboring Lebanon. At a dock bordering the sea, the Talismans' possessor cautiously arranged the extraordinary four stones inside a newly-acquired metal box, and after hiring the use of a small rental boat, Malik Kannan started the motor and sped a half-mile off shore. And there, the rapidly aging mortal gleefully deposited the small locked chest into the depths of the Mediterranean Sea.

Unfortunately, a twelve-year-old fisherman's son named Bashar Wasem was curiously viewing Malik's surreptitious offshore activity through a weatherworn pair of cheap binoculars. Young Wasem rushed along the marina pier and immediately borrowed his older brother's SCUBA gear, along with his father's leaky spare dingy, all being done without obtaining proper permission. Then, the elated lad proceeded to row out to sea to inspect the particular area of interest that his perceptive eyes had witnessed.

After ten-minutes of random underwater searching, jubilant Bashar Wasem incredibly managed to locate the abandoned metal container. 'I don't like being reprimanded. I'll secretly hide this odd discovery from my older brother and parents,' the young dreamer silently vowed. 'Who knows what the rattling contents might be? Whatever is inside,' the formerly bored lad conjectured, 'I'll visit the local library tomorrow to see if I can somehow identify the items that are oddly banging-around inside!'

As the next ten-years passed, Malik Kannan observed that his facial appearance was no longer aging at an accelerated pace, and his prominent features were no longer being altered and distorted. Slowly-but-surely, after much introspection, the now-relieved college graduate finally fully appreciated the magnitude of his past extraordinary exploits involving the incomparable four Talisman Stones.

278

'I now know the true meaning of 'Arabesque',' the persistent seeker-of-wisdom feasibly determined. 'Actions of any kind have their own potential consequences! The arcane Talisman Stones were both a superb blessing and a mendacious curse! Hopefully and truthfully,' Malik sincerely concluded, 'I pray that in the future that no one else on Planet Earth will ever have access to the four spectacular Talisman Stones' omnipotent secrets! May Allah be praised!'

"The Tattoo"

At noon on August 22, 2010, twenty-seven-year-old Dennis Kinkaid anxiously left his small Midwestern town, and six-hours later, arrived by train at his eastern destination, Philadelphia. Having little money in his faded leather wallet, young Kinkaid eventually discovered a very modest upstairs apartment located in a seedy section of the historic city, the room being a mere block from the historic Delaware River.

Dennis was a burly, muscular, physical specimen, standing six-feet-four-inches in height and weighing a hefty two-hundred-and-fifty-pounds. The new Philly' resident possessed jet black hair, a full mustache, along with a small cropped beard, and as was his shy disposition, the recently-arrived, indigent, freight train-traveling-itinerant seldom sought the company of other tenement house dwellers, whose closed wooden doors incidentally bordered his very modest second floor flat.

Kinkaid had been on government disability the past five-years, and practiced no specific purpose in life other than his daily drinking of beer and whiskey. Quite seemingly, the non-motivated, rather content resident tolerated living in positively squalid conditions. Much to Dennis's satisfaction, the other second floor apartment occupants were of a similar ilk; being mostly chronic alcoholics and drug addicts, and so Kinkaid easily blended-in with his newfound, apathetic, anti-social, tenement environment.

'If I need extra dough to support my drinking habit, I'll take a job working for cash on the docks,' Dennis reluctantly presumed. 'Big, strong stevedores are always in demand! But for a lazy man's sake, let's hope that *that* unfortunate day never materializes!'

An obscure-but-popular tattoo parlor existed in a side alley several streets away from where Dennis now lived. Although the curious newcomer was quite deficient in his knowledge of Entomology, young Kinkaid had always been enamored with the idea of learning about myriad insects of all sorts. And so, one late sultry August afternoon, while still experiencing a fairly drunken stupor, the lackadaisical derelict staggered into the musty 'ink shop' and insisted on receiving a whole repertoire of assorted bug and arachnid tattoos.

The first rendition administered by the "ink artist" was that of a menacing-looking, six-legged tarantula. The grotesque arachnid was an inch in length, and the newly acquired hideous tattoo design that became embedded upon the loner's right wrist appeared to be so real that its image startled anyone in public who later had occasion to incidentally view it.

Upon Dennis's slurred-speech insistence, other various insects and assorted bugs such as a docile caterpillar, a miniature eight-legged scorpion, a mosquito, and an antagonistic-looking wasp had been carefully etched upon his right arm, and next, a chubby bumble bee, a fly, a roach, and an Amazon Jungle fire ant was drawn upon the customer's upper chest. The peculiar body ornamentation was complete with the fly and the roach finally being applied upon his chest, and last but not least, a Black Widow was eerily drawn upon Kinkaid's neck, being positioned just adjacent to the drunken dreg's very prominent, projecting Adam's apple.

At first glance, the horrifying-in-appearance tarantula tattoo seemed absolutely harmless, but after several months' existence, the weird creature was frightfully growing in size, and remarkably, began sprouting hair, giving an astute observer the impression of actually being three-dimensional. Overnight, the ugly arachnid manifestation had astoundingly developed a width of two-inches in magnitude, and its new position upon the inebriated derelict's arm was now detectable midway between his right wrist and elbow. But every night, as the intoxicated apartment dreg admired the strange 'epidermal illusion', Dennis's fertile, overactive, drunken mind began concocting a mental newsreel of nightmarish horror movie scenarios, that to Kinkaid, seemed entirely delusional.

'It must be a queer optical illusion that my pupils are noticing,' Dennis conjectured before ambitiously guzzling-down several ounces of potent *Jack Daniels*. 'I think it's all a definite aberration, or maybe a visual anomaly of some kind!'

The bewildered observer awkwardly measured the space between his mobile tarantula tattoo and his elbow, and the distorted metric was now an unbelievable eight-inches in length. And a month later, being sedate and thinking with a more-sober disposition, Kinkaid determined that the space between the traveling tarantula and the motionless caterpillar had decreased to a mere seven-inches. But still, there remained three other rather diminutive-but-interesting bug tattoos impressively exhibited upon the drifter's upper right arm: a scorpion, a mosquito, and a wasp.

By mid-November, the distance separating the tarantula and the caterpillar had decreased to less than an inch, but upon closer inspection, the all-too-sensitive skin surrounding the active spider was indeed becoming inflamed; the insect's characteristic features being risen, as if existing in bold relief above the surrounding epidermis, and most certainly appearing more-hairy than its original, two-dimensional skin flatness.

282

But more significantly, and to Dennis's utter astonishment, the caterpillar seemed to be forming a cocoon around itself, apparently readying to transform into either a moth or a butterfly. This evident, extraordinary metamorphosis-in-progress then prompted the addicted drunkard to imbibe a large quantity of very potent whiskey, and predictably, his captivated and intrigued intoxicated mind entered into a very deep slumber.

Each consecutive morning, the growing tarantula presented itself as methodically and stealthily approaching the equally-exceptional, in-transition, developing chrysalis. 'What'll happen when the aggressive spider tattoo finally encroaches upon the vulnerable cocoon?' Kinkaid imagined before belching. 'Predators always vanquish their weaker prey! The moving tarantula looks pretty hostile!'

At daybreak the following November morning, the tattooed slouch awoke amidst a tossing and turning frenzy, and upon instinctively examining his right arm, Dennis realized that the camouflaged caterpillar inside the cocoon had stunningly vanished, and that *that* part of his right arm was presently covered in dried blood. And after fearfully scrutinizing the carnivorous black spider, the raised-in-appearance creature seemed to be much fatter and indeed, much more menacing.

'This whole matter is totally incomprehensible!' Kinkaid fearfully acknowledged, as the apartment dweller quickly entered his tiny bathroom and vigorously washed and scrubbed the red stains from *that* vicinity of his right elbow. Still in a state of emotional confusion, the addled lush's mind automatically considered a terrible worst-case-scenario; a rather frightful contemplation where the hungry spider would cause additional havoc over his upper right arm, his chest, and possibly even savagely encroaching upon the Black Widow that was still immobile and permanently situated next to Dennis Kinkaid's Adam's apple.

'I'll attempt to be patient and more rational. I'll try to objectively observe what happens when the hideous tarantula confronts the scorpion, which should represent more of a direct challenge than the helpless cocooned caterpillar did,' Dennis decided. 'I gotta' be prudent about understanding all of this mysterious, illogical, outlandish stuff! If I consulted a doctor about the unbelievable phenomenon I've just witnessed,' Kinkaid hypothesized, 'he'd immediately recommend me for a thorough psychological evaluation! There must be some plausible explanation for all of these abnormal supernatural occurrences that seem to defy both common sense and natural science! I just hope and pray that my present poor health and my melancholy brain are not being somehow placed in immediate jeopardy!'

By mid-December, the pugnacious tarantula was showing signs of becoming intensely hostile and bellicose as the aggressor deliberately encountered the stationary scorpion, and by Christmas Eve, the famished arachnid was less than a half-inch from its designated target. 'Another sleepless night accompanied by a painful bloody battle above my right elbow awaits my special attention at dawn!' Dennis fretfully speculated. 'I wish I had gotten a heart with an arrow pierced through its center, or an ordinary-looking sailor's anchor tattoo instead of getting the various inked insects,' the nervous former merchant marine regretted. 'I dreamed last night that the tarantula had viciously attacked and then devoured the scorpion. Tomorrow, I'll no doubt notice if my horrid thought becomes the ghastly violent deed!'

Upon awaking from his restive sleep, the apprehensive vagrant experienced what his distressed mind had indeed dreaded. 'My upper right arm is entirely soaked with blood, and the villainous tarantula seems to again have a most satisfied, smiling expression upon its ugly face. This whole matter is rapidly evolving into a most terrifying series of worrisome events!'

The distressed tenement dweller then imagined more fleeting ruminations. 'The two-dimensional scorpion no longer exists as a simple tattoo located above my right elbow!' Dennis almost-soberly marveled and fearfully assessed. 'And the evil, on-a-mission tarantula is definitely more bloated than ever, after enjoying its last gluttonous feast! It's a good thing I didn't have a plethora of assorted insects inked all over my body! I'm really terrified beyond belief!' ascertained the now-neurotic fellow. 'And I'm starting to think that I require advanced mental services beyond those of a psychiatrist! I truly believe that I need the skills of a qualified Catholic priest to effectively exorcise this devilish tarantula that's quite intent on devastating my entire body! I need an immediate remedy! I must do something drastic right now! I have no time to procrastinate!'

On New Years' Day of 2011, two peculiar scars had formed on Kinkaid's sore right arm; the former showing below the elbow, representing where the caterpillar had been devoured, and the latter scab, developing between the elbow and shoulder, where the idle scorpion had been engraved. 'I'm pretty sure that the ravenous tarantula will greedily consume the rest of the insect tattoos in like manner! I just know it'll happen!' Dennis pondered and worried. But the indigent's compelling assumption would in time constitute the least of the psychotic fellow's major concerns.

As heavy February snow descended on that run-down riverfront Philadelphia neighborhood, the onerous spider was again advancing daily upward in the direction of the inked mosquito and wasp, and the now-paranoid alcoholic alertly watched the carnivorous bug's slow movement as it would soon wickedly encounter the two motionless insects. Again, after midnight, the perimeter around the targeted bug tattoos became irritated, and the hungry encroacher oddly transformed to being bright red in color. Heavy-breathing Dennis Kinkaid lay restive upon his unkempt bed with his disheveled brain being rather terrified. The immobile sleeper's erratic cerebrum was contemplating the spider's lustful *killing* and the tattoo's subsequent consumption of its inanimate victims. But overnight, only the mosquito had suffered earthly elimination. The stationary wasp was still there.

With the advent of spring approaching in late March, Dennis Kinkaid's vacillating emotions were alternating between being unmistakably psychotic, and next, being saturated with depression. The boozer's nightly bouts with insomnia were gradually wearing-down Dennis's general spirit, along with his overall desire to find necessary drinking pleasure in living.

On what should have been the glorious morning of the March 21st vernal equinox, the troubled soul woke-up, only to detect that a large crimson stain was showing near his right shoulder, indicating that the warlike wasp had disappeared, and that the 'diabolical spider' was now plumper in diameter than ever before. Obviously, the vanished wasp was no match for what the drunken observer had described as 'the formidable Hades tarantula'.

'I should've remained an unhappy bum living in good old Macedonia, Ohio!' Dennis sadly lamented. 'The combination of Philly' slums and that accursed side alley tattoo parlor have deluged me with an abundance of hellish bad luck. I could've married my high school sweetheart, settled down, and became an ordinary family man with two or three bratty kids,' the penitent alcoholic recalled. 'But three-years of detrimental isolation while dutifully serving Uncle Sam in two different submarines had slowly dissolved and destroyed my sanity, and most certainly, made me resort to relying on hard liquor and powerful German beer. And my stint in the merchant marine didn't help me any, either. Over the years, I've deviated from truly relishing a responsible, normal adult life! Now I deeply regret my decision.'

In the ensuing spring months of April and May, Dennis Kinkaid no longer trekked eight blocks to buy fresh fruit and vegetables at the popular Ninth Street Italian Market, nor did he hike an even greater distance to purchase Sicilian pizza and delicious hoagies at the City of Brotherly Love's all-too-familiar Reading Terminal. The deadbeat's diet and eating habits negatively shifted from healthy to self-destructive, with the fazed and rattled mendicant spending his daily lunch and supper hours at the local Burger King, at the corner

McDonald's, and at the lackluster Chinese fast food restaurant, and at the filthy convenience store that was situated directly beneath his shabby apartment. Undoubtedly and most telling, the anxious-and-desperate Pennsylvania transplant had become more despondent and wary with each passing sunrise and sunset.

'I'm beyond the point of receiving any recuperative mental health help, so why should I even bother exploring *that* remote possibility?' Dennis admitted and concluded. 'I even envy the lousy panhandlers and the hapless street people wandering about this dismal part of the city. If only I had stayed back in tranquil Macedonia! But my foolish fascination with insects and arachnids, along with my desire to achieve asylum from harsh reality, are abnormally uniting to erode my basic confidence. Escapism be damned!' Kinkaid concluded. 'How have I ever become the victimized main character in a nefarious and satanic sci-fi movie? Am I hallucinating this terrible horror? This haunting fantasy I'm enduring can only end in disaster!'

Dennis was indeed quite aware that no more bug tattoos remained as obstacles upon his right arm, since the invincible tarantula had presently exited the right shoulder area, and now had made a deliberate linear path directly towards the rotund bumble bee, the tiny fly, and the disgusting cockroach, which had been inked onto the vagabond's massive, hairless chest.

Several weeks after the stalking spider had eliminated the vulnerable wasp and the harmless bumble bee, the illustrated black fly happened to be the next insect to be *killed,* or as Kinkaid's afflicted mind pondered, 'intentionally *murdered*'.

And next, during a very rainy late April day, the vulnerable roach and the flesh-eating Brazilian fire ant (all of which had formerly formed a semi-circle next to the crazed fellow's right nipple) had also been efficiently eliminated from existence; each 'bug martyr' had left behind an ominous trace of wet, red blood. Each devoured insect accurately demonstrated itself as being pure-proof evidence of 'the 'night crawler's' incessant pursuit of bug consumption. But scared-out-of-his-mind Dennis Kinkaid had no viable plan as to how to effectively respond to the ever-emerging carnivorous crisis.

'The heinous spider has a foul life of its own, and my tortured mind is trapped in a baffling quandary about how this *enemy* should be either eradicated or destroyed,' Dennis apprehensively reckoned. 'Now, I'm very much afraid to make an appointment with a Jefferson Hospital skin surgeon to remove the baneful tarantula, for surely, after I would reveal the true nature of my overwhelming malady during the preliminary office interview, he or she would recommend that I seek the professional services of a qualified mental health facility. I pray to

286

God that my fate is not doomed! My God! This ongoing nightmare is quite evil! The voracious spider seems to be moving and attacking faster with every passing week!'

A whole series of scars had appeared in a straight path extending from the former sailor's right clavicle and then across his thorax, and soon, the large, corpulent, defenseless cockroach was systematically 'executed and exterminated' in the same manner as had been the nearby bloated bumble bee, the frail fly, and the accessible flesh-eating fire ant. In each instance, the residual result of the dangerous tarantula's indomitable persistence was a 'signature blotch' of wet blood left upon the hairy-but-irritated skin wound, appearing alongside Dennis Kinkaid's sternum.

Only one remaining adversary existed for the clutches and mandibles of the avaricious, famished tarantula, and that seemingly worthy opponent was the awesome-looking Black Widow, which had been tattooed next to Kinkaid's protruding Adam's apple. And by early July, the dual spiders were ready to engage in definite lethal combat. 'I'm about to die from extreme terror even before the horrible struggle ever begins!' Dennis fretfully considered. 'I feel like I'm helplessly being devastated by the black spider's dominant insect instinct! I wouldn't wish this atrocious curse on my worst enemy, or even upon demonic Lucifer himself!'

Suffering from a lack of sleep, the tattooed 'victim' gradually lapsed into a coma on the morning of Independence Day, July 4th while the pair of dedicated foes were engaging in a drastic, intense, death duel. Upon regaining consciousness, Dennis slowly and drowsily arose out of bed, cautiously stepped to the bathroom mirror, and soon perceptively gazed at his physical reflection. Immediately, in horror, Kinkaid's eyes recognized that his entire neck had been covered and smeared with arachnid blood. But much to his utter dismay and total shock, a two-inch wide cavity had somehow been carved-out next to his voice box, and then, much to the 'victim's befuddlement and dismay, there was no sign of either a tarantula or a Black Widow anywhere near Kinkaid's penetrated neck.

With his agitated mind now in total bafflement, while using the bathroom mirror to meticulously study the dark hollow existing in his throat, suddenly a hairy spider leg steadily emerged from the recently-created black circular pit. Instantaneously, Kinkaid's shocked body felt paralyzed, as the petrified spectator stared with amazement at the genuine-but-bizarre mirror phenomenon that his gaping eyes had been witnessing. The first gruesome leg was soon followed by a second, and next, all six appendages were grimly visible and reflected from the medicine cabinet's mirror. Dennis Kinkaid was completely horrified, and his weak knees were buckling and on the verge of collapsing as the illogical. in-progress, hellish episode was frightfully evolving, virtually in slow motion.

'Maybe I should imitate the old superstitious Italians and wildly dance the Tarantella,' Dennis's tormented mind conjured, obviously alluding to a legendary folk dance that was often performed in Naples or in Sicily, after a native had been accidentally bitten by a defensive tarantula. Then, a rather salient thought entered the perplexed resident's distressed mind. 'There's little time left. I must survive this fiendish spider curse if it's the last thing I ever do! How pathetically ironic! Me, an intelligent human being at the top of the food chain being maliciously exterminated by a despicable spider! How ironic and detestable! I'm supposed to be at the top of the food chain!'

After exiting the dark hole that had been dug inside the victim's neck, the clawing three-dimensional tarantula had conspicuously grown in size to an outstanding three-inches across, but it was now much hairier than it had been hours before the insect monster had entered its secretive dark hiding place, next to Dennis Kinkaid's Adam's apple. The aggrieved tattoo lover's appalled and suspicious eyes then fully noticed, and entirely understood, the ongoing graphic paranormal spectacle, and a moment later, the man's erratically beating heart ceased its automatic rhythm. Dennis's forced breathing had stopped, and at that particular second in time, Death had mercilessly enveloped the bad-luck tattoo lover. Kinkaid had very willfully surrendered his vanquished soul to the heartless afterworld, and no other apathetic, neighboring mortal seemed to care.

Soon, the bloated tarantula, seemingly fully cognizant of its abominable accomplishment, victoriously wandered-off of the dead man's face in a very ostentatious manner, and then the toxic creature hastily moved across the dirty linoleum floor. After performing its latest *murder,* the triumphant, on-the-prowl arachnid was never again seen wandering and roaming anywhere on the face of the Earth.

On the bright and sunny morning of Independence Day, 2010, just five short blocks from historic Independence Hall, Dennis Kinkaid's soul had declared its irreversible liberation from its spiritual captivity inside the 'victim's' tortured body. As the former sailor's inanimate corpse lay upon the dilapidated apartment's bathroom floor, the furious landlord was seen pounding on the entrance door with an access key in fist, the slumlord futilely and incessantly knocking in quest of a late June rent payment.

288

"The Black Magic Pen"

The publishing house editor frowned at Joseph Perna and negatively shook her head. The rejection was another demoralizing defeat for the aspiring author, the last failure in a rather long skein of similar disappointments. Another large New York distribution powerhouse had declined to offer a lucrative contract and print the ambitious writer's precious book manuscript.

Joseph Perna was a struggling author in his mid-thirties. and still quite idealistic about realistic world matters. The hopeful novelist had a strong desire of attaining international literary fame, but his futile career as a prospective literary savant had been a terribly frustrating, continuous, three-year failure.

"I read your work out of courtesy and loyalty to my secretary, who as you aptly know, Joseph," stressed the austere-looking editor, "also coincidentally happens to be *your* sister."

"Annie would do anything she could that would support me in realizing my dreams," the dejected author replied. "She's a wonderful sister and is always looking-out for my benefit."

"Right you are," agreed the stern-looking editor. "But frankly Joseph, you're definitely no modern *Steinbeck* or *Hemingway*. Your work is fairly good, but it lacks that certain special quality that would elevate your style to the level of excellence."

Perna's fatigued mind was drowning in a totally deep quandary. Joseph's work had been harshly evaluated as 'mediocre' and 'run-of-the-mill', despite his many years of hard diligence. The poor fellow knew that the steep author pyramid was extremely difficult to ascend, with only three-percent of the writers enjoying fame at the top of the burgeoning matrix, making the big dollars.

"I don't want to go back to mundane newspaper reporting," Joseph confessed to the dispassionate editor. "Every story is basically the same. Only the names, dates, and places change, but the murders, the muggings, the suicides, the kidnappings, the fires, and the front-page catastrophes are always pretty much the same."

The editor pondered and analyzed Joe Perna's apparent disgust for a moment. Her characteristic habit was to never mince words. Then, Mrs. Dixon gave her blunt reply. "Mr. Perna, you need to develop an individual style that distinguishes you from the rest of the competing pack. You need to have a clear, distinct *writing voice*. That's the primary area where you're obviously most deficient!"

Joseph Perna thanked Mrs. Dixon for her valuable time and critical advice and then stepped out of the mahogany paneled Manhattan office with his head crestfallen. The melancholy fellow hated the thought of his only viable alternative, lackluster newspaper journalism. The woebegone writer despised the simple monotony of the daily routine of a 'hook' followed by 'who, what, where, when, why, and how'. But every time Joseph tried creating a fabulous fictional masterpiece, Mrs. Dixon would deflate the air out of his all-too-sensitive ego. The sensitive scribe's delicate self-esteem was now plummeting to its lowest vulnerable point.

It was a rainy late April afternoon in New York City. Joseph trudged his way down Madison Avenue toward the high concrete garage tower where his rusty 1978 red *Ford Fairlane* had been parked. As the sulking author increased his gait to escape the steady, miserable spring rain, an annoying panhandler accosted him. The unkempt-looking bum was aggressively attempting to sell Joseph *his* last "souvenir pen". The sudden cloudburst had dispersed most of the gullible tourists from uptown *Gotham,* and so Joseph Perna had been especially targeted for direct solicitation.

"I'm desperate. I'll sacrifice and sell you this souvenir good luck pen for only one dollar," the grimy fellow obnoxiously offered. "It works like magic!"

The downtrodden, prospective customer could easily identify with the pathetic vagrant's luckless plight. The failed novelist felt a measure of sympathy for the panhandler because the disconsolate author's own pessimism had related to the poor man's squalid, pauper-oriented existence. Joseph prudently reached into his pocket for a loose dollar bill, and then slowly grabbed the poor solicitor's last black pen in the exchange.

As the wary novelist examined the purchased black writing tool in the drizzling rain, the aspiring author noticed that the unusual device was rather antiquated in appearance, having a long-stemmed black ostrich feather, similar to the ones used centuries before by sages *William Shakespeare* and *Miguel Cervantes.*

"Here," insisted the derelict-looking vagabond/salesman. "Take this bottle of black ink, too. Since it's a dreary day, I'll give you a bonus to add to your terrific bargain."

Joseph Perna stared incredulously at his most recent purchase. "It's simple but beautiful," the former newspaper columnist answered as he touched and closely studied the pen's soft black plume. "What's your name? I might mention this strange event in my next novel," the depressed pedestrian asked the disheveled-looking tramp.

"Raymond Pierre Girard," the vagrant answered quite proudly. "Raymond Pierre Girard," the mendicant emphasized and repeated.

The drenched, shivering writer easily soon located his antique automobile inside the half-empty parking garage, which at that moment, reminded his fertile imagination as being a gigantic, vertical concrete mausoleum. The chronic dreamer was soon heading south on *Broadway* to his humble residence. The quaint old-fashioned pen was quickly stashed in a side pocket of Perna's out-of-style jacket, and the unique "souvenir" was soon forgotten. After the discouraged author reached his dismal Soho apartment, the defeated fellow found some minor consolation in finally securing shelter from the April Fool's Day pelting raindrops.

Joseph was in no mood to begin cooking his standard supper of cheap pork chops, mashed potatoes, and yesterday's leftover baked beans. The disenchanted small-flat dweller was besieged with worry. Where could Perna earn the remainder of the rent money that would be due in two short days?

The despondent writer's own logic dictated that he should ferret-out another less costly apartment in an even seedier part of the city. Locating a nearby standard legal writing pad, Joseph Perna began drafting a personal letter, advising his inflexible, arrogant landlord of *his* decision to seek a cheaper residence. The jotter's ballpoint pen suddenly expired its ink supply, and it was then that the resident searched his coat pocket and retrieved the black plumed pen along with the accompanying bottle of black ink, which also had been provided for the 'bargain sum' of one dollar by the begrimed panhandler.

As Perna thoroughly scrutinized the features of the ancient-looking replica, the observer keenly noticed that the object seemed to possess a distinct authenticity that compatibly matched its '*Age of Enlightenment*' appearance. The pen's black stem and dark black plume seemed to admirably sparkle and glow in the small apartment's quiet shadows. Joseph took an immediate liking to the pretty one-dollar acquisition, and soon the starving wordsmith contemplated composing the necessary vacancy letter addressed to his temperamental landlord.

A salutation was soon scribbled onto loose-leaf paper, and it wasn't long before the saddened novelist perceived that the words he had written-down were different than the words that his mind had imagined. It was almost as if a powerful literary genie had been rewriting and editing the intended content of the missive. Even the penned 'script cursive' was peculiarly different than Joseph's sloppy handwriting! Being intrigued, Perna completed and carefully recited the letter, and when he carefully read its almost lyrical sentences, Joseph was rather amazed at the final composition. No instruction had been given to the landlord of his intent to move to another less expensive address as *he* had initially written.

'Why write fiction when reality is much stranger?' marveled the very astonished man in an improvised imitation of *Lord Byron's* famous quotation. "This is absolutely extraordinary!"

Joseph had a strange sensation that soon surged throughout his total being. The newfound inspiration afforded Perna a sudden rare burst of confidence. All semblances of depression had somehow evaporated from his formerly defeated soul. Indeed, no plausible explanation could account for the writer's changed mental attitude, but the apartment occupant instantly accepted his new perspective without challenge, as the man's spirit was honoring his life's goal to organize a dynamic and original work of fiction.

Joseph momentarily reveled in his instantaneous zeal. This newly-discovered motivation was to be the fantastic genesis of an extraordinary chain of events. The frequently ignored author now felt an overwhelming compulsion to deftly write a classic piece of American literature.

* * * * * * * * * * * *

Joseph couldn't wait another minute to outline his strategic plot ideas for a fresh novel. It wasn't long before the determined young Hawthorne had organized his all-important chapter divisions, creating a promising 'freedom theme' for his next literary endeavor. Midnight was approaching, and after defining the personality profiles for his main characters, Joseph persevered, meticulously arranging his ideas in chronological order. The writer worked obsessively past midnight and well into his normal sleeping hours. Unique scenarios flashed into Perna's rejuvenated, inspired intellect. The plot producer was euphoric about the splendid progress his effort was making.

"I've never felt so profound and erudite in my entire life!" the word creator quipped out loud. "I'm finally crossing the bridge from commonplace journalism into the realm of true literature!" Perna loudly exclaimed to the inanimate black-plumed pen. "I'm finally finding my *writer's voice!*"

The 'freedom theme' novel progressed in development with incredible ease. Joseph Perna was exhilarated with the adroitness with which his right hand and pen moved rapidly in horizontal successions across the yellow legal pad. Around three o'clock in the morning, the novelist eventually succumbed to exhaustion and retired to bed. Finally relaxed and at ease with his reinvigorated spirit, the rejuvenated author's weary mind dwelled-upon the marvelous black pen. In fifteen minutes, the exhausted story composer was sound asleep and dreaming about the black-plumed writing instrument's rather remarkable motivating qualities.

The following morning, Joseph abruptly awoke from his sound slumber. The inspired writer's mind was refreshed and eager to pursue the completion of *Chapter 1* of his 'freedom masterpiece'. Perna showered, dressed, and hurriedly made himself a pot of strong coffee. The aroma immediately elevated his mental awareness into its optimal writing mode. Soon, the stimulated scribe was comfortably seated at his dull-looking roll-top desk while having the exceptional quilled pen gripped in his right hand.

"This remarkable black pen must be a lucky charm. *Jonathan Swift* must've had one just like it when he wrote *Gulliver's Travels*," mused and chuckled the now-jovial novelist.

The correct words seemed to flow especially smoothly and majestically out of Joseph's newfound plumed possession. No matter what ideas Perna erratically imagined and scribbled, the aforementioned black pen automatically synthesized its own magnificent parallel phrases and clauses in exquisite cursive. The 'freedom theme' described in the writer's fictional sketch was completely different than the embellished 'loyalty theme' that soon appeared as words upon the long-length, yellow legal paper. The astounding, inimitable word patterns applied to the yellow paper had a very singular, rhythmical coherency, and the perfect paragraphs exhibited a brilliant evolution of extremely imaginative time and setting transitions.

Joseph was absolutely fascinated with what was happening. His crude handwriting was even wonderfully improved when using the fantastic 'black writing utensil.' His formerly illegible chicken-scratch now appeared on paper as flawless classical penmanship. The delicate letters that formed the rich vocabulary flow definitely were the product of an inexplicable alien origin. Perna was fully intrigued by what his brown eyes were witnessing, and what his quivering right hand had been experiencing.

The formerly unsuccessful author decided to attempt an innovative experiment. The language composer found a common blue ballpoint pen kept in a kitchen drawer, and jotted-down some random thoughts on paper. The experimenter then compared the ballpoint- pen's results with that which had been generated by the incomparable quilled pen. The outcome of the demonstration was quite unbelievable. The ball-point pen handwriting was most definitely *his*. The words, however, did not stream-out smoothly and perfectly as the flawless grammar had exhibited when Joseph had been using the 'magical, plumed black pen'.

That startling realization convinced the former 'flunky newspaper reporter' that he must continue utilizing the new pen, and follow its astonishing capabilities to the very end of its limited blank ink supply. As the still-shocked novelist pursued his ingenious art, Joseph was particularly cognizant that his writing arm, wrist, and fingers never tired. The word architect could now scrawl in longhand for hours with sophisticated sentences and paragraphs streaming-out of the quilled pen as if they were liquid matter. The compulsion to write was suddenly both addictive and unstoppable. The merry-minded story creator totally relished his sensational enterprise along with his newly discovered energy.

"I'll bet that *Mark Twain* and *Charles Dickens* owned enchanting pens similar to this one," the young scribe theorized and mumbled to himself. "How else could those great contributors to literature ever have been so prolific! I truly believe that with the assistance of the black pen that I can now rival their transcendent *voices.* Now, I'm most certain I can, and that I will!"

Joseph then examined the time displayed on his cheap watch. It was already 12:00 noon. A lunch break was definitely in order. The thrilled young man stepped outside and sauntered to the all-too-familiar greasy spoon diner, located two blocks down the city avenue. The frequent patron ordered his customary corned beef sandwich, which he devoured quickly. The thirsty diner next lustily quaffed-down a large cup of *Coca Cola,* inadvertently reacting to his extreme enthusiasm about continuing his lonely work with the mysterious 'black magic pen'. The enamored author soon exited the dining establishment's swinging glass and metal door, and in the midst of his brain's intense 'sugar rush', dynamic 'William Shakespeare Perna' anxiously ambled back to his modest Soho apartment. 'I think I'll stay in my little apartment,' the occupant decided. 'I have enough money in my bank checking account to cover another month's rent.'

That entire afternoon, Joseph kept writing and writing like an obsessed ancient Egyptian scribe. The story's complex plot being created was so original and so sagacious that Mrs. Dixon would never be able to find a single fault with the overall narrative and with the dialogue's present level of unrivaled excellence, or for that matter, with the inimitable story's error-free grammatical articulation.

'This superb 'loyalty novel' is guaranteed to surprise the faculties of my demanding Mrs. Dixon, of the grumpy publisher, and of the myriad scathing media critics, and finally, of the fickle public,' thought the now-confident writer while sporting an intense, permanent smile, seemingly monopolizing his lower face. 'I'm finally on my way to world fame and fortune!'

294

With unprecedented incentive, Joseph assiduously pursued his lofty literary quest. The jubilant storyteller believed that the loyalty masterpiece which he was engineering would only require a brief two-additional-weeks to complete. His stellar language mechanics being flawlessly employed were impeccable, his spelling and punctuation were infallible, and his 'distinct writing voice' currently seemed virtually invincible.

Even when Joseph deliberately tried making a grammatical error, a simple mistake could not be achieved and appeared positively correct on the yellow notepad. Revision and rewrites were completely unnecessary. Essentially, Joseph Perna's entire text was positively perfect. An editor's only function would be to approve the spectacular 'object d'art' for immediate, profitable, best seller publication.

"No wonder why William Sydney Porter had adopted the catchy *nom de plume* of *O. Henry!*' laughed Joseph as the thinker closely gazed at the magical *plume* atop his magical pen. 'I'm now a literary Mozart creating impeccable work, without any specific modifications or alterations being needed!'

Joseph's four-hundred-page literary gem consumed only thirteen days of continuous writing to finish. When the magnificent work was completed, the author nonchalantly placed the stellar achievement inside a standard manuscript box. His clever plan was to personally deliver the package to rigid-minded Mrs. Dixon's office. The often-feared editor had previously rejected his other grandiose endeavors with great cynicism. Joseph reread the preface to his most recent labor, and the former newspaper reporter concluded that the publisher's principal literary critic would not find one iota of a misspelled word, or one trace of an uncrossed T anywhere in his sublime novel.

The elated author was convinced that his most outstanding project would be automatically accepted without a hint of challenge or criticism. It was indeed without a doubt *his* best literary effort ever, but as the all-too-biased author further reassessed matters, Joseph curiously wondered whether the prodigious masterpiece was genuinely his own work. Or was the new 'literary jewel' someone else's accomplishment, perhaps the genius of an obscure phantom prodigy whose superb expressions were somehow anonymously transmitted through the phenomenally resourceful black pen?

"Writing a novel is an easy task once the stress of thinking is erased from existence and once the accompanying finger and wrist pains have been eliminated," Perna snickered. "It was as if the pen were a benign supernatural force, and also as if I'm simply the occult object's robotic, mechanical puppet!"

Whatever was happening at present, the literary artist desired to fully exploit his unique advantage to the hilt, as would any other opportunistic human being would certainly pursue in similar circumstances. What a remarkable reversal of fortune for a former failure-oriented novelist to miraculously turn into a major literary benefactor to *Western Civilization!*

"Let the chips fall where they may!" boldly proclaimed Joe Perna to his indispensable black magic pen, speaking as if the writing instrument were his best and only friend. "I'm taking this most profound manuscript to *my* grouchy editor as soon as possible. I hope she doesn't have a stroke or heart attack!"

The self-assured author made an appointment with Mrs. Dixon for 9:00 a.m. on the following Tuesday morning. The hard-to-please editor/critic comprehensively inspected the first several pages, certain to find a misplaced modifier, or a minute punctuation problem to assault, or maybe a glaring pronoun-antecedent error, or any other microscopic grammar mistake or minor phrase defect that would justify a scathing remark.

The manuscript's accuracy and integrity were above and beyond editorial criticism. Mrs. Dixon was both absolutely dumbfounded and flabbergasted. "Joseph, I want the distinct privilege of showing your impeccable work to Mr. Allen," the fussy woman politely requested. "I'm certain that his office personnel will contact you when *our* thorough evaluation has been completed."

It was then and there that Joseph finally felt exceedingly proud of his newly attained level of earned respect within the literary universe. The fledgling author promised his fragile self-esteem that he would never once reveal the magic pen's secret to another human being. 'I don't wish to be accused of plagiarizing an inanimate black pen!'

The next few days would have seemed endless under normal circumstances, but Joseph was positive that the anticipated contract call from the publisher's office would be 'most favorable'. Mr. Perna temporarily abandoned his shabby apartment to procure some nourishment at the familiar, nondescript greasy spoon eatery. While the customer was seated on a counter stool at the commonplace eatery, happily preoccupied munching an ill-flavored hamburger, his apartment phone rang.

Upon returning to his unenviable living quarters, Joseph Perna glanced at his table phone's caller *ID* and immediately recognized that the seven digits being displayed belonged to the influential publisher's office phone number. The excited wordsmith returned the call at once, but unfortunately, the writer/caller was not able to speak with either Mrs. Dixon or with always-busy Mr. Allen. The pair had evacuated the teeming Manhattan corporate offices early Friday afternoon for the purpose of enjoying a tranquil weekend at a well-publicized writer's conference on Cape Cod.

Joseph was angry with himself for foolishly leaving his dimly lit apartment when such a vital call was predestined to be forthcoming. Now, *he* would have to wait two seemingly eternal days before ascertaining the prestigious publisher's crucial verdict.

Much to the writer's mounting anxiety, Joseph's phone rang early Monday morning. On the line was Mr. Allen, the normally all-too-busy, sanctimonious publisher. The corporate mogul nervously insisted that the young writer immediately come to *his* uptown office without delay.

It didn't take the former amateur novelist long to rush from the mediocrity of Soho to glorious Madison Avenue in almost a "New York minute". After parking his old red *Ford* sedan inside the all-too-familiar multi-tiered parking garage, the author was soon occupying a plush green leather chair inside Mr. Allen's spacious and luxuriously-appointed office. Joseph Perna was convinced that his latest labor of love would meet with the publisher's reputable, lofty expectations. Strangely, at *that* unreal office moment, both Mr. Allen and Mrs. Dixon appeared more fidgety than the apprehensive and naive novelist was. Young Perna smiled upon witnessing their dual nervousness.

The gathered threesome chatted small-talk preliminaries for a few awkward minutes, but then the stuttering publisher deviated from the standard mundane introduction and swiftly switched his rhetoric to the topic of the writer's extremely riveting "loyalty-theme manuscript". The faces of the impressed evaluators were florid and beaming, and the neurotic gesticulations of the normally stringent nitpickers were quite animated. The erratic, out of character mannerisms of Mr. Allen and Mrs. Dixon were more unnatural than the suave expressions exhibited by the calmer, more reticent greenhorn author.

"Your well-organized story is one of the best I've ever read in my entire career," lavishly praised the wealthy publisher. "I would like to publish, to market, and to distribute your work, that is, with your permission," Mr. Allen courteously requested. "We'll draw-up a handsome royalty contract with a hundred-thousand-dollar advance. We'll begin setting the galley proof type immediately, since fastidious Mrs. Dixon has detected no content problems whatsoever."

Mr. Allen only had to state his expressed intentions once, and then Joseph eagerly signed the stupendous agreement. Mrs. Dixon and Annie (the author's dedicated sister who doubled as the editor's professional secretary and notary) applied their signatures as authentic witnesses to the 'very generous covenant'.

The incredible contract-signing event marked the true genesis of the author's most fabulous, budding, writing career. Joseph Perna was fated to reside on cloud nine, at least for one phenomenal novel, or until his black magic pen exhausted its limited black ink supply.

* * * * * * * * * * * * *

Joseph Perna left the distinguished publisher's office after receiving his handsome advance check, and the very timely bonanza alleviated a heavy emotional and economic burden from his troubled mind. Now, the writer had sufficient funds that could satisfy his immediate debts, including his overdue rent.

As the novelist drove his ancient red *Ford* sedan home through the Theater District to Soho, the motorist had a vivid recollection that something had seemed rather peculiar when *he* had signed the attractive publishing contract. The young author could not provide a plausible explanation to account for his 'unusual feeling'. The satisfied driver nevertheless continued on his merry route down highly congested *Broadway* toward his Manhattan Soho apartment. 'I was so excited that I hardly remember ever signing my name.' the puzzled author wondered.

The first copy of the "loyalty novel" would not be available on the literary marketplace for three months, and having excess stamina to spare, the enthused author contemplated commencing with a second meritorious enterprise. 'Who needs to go through the process of galley proofs and ridiculous page proofs? No more over the transom stuff. The next manuscript that'll be sent by certified mail directly to Mr. Allen's plush office will be perfect, just as it is,' Joseph critically and cavalierly mused.

The haughty writer's mind then reflected for a moment; his normally anemic ego was swelling-up with self-destructive pride. 'No silly changes are necessary,' Perna thought and believed. 'The final printing should be initiated right away. My next stellar rendition will require no enhancements.'

After arriving at *his* humble flat and feeling extremely ambitious, Joseph stationed himself at his antique cherry wood roll-top desk and began composing a new spectacular work of fiction. Perna had no outline or literary blueprint to consult as a guideline. He had no notes or character sketches. He had no plot constructions. He had no theme, either. But from living his unprecedented publishing experience over the past several weeks, the revitalized writer didn't need any of *those* conventional methods of organization. Joseph Perna's goal was to simply create superior literature through his own recently-discovered, enigmatic 'black pen stream of consciousness method'.

With his invincible magic plumed pen in hand, Joseph began composing the first chapter to his second major literary masterpiece. As the 'New Age Jack London' adroitly progressed from paragraph to paragraph, the inspired wordsmith became increasingly aware that the magic pen regarded *his* personal thoughts as being both expendable and immaterial; the first chapter was produced as if *his* right hand had been mystically guided by some alien supernatural intervention. The various letters, words, sentences, and paragraphs flowed liberally out of the quilled *Shakespearean* pen as easy as flowing water rapidly being cascading over *Niagara Falls*.

Joseph Perna's latest fictional prose was very dissimilar to any of his prior literary offerings. The uncanny, unearthly guidance (which apparently used the magic pen as its selected conduit) confounded the writer's sense of reason. Everything about his strange authorial experience seemed abundantly surreal. The puzzled young gentleman could not fathom one iota the vast mystery haunting his soul; its cryptic nature seemingly transcended ordinary scientific logic and acceptable human comprehension.

'I only hope that this is not the devil's 'black magic' work,' Joseph frightfully considered. 'I pray that I'm not selling my immortal soul for mortal fame, fortune, and greed. If this is some hellish barter involving the magic pen and me, then *Lucifer,* I insist that you show yourself now!'

Joseph kept mumbling while writing feverishly and diligently. Minutes converted into hours, and soon hours transformed into days, and the eighteen-hour workdays evolved into a full week of sheer pleasurable labor. In nine days, another 'perfect novel' was easily finished. The fatigued-but-happy 'modern nomenclature authority' then packaged the 'perfect text' that he planned to send by means of FedEx, directly to Mr. Allen.

The second outstanding tome was of the gothic romance genre, and the manuscript had the staggering length of 180,000 words; a truly remarkable feat to be accomplished in a mere nine consecutive grueling workdays. But Joseph promised his prestige-starved self-image that he would not submit the second work to Mr. Allen until the first "loyalty" hardcover and paperback book would become available in print on the retail market.

"Who needs Mrs. Dixon, that sarcastic, nitpicking martinet editor?" the author egotistically exclaimed to his new best friend, the infallible black magic pen. "I'll go straight to the main man."

But placing caution before haste, Joseph had to objectively see exactly how many copies his first novel would sell. Heir Perna greatly-desired to be accepted and admired by the reading public before ever proceeding with releasing the much-heralded additional *Nobel Prize* caliber piece of fiction. In the grotesque past, the failed fellow had encountered too much rejection to suddenly now become too overly optimistic about his chosen career.

No sooner had Joseph finished authoring the second magnificent manuscript that he soon commenced with a third. The prolific historical fiction creator had more inspiration and more energy than he had ever known, felt, or exhibited before his lucky acquisition of the black magic pen. His right hand now knew not cramps; his fingers knew not arthritis, and his brain knew not rest. The neurotic novelist could not stop relentlessly writing, jotting-down words and paragraphs like a possessed maniac.

The seated author had a strange premonition that someone omnipotent, or something sinister had been controlling his creative behavior. That fearsome notion greatly disturbed Heir Perna's sense of awareness. But Joseph's arrogance, along with his abundant confidence, easily dwarfed and suppressed his weaker, ascending suspicions. How long would the ethereal power of the pen last? The emancipated former vagrant's 'bonus black ink bottle' still remained half full!

'What would happen when my fabulous ink supply runs dry? Would a bottle of ink from a stationery store work the same way?' These were some of the more major considerations that greatly perplexed and worried Joseph's convoluted mind.

The third novel had a superlative 'revenge theme', and it was quite different in tone than the first two meritorious manuscripts. The writer had no explanatory theory that adequately accounted for the phantom source of his sensational ideas. He only knew a compelling compulsion to persist in pursuing his crazed mania. Amazingly, the third literary contribution had been completed in record time. It was cautiously stored inside his bedroom's locked bureau drawer, right beneath his *Federal Express* wrapped Gothic-romance manuscript.

Two weeks had elapsed since Mr. Allen had offered Joseph his first contract, and the 'fortnight duration' was now equivalent to producing two perfectly edited novels. The aspiring writer calculated that when the first 'loyalty story' would be ready for mass production, he would have already masterminded a minimum of five additional fantastic, original, awesome, novels, each composition being a literary treasure so impeccable in content and presentation that their 'pure perfection'

300

would be impervious to the vain sarcasm of envious New York City TV and newspaper critics.

"At this rate, I can write fifty-two novels a year," marveled and spoke the workaholic to his seemingly apathetic magic pen; "With co-opting *your* most excellent, supreme help, of course!"

Three more weeks elapsed, and Joseph received the expected call from the normally insufferable publisher. Mr. Allen informed the word genius that *his* manuscript remarkably contained no errors in grammar, logic, or punctuation. It was "absolutely perfect" as submitted. Such an accomplishment had never before been recorded in *his* company's long history. Advance copies of the second novel would be rushed and stocked on bookstore shelves within a month. All systems were now "full speed ahead" for the dedicated book producer, since Mr. Allen's revelation constituted very elating news to the upstart author. The encouraging phone call only propelled Joseph back into his humble apartment in order to resume his wild creation of literary gems.

"I'll write as long as my pen and my ink give me inspiration and a plentitude of words," Perna uttered while admiring the black pen's colorful plume. "Mr. Pen, you indeed were a Godsend!"

Joseph proceeded with his prodigious enterprise, and the words on paper kept their full, smooth fluency. It was as if the transcendent pen had a mind and a style all of its own. Young Perna wholeheartedly coveted the plumed object, and the hubristic owner wouldn't trust its great secret to any other living soul, for all the accumulated gold stored in *Fort Knox*.

A certain other-world quality about the magic pen captivated Joseph's attention; consequently, the concerned possessor was extremely fascinated by its undeniable domination of his lengthy writing sessions. *It* was the master, and *he* was presently its obedient servant. Joseph paused to closely analyze the pen's appearance more in detail. "Your wish is my command," Perna whispered to the sparkling black-plumed quill, his glib utterance being a genuine impersonation of *Aladdin's* swarthy lamp genie, rising and respectfully addressing its Arabian master.

Joseph Perna put the pen down for a moment to savor a brief respite from his extensive sacrifice. The about-to-become famous word-master then entered his very commonplace kitchen to drink a glass of cold water. His first exposure to a terrifying spiritual event was about to interrupt his present state of tranquil contentment.

* * * * * * * * * * * *

Joseph gulped-down the cold water and it indeed refreshed his mind and body. The determined story plotter then stepped to the bathroom where he washed his face, and that simple act made the re-energized writer feel even better. While rubbing his cheeks and eyebrows with a cloth towel, the quixotic author thought he had heard some unexpected sound originating from the main room; the place where *he* had just been writing. The low, odd, distant rustle resembled that of the sound of loose sheets of paper being softly shuffled.

Joseph glanced into the mirror of the open medicine cabinet. Above the object's dull reflection of the aforementioned cherry-wood desk was an outlined aura of someone sitting stationary; a two-dimensional figure wildly writing cursive language from left to right.

This paranormal observation instantly horrified the reclusive Soho apartment occupant. With his heart feeling as if it were ascending into his mouth, the awed viewer quickly pivoted around and looked in the direction of the living room's cherry-wood desk to visually verify if his imagination had momentarily gone amok. Nothing extraordinary was there; only the familiar yellow legal pad on the desk, the tablet eerily accompanied by the inimitable black-plumed pen.

The 'super-ghostly mirror image' was too incredulous for the observer to mentally believe. Joseph speculated that he must have been hallucinating from sheer physical and emotional exhaustion. The guesser was certain that he had seen someone or something sitting and assiduously writing at *his* cherry-wood desk, and being warily on his guard, the suspicious writer then hesitantly stepped gingerly into the adjoining room. Heir Perna cautiously scanned the walls and floor for any indication of irregular activity. The anxious young man soon determined that *he* was at present the sole inhabitant of the shoddy apartment. Joseph's apprehension soon reduced to intrigue, and then his captivating concern instinctively diminished to natural curiosity.

The about-to-be-famous novelist's mind rationally hypothesized that *he* had suffered a 'mental delusion resulting from overall fatigue.' The emotionally recomposed gentleman stridently paced over to the roll-top desk, and then cautiously sat-down to again contemplate 'the strange anomaly.' The hard, oak chair felt unusually warm; someone had recently been sitting there other than himself. 'But who and how could it be?' Perna deeply wondered. 'Ghosts don't radiate body heat,' the apartment dweller plausibly thought. 'This is too unearthly to either believe or fathom.'

The apartment's door lock was still dead-bolted. It never had been opened that evening to allow anyone entry or exit, because the renter's huge fear was that the two potentially invaluable manuscripts might be stolen. Being wholly petrified, the harrowed writer detected that a small puddle of ice-cold water was now on the desk's rectangular brown ink blotter, and several other patches of frigid water were evidenced lying upon the squeaky, wooden floor planks.

'Maybe I've been spending too much time overly engrossed in my third fictional volume,' Joseph worriedly supposed. 'I'll admit that a lengthy nap is the only suitable remedy for my exhaustion. But how did the icy water puddles get in here?'

The alarmed writer had always taken great pride in being especially neat and tidy. Joseph decided to file his utilitarian yellow writing pad flush against the desk's lower right-hand drawer. As the unnerved sitter picked-up the amber-shaded stationery, his wandering eyes nervously surveyed the most recent text paragraphs that his active brain had been plotting and recording.

Joseph Perna read the first three expository passages to *Chapter 1*, and the confused interpreter was certain that several current allusions and descriptive metaphors were not expressed in the same language that he had hours before applied to the yellow paper. Some of the dialogue now appearing on the tampered-with pages had been expressed in *Latin,* and Joseph was positive that he had not scripted those particular language exchanges to his original text. The realization of *his* involvement in an insane metaphysical interaction was making the literary artist's erect body immediately cringe and sweat. Perna instinctively rushed from his meager Soho apartment, locked the door, and was soon outside the premises, walking south on the cold Manhattan sidewalk. The trekker decided to take a brisk hike *to Washington Square* in *Greenwich Village.*

'I suspect that I'm being punished by alien spiritual forces for capitalizing on someone else's brilliant talent. I've evilly compromised my immortal soul,' the remorseful ambler conjectured and grieved. 'I'm guilty of being little more than a literary phony, a colossal hoax, a blatant plagiarist! But who or what was the anonymous specter that my eyes had seen sitting and editing my work at my cherrywood desk?'

* * * * * * * * * * * *

Joseph recollection sharply remembered that the new manuscript's remarkable first chapter was now more lucid than it had been structured before Perna had entered the bathroom and had inadvertently glanced into the vanity's mirror. The greatly modified text had vastly improved both the 'formerly perfect' manuscript's harmony and the tome's general integration, even though the priceless black magic pen had beautifully organized Joseph's original version, without the spooky *ghost writer's* alternations.

"How could it be that perfection has been improved upon!" Joseph uttered to a lonely *Greenwich Village* streetlight. The totally baffled writer considered the exact words written upon the yellow legal pad. 'What is happening?' the now-disconcerted novelist wondered. "Will I ever know?"

Perna walked many blocks of cold city pavement for well over an hour. Frightening impressions of eternal damnation described in *Dante's Inferno* raced through his fully disheveled consciousness. The itinerant pacer was extremely confounded by the recent series of inexplicable phenomena that had transpired and occurred inside his humble apartment. The trekker was so terrorized from the paranormal mirror and uncanny desk experiences that he presently lacked the courage to return to his tiny Soho apartment. Finally, after drinking down two double *Southern Comforts* on the rocks at a local corner bar, the disturbed man finally garnered the boldness to amble back to his 'haunted' residence.

Joseph meticulously opened his dingy apartment's creaky door. After flicking on a light switch, the arriver slowly craned his neck in both directions. Nothing inordinate was evident so, the very wary fellow proceeded into the main room, which the quaking coward had hastily and cravenly dashed out of just several hours before. Perna's warranted apprehension honored a sudden inclination, and the faltering novelist walked rather prudently over to the insular roll-top, cherry-wood desk.

'Ghosts are as implausible as interstellar alien Earth visitors,' the very scared writer fancied. 'I need to be cynical. Jacob Marley's awesome specter exists only in *Charles Dickens'* exotic Christmas fiction, and nowhere else.'

On top of the cherry-wood desk rested a small box of paper clips. Joseph then noticed *his* plastic cup filled with disposable, used ballpoint pens. The astute searcher next eyed the familiar stack of yellow legal stationery pads. But something was highly different and quite anomalous.

Many more sheets of written stationery had been accumulated in the now-mystical pile that Perna had hours before left upon his desk, and much to his heightened bewilderment, the heap had been stacked-up during his recent absence, piled in a very neat and orderly manner. Feeling quite intimidated and Lilliputian, the hesitant witness picked-up the first page and started to avariciously read the words.

Upon the staggered man's further examination of the finely written literature, the perplexed inspector immediately discerned the existence of several additional text chapters that the magic pen had neither conceived nor written. 'What on earth has happened?' the beleaguered author mentally questioned the magic pen. 'Do you have a ghostly accomplice?'

Joseph was then in a heightened state of panic, but despite *that* mental handicap, he still had the wherewithal to devise a clever strategy. The novelist would continue writing the incomplete chapter to see exactly where his unorthodox experiment would eventually lead. *His* faithful magic pen proceeded with the draft (as if it had interfaced with the words of the new 'ghost text' and had established a symbiotic relationship with the extended, mysteriously written narrative). "I just have to solve this double-bladed baffling riddle.'

Looking at his primitive table telephone, Joseph observed a specific number registered on the caller *ID,* and it was the private line to Mr. Allen's plush Long Island estate. The call had been made Saturday at 9:33 p.m. The frantic fellow picked-up the phone from its cradle and promptly dialed the influential publisher.

Mr. Allen informed Joseph that *his* first novel had been printed and that the tome was ready in hardcover edition for bookstore distribution. This initial dissemination process would take a full week, and the novel's national bookstore and library promotion would soon be initiated. Mr. Allen also informed the thrilled writer that a coordinated network of booksellers and sales representatives would be doing the primary marketing promotion. In a few more days, the public would learn of Joseph's superb genius. The hypocritical critics and pundits would have no choice but to submit their laudatory newspaper reviews to their respective editors.

The following Sunday, in the book section of the *New York Times,* the first of many complimentary articles pertinent to Joseph's maiden novel appeared in print. After purchasing the thick Sunday Edition of *The Times,* young Perna opened the desired section and eagerly scanned the sundry book reviews.

One of the city's leading reviewers had been assigned the task of evaluating Joseph's first major literary effort. The article gave a glowing report on the book's noteworthy theme, "Loyalty," on its intricate plots and subplots, and on its extraordinarily dynamic characters; and then, the complimentary newspaper summary also generously commended the author on *his* "very evident linguistic, neoclassical brilliance."

Joseph was ebullient at seeing the many kudos relevant to his masterpiece, the praise conspicuously appearing and being showered in the prestigious *New York Times* book section. His name would soon be recognized in every major national newspaper, in every American bookstore, and in every city and town library in the entire country.

"I only wish that the work had been the product of my own arduous labor," Joseph lamented to the inanimate magic pen. "But I'll bet that *Edgar Allan Poe* and *Herman Melville* had similar magic pens, also. How else could their splendid masterpieces have been created, and later attributed and credited to their immortal names?"

Joseph's keen eyes sieved through the glowing newspaper article four consecutive times, but then, the stunned reader became angry when he determined that a disturbing error had been made in the presentation of the author's name. Joseph Perna's identity was nowhere to be found. Instead, the aforementioned name *Raymond Pierre Girard* had been given the abundant acclaim and accolades. Joseph couldn't believe that the venerable publisher, Mr. Allen, could have made such a grievous oversight.

"I never *author*ized or consented to having a ridiculous pseudonym!" Joseph lividly stated and protested to the black magic pen. And after the fully disgusted article reader gazed at the accompanying black *plume* that remained slightly glimmering upon the magic pen, Perna verbally added, "And I never agreed to a lousy nom de *plume,* either!"

On Monday morning, the upset author parked his old red *Ford Fairlane* sedan in the familiar high-rise Manhattan garage, rushed to the Madison Avenue publisher's office, and vociferously demanded to see the head honcho, Mr. Allen. Mrs. Dixon instantly conducted the infuriated neophyte into the publishing mogul's mahogany-paneled office. The corporate guru was smugly sitting behind his gigantic walnut desk, and the egocentric rich tycoon's florid face was beaming with apparent joy.

"Isn't it great that you got such a rave review from the foremost critic in the entire city?" Mr. Allen asked his unexpected visitor with a broad smile. "Joseph, you should consider yourself' quite fortunate indeed! It's extremely rare that a writer's first novel receives such fabulous praise!"

The publisher's entirely false comment made Joseph furious that overbearing Mr. Allen would show such fraudulent exhilaration, while seemingly ignoring the newspaper's oversight of never mentioning the author's true identity. Instead of being apologetic about the mistake, Joseph immediately thought that Mr. Allen was being selfishly devious and dishonest.

The out-of-kilter author instantly enlightened the publisher about the "irresponsible omission", and about the obvious "credit misprint." And then Joseph audaciously pontificated on how "stupid" it was for

Mr. Allen, or his dunce-like staff, to have made such a horrendous informational discrepancy.

The astonished publisher couldn't decipher exactly what Joseph was complaining about. "Joseph, I had submitted the exact name that had appeared on the contract," Mr. Allen declared. "And Mrs. Dixon and I were certain that it was the correct credit, and I'll swear to you on a pyramid of sacred *Bibles* that the name on the contract was the exact appellation that you had provided in my office."

"Don't play me for a silly, asinine fool, Mr. Allen!" Joseph vehemently accused and protested. "I'm no wet-behind-the-ears, naïve and gullible hillbilly dolt, you know! I insist on seeing irrefutable proof you're describing right this very instant! Show me my signature on the contract right now!"

Mr. Allen was somewhat chagrined by Joseph's out-of-character display of combative petulance. The corporate executive advanced to his personal file cabinet, located the original publishing contract, and then presented the material documentation to Joseph, who almost fainted upon the posh office's elegant Oriental rug.

The author's name that had been oddly listed upon the contract was *Raymond Pierre Girard,* and the scripted signature had been written in majestic royal black ink. Joseph immediately interpreted the handwriting as being the same calligraphy as that which had appeared on the phantom manuscripts inside his Soho apartment. That same unique, inimitable penmanship had somehow cleverly overridden the mighty power of the magic pen's authorship. The splendid, formal handwriting shown upon the contract was the same impeccable cursive lexicon that had formed marvelous English prose upon the yellow legal stationery paper, conveniently situated on Joseph's antiquated cherry-wood roll-top desk.

The dumbfounded writer couldn't argue against the obvious truth that had been convincingly provided by the now-insulted, eminent publisher. The handsome penmanship exhibited upon the altered manuscript, and evident in the beautiful signature displayed upon the publishing contract, shared the same identical, sublime, fantastic characteristics. The remaining signatures of the two witnesses and also that of Mr. Allen were deemed absolutely genuine.

"Joseph, I was going to give you a copy of the contract as soon as the book would be available off the presses. I have to admit something, Mr. Perna. That's a wonderful pseudonym you've created, Raymond Pierre Girard," Mr. Allen suavely commented. "It has both integrity and imagination!"

"Yes," affirmatively added Mrs. Dixon, who had just entered the mahogany-paneled office. "And Joseph, please give me your social security number before you leave so that royalty checks can be promptly sent to your real self, and not to someone in the phone book anonymously named Raymond Pierre Girard. Our accounting department has been known to make idiotic errors in the past over wrong royalty payments being sent!"

"That's right," the still somewhat-perturbed publisher concurred. "The *Internal Revenue Service* doesn't give a hoot about fictitious Raymond Pierre Girard. The Federal Bureau only wants to receive tax payments from Joseph Perna!"

No one would ever believe Joseph's preposterous fantasy about a black magic pen and about an actual honest-to-goodness *ghost*writer. Mr. Allen and Mrs. Dixon would regard the magic pen tale as being both ludicrous and also absolutely preposterous. Feeling exceptionally guilty and embarrassed, Joseph decided to swiftly terminate the mortifying discussion. The office guest even felt obligated to sincerely apologize to Mr. Allen for challenging the reality of the unique "Nom de plume". Then, the ashamed visitor candidly bade Mrs. Dixon an honest "goodbye", and rapidly exited the executive's office in a complete stupor.

The following week's media events enhanced and embellished Raymond Pierre Girard's ascending reputation, coast-to-coast. More rave reviews appeared in other major metropolitan newspapers from Boston, to Philadelphia, to Chicago, and to Los Angeles. Mrs. Dixon appropriately scheduled the author for numerous public speaking engagements, and also for a series of vital interview appearances on afternoon national television talk shows.

The only salient problem haunting the accomplished author's mind was that Joseph had been blatantly masquerading in the media as the anonymous "Raymond Pierre Girard", and soon, his alter ego's existence would be truly bothering *his* increasingly confused conscience. The fledgling writer was in the throes of a massive, serious identity crisis, and the emerging TV celebrity was simultaneously suffering from an acute, emotional breakdown.

Confounded Joseph Perna feared that his mental state was rapidly becoming schizophrenic, and the out-of-wits, now-renowned writer determined that he would have to learn to live with *his* incompatible dual personalities. It was in the literary impostor's best interest that no other individual on the planet should know anything at all about the enchanted pen's dynamic secret powers.

* * * * * * * * * * * *

Joseph's next endeavor would be having his latest pair of ingenious novels published. A great demand was quickly building for the newcomer's highly-lauded work, which had already caused more than a mild sensation in periodicals, in bookstores, and in the story-hungry American press. The "Loyalty Novel" was already selling by the tens of thousands, and substantial retail and *Internet* revenues were accumulating faster than Joseph could possibly spend the bountiful income. Still, several powerful questions plagued the author's sleepless nights. 'Was the black pen the *Devil's* sorcery? Was the black magic pen really a *black magic* pen? What about the accompanying black ink? Would the talented medieval-looking pen work its magic with the inkbottle eventually being empty? And finally, what was the nature of the strange coincidence of the pen name Raymond Pierre Girard and the mendicant New York City plumed pen salesman, Raymond Pierre Girard!'

* * * * * * * * * * * *

Joseph had always dreamed of comfortably living in a mountain chalet featuring a panoramic view; the imagined structure being situated somewhere near a European alpine city. The writer's book advances had afforded adequate remuneration for young Perna to be in the market for any obtainable rustic Swiss chalet, preferably in a resort area where the elite lived in isolation from 'wanton metropolitan crime' and from 'hedonistic urban immorality'. The mountain retreat would have to be quiet, scenic, exclusive, isolated, and finally, quite perfect for writing.

The successful fake wordsmith gladly contacted a leading Realtor in Bern, Switzerland. The now-famous author instructed the real estate broker the about the essence of his fondest dream. If something suitable should become available, then the firm of *Schmidt and Suhmann* should contact the prospective buyer at once. The potential purchaser had one principal stipulation that he had made over the long distance international phone call to Mr. Schmidt. Whoever had occupied and owned the desired Swiss mountain retreat in the past had to have also been "a writer".

Two weeks later, Joseph received a surprise phone call from the aforementioned real estate agency. Mr. Schmidt had located a fine chalet currently owned by a struggling poet. The woman was now vacating the premises in order to move back to Lucerne to be closer to her ailing parents. Mr. Schmidt advised Joseph that the female poet was serious about moving-out of her secluded retreat as soon as possible, and the lady writer wanted to know if "Mr. Perna" was still interested in negotiating the acquisition. If so, the prominent author, known to the public as Raymond Pierre Girard, should immediately come to the Alps to inspect the property and make a "bona fide offer".

The American writer was assured by the Swiss reality agent that the terrific mountain chalet was located in a spectacular setting, and that the home was exactly what Perna was searching to own. In addition, the asking price was quite moderate, and what low-pressured Mr. Gunther Schmidt aptly described as "a sacrifice!"

Joseph immediately made arrangements to travel by jet to Switzerland. Two days later, the intercontinental *747* landed at *Bern International Airport* with on-a-mission Joseph Perna attentively seated in the first-class section.

The jovial, corpulent realtor Gunther Schmidt met Joseph inside the main airport terminal, after the 'anonymous author' had passed through standard customs. Without delay, the inquisitive buyer was driven to the remote mountain chalet where the young female writer was waiting to meet him. The poet's home was ideally situated off a steep, winding, stone road, a mile high-up in the majestic *Swiss Alps.* Mt. Finsteraarhorn, which has a scenic snow-clad summit of over fourteen-thousand-feet, was located a only few miles away.

The pleasant, garrulous Realtor cautiously drove the American passenger up the final incline, and parked his *Chevy Blazer* upon the crushed-stone driveway. The attractive seller was standing at the front door to greet the new arrivals.

"Elka, I would like to introduce you to Joseph Perna, and Mr. Perna, I would like you to meet Miss Elka Zimmer," Mr. Gunther Schmidt said with a smile.

"I'm very pleased to meet you, Mr. Perna," the pretty blue-eyed blonde stated. "I hope you enjoy your visit to Switzerland."

"Likewise, I'm sure. Elka. I see you have a lovely home," Joseph praised. "Would you' folks mind showing me around?"

Ms. Zimmer had no objections, and she and Mr. Schmidt cordially conducted the Swiss visitor on a thorough home tour. The chalet was lavishly furnished with expensive *17th Century* wooden tables, chairs, and decor. The home had a specially built living room with a magnificent alpine view, along with a sporting a handsome stone fireplace, and the author instantly surmised that (in that scenic setting) he could ardently practice his craft without being interrupted, disturbed or distracted.

The New York City visitor gazed-out the living room's large window with great appreciation. The serenity of the noble snow-capped *Alps* was indeed inspirational. Their towering peaks were easily visible from every chalet side window. Joseph visualized himself meditating inside the quiet den where he then believed the productive "miraculous magic pen" could achieve *his* finest work. The admirable stone fireplace added a cheerful, warm atmosphere to the 'Old World grandeur' of the appealing chalet's design.

"I'm very impressed, and that's no exaggeration!" Joseph sincerely commented. "It's precisely what I was looking for."

"There's also a garage that had been converted from a stable, which incidentally accompanied the original home, which had been built in 1720," the multi-lingual poet informatively added.

"Elka, I can't believe you want to sell this terrific chalet!" the potential buyer exclaimed. "It's a perfect fit to satisfy both my emotional and introspective needs!"

"I'm from Luzerne and my parents are both suffering from various old age maladies," Elka Zimmer sadly explained. "I must leave as soon as possible to be with them. My loss will be your gain!"

Joseph was already advised of the home's asking price, which he considered being more than reasonable. The American made a generous offer that exceeded Elka's selling price by $20,000.00, and his proposal was immediately and graciously accepted. Papers were presented and soon signed, consummating as Mr. Gunther Schmidt put it, "a bona fide legal real estate contract".

"Good luck, Mr. Perna with your new home," Elka Zimmer thankfully remarked. "And I'm sure you'll just love living here. Perhaps one day I can visit you when you're finally settled. But please tell me, why did you offer more than the asking price?"

"I already immensely loved this grand home, and I didn't want someone else who also loves serene isolation to outbid me for it!" Joseph frankly confessed. "And since it came fully furnished, I don't have to go shopping for sofas, chairs, tables, and beds."

"Mr. Perna, I'm very grateful for your sincerity and generosity," thanked Elka. "Honesty is a rare attribute among so-called civilized people meandering-about in this complicated day and age."

"Elka, I'll be more than happy to have you call on me," Joseph verified. "Perhaps you can show me some local sites of interest. You know; restaurants and museums."

The purchaser was very pleased with Fraulein Zimmer's hint at a future visitation and quite genuinely, Joseph Perna also was rather attracted to the gentle poet's natural beauty. In his lonely heart, the homebuyer candidly hoped that Elka Zimmer was serious about her innocent proposal of cheerfully returning for a possible romantic visit to her former mountain abode.

With the real estate transaction being completed, the novelist and Mr. Schmidt happily departed the 'newly acquired chalet' in the realtor's rugged *Chevy Blazer*. The passenger informed the driver that he would be ready to move in as soon as his clothes and personal belongings would be shipped from New York to Bern.

Joseph stayed in a Bern hotel for three days to allow Elka sufficient time to move her personal belongings out of the enchanting "post card chalet". In the interim, the magical black pen dominated most of Joseph Perna's fleeting thoughts. His literary glory and international reputation highly depended on the item's sustained performance. Another consideration that alarmed and often haunted Perna's psyche' was his graphic recollection of the spectral silhouette that had been viewed, sitting at *his* Soho, desk just after the author had witnessed the distinct, ghoulish reflection from inside his dingy apartment's bathroom mirror.

The bizarre mystery of the additional written chapters of Joseph Perna's third novel, which had been found atop *his* cherry-wood desk during his unproductive South of Houston-New York City trek, also tormented Joseph Perna's restless soul. 'Is there any feasible explanation to solve this extremely difficult riddle?' the skeptical Swiss sojourner pondered. 'And who in God's name is *Raymond Pierre Girard?*' The mercurial-tempered author would soon be able to comprehend those gravely-complicated conundrums that greatly was torturing both his mind and his heart.

* * * * * * * * * * * *

Three days later, Joseph was resting inside his new chalet and reminiscing about his inexplicable past spectral experience. Heir Perna didn't do any significant novel writing those first several weeks while still getting adjusted to country life in the panoramic *Alps*. The incognito Raymond Pierre Girard's principal objective was to piece together the very cryptic puzzle that had been bewildering his fears ever since departing Soho. But the writer's overall ordeal concerning his 'communion with a benevolent spirit' was as much of a giant mental maze as it was an annoying "massive jigsaw puzzle". 'What if the ghost I had witnessed is malevolent besides being benevolent?' Joseph contemplated. 'What if the apparition I had seen is an itinerant partner to the black magic pen I plan to use here in Switzerland?'

But conversely, on the positive side, Joseph was quite excited about his acquisition of the handsome mountain lodging, and the young man's very comfortable accommodations provided him with a degree of emotional consolation to balance-out his myriad apprehensions. The writer was then motivated to begin generating his next prolific manuscript and industriously bringing the finished product to fruition.

His very demanding and emotionally volatile New York publisher was in constant communication, and Mr. Manuel Allen was pressuring Joseph to produce more literary masterpieces in order to supplement the current ones that were now commanding five-hundred-thousand-dollar advances.

"Raymond, or I meant to say, Joseph," Mr. Allen pleasantly corrected himself over the phone. "You must get to your desk and start creating another best seller. Your burgeoning international audience insists on it."

"Mr. Allen, as soon as I get fully situated here in Switzerland, I promise I'll be rejuvenated and productive once again," Joseph pledged. "My spirit will again be synchronized with the mystical forces of the universe, and I'll fabricate incomparable stories that would've made Alexandre Dumas or Victor Hugo envious."

The young story fabricator had brought-along to Switzerland a new computer with sophisticated features, and immediately had a team of technicians install the advanced machine at his new Swiss mountain chalet. Convenient *Internet* access would be the indispensable tool that the author would need to successfully conduct *his* special black magic pen research.

The remote retreat afforded Joseph essential solitude, but since the self-proclaimed introvert was so far removed from civilization, 'web e-mail' communication with the outside world would still be vitally necessary in case of him having a dire emergency, or an urgent need to respond to important business developments. Just like *Henry David Thoreau*, Joseph Perna, alias Raymond Pierre Girard, had for all intents and purposes had transformed into an insecure recluse. The Swiss mountain chalet had become the eccentric loner's version of Thoreau's *Walden Pond*.

Outside the cozy alpine lodging was a rusty set of wind chimes that had been dangling from the shingled roof for countless decades. Even a mild breeze would cause the objects to harmoniously clatter. Joseph soon became accustomed to listening to the 'dissonant clashing chimes'. The Swiss fall weather had so far been relatively mild, and so Perna regretted that he could not appreciate the full intensity of the chimes' 'entrancing winter rhythms.'

Except for the Madison Avenue publisher's incessant nagging phone calls, the hermit writer had enough 'quality time alone' to alleviate his many conscious fears, and to fortify and embellish his growing vanity. Classical music often filled the chalet's den, and the familiar vibes frequently permeated into the remote home's living room. *Beethoven's Fifth Symphony, Tchaikovsky's 1812 Overture, Mozart's Number 41,* and *Richard Wagner's The Valkyries* stimulated

Joseph Perna's writing confidence and enabled his in-jeopardy spirit to rise from the depths of his heart, like a newborn *Phoenix*.

Already feeling inspired and in complete harmony with his new-found mountain environment, the chalet resident located his invincible black pen tucked-away inside a small carry-on case, which the author had safeguarded with his life on the long flight from New York. Upon moving into the delightful dwelling, Joseph had hidden the revered instrument behind an ancient loose log he had accidentally discovered, lodged inside the bedroom wall, and after removing the chunk of forest wood, the doubting writer fondled and worshipped the black object that was now indeed his most cherished possession.

Heir Perna then gave a lusty sigh of relief as his eyes were valuing his precious treasure piece. 'Heaven forbid if *you* had been lost, or if *you* didn't work in your new Swiss environment,' the owner mused to the pen as if it were a living, breathing person. 'You're all that I've yearned to be. You are my vital lifeline to worldwide success! You are my soul and all that it desires!'

The yellow stationery pads were available upon the chalet's antiquated desk, and the good-mood author was desperately eager to proceed with initiating his 'craft'. It was early morning, and Joseph was especially energized by the sun's radiance refracting through the chalet's eastern windowpanes. Again, just like in Soho, a cascade of words mysteriously began streaming onto the paper as the enigmatic power embodied inside the magic pen directed the first chapter's development with effortless facility. To Joseph's fond acceptance, the 'uncanny miracle' had now become a very routine exercise. The pen's supernatural influence had again wonderfully elevated Perna's prowess as a powerful literary force, and the excellent utensil allowed Heir Perna's reputation to migrate from "unknown national author" to the level of "international master wordsmith".

Joseph was quite resolute to investigate the arcane wizardry of the wondrous black plumed pen. "I must discover the source of *your* tremendous magic," the word-master insisted to the faintly glowing pen. "Perhaps you can communicate with me in heretofore undiscovered ways, other than written language!"

The writer/dreamer deeply contemplated his annoying dilemma and soon devised a clever breakthrough plan. Joseph's scheme was to confirm the reality of the apparition's reflection that had formerly been seen seated at his Soho apartment's cherry-wood desk.

The now-established novelist then recollected something rather salient. When the literary savant had turned-around from the mirror of his New York apartment's bathroom wall mirror, Perna recollected that the somewhat-nebulous image had disappeared in an instant. "I'm certain that there was someone there before the manifestation vanished into thin air," the worried word composer remarked to the inanimate quilled object being held in his right hand. "My cherished pen would need an author, just like a ship needs a captain."

Undeniably, the mystical pen with the dark black plume, along with its characteristic bottle of black ink, could not have written those phantom chapters by itself. The great mystery just had to be answered because the special pen's unearthly intelligence substantially defied the common operable tenets of both science and reason.

The same day that Joseph had witnessed the elusive reflection in Soho, his astute memory recalled that in the afternoon, he had hurried out of his modest apartment and had scurried down the street toward midtown Manhattan. The author had ended-up at the Public Library at Fifth Avenue and 42nd Street; when there, the literary artist had read ravenously for several hours. The topics that the curious library patron researched and explored dealt with metaphysics, the occult, and finally, the documented habits of wandering ghosts and spirits.

'Is it possible?' the bemused library guest pondered, 'that I had encountered a restive, mobile apparition, sitting at my cherry-wood desk?' Naturally, Joseph's overactive mind enjoyed having the liberty of swimming in its self-induced, idyllic fantasy dimension, employing the thriving freedom to revel while simultaneously drowning in a sea of pure creativity, which was a true advantage when most other human beings on Planet Earth had to toil and sweat daily, just to sustain his or her mediocre earthly existence.

"I once lived from day to day like most ordinary people, and now that I don't have to be a slave to drudgery anymore," Joseph lectured to his magic pen, "I now feel guilty, because my great wealth is not a direct *effect* of my own *cause*. Do you comprehend my gist?"

Joseph essentially was a bashful loner, and did not want or seek the assistance or collaboration of others. He was adamant about 'pursuing the talented specter's identity, without the direct *collaboration or the assistance* of other 'bothersome mortals'. Heir Perna was now overly impulsive about implementing his shrewd 'ghost communication strategy'. The idea of encountering an authentic '*ghostwriter*' was beginning to consume his entire imagination, and starting to govern and control his very soul.

"Every 'ghost*writer*' in history that I've studied had been made of human flesh and blood," spoke the writer to his silent magic pen. "Someday you'll have the wherewithal and the decency to expose your true identity to me!"

First, Joseph initiated an intense *Internet* search of all authors who had lived during the past three-centuries. *Yahoo, Google,* and *Bing* search engines would be able to narrow-down his elusive subject inquiry, namely, the seemingly indecipherable enigma, *Raymond Pierre Girard*. The truth pursuer's trustworthy desktop computer would be the appropriate tool to further subdivide the newfound information into discernible research elements.

Joseph was very zealous in organizing his calculated quest, and obtaining 'the truth' was his sole incentive to persistently investigate the relevant sought-after data. The 'mountain recluse' was resolute about tapping into all of the major European libraries data bases, and then scanning their extensive autobiographies in quest of every possible list of published writers. Determined Mr. Perna was persistent in cracking-open the cruel mystery of whom actually was *Raymond Pierre Girard;* besides the stated appellation of the scruffy beggar who had sold the black magic pen and the bottle of black ink to the aspiring author.

The crazed Internet researcher started his literary manhunt with an analysis of *20th Century Literature.* After viewing thousands of names of deceased European authors, Joseph failed to locate any trace of his evasive subject, *Raymond Pierre Girard*. Being disappointed but not vanquished, the obstinate investigator then methodically searched all of the *19th Century* European authors. This demanding activity was very time consuming, but the strong-willed web explorer was driven by extreme zeal. Perna was absolutely devoted to pinpointing the obscure personage, *Raymond Pierre Girard*. That dedication was an extraordinarily fascinating 'time consuming experiment', which if successful, would possibly unlock and reveal the true secret of the magic pen's origin and nature.

"I would rather die than not know the key to this troubling riddle that I believe would've even frustrated the winged sphinx of Greek mythology," Joseph emphasized to the mute pen, as if it were another person. "Perhaps the ghost of Oedipus could appear and render its solicited assistance!'

Joseph had to strategically budget his time so that he could maintain a decent balance between his arduous writing schedule and his addictive computer research. Each evening, the chalet's stone fireplace roared with bewitching, dancing flames. The living room was always kept as warm as toast. As the undaunted researcher peered out the window above his now-familiar 'alpine desk', his consciousness was enamored with the general grandeur of the distant imperial snowcapped *Alps*. The high peaks' splendor easily stimulated the writer to again concentrate on his dual projects of authoring quality literature and of performing background computer research. The speedy, classical rhythms of the "William Tell Overture" and "The

316

Flight of the Bumblebee" were heard blasting through the walls' stereo speakers, the ascending rhythms also accelerating Joseph's hectic pace. 'I'll search and then I'll search again,' the lonely gent vowed. 'That redundant process, I believe, is the true meaning of the common word re-search!'

"This dual obsession I'm confronted with has without a doubt both possessed and consumed me. I've lost control of my free will. Do you understand me, Mr. Magic Pen? I'm either *your* marionette or *your master's* puppet, or perhaps I'm the enslaved subordinate of both of *those* incomprehensible prospects. Much to my chagrin, I'm now more *Raymond Pierre Girard* than I am Joseph Perna. In the final analysis, or perhaps in *my* primary psychoanalysis, I've essentially become a most insane, neurotic, desperate ingrate!"

Heir Joseph had spent over three weeks on his colossal, painstaking European author research, but the distraction of his addictive computer inquiry did not compromise the fabulous rhetoric being embodied and incorporated into his new manuscript.

"Thank God for this singular gifted pen, for without it, I'd have to make a very difficult choice between my obsession and my profession. Thanks to you, dear *Magic Pen*, I can devote six precious hours a day to delving into the wild mystery of my two-dimensional *ghost*writer. Thank God for library and Internet academic education!"

It wasn't long before Joseph finished his search of all the deceased *19th Century* authors, but still the name explorer enjoyed no particular satisfaction or basic luck. The self-appointed scholar's next enterprise would be to investigate the litany of latter *18th Century* American and European authors. Detective Perna's remarkable due diligence was both enviable and noteworthy, but his continuous attempt at achieving biographical success was fraught with failure and futility.

"Finding a cure for cancer might be an easier task than finding the evasive *Raymond Pierre Girard,*" the American transplant articulated to the reticent plumed pen. "The evasive phantom must've lived his life on another planet in another solar system."

The very stressful, ongoing computer investigation was, to say the least, challenging, tedious, laborious, and monotonous. A lesser man's will would have either surrendered or succumbed to the anguish of continuous disappointment and perpetual frustration.

Two more aggravating, fruitless weeks elapsed, but still no 'missing link' had been discovered by the faltering 'Darwin literary impersonator'. Joseph felt as if he had been participating in a losing one-man wild goose chase, but the 'never-say-die' Swiss resident was extremely obdurate, and the 'truth champion' gallantly persevered in completing his Promethean quest.

In *that* incredible fourteen-day time frame, another two books had been expertly 'word-smithed', thanks to the attributes and the supernatural contributions of the superlative black pen.

The voluminous catalog of famous and secondary authors was finally becoming reduced to an abbreviated list of names; and soon, the *Internet* navigator was ready to finish his unilateral expedition into the early *18th Century*. Joseph had a good feeling about the outcome of his 'colonial era' analysis. The 'student of immaterial names', as Perna sarcastically called himself, relentlessly probed the new century's parameters, waiting and hoping to find the cryptic name *Raymond Pierre Girard* to appear onto the *IBM* screen.

Another two weeks elapsed, and Heir Joseph now suspected that his exhaustive 'data-expedition' was nothing more than a childish whim. Skepticism reigned supreme within his very weary, almost-conquered mind. 'This fanciful travesty is like a horrendous Shakespearean tragedy!' Joseph sadly evaluated. 'I'll die before I ever solve this impossible Gordian knot mystery!'

Suddenly, and without warning, on that *April Fools* morning, the name ***Raymond Pierre Girard*** finally appeared upon the *IBM* computer monitor. The tired key tapper was temporarily spellbound by 'the illusion'. Joseph was so euphoric that he had to postpone writing the next chapter of his novel, just to savor the rewarding moment of ultimate triumph. The seated young man had little time to relish his extended study. The ecstatic computer guru happily quaffed-down a shot of blackberry brandy, which was then quickly followed by a double. Joseph Perna felt both mellow and mentally drained, and the fagged-out fellow soon fell sound asleep without any further overt or quiet celebration.

The following dawn arrived, and the rejuvenated writer awakened and ambled in a beeline to the computer terminal, wanting to verify his most prodigious identity discovery. Was it all a tantalizing dream? No, it wasn't. The wonderful name ***Raymond Pierre Girard*** was still prominently represented and described upon the *IBM* screen.

The researcher's next objective was now perfectly clear. His focus was to glean every smidgeon of important information he could gather concerning the obscure, early *18th Century* author. That particular endeavor would again require a daring, assiduous undertaking. The American researcher's next Swiss adventure would prove to be absolutely mind-boggling.

* * * * * * * * * * * *

Joseph Perna eagerly retrieved additional utilitarian information from his reliable *IBM* computer, and downloaded everything which he obtained into a specially prepared *Microsoft Word* file. After conscientiously initiating his intensive search for specific background on *Raymond Pierre Girard,* several leading European libraries supplied subsequent pertinent data. The essential question posed to each library's database was this inquiry: "Biographical background, Author *Raymond Pierre Girard,* early *18th Century.*"

At first, no germane personal records could be gleaned from any bibliography or national archive. Later appendix excavations revealed two possible clues. One was from the *Bibliotheque Mazarine* in Paris. The reputable library had been founded in 1643, and it was one of the greatest fact-based facilities in France. The other dependable and beneficial source was the revered *Swiss National Library* in Bern. At last, favorable progrsss was being made.

The worthwhile information Joseph mustered re-activated his former enthusiasm. The inspired novelist now commanded refreshed vitality along with much-needed dogged resiliency.

The obtained resumés on *Raymond Pierre Girard* were brief, but nonetheless, quite important. The man was born in Schoeneck, France in 1680. Girard had attended the *University of Paris,* where he had studied *Plato's Republic* and also various academic medieval and neoclassical literature. The serious-minded 1680 student had become an eminent authority on *Greco-Roman* mythology and pre-colonial 'enlightenment political philosophy', specializing in Voltaire.

As an active middle-aged man, *Girard* became a political radical who intrepidly wrote revolutionary pamphlets, which a century later, helped inspire the storming of the *Bastille,* and his anti-monarchy writs contributed to the violent escalation of the *French Revolution.* His firebrand rhetoric proved to be valuable propaganda a hundred-years later for the rebellious French dissident 'anti-imperialists'.

Raymond Pierre Girard was indeed a political prophet, but the avowed revolutionary also derived much pleasure from writing operas and composing romantic stories. posthumously, the currently obscure French philosopher/writer became fairly popular in certain cognoscenti literary circles, his short fame arising prior to Napoleon's dramatic defeat at *Waterloo.* According to accurate European library records, towards the end of his noble life, *Girard* began organizing dynamic historical novels with freedom, loyalty, love, and friendship abstract themes.

Encyclopedia records revealed that *Raymond Pierre Girard* had a devoted wife, Catherine. Salient biographical information disclosed that the 'messenger intellectual' always had a strong desire to live in

Switzerland. After his cozy *Alps* chalet had been built, Girard then moved to his secluded mountain retreat near Bern in 1720. Records also indicated that Raymond had sent for his wife to arrive from Paris at a later date. But shortly thereafter, Catherine had received one final letter from Raymond Pierre. The short missive stated that her husband was getting situated in Switzerland, and that the 'French Plato' still deeply loved her. Then, Catherine never again heard a word from her devoted spouse, the clandestine *Raymond Pierre Girard.*

"My God!" Joseph exclaimed to the magic pen. *"Raymond Pierre Girard* was a contemporary of *Jonathan Swift* and *Daniel Defoe,* and the *sage* had lived before eminent *Jean Jacques Rousseau, Sir Isaac Newton, Ludwig Beethoven,* and *Wolfgang Amadeus Mozart."* gasped Joseph, while the contemporary author almost-hypnotically sifted through the fascinating biographical facts and statistics.

The renowned *Swiss National Library* in Bern provided added substantiating information that also proved to be of great importance. The famous author's new delving confirmed that *Raymond Pierre Girard* had moved to Switzerland in 1720, and had lived in a newly constructed chalet situated upon a scenic mountain not far from Bern. The political dissident had made arrangements with a reputable Swiss publisher to submit a full portfolio of original manuscripts for critical scholarly evaluation. Suddenly, *Girard* had seemingly disappeared from the face of the Earth and was never seen or heard from again. Joseph Perna's extraordinary computer search ended precisely there, with part of the cryptic mystery being revealed.

"Could the ghost in my Soho apartment have been none-other than *Raymond Pierre Girard?"* speculated and uttered the dumbfounded writer to the plumed black magic pen. "Come forth, my benign ghost! Are *you,* by any chance, he?"

* * * * * * * * * * * * *

The next vital phase of Joseph's intensive investigation was to bravely establish physical contact with the transient spectral wanderer. A decisive plan was needed to communicate directly with the 'restless, meandering time trekker' who had been visiting Perna from the mystical spirit world. The very thought of an actual supernatural confrontation was quite staggering to Joseph's already disoriented imagination. 'If there really is a ghost behind the magic pen's surreal function, is Girard's specter a benevolent messenger, or is the erratic ghoul an invisible. shrewd creature having malicious designs?' Joseph considered. "The moment of truth has arrived. I'll endeavor making contact with the apparition and risk what might be the ultimate consequences," repeated Joseph quite brazenly to the marvelous black plumed pen being held in his right hand.

Establishing contact with someone who had died in the early 1720s would ordinarily be an impossible undertaking, but the audacious novelist had one indispensable resource, the magical plumed pen, which would be the obvious 'time bridge' connecting the early *18th Century* with the atomic age. Certainly, in the past, no human being had ever before been afforded such a fantastic opportunity to exchange dialogue with a restless, migrating spirit. Joseph felt that 'midnight' would be the most advantageous time to establish direct contact with the 'ultra-talented roving spirit.'

The knowledgeable author believed in the popular superstitions that ghosts had unfinished earthly business to attend to, and that their migrating souls also felt more secure during the presence of the dark New Moon. Joseph checked his chalet's hanging kitchen calendar and quickly decided that *that* night would be the most opportune time to conduct an 'unprecedented spiritual experiment'.

The intrepid, American planned to compose a friendly letter to *Raymond Pierre Girard,* using the singular services of the black magic pen. If *Girard's* ghost were in need of mortal assistance, the rational apparition would naturally divulge its intent to Joseph, and cooperatively reciprocate with the functional magic pen, the writing device serving as an accommodating interpretation medium.

Writer Perna very deliberately placed the quilled utensil down upon the old, solid oak desk, and then placing the pen adjacent to his informal letter of introduction. The novelist really felt that writing a brief message would be the best way to preface a viable discussion with the wayward spirit from the Swiss past.

The die had been cast, but the new *Rubicon* would be the uncharted gulf existing between the world of the living and the kingdom of the dead. In his missive addressed to the wandering spirit, valiant Sir Joseph stated his identity and specified his sincere desire to render valuable earthly assistance to the 'woebegone lost benefactor'. If the shade of *Raymond Pierre Girard* would read and comprehend Joseph's letter of appeal, the apparently shy contributor to the fomenting radical principles of pre-*French Revolution* democracy would then favorably jot-down his exact purpose (as requested) upon the yellow legal pad that had been conveniently placed upon Joseph Perna's 'lucky brown desk blotter'.

After the Swiss chalet owner wrote a brief paragraph of salutation, the magic pen was carefully laid next to the yellow legal pad. In addition, Heir Perna made sure that the first three paragraphs of the first chapter to *his* new manuscript accompanied the introductory letter along with the ingenious pen.

"*Raymond Pierre Girard* will re-cross the *River Styx; Lord Charon,* I advise you to start rowing your macabre barge!" the chalet resident uttered to himself in an almost trance-like state of mind. "My letter and the magic pen constitute dear Raymond's official invitation to pay me a cordial visit."

Nothing of ghostly significance occurred until the following winter. It was February and bitter winds were circulating swirls of cold air outside the wooden-framed chalet. The stone fireplace was roaring, its heated hearth emitting steady waves of comforting warmth. At 11:00 p.m., Joseph yawned, stretched his arms above his head, and retired to the main bedroom. 'What will the morning bring?' the tired author wondered. 'Where is *Raymond Pierre Girard's* ghost? Is the presumed spirit a fake, a fraud?'

The disappointed *Good Samaritan* then fell into a deep sleep. At 4:15 a.m., Joseph awoke, and his ears heard the metallic wind chimes rattling outside the isolated chalet. Their repetitious clatter foreshadowed evidence of a highly irregular in-progress event transpiring. Strangely enough, the howling winds had suddenly reduced to a virtual calm, and there was no special reason at all for the windchimes to be incessantly clanging. The fireplace flames were now slowly burning, and their tongues of fire dimly lit the living room.

As the fascinated writer slowly stirred and stepped in the direction of the main room, the cautious ambler became aware of a pool of water, and then Joseph's eyes noticed a trail of ice that led to a pool of water underneath the old oak writing desk. This experience immediately reminded Heir Perna of the icy water that he had first found on his 'lucky brown ink blotter' back in Soho.

No one human intruder, or anyone else, was noticeable meandering inside the room, and there was no evidence of the chalet's front door having inadvertently been opened. Joseph advanced forward with exaggerated concern and with his trembling knees buckling. He nervously examined the formal writing parchment that had been repositioned on the familiar yellow notepad. The astute observer gasped with astonishment.

A handwritten note read...

Greetings, Joseph! My name is Raymond Pierre Girard, born in the year 1680. My restive spirit has been aimlessly wandering about from continent to continent for almost three centuries in dire quest of a pure-hearted mortal that could discover and rectify a personal tragedy that had happened to me in the year 1721.

This chalet in which you are living is the same one I had built and resided in with my faithful St. Bernard, Niko. In 1721, an abundance of snow had surrounded this home almost all that bitter winter, and the massive accumulation had especially drifted on the west side that receives less sunlight. It was a bitter, agonizing February day, and there were sheets of thick ice all over the nearby mountainsides. My food and my vital supplies were running low. I was forced to leave my comfortable abode and its corresponding safety in order to travel to lower ground and purchase necessities. The stone road to Bern was too slippery and too treacherous for me to take my large sleigh and horse, so out of sheer desperation, I attached my smaller sled to a harness that had been custom-made for my dog, Niko.

Over my lifetime, I had written a portfolio of novels that I was intending to bring to the Swiss National Library for scholarly evaluation. The library had already documented my first two novels in its official archives, and I wanted to add to my collection with my new accumulative literary works. I had placed the freshly prepared manuscripts nestled inside a leather-bound case to properly protect them from the hostile winter elements.

Now Joseph, the sled was very difficult and too weighty for beloved Niko to pull, and it took my canine several hours simply to move the contrived vehicle seven-hundred-meters. It was getting late in the afternoon, and I had several more arduous kilometers to finally rendezvous with the library authorities in Bern, and also to purchase much needed supplies. There were no other occupied chalets in the vicinity to provide me with basic shelter and food.

My faithful St. Bernard was suffering from exhaustion, and so, I wound-up pulling the sled with loyal Niko by my side. The sled held my cherished portfolio of manuscripts on the way down the treacherous snow-laden mountain, and I intended to also use my wrongly chosen mode of transportation to transport equipment and groceries on the way back up to the chalet. This plan was indeed a major mistake in judgment.

Joseph, I had to risk frostbite if I boldly continued my hazardous trip, or else flirt with death if I attempted to return to my secluded chalet. I started trekking around a steep curve present on the dangerous, icy road. All of a sudden, the sled's reins slipped from my faulty grip. I frantically lunged forward to grab the reins but could not reach them. In desperation, I rushed as fast as I could, but the improvised sled was moving faster than I could ever control its forward motion.

I had made a last vain attempt to stop the sled's momentum and progress, just as the object approached the edge of a precarious cliff. I managed to grasp the leather case containing the precious manuscripts, right before the runaway sled flipped over the edge, and then plunged directly into a narrow glacial crevice.

However, Joseph, at that moment, I had lost my footing and accidentally wildly slipped. I still clutched the precious manuscripts inside the portfolio, and then I swiftly followed the sled down the steep slope, plummeting with my doomed body helplessly falling into the fifty-foot-deep frozen fissure. As I descended, I could hear Niko barking loudly from above. Try as I might, I had been wedged against solid walls of ice, and could not possibly escape and dislodge myself my pathetic glacial entombment.

Minutes later, I saw my trusty St. Bernard also sliding into the accursed lips of the slippery crevice, and then my eyes witnessed my cherished canine finally landing next to my frostbitten feet. In a short time, the frigid cold made my hands and feet excessively numb. Before long, my entire body had become virtually frozen like a frigid polar igloo. I slowly blacked-out, and my mortal life (along with my loyal Niko's) was soon extinguished.

It is my sincere hope that through you, Joseph Perna, alias Raymond Pierre Girard, an earnest attempt will be made to recover the leather case containing my treasured manuscripts. If this requested task can be accomplished, the portfolio could then be brought to the Swiss National Library for academic and literary evaluation. My life's work could be published so that the world will finally be able to read and appreciate my long-neglected, virtually ignored talent.

For almost three centuries, my itinerant spirit has been distraught. I had to find a sensitive soul with admirable human compassion that only a genuine writer like yourself could possess or exhibit. Only a sentimental fool such as you (or me) would find his way to this obscure mountain chalet. You, Joseph, were selected by the eternal laws of justice to unselfishly render your most valued assistance to a lost, wandering soul.

After my name is conferred the credit and recognition that it rightfully deserves, then I could joyfully be reunited with my loving Catherine, together resting in eternal peace. You, Joseph Perna, are my sole hope for me achieving honor and redemption. You are both my validation and my vindication. Your solicited intercession will mark the end of my many centuries of misery, searching, searching and more searching.

Gratefully yours,

Raymond Pierre Girard

Joseph read and reread the very convincing letter and was overwhelmed and greatly moved by comprehending its noble nomenclature. Tears immediately filled his bloodshot eyes. The affected author determined that a solo mini-expedition to the icy burial site of *Raymond Pierre Girard* and his beloved St. Bernard Niko should be conducted with urgent dispatch. Their glacial sepulcher that had been wedged inside the ice-laden mountain seam needed to be successfully located and explored.

Joseph's mind and heart were still stunned by his fathoming that the impeccable handwriting which had appeared on Stephen Pierre Girard's ethereal cursive letter was identical to that of his own when he had employed the distinct privilege of writing with the 'Black Magic Pen'. Perna also noticed that the three-paragraph manuscript *he* had written on the chalet's desk had been miraculously transformed and had been inexplicably expanded into a resplendent twenty-five-chapter adventure novel.

* * * * * * * * * * * *

When Joseph Perna had moved to Switzerland, the avid dreamer knew that there would be certain occasions where he would have to leave the chalet in the wintertime. The American had come equipped with an adequate supply of snow gear; boots, sled, shovel, rope, pick-ax, and flashlight, all initially purchased in Bern. The relocated author planned to commence his daring expedition the following February morning in order to find the priceless lost manuscripts of deceased *Raymond Pierre Girard*. The single-goal ghost explorer meticulously packed everything that he would need, neatly tucked into his silver *Mercury Mountaineer* sports utility vehicle. 'This reliable auto' is going to make the seven-hundred-meter distance search to the crevice much easier than the horribly difficult hike that poor *Girard* had to make,' Perna thought. 'Thank goodness for modern technology!'

It would be slow going while maneuvering along the perilous Alpine precipices and icy embankments. Joseph vowed to loyally adhere to the directions that had been so competently described in the roving spirit's expository letter. Hopefully, the bold rescuer would be able to eventually locate the ice-laden separation, along with the frozen forms of *Raymond Pierre Girard* and his trusty St. Bernard, Niko.

In Joseph Perna's estimation, the discovery of the manuscripts concealed in the leather case was even more important than the actual finding of *Girard's* body, because then the early *18th Century* author could finally rest in peace once, the non-acclaimed novelist had received the rightful world recognition that mindless fate had maliciously denied him. In Joseph Perna's determined mind, *Raymond Pierre Girard's* manuscripts just had to be found.

The next morning was clear and cold, and the prospect for a sunny day was highly probable. Joseph hastily consumed a hardy breakfast and packed a thermos of hot coffee for his intended expedition. The hopeful 'truth prospector' had also prepared two ham and cheese sandwiches to devour for lunch, as Heir Perna wasted little time in finishing his thorough preparation. The efficient completion of Joseph's honorable salvage operation was *his* only focus; time was waiting for no one.

Soon, the aspiring, crusading ghost liberator had loaded his *Mercury Mountaineer* and was carefully steering his way down the slanted icy stone trail. Perna scrupulously thought about how Raymond Girard had managed *his* similar trip almost three-hundred-years before, having only a small sled and a faithful dog. And now, the truth searcher was stubbornly duplicating the exact same course taken by *his* ghostly mentor inside a modern sports utility four-wheel-drive *Mercury*. The challenging passage was slow-going and precarious, but Joseph was satisfied making gradual forward progress.

The *Mountaineer* cut a steady path through the thick snow and patchy ice-covered road in order to approach the author's noble appointment with destiny. The driver stopped his SUV for a brief interval, drank his hot coffee, and ate his delicious ham and cheese sandwiches around noon. But little time was required for the indulgence in mere biological sustenance. Spiritual fulfillment and

Girard's indomitable will, along with the prospect of intellectual gratification, were the compelling forces that made Joseph Perna's surging adrenaline effectively neutralize the numbing effect of the frigid Alpine air.

When the driver estimated that he had traveled the mentioned seven-hundred-meters (according to the *SUV's* odometer reading), Joseph kept a keen surveillance for the precise steep curve that Raymond Girard had reported when *he* and his sleigh had vanished over the icy ledge. 'During the last three-centuries, there had to be some topographical alterations to the terrain,' thought the mountain rover sitting behind the steering wheel. 'Soil erosion, rock slides, and avalanches could've changed the entire contour of this section of the road.' But the unwavering explorer had no doubt that in the end, *he* would be equal to his lofty goal.

As the sports utility vehicle slowly inched its way through an awesome snowdrift, Joseph skillfully maneuvered his four-wheel-drive SUV across the obstacle's center, and finally managed to arrive at what his mind theorized could have been the steep, curved section of the descending trail, which had been alluded to in *Raymond Pierre Girard's* wondrous letter. The *Mountaineer's* dashboard odometer now registered that Joseph had traveled approximately seven-tenths of a kilometer. Perna stopped the *Mercury* to get an accurate reassessment of his bearings. Rather than continue, the driver decided to find and examine the described ice seam, which he now hypothesized to be near the bottom of the narrow slope.

A slight human miscalculation in judgment or footing would mean a lethal plummet directly into the God-forsaken mountain ravine. The *thinker* audaciously carried his dependable pick-ax and rope to the exact position where the encroaching explorer believed *Raymond Pierre Girard's* frozen entrapment was located.

Joseph Perna feared that *he* was trespassing into the exact 'cusp zone' that separated the primitive three-dimensional world of mortal humans from the preternatural infinity (or proximity) of *Raymond Pierre Girard's* nomadic soul.

The jittery, shivering novelist then recalled the faint, outlined image he had seen sitting at the cherry-wood desk inside his Soho apartment. The morbid, deceased figure had been clad in a neat ruffled colonial shirt that protruded beneath the collar, a garment similar to *George Washington's* apparel shown in his famous portrait appearing on the one-dollar bill.

"My God!" the frigid trespasser gasped and exclaimed. "I'm not alone! I insist that *Miguel Cervantes* and *William Shakespeare* had to have magic pens assisting them, too!" More raw reflection (by the out-of-place fanatic) regarding the renowned alluded-to literary geniuses then formulated a new realization in Perna's awed mind. "But Bill and Mike both died on the exact same day in 1605, seventy-five years before *Raymond Pierre Girard* had been born. So, therefore, *Cervantes* and *Shakespeare* must've been privy to different magic pens than the one which has been ingeniously employed by the radical social philosopher *Raymond Pierre Girard,* and me!"

The uncanny, magnetic, paranormal attraction of *Raymond Pierre Girard's* nearby spirit had transformed Joseph Perna's mind into a semi-hypnotic, obedient, state of existence. The writer/rescuer's rampant imagination kept rehashing several incredible parallel coincidences. Not only had *Cervantes* and *Shakespeare* died on the exact same day in 1616, but also ironically, *Thomas Jefferson* and *John Adams* had also died on an exact same day, *July 4th, Independence Day* in 1826.

Those particular literary and historical coincidences made the recently acclaimed novelist shudder with absolute terror about commencing with his major task at hand. The chalet's wall calendar's coincidental date of February 15th was the precise date of *Raymond Pierre Girard's* documented disappearance in 1721. Could the benign, genteel spirit of the dead *18th Century* author have a diabolical dark side that had been diabolically luring Joseph to impending doom? 'It would be grossly unfair for *the supernatural* to get involved in either thwarting or harming my *natural* human endeavor!' Joseph admirably considered and concluded.

While Heir Perna's active mind attempted avoiding self-imposed academic distraction, the on-a-mission author managed to slowly climb to the bottom of the icy slope, and next began edging his way around a slippery crag during his deliberate clamber down to the alluded-to narrow crevice. The ice-covered cliff was indeed very dangerous. One misstep or tumble and Joseph Perna's fate would be the duplicate of the ice-entombed *Raymond Pierre Girard, who* had been adeptly guiding the creative words being generated from the inscrutable black magic pen.

Joseph very methodically tied the strong thick rope to a large snow-covered boulder. After next tethering the thick hemp around his midriff, the tenacious man squeezed his frame slowly down into the narrow fifty-foot-deep crevice. The glacial crack was slick with a layer of smooth ice, and the rope attached to the giant rock represented the gritty man's only means to allow for either descent or vertical escape. Perna very gradually retreated from his temporarily safe, stationary position, and soon very assiduously clambered-down into the suspected icy grave of *Raymond Pierre Girard.*

The crevice further narrowed around forty-feet below its surface aperture, and Heir Perna felt it would be certain suicide to lower his depth any further by using the lengthy rope that had been secured to the ground-level boulder. 'It's now or never,' the grave searcher grimly reckoned and concluded. 'If I proceed any deeper, my fragile life will surely be in jeopardy."

The fervent excavator lifted his hand-axe and began strenuously chipping-away ever-so-forcefully in order to provide himself with more working area in which to maneuver. As Joseph chiseled-away at the dense mass of ice, the toiler was soon aware that only minor progress was being made. The obsessed man labored onward, strenuously enacting his ice axe sculpturing, but all along the 'death prospector' had a peculiar sensation that someone, or something, was spying on him. A sharp chill suddenly rushed through Perna's entire anatomy. As the now-possessed man wildly hammered and chipped away, Joseph again perceived through his sixth sense that his frenetic activity was being monitored by some eerie alien vigilance.

"I might as well be stranded in the middle of *Antarctica,*" Joseph sniffed, momentarily pausing his mania to take a healthy, deep breath. "I *will* certainly die from frostbite if I falter here. Guide me to your icy remains, Raymond. Please guide me."

The laborer's eyes suddenly perceived what vaguely appeared to be a lifeless, bearded human face, seemingly frozen and ensconced in solid ice. Joseph was instantly startled, and his body was immediately paralyzed. A dead man's chin and nose was noticed protruding from the frontal ice layer, and at first impression, the corpse's facial features seemed to have been carved out of glass. Joseph flicked on his flashlight, and his keen inspection was soon frightened; his wits suddenly being stunned beyond belief.

The projected light-beam had illuminated the frozen 'glacial man's macabre features, that were now adequately transparent as being witnessed by Heir Perna through six inches of thick glazed ice.

Joseph had undoubtedly located the three-century-old tomb of his noble benefactor, whose body had amazingly been preserved for over thirty decades inside the frozen glacial fissure. The explorer garnered courage and meticulously cleared-away the six-inches of excess ice. The more chipped shavings that the possessed axe-thruster carved away, the more horrifying, stark facial features of *his* literary mentor readily became distinguishable inside the dark, frigid crevice.

"God rest your benign soul," Joseph recited to the morose-looking countenance that seemed staring directly at him, still exhibiting opened blue eyes. "May eternal light shine upon you, and after I take your magnificent, official manuscripts to the reputable Bern Library for copyrighting, may your troubled spirit rest in peace with warranted dignity. God bless you, august Raymond Pierre Girard."

After a third hour of very cautious carving, the perfectly horrendous, hideous-looking morbid face was now staring directly at Joseph with its penetrating pale blue eyes still wide open; and yes, the duration of *Raymond Pierre Girard's* ghastly death had incidentally also been frozen in time.

As the salvager stared in hypnotic trepidation at the grim face before him, the dreamer's mind again recollected the dim reflection his eyes had seen while sitting at his Soho apartment's cherry-wood desk. The exasperating glacial corpse wore a ruffled shirt that was an exact duplicate of the one worn in the bathroom mirror reflection. The New York City two-dimensional apartment ghost and its three-dimensional Swiss glacial counterpart were one and the same.

The maniacal ice-chiseler paused for several seconds to reorganize his presently disheveled scruples. Daylight was on the wane. Vast shadows were beginning to encompass the tight depths of the narrow fissure. Joseph anxiously examined the freed brown leather portfolio that contained the highly sought-after manuscripts. The case had slightly left the grip of ill-fated *Raymond Pierre Girard* when his precious human spirit had slowly oozed-out from *his* frostbitten body. The case's recovery would be easier for Joseph to confiscate than if the handle were still firmly held within the corpse's grasp.

As the portfolio emancipator pointed his trusty flashlight further down to inspect the frozen man's feet, a mass of brown and white fur became quite discernible. A closer perusal revealed the notable outline of Girard's faithful St. Bernard, Niko.

Aside from the frozen remains of *Raymond Pierre Girard*, the long-forgotten early *18th Century* writer's illustrious manuscript portfolio, in essence, constituted the discovery of a major literary bonanza. Removing the ice encrusted brown leather case would require another hour of persistent chipping away, but Joseph Perna would be equal to accomplishing his deceased mentor's instructions.

Joseph used his hand-held axe to then carefully chop-away the thick layer of ice surrounding the sought-after leather case. He next meticulously picked-away until the desired object had been loosened from the ice that had enveloped it. Heir Perna was able to seize a grip and gently wriggle the leather case out of the right index finger of Raymond, who weirdly seemed to gladly surrender his three-hundred-year-long possession of the coveted literary treasure to Joseph, who intelligently chose not to open the item right then and there while standing deep inside the glacial abyss. The retriever feared that even a slight tug or pull might accidentally crack the case's beautiful brown leather exterior, or perhaps external hand pressure might unexpectedly damage the valuable manuscripts contained inside.

The afternoon sun was setting, winter dusk was descending, and vital time was absolutely crucial. The young rescuer felt compelled by circumstances to proceed his mission with dispatch. The out-of-his-environment writer hoisted his tired frame, along with the treasured portfolio, slowly up the side of the treacherous crevice. As Joseph ascended from the ice-laden tomb, still tugging on his taut rope, the respectful climber turned and took one final glance at the wonderfully preserved corpse of *Raymond Pierre Girard.*

In a matter of fifteen nerve-racking, extremely dramatic minutes, Joseph managed to manipulate his careful ascent to the mountain crag's crown. The elated conqueror rejoiced by shouting "Hallelujah!" And as the euphoric hero held his truly invaluable prize up to his face, his hoarse voice instinctively yelled "Eureka!" so loudly that his boisterous shout resounded as a shrill echo several valleys away.

Joseph continued his surreal odyssey as his weary feet shuffled and trudged his path through the perilous winter ice and across bountiful February snowdrifts, trudging all the way back to his silver *Mercury Mountaineer.* The cumbersome snow gear was swiftly deposited into the rear of the vehicle, but the coveted leather-bound portfolio was gently placed on the passenger seat, where the jubilant acquirer could randomly admire it from glance to glance. Joseph then turned the four-wheel-drive vehicle around and drove back up the snowy mountain road toward the warmth and comfort of his chalet. It was almost early evening when the dependable SUV arrived at the domicile-retreat, which looked so wonderfully inviting after the driver had experienced such an exhausting adventure.

The fireplace embers were still glowing, and with the addition of three fresh pine logs, the hot flames soon caused the new wood to blaze. Joseph removed his heavy wet clothes, dried-off with a large bath towel, and then thawed-out in front of the radiant fire. Next, the hungry man grilled a plump juicy steak above the alluring, leaping fireplace flames.

Feeling relaxed, Perna next sat in his favorite cushioned armchair, put some relaxing *Chopin* music on the stereo, and graciously sipped a draft of blackberry brandy while waiting for the second delicious steak to broil to 'well-done'.

The leather portfolio was also warming-up on the hearth, and in the morning, the now-famous author would be able to open the attache case without the risk of causing unwanted damage. While the delighted finder was gazing and marveling at the 'leather treasure trove' and imagining the nature of its outstanding contents, the room's tablephone rang. Perna robotically picked-up the communications device out of its cradle. "Hello!"

"Joseph, this is Elka Zimmer," the caller cheerfully informed. "I was visiting a friend of mine in Bern and thought I'd call you to see how you're surviving this nasty winter weather we're having."

"Elka, it's so nice to again hear your pleasant voice," Joseph sincerely replied. "I thought you had forgotten all about me."

"Not at all, Joseph. In fact, I found you to be quite charming," the quixotic poet rather earnestly answered. "Philosophers often say that first impressions mean a lot."

"Elka, would you like to pay me a visit at your old home?" the chalet's new occupant requested. "You can come to the mountain retreat tomorrow afternoon, and we can have a friendly chat while I prepare something special for dinner. Cooking happens to be my favorite hobby, you know."

There was a five-second pause as the pretty caller took time to evaluate Joseph's unexpected proposal. "That'll be great. I'll be there at around four o'clock this afternoon," Elka agreed. "It'll be good to see you again, and I hope to learn how you're getting along."

Joseph was happy that Elka had the courtesy to contact him. The lonely hermit had found the young woman to be quite charming and enticing, and the prospect of romance put the world-famous author into the perfect frame of mind to savor his present dinner of luscious filet steak , which his active mouth then devoured rather ravenously.

By noon, the leather portfolio had sufficiently thawed-out, and its interior could then be thoroughly examined. Opening it was a bit difficult, but working patiently without cracking the archaic leather, Joseph immediately identified the valid existence of the prized antiquated manuscripts. *Raymond Pierre Girard's* penmanship displayed the beauty of professional calligraphy.

Five novels, eight novelettes, and twelve priceless novellas comprised the long-lost, esteemed collection. Although the papers were matted, and even though some of the parchment was a trifle faded and a tad tarnished, the beautiful handwriting was still very legible. The excellent "script" was further flaunted by the usage of impressive black ink, the exact same color and texture that the magic pen had majestically implemented for Joseph. Each successive story was proudly and prominently signed '*Raymond Pierre Girard*'.

Raymond's plots and themes (of all the prolific stories and novels) appeared to be quite precocious and very much advanced for a stagnant time period when published literature was controlled by the closed-minded authoritarianism of tyrannical kings and popes.

'Raymond probably feared persecution and retribution from the established institutions of his time,' Joseph conjectured. "Freedom, truth, and romance were almost taboo subjects to publicly elaborate on in the late *17th* and early *18th Centuries*," concluded and orally expressed the sympathetic writer as his words again solemnly addressed the magic pen as if it were a distinguished colleague.

Joseph's next travel destination was scheduled to be the *Swiss National Library*. The writer's grand scheme was to donate the entire portfolio to posterity in *Raymond Pierre Girard's* stellar name, which happened to also be Heir Perna's own involuntary *nom de plume*.

But the *Swiss National Library* would have to be temporarily put on hold because Elka would promptly be arriving at three p.m. Joseph 'Hemingway' furtively didn't wish to divulge his singular discovery to anyone, including Elka.

The faded, brown leather portfolio and the associated manuscripts were surreptitiously concealed by its guardian inside a bedroom bureau drawer, and soon Joseph decided to take a well-deserved nap. His final thoughts before dozing-off were of the fantastic discovery of *Raymond Pierre Girard's* incredibly preserved body, the salvaging of the precious manuscripts, and finally, Elka Zimmer's highly anticipated afternoon visit.

* * * * * * * * * * * *

Elka Zimmer pulled-up into the snow-covered driveway in her light blue *Renault* at precisely four o'clock. Joseph enthusiastically greeted the vivacious blonde-hair woman at the chalet's front door.

"Elka, it's so good to see you again," genuinely began the resident author. "Please come in and make yourself comfortable."

"It was quite a winter adventure driving-up the snowy road," Elka stated. showing a degree of relief in her delivery. "Ever since *Christmas,* I was planning on visiting you on my next trip to Bern. Actually, this is the first time I've been in the Bern area since the day after you had purchase the chalet."

Joseph was fascinated by a special 'interested' quality that was evident in Elka's calm voice. The woman's eyes sparkled and her pearly white teeth gleamed. Fraulein Zimmer seemed authentically glad to see her former residence maintained in such good order, along with its new, very delightful, handsome occupant. The pretty woman stepped further inside her former dwelling, and Joseph quietly closed the front door.

"Well, Elka, it's really very nice to see you again," Joseph nervously reiterated. "I simply adore this chalet; it's everything I ever dreamed of, and I couldn't be happier. I still can't believe you sold it. Say, how would you like a cup of fresh hot coffee served with some tasty cheese and crackers?"

"That would be lovely. I could use something hot and munchy to help thaw me out," Elka replied with a smile. "I do appreciate your kind hospitality."

While the aroma of freshly brewed coffee permeated throughout the rustic mountain retreat, Joseph turned-on the stereo, and soon soft classical music functioned as the appropriate background to their semi-formal conversation.

The reunited cauual friends sat and chatted in the cozy, furnished living room. Elka was impressed with Joseph's traditional lifestyle and also with his shy, congenial demeanor. All the enchanting things that the visiting beauty truly enjoyed in life were now being lived by model human being, Joseph Perna, who in truth, believed that he was a literary fraud masquerading as Raymond Pierre Girard. But to put on fake airs to impress Elka, the host spoke about his strong commitment to writing, about the best classical music arrangements, about peaceful surroundings, and most of all, about utopian heavenly contentment. Elka Zimmer had also led a secluded life, and did not know much about passive introvert Joseph Perna, except that the aspiring author was a dedicated foreign writer, and that the shy wordsmith appeared to be financially secure.

Joseph had taken a fine filet out of the freezer, and soon placed the tender meat in the kitchen stove's oven. Living alone over the years, Perna had developed a decent culinary talent, and now the in-house chef would have the chance to aptly demonstrate his proficient skill to his elegant guest.

"Elka, for the life of me, I don't understand why you had sold me this exquisite chalet," the curious author, known publicly as Raymond Pierre Girard, commented. "I wouldn't have parted with it for all of the vintage wine in France. I fully understand your plausible reason about your ailing parents. But is there something else you aren't telling me about this place?"

That sudden honest inquiry caught Elka off-guard, and finally, the young woman felt obligated to divulge something irregular that had always had her worried mind on edge. "When I lived here, I was very happy being alone, writing my poetry. I had been in the chalet for several months, but one winter night, Joseph, February 1st, I believe, as I was lying in bed ready to fall asleep, I heard the loud clatter of wind chimes," Elka related. "It was an unusually calm winter night, and there was no reason for the metal chimes to be clanging in such a loud manner. That strange auditory sensation sent a major chill rushing through my entire body.”

Joseph was intrigued by Elka’s voluntary disclosure. He begged for more pertinent background. “What happened then?”

“After several minutes, the disturbing noise finally stopped,” the lovely blonde-haired woman continued with her vivid recollection, “and soon the uncanny occurrence had occurred several more times after that. But then, another unnatural. peculiar event transpired that I could not rationally explain. On several mornings, when I walked to yonder desk,” Elka proceeded with her rather profound exposition, “I noticed that the floor and the tabletop were wet with melted ice. These odd incidences were unexplainable, and each one unnerved me to the point where I finally decided to sell the chalet. Ever since I was a young girl, I was always greatly afraid of hearing witches and ghost stories.”

“Thank you for being so honest with me about *those* most irregular happenings,” Joseph sympathetically replied. “Is there anything else you’d like to say?”

“When you came along and purchased the chalet,” Elka divulged, “I was very relieved, but I always felt a sense of guilt for not mentioning those strange memories to you. I felt that if you knew about the weird anomalies, you would not want to buy the home.”

The listener’s mind was captivated with what Elka had forthrightly confessed. Now, it would be a difficult revelation for the nervous author to objectively share with Miss Zimmer his empathy without disclosing his collective knowledge of *Raymond Pierre Girard.* ‘I feel that I must tell her,’ Perna woefully decided. “I don’t want to think of myself as a bungling, dishonest hypocrite.”

“Elka, if this will make you feel any better, I too have heard the windchimes clanging, and also have seen water and ice on the desk and on the floor, especially in the early morning,” the reclusive fake-author disclosed. “I then rationalized a logical explanation. I reckoned I could’ve tracked-in the floor water when I had gone outside for firewood. My gloves and coat could’ve accidentally gotten snow on the desk’s flat surface,” Joseph related. “The chimes could’ve clanged as a result of a small gust of wind, or even by virtue of a squirrel disturbing them from hopping about on the side roof. I didn’t dwell on thinking about the separate events, and the separate instances never really bothered me.”

The introspective chalet owner could not find the moral strength to candidly reveal the true source of the shared strange aberrations to Elka. But most importantly, the prevaricating resident also did not want his gorgeous guest to know *his* true literary identity being, *Raymond Pierre Girard.*

The affable host, acting as a butler, served his lady guest a special her mouth-watering meat dinner. Elka had been seated in the dining room, perusing a real estate magazine, and Heir Perna soon joined his visitor for mutual consumption of the dual fillet feast. For drink, a popular French *Chardonnay,* accompanied with homemade bread and a variety of green-steamed vegetables, also graced the dinner table. Joseph opened the wine bottle's cork with a loud pop and slowly poured two glasses full, politely handing one to Elka.

"Here's to your good health, Fraulein Zimmer," Joseph Perna affectionately toasted. "And may this meeting be the first of many happy occasions together."

"I'll gladly endorse your heart-warming toast," the former chalet owner concurred, clicking glasses. "You definitely have enviable discretion, and also, a certain way with words!"

The two sipped the vintage vino. The prime-cut meat was sliced, and their plates were generously filled. The soft instrumental *Chopin* background music, the savory white wine, along with the couple's compatible company all made for a rather romantic evening.

The couple loosened their formal, culturally-learned inhibitions and continued randomly gossiping more details about each other's hopes and dreams. A definite emotional attraction was being bonded between the pair of kindred spirits.

The main meal ended with the host pouring cups of steaming tea. Then, for dessert, Joseph offered his guest ample slices of chocolate mousse cake. Elka was impressed with her host's sophisticated gourmet tastes in food and in beverages, and finally, an after-dinner drink of *Creme de Menthe* complemented the warm dining experience.

A sizzling fire was still ablaze inside the stone fireplace. The pair comfortably sat and solemnly watched the dancing flames, as the introspective host and his starry-eyed female guest continued their cordial conversation. Neither he nor she wanted the memorable evening to end.

Snowflakes began descending upon the chalet's roof, while the two writers were still prattling-away, and when the time came for Elka to return to Bern, Joseph insisted she stay, because of the "extremely foul weather pattern". The developing hazardous weather conditions on the mountain roads were not worth the risk of sustaining permanent injury. Under the harsh and bitter winter ice and snow conditions, Elka Zimmer felt she could not discreetly refuse Joseph's concerned gesture of human hospitality.

"Elka, never take chances with the formidable forces of *Mother Nature,*" the author awkwardly prattled. "We're all too fragile and quite ephemeral!"

336

"Joseph, thank you for being so worried about my welfare," Fraulein Zimmer suavely answered. "You're so sensitive and so caring! I really like those aspects about you."

Elka retired to the guestroom, where she laid in bed thinking about the resplendent evening which she had spent with her new friend Joseph Perna. Four glasses of wine had also made the host groggy, and as soon as the author cleaned and washed the dishes, he clumsily stepped to the master bedroom. The last thing the callow fellow heard before dozing-off was the chronic clattering of the metal wind-chimes, and the resident-writer was certain that Elka had also heard their symbolic beckoning. A smile appeared upon Joseph's face, for the grinning ghost-finder knew that the noise signaled another visitation from *his* noble and revered spirit friend, *Raymond Pierre Girard*.

The following cold February morning featured a beautiful winter sunrise. The snowfall had terminated overnight, and the brutal mountain weather had finally calmed. Joseph prepared his standard pot of coffee on the stove, and next concocted an inviting breakfast of fried eggs, French toast, and orange juice. Soon, Elka joined alias Raymond Pierre Girard inside the kitchen nook. The compatible twosome sat at the table, which like the living room, offered a terrific view of the snow-clad *Alps*.

"I can't remember when I had a nicer evening than I enjoyed last night, Joseph," the attractive blonde guest admitted. "It was simply wonderful! And I want to thank you for inviting me."

"The pleasure was all mine," Joseph replied with a cute laugh. "I hope you'll be back again to further our relationship. Just look at all the tremendous nostalgia you'll be missing."

"I'll agree to that. Joseph, you have some unique sterling ideas to share. You'll see me again, soon," Elka promised.

"That's just great. Maybe we could collaborate on a future writing project," Joseph suggested in an impromptu fashion. "We can combine our separate talents and produce a modern classic."

Elka planned on leaving shortly after breakfast. The appreciative woman kissed Joseph goodbye on his receptive cheek, and Fraulein Zimmer was soon driving slowly down the snowy mountain road in her light blue *Renault*.

The chalet owner relaxed on the sofa and listened to music for the remainder of the morning. At noon, the Beethoven fanatic focused his attention on delivering the priceless leather-cased manuscripts to the *Bern Library*. That noon, the notable institution had been contacted by phone, and an appointment had been made with the President.

The following clear morning, Joseph entered and drove his *Mercury Mountaineer* down the steep mountain roads, motoring toward the city.

At the library, an elderly, all-too-business-like secretary, ushered the visitor into the president's wood-paneled office.

"I wish to introduce myself, Mr. Zingher. My name is Joseph Perna. I often use the nom de plume *Raymond Pierre Girard,*" the acclaimed world novelist tersely prefaced. "I have an unbelievable story to tell, if you have the time to hear it."

"Won't you have a seat!" invited Mr. Zingher. "I have an open schedule until later this afternoon. I would be delighted to hear what you have to say."

Joseph sat-down in a red leather chair and peered straight into his listener's large brown eyes. The library guest didn't know precisely how to begin disclosing his fantastic ice crevice account. "I have with me a number of literary masterpieces that have been insulated from civilization for several centuries. I'd like for you to examine and value their worth."

Joseph next went on to explain how the ice-buried manuscripts had been recently recovered inside the mountain's glacial crevice. A full hour later, the *Bern Library* President was wholly overwhelmed after hearing the entire, incredible sixty-minute rendition. The wide-eyed official incidentally remained sitting still as a statue, having an astounded expression showing on his florid face.

"The *Bern Library,*" Mr. Perna, is extremely grateful to be the proud recipient of such stunning Age of Enlightenment classics you've brought to my attention," Mr. Zingher declared, clearing his chubby throat. "The documents you're donating are assured a lofty position in the fine heritage of our beloved Swiss literature. The eminent *Raymond Pierre Girard* will be honored posthumously, certainly with our highest and most revered commendation," the dignified library President vowed. "We already have several of *his* excellent books on our shelves, and we'll be honored to have these others! Thank you for making your wonderful surprise contribution to our national archives."

Joseph still intended to assume the authorial pseudonym *Raymond Pierre Girard,* and Heir Perna relished the realization that he would be the *heir* to the *18th Century* wordsmith's new-edition reproductions of the genius's prolific collection of freshly-discovered short stories and novels. The royalties would be positively astronomical and expected 'Demand would certainly dwarf Supply,' Joseph Perna surmised. 'A fantastic fortune will soon be generated,' thought the now-content-with-the-world author. "I could be the next Horatio Alger."

* * * * * * * * * * * *

The library visitor arrived at his mountain chalet late that afternoon and settled-in for another chilly, howling night. The proud man lit a pile of logs inside the stone fireplace, poured a hefty draft of blackberry brandy, and proceeded to meditate about Caesar's Ghost and about Hamlet's father's haunting specter. *Brahms, Bach,* and *Strauss* musical compositions were being softly played in classical succession on the den's stereo. The glad-to-be-alive author pondered the evolution of sensational events that had occurred during the course of the past several days. People would be hard-pressed to place any credence in such actual truth that superficially disguised itself as pure vivid fantasy.

"I pledge that I'll never disclose my true secret to an agnostic, cynical humanity," the lonely writer promised to himself. "People are just too negative to believe anything out of the ordinary! The general public is a gaggle of mostly mindless apostates that values TV propaganda over basic truth!"

Joseph felt a sudden urge to compose an argumentative letter, utilizing his now 'exquisite' black magic pen. As the scribe sat-down at his solid oak desk, the perceptive writer observed a few words appearing in fine calligraphy, artistically written upon the familiar yellow pad. "Thank you so very much, Joseph; I vow that you will be rewarded for your loyal assistance." The prophetic handwritten memo' was signed "***Raymond Pierre Girard***".

Joseph momentarily stared at the remarkable revelation, smiled, and then shook his head in disbelief. The author resumed to attempt drafting a strongly-worded letter to his greedy publisher, Mr. Allen. Perna hastily picked-up the black magic pen, but it would not write either a single vowel or syllable. The plagiarist looked inside the accompanying bottle of black ink, but it was bone-dry. The writer was both visibly shocked and most dismayed.

"Oh well, it was great while it lasted," the saddened dreamer lamented. "I suppose I'll have to now achieve fame and fortune, exclusively on my own ability!"

The world-famous author swore that he would adopt the harmonious-sounding name "Raymond Pierre Girard" as his real name, since the appellation had already served him well as *his* functional pseudonym.

The pen's sudden failure to write neither prose nor fiction was psychologically shattering to Joseph's diminishing confidence. Without its unparalleled wisdom originating from an ethereal source, the melancholy novelist felt he would never again be capable of manufacturing those wonderful, brilliant plots and themes. What should or would he do? Could his frail ego live without the pleasure of enjoying continuous notoriety? The woebegone storyteller fell fast asleep, and that very night, suffered a sequence of outlandish nightmares, which Joseph Perna believed would dominate the artist's grossly-interrupted literary career.

* * * * * * * * * * * *

During the ensuing weeks, Elka and Joseph were in constant communication. The mutual respect that the pair had cultivated for each other was plainly apparent, and their mutual affection was palpably abundant in all of their lengthy phone conversations. Plans were made to meet again on subsequent weekends.

Elka Zimmer drove her blue *Renault* to the mountaintop chalet each Saturday to renew her budding romance with the fraudulent author, who used to write under the famous pseudonym, Raymond Pierre Girard. Constant weekly anticipation grew into constant longing for each other's company. The dual attractions were both strong and real. The love-birds' admiration for each other had evolved into pure, unadulterated desire.

The couple's discussions originally embodied Joseph's creative writing and Elka's avant-garde poetry, but then the enraptured pair found that their sports and reading interests were also congruently similar, and truly worthy of sharing. One summer day, while discussing popular book titles, Elka asked her soulmate a pertinent question her mind had been contemplating.

"Joseph, have you ever read anything by the renowned New York author, *Raymond Pierre Girard?*" the blonde girlfriend innocently asked. "I've recently read several of his novels, and frankly, they're the most imaginative stories I've ever enjoyed."

Joseph reflected for a moment, not wishing to divulge his secret identity to anyone. The frivolous listener wanted to be sincere, but at that moment, the former Soho native needed to be facetious. "Yes Elka," Joseph acknowledged and replied in a somber tone of voice. "I've also occasionally read some of *his* books, and I wholeheartedly have to agree with your assessment of the gentleman's outstanding writing ability. Some say he's a veritable modern-day Charles Dickens! Mr. Girard is gifted in creating both outstanding narrative descriptions and fascinating character dialogue."

Joseph knew then and there that Elka would sooner or later find-out that ordinary *he* and dynamic *Raymond Pierre Girard* were absolutely one and the same individual. 'What should I do?' the distressed male regretted and mentally debated. The puzzled writer had always desired disclosing the truth to his newfound love, but now the poor fellow also wanted to wait for a more propitious time, when *their* relationship would be more 'serious and committed'.

The self-effacing, former Charles Dickens impersonator had been considering proposing marriage, for the idealistic protagonist thought that Elka should wed him for whom he was, and not for the sake of mere worldly fame and fortune. Six months quickly elapsed, and then one late August day Joseph garnered sufficient courage to orally present *Cupid's* hackneyed question.

"Will you marry me?" the internationally acclaimed author under another name asked his Swiss sweetheart. "Elka, please forgive me for being so intolerably blunt."

The young lady's instant answer was a most resounding "Yes, yes, yes!" And then, the starry-eyed pair happily embraced. The notorious writer under another non de plume believed that Elka's commitment to matrimony would inspire him to author praiseworthy novels without requiring the aid of the mystical black magic pen. A quiet wedding had been planned for the second Sunday in October.

Summer quickly ended, autumn leaves abounded, and a brief wedding ceremony was held in a Bern Catholic Church with just the couple's aged parents attending as witnesses. Then, the totally thrilled newlyweds immediately departed to partake in a nondescript, quiet honeymoon at placid *Lake Como.*

After two weeks of rapturous marital bliss, Joseph and Elka left the beauty of *Mt. Blanc,* and without fanfare, returned to the insular chalet to begin their new roles as husband and wife. Joseph drove the blue *Renault* through the splendid autumnal scenery that the majestic *Alps* had recently created. The husband and spouse arrived at the chalet early on a mild Thursday evening.

In the morning, the phone rang incessantly until the blurry-eyed, acclaimed writer under another name finally answered. The caller was the financial manager of the principal Swiss Bank in Bern, *Armond Von Ernst and Cie.AG.* The treasurer insisted that Joseph speed over to the bank "with dispatch". "Wonderful news has to be personally communicated," the excited caller declared and informed.

"What was that loud shouting on the phone all about?" inquired Elka. "Were your parents in an automobile accident?"

"No accident, Elka. And I have no idea of our awaiting good fortune, but we'll soon find out," the husband assured his overly concerned wife.

Mr. and Mrs. Joseph Perna departed in haste for Bern in the silver *Mountaineer,* and in less than a half-hour, the newlyweds had arrived at the world-renowned gold depository. The nervous manager greeted the duo and invited the curious "newlyweds" into his stately office.

"*Mr. Girard,* please sit down because you might faint when you hear what I have to tell you."

"Mr. Girard?" Elka exclaimed in disbelief. "My husband's birth name is Joseph Perna!"

Joseph asked Elka to "please listen" with undivided attention to the bank executive's specific instructions. The husband and wife sat-down in compliance with the treasurer's imperative request.

"When *Raymond Pierre Girard's* original manuscripts were brought to the *Swiss National Library* in the year 1721, the talented author never returned to receive any accrued royalties," the bank's money manager explained. "Because *Mr. Girard* feared ostracism and censorship from the political and religious establishments of his time, the literary genius had adopted the strange pen name of Joseph Perna to conceal his true identity from vengeful political and religious enemies. The accumulated royalties that Mr. Girard had legally earned were then put into a trust and never touched, that is, until a legitimate heir would come forward and legally claim the account," added the corpulent, mustached bank official. "Well, *Mr. Raymond Pierre Girard,* quite apparently you are the rightful heir and can claim the massive fortune, which has been amassing interest for almost three-hundred-years. You're now a very rich and fortunate man."

Raymond Pierre Girard (alias Joseph Perna) was overwhelmed at receiving a fantastic gift. His limp form collapsed deep into his leather chair in response to the startling revelation that the bank's financial manager had just disclosed. Then, Joseph felt obligated to responsibly retell the entire phenomenal story from beginning to end, both to Elka and to the informative financial administrator.

"I wonder, Mr. Von Ernst," the euphoric writer finished a full hour later. "How did you know that I had been using the pseudonym *Raymond Pierre Girard?*"

"Yesterday, your publisher Mr. Allen, had called me from New York. He inquired about opening an account for you in Bern for direct deposits to the name, Joseph Perna, alias, Raymond Pierre Girard," the bank executive explained. "That's how my staff happened to learn about your dual identity from your Manhattan publisher, Mr. Manuel Allen. My employees quickly searched our bank's database, and we were immensely stunned to discover that a certain Raymond Pierre Girard, after *his* death, had willed a massive sum of money to another certain Raymond Pierre Girard."

"Mr. Von Ernst, is there anything else I need to know?"

"I hope you don't fall out of your chair after hearing *this* summary," the wide-eyed bank official stated, before clearing his throat. "How can I best explain this incredibly bizarre scenario! Our

342

extensive research has discovered that Raymond Pierre Girard had used the pen name Joseph Perna, and you have used the non de plume Raymond Pierre Girard. And so, Joseph Perna, you owe your fantastic inheritance to Joseph Perna, alias, Raymond Pierre Girard."

There was a momentary pause as the pompous bank manager again cleared his throat, and then the executive prodigiously sneezed into a handkerchief. Elka's face turned ashen, as if thirteen terrifying ghosts had just savagely antagonized her existence.

"Forgive me, for my seasonal sneezing fits are acting-up. And now Mr. Girard, er, I mean Mr. Perna. It gives me great pleasure to present this wooden chest to you as your inheritance-in-full from your *18th Century* namesake," Mr. Von Ernst formally proclaimed.

Joseph was very cautious about handling the mysterious surprise gift. The bank's ancient copy of *Raymond Pierre Girard's* personal last will and testament was verbally read aloud by the portly bank treasurer, and the centuries-old document clearly stipulated the exact conditions upon which an eligible recipient would inherit the wooden chest's lucrative contents.

The shocked bank visitor slowly lifted the chest's squeaky lid. Inside were twelve remarkably preserved, full bottles of precious black ink to be used by the secret, occult black magic pen. The new supply would activate and further enhance *Raymond Pierre Girard's* ascending literary reputation for many years to come.

Joseph and Elka left the marble-walled bank with his mind swimming in astonishment, and with Elka incessantly asking a litany of now-answerable questions. While deftly guiding the silver *Mercury Mountaineer* from Bern up to the serene mountainside chalet, Joseph blandly explained the entire incredible sequence of events, filling in all of the missing details from the time *he* had met the New York City beggar Raymond Pierre Girard, who had solicited and sold the aspiring novelist a one-dollar "black magic pen", up to Joseph receiving the present dozen bottles of magical black ink.

"I can't believe that *my* husband is also *my* favorite author!" marveled and praised Mrs. Elka Perna. "I couldn't have prayed for a more perfect marriage! And now, I understand the entire history perfectly. Both the black magic pen and the magical black ink supply needed to be utilized in order for Raymond Pierre Girard's ghost to again be summoned to competently compose additional sublime manuscripts for Mr. Joseph Perna."

Yes, Elka. I'm glad to realize that the supernatural black magic pen was not evil *black magic,* after all!"

On December 1st, one more surprise awaited Heir Joseph. The City of Bern had arranged to have *Raymond Pierre Girard's* remains exhumed from the mountainside's dark, frozen fissure. A formal state funeral was conducted and attended by self-centered local authorities, and a dignified posthumous burial was performed on the lawn in front of the *Bern Library*.

A huge monument was later erected to pay tribute to the memory of *Raymond Pierre Girard,* who now has finally received the literary accolades that his short, dysfunctional life so rightfully deserved. "I now understand that when I wanted to write a negative letter, the ink bottle had gone dry, and the black magic pen became useless. The black ink and the black magic pen only worked when my thoughts and moods were positive and optimistic. The black magic pen was not at all involved in black magic! May *his* enviable soul now finally rest in peace," Joseph eulogized his literary mentor to his beautiful blonde wife. "And may perpetual light shine upon him!"

"Amen, Joseph!" Elka aptly replied. "Amen!" Mrs. Joseph Perna sincerely reiterated.

About the Authors

Dr. Leonard Streitfeld (1922-2019) was a retired optometrist, who maintained his offices in Hammonton, New Jersey from 1950-2012. In fact, Dr. Leonard Streitfeld (along with his son Dr. Stephen Streitfeld) had been John Wiessner's eye doctor for many years. Len Streitfeld and Jay Dubya had written and rewritten the stories "The Chess Set", "The Cups", "The Incense Burner", "Reflections", "Stained Glass", and "The Black Magic Pen" many times, until all sixteen tales appearing in *The Arcane Arcade* have evolved into their present, quality, literature form.

During *World War 11,* Leonard Streitfeld had been a bombardier on a *B-17* with the *Eighth Air Force,* and he remarkably participated in thirty-one aerial raids over Nazi Germany and France from 1942-45. Dr. Streitfeld had kept an accurate diary, and had recorded his fascinating war experiences in the biographical book *Hell from Heaven*, Second Edition. Dr. Streitfeld has also authored the paperback book titled *Unexpected.* Len and wife Mary had two sons (Stephen and Rick) and a daughter (Linda).

Jay Dubya is author John Wiessner's pen name, a corruption of his initials, J.W. John is a retired New Jersey public school teacher, having diligently taught the subject for thirty-four years. John lives in Hammonton, New Jersey with wife Joanne, and the couple has three grown sons (Joe, John Thomas, and Stephen).

John has written and published fifty-three books. Besides his latest satire titled *PLOTS,* Jay Dubya (J.W.) has also written books in other genres besides satire, including novels and short story collections.

Other Jay Dubya adult-oriented fiction works are *Black Leather and Blue Denim, A '50s Novel*, and its exciting sequel, *The Great Teen Fruit War, A 1960' Novel,* with *Frat Brats A 60s Novel* completing the coming-of-age trilogy.

www.ingramcontent.com/pod-product-compliance
Lightning Source LLC
Chambersburg PA
CBHW060226100726
47907CB00003B/518